A Stranger Here myself

BEING THE LIFE STORY AND REVELATIONS OF MISTER RAB C. NESBITT OF GOVAN

IAN PATTISON

A Stranger Here myself

BEING THE LIFE STORY AND REVELATIONS OF MISTER RAB C. NESBITT OF GOVAN

PICADOR

First published 2000 by Picador
an imprint of Macmillan Publishers Ltd
25 Eccleston Place, London SW1W 9NF
Basingstoke and Oxford
Associated companies throughout the world
www.macmillan.com

ISBN 0 330 48493 1 (Hardback)
ISBN 0 330 48672 1 (Trade paperback)

1 3 5 7 9 8 6 4 2

A CIP catalogue record for this book is available from
the British Library.

Typeset by SetSystems Ltd, Saffron Walden, Essex
Printed and bound in Great Britain by
Mackays of Chatham plc, Chatham, Kent

ACKNOWLEDGEMENTS

THANKS

Mr Nesbitt would like to thank the following who have, in their various ways, made this memoir possible:

Doctor Helen Mackie, Max Eilenberg, Peter Tummons, Katie and Margaret, Bob Thompson, Tonga McIntyre, Robert Kirby at P.F.D., Maria Rejt at Macmillan, not forgetting her serene loveliness Andrea H.

BLAME

Mr Nesbitt would like to name and shame the following who, for the past dozen years, have grown fat and rich by turning his life into televisual pap, fit only for armchair-class tourists and media lickspittles. They are:

Messrs Fisher, Pattison, Smith, Roper, Rafferty, Fairley, Cullen, Gilbert, Ewing, McNeil, Wild, McNiven, et al.

CHAPTER ONE

IT'S LATE 1950.

I'm minus three months old, a precocious child, and I have my ear pressed up against the wall of my mother's womb. A man and a woman, my parents, are arguing the toss. 'I'm having the kid,' she's yelling. 'You're not having any kid,' the man's yelling back. There's a noise like a soup pan bouncing off a head. A moment later a knitting needle, size eight, appears like a periscope, trying to jab me up the sac. I cling to a membrane, out of harm's way. The needle retracts. There's more yelling, screaming, a flurry of expletives barked in rage. A door slams. All is silent but for a background muzak of gritty female wailing, a comforting noise, since it always precedes the onset of a tobacco binge and I'm twitchy and eager for a fix. Indeed, I look guiltily at the nicotine stains on my unformed fingertips and make a mental note to cut down. Lately I've been finding myself out of breath after a couple of circuits of the womb and in the mornings I've been coughing up tar. Maybe tomorrow. Right now I take a deep grateful double lungful and lie back in the sac, surveying my situation. I've no idea where I am as yet, but I'm pretty sure it isn't Hampstead. My parents appear to speak little English, which makes them either foreign or ignoramuses. The third option, that they have very little to say to each other, dawns on me only later.

People say puberty is a bad time for a kid but in my view it's not a patch on getting born. Getting born is a bastard. It's a free-fall bungee jump without the rope. The secret's in the timing. I've seen many a good foetus hit the slop pail because he screwed up on when to surf the placenta. I've vowed it won't happen to me. Not that I haven't had my share of near misses. Like that time in the butcher's when the sight of a pig's head made Mother queasy and her sudden contractions spooked the queue. They laid her on the floor and called for help but if they'd had the good manners to speak to me first I could have saved the room a lot of anxiety. Call me fussy but a sawdust floor and a guy in a straw hat with a meat hook isn't my idea of a sympathetic environment, so I curled up like a fist in the sac and stayed put.

You get a lot of time to think when you're banged up in a womb all day. Will I be handsome? Will I be rich? I pondered these questions long and hard till in the end I just thought, 'Que sera, sera.' I don't care what I am so long as I'm healthy and don't have an extra head or any extraneously hideous debits or credits in the biology state-ment of existence. I just want to get by. To tiptoe through no-man's-land without taking a fatal shot, before my time, from either side. Or worse, a shot that isn't fatal but leaves me crippled and tetchy in the waiting room of life, clutch-ing a balloon and gurgling. Say what you like, it's hard to be taken seriously by women when you're twenty-eight and still pissing into a romper suit. No, I ask only two things of life, courage and dignity. Well, three things if you include the ability to shit Maltesers. For I am human. I strive toward the light of the divine godhead. I come trailing clouds of glory. I have lingered in the chambers of the sea and heard the mermaids singing, each to each. But then, what do you expect, my mother's on medication.

*

So it was in the early hours of late October, on a wet night as the drunks sang and cursed in the park, that Mother gave me the precious gift of life.

2

'Aaaaachhhhhhhnnnnnnnn . . . !' she said, as I slipped from her womb into the safe waiting hands of the old doctor, then back out of the safe waiting hands of the old doctor to land with a greasy *dunk* on the floor of the delivery ward.

'Well, there'll be no need to smack this one's behind,' chuckled the healer, attempting to hide his malpractice with a mask of joviality, 'he's bawling his lungs out already.'

Mother, exhausted, propped herself on one shoulder and peered down at me where I lay. In lieu of legal damages the doctor offered her a Bristol and together they lit up.

'Shouldn't he be squirming, Doctor?' asked Mother, finally, after a long thankful draw.

'How do you mean?'

'Well, babies squirm, don't they? I've seen it in the films and that. Sort of squiggle about, full of vitality and bubbly joy.'

The doctor looked at her gravely. 'M'dear,' he said, 'this is Govan, not Hollywood. There's not much worth squiggling about for round here.'

Mother nodded. Her fag drooped, disappointedly.

Seeing this, the doctor attempted kindness. 'This is your first, isn't it?' he said, squeezing her hand. Again Mother nodded. 'Then I'll see what I can do.' Turning to me, the doctor drummed a short stabbing tattoo in the small of my back with his toecap. I squirmed. 'Happy?'

Rather than displease, Mother beamed dutifully and I was lifted, flannelled and placed whimpering into her arms. 'Who's my wee man, then?' she enquired of me. I was surprised. It seemed that since she was responsible for half my gene pool and would be doubtless instrumental in furnishing me with a name she was in receipt of more information about me than I was myself and therefore if there were any awkward existential questions to be asked I ought to be the one posing them. My mother repeated her question and as she did so vibrated my lower lip with her pinkie. 'Who's going to grow up to be a big strapping boy, just like his daddy, eh?'

I'd glimpsed my father in the distance on one of my surreptitious peeks from the womb and was not favoured by the comparison.

'Eff off,' I muttered, incoherently. It was an uncharitable sentiment but it had been a difficult birth and I was dog-tired.

The doctor drew a coarse hand over my smooth head then excused himself to dress a rivet burn. I watched dimly, in horrified fascination as Sister Friel, squatting, destapled a *Titbits* and placed the pages on the afterbirth on the floor, pending a cleaner.

Then I fell into a troubled sleep.

*

I opened up my eyes and looked about me. Either I was now out of the womb or my mother had redecorated the place in black enamel while I'd slept. Everything was blurry but that might just be the drugs from the night before. Then I remembered the birth and had to fight panic. The first thing they drum into you when you become a foetus is a sense of racial memory. I flicked mentally through the back pages of my survivors' training guide and came to rest at the chapter headed 'Environment'. Hitching myself up on one elbow I tried to get a grasp of the terrain. There was no doubt about it, the world was a dark and narrow place. All the same, I had expected it to measure substantially more than around two foot six across. When my groping fingers found a shiny metal logo things started to fall into place. 'Silver Cross.' So that was it, I was in a pram. It all made sense. That faint reek of vomit. The stretched line of plastic bunny rabbits on the horizon that rattled when I touched them and which, up until now, I'd assumed must be the equator. And that big glass dish up there, hanging from the chains, the light behind it highlighting its mottled sediment of fried dead flies, that couldn't be the sun after all. Elated by the wondrous clarity of my powers of deduction, I let out a little cocky self-satisfied chortle. This was a big mistake as instantly the pram was surrounded by some of the most ghastly examples of the will to live any reasonable infant could expect to countenance without toddling over the pink fluffy line into insanity.

'Hello, wee fella,' said a thin tremulous voice I recognized as belonging to my mother, 'we're your mummy and daddy.'

I had had no idea what I expected my parents to look like. I had hoped vaguely they might resemble Bogart and Bacall, of whom I'd heard them speak in awed tones. In this, I was half lucky. My mother looked like Humphrey. I gazed up at her thinning hair. 'If her husband doesn't die soon,' I thought, 'she's ordered that widow's peak for nothing.'

A stocky male in the cheap dark serge of a bus conductor's uniform stepped into view. His features were taut and clenched and as I perused them I had the uneasy feeling he interpreted my scrutiny as a challenge and that he might invite me to take off my shawl and step out into the hall for a doing. I hoped, optimistically, he might reveal himself as the family's dour but faithful chauffeur but when he held up a ticket machine and clicked off a couple of low fares to entertain me, I knew my original surmise was, unfortunately, correct. 'Oh fuck,' I thought, 'I'm poor.'

'Look at him, Robert,' beamed my mother, 'he's your double.'

'Oh fuck,' I thought, 'I'm poor and ugly.'

My father, heartened, thrust his face in close for a better inspection. I gurgled amiably, trying to dispel the threat of violence whilst regarding, more furtively this time, his coarse and quizzical features. Lines of premature worry on his ample forehead had drawn his pale grey eyes up into a frozen look of anguished bewilderment. Under an over-large fleshy nose his mouth was drawn tight as a purse string, though his chin, thankfully, was square, lightly dimpled and might have held its own in better facial company. They say true poverty smells filthy sweet. In that case my father was not truly poor. He smelled of stale tobacco, damp cloth and bad temper. More than anything, as he rose to take his leave, his rounded shoulders spoke of disappointment.

'That's me away, Issy,' he said, picking up his badged cap from the sideboard. 'I'm on the thirty-four run today, Govan Cross to Castlemilk.'

This information provided me with a further damning clue to my inheritance. 'Oh, fuck,' I thought, 'poor, ugly and Scottish. What a bastarding hat trick.'

The door slammed and I fell into a troubled sleep during which I entertained many strange dreams and fancies. Of course at two days old you'll understand my symbolism was still pretty basic, nonetheless it seemed my unconscious mind was striving to convey a message.

In a dream, I stood alone at the gates of Hades carrying the Sword of Truth and the Mighty Shield of Kran, and dressed in a pale-blue romper suit. Before me stood the Fearful Rusk of Alastair, forty feet of ruthless biscuit with no chink in his daunting armour save at the edges where the drizzle had made him slightly soggy.

'None shall pass!' boomed the Fearful Rusk. He had a Perthshire accent and a Fettes College badge on his helmet.

He tore off crumbs and rained them down on me like mighty boulders which I deflected with my Shield of Kran. This went on for, oh, an hour or two until the Rusk was about a foot and a half high and his breastplate hem was trailing in the mud. 'I told my mother this armour was too big but she swore I'd grow into it,' he mumbled, embarrassed.

'They always say that,' said a rough voice behind me. I turned, startled. A young guy of around my own age stood, looking sheepish. He was wearing a pale-blue romper suit. 'Is that the Sword of Truth and the Mighty Shield of Kran you've got there?' he asked.

I nodded.

'Me, too.' He held up his sword and shield half-heartedly for me to see. 'And them,' he added.

I looked up. Hundreds of poor-looking guys in pale-blue romper suits stood, shuffling awkwardly and holding Swords of Truth and Mighty Shields of you know what. We looked at each other, feeling foolish.

'None shall pass,' muttered the Rusk by way of a social filler. It was unnecessary. We had already started to disperse.

'I thought I was the only one,' I said, my voice reedy with disappointment.

'Me too,' said the rough boy.

'I wonder who Alastair is?' somebody asked.

'Let's ask the Rusk,' said someone else.

'What the fuck does he know?' said the rough boy. 'Fucking broken biscuit.'

I turned to see the Rusk sink further into his armour. He was a nice middle-class kid but he'd never make it as a bouncer at the gates of Hades if he couldn't hack the abuse. With luck he wouldn't get killed before the college term restarted. His was a tough gig but being poor was tougher. Not only did you share an outside toilet, you couldn't even afford your own neurosis.

With that thought I resolved to escape.

* * *

My parents occupied what was termed in Glasgow a 'room and kitchen'. This implied that the kitchen was a separate entity, distinct from 'the room'. It was. But it was not complete unto itself. The room was a living room, not a bedroom. The bedroom was in the kitchen, or perhaps vice versa; in any event the net result was that it was possible to lie in bed and have one's pyjamas spattered by hot lard from someone cooking chips not an arm's length away. The bed was lodged in a recess near the door of the kitchen. Because the bedroom was in the kitchen, there was no room for a wardrobe or dressing table, so the bedroom furniture was in the living room. Consequently the living room looked more like a bedroom than the kitchen which was the bedroom. It followed that when guests visited they were shown into the bedroom not the living room, even though the bedroom was the kitchen. Therefore by extending the previous net result it became possible to lie in bed and have one's pyjamas spattered by hot oil from someone cooking chips whilst exchanging social pleasantries with a person or persons one had never laid eyes upon in one's puff.

Such an occurrence befell my parents a few months after my birth. My own involvement was purely tangential. I was crawling, barefoot, along the floor of the kitchen/bedroom, gurgling happily, for camouflage, whilst perfecting my escape plan. At the cooker my mother hummed happily, fleetingly content with her lot in life: to have married a mirthless bully and spawned a dribbling devious brat.

8

'Just look at him, Rab,' she beamed, 'he's right good at the crawling, isn't he?'

'So what?' said my father, unimpressed. 'He's a kid, isn't he, he's supposed to crawl. If he was tap dancing while swallowing fire that might be worth a peek up from my *Daily Worker*. Until then let's assume we've not got the new messiah on our hands, eh?'

My father sniffed the air. He peeked up from his *Daily Worker*. 'Is that chips again?'

'Aye,' admitted my mother.

'Good God, does everything we eat have to be cooked in grease? Can you not cook anything healthy?'

'Aye,' said my mother, 'I'm frying a packet of crisps to go with them.'

My father flashed her a warning look. She backed down. 'I'm grilling some whiting,' she mumbled.

With their attention distracted I'd stood wobbly-legged, clutching the drop leaf of the kitchen table. Deftly, I'd removed a caramel wafer from a plate and hidden it down the band of my nappy. It'd mean going without a piss for a full twenty minutes or so until I could sneak away into the lobby to deposit the ration in my stash under the coal bunker but, hell, if was it was that easy to bust out of a crib, kids would be doing it all the time.

I knew the secret of a successful escape lay in determination and planning. During the long hours banged up in my pram, when I should have been idly dribbling and whining, I had been secretly working on my fitness. A couple of rattles swaddled in plasticine could make a pretty effective dumb-bell. A quick bum-shuffle down the pram and those cutesy booted high kicks became dynamic horizontal squat-thrusts. Some instinct deep inside told me I had to escape Govan before I became conditioned. I'd seen those sad old institutionalized toddlers in the swingpark, hanging around the banana slide uselessly, sweet cigarettes wilting in their mouths, too gutless either to scale the steps alone or make the break for it while their headscarved mothers gibbered together about the price of mince. What would become of them? Most likely they'd grow up, fall in love, get married and have children. What a terrible waste of existence! I cursed the society that could take people's lives and give them nothing in return but happiness. Why, I only had to look at my parents to see the misery that happiness could bring. Two deformed and stunted souls, bound together by fear and custom, the tension between them a terse and murky current, like Strindberg with glottal stops. In short, two Govan newly-weds.

Troubled by these dark thoughts, I sought balm for the soul in my pop-up Noddy. After eating around half a page I felt better. Noddy was colour, colour was different, different was other than Govan and my parents. Hunger presupposes the existence of food; what existed in my imagination could, with effort, become a willed reality. All I needed was a renegade soul to show me the way. A cold draught around my bare legs made me shiver. The front door was open. I peered up from my daydream to see a matching grave and ashen look on the faces of both my parents. In the middle of the floor two policemen stood, thick of boot, girth and trouser. One was asking sharp questions in a blunt manner while the other searched the room with a rude unhurried gaze. Alarmed and intimidated, my parents bowed to their authority with the servile diffidence of the respectable poor.

'And you say you haven't seen Bobo?' said Blunt.

'No,' said my mother.

'But he's your brother-in-law.'

'She's got an atlas but she's not seen Honolulu,' grumbled my father, raising himself in his chair.

'You causing trouble?'

'No,' said my father, lowering himself in his chair.

'What is it he's done?' asked my mother, to deflect attention.

'Never you mind. But if he knocks on this door, you tell us. Understand?'

My mother nodded. The policemen grunted and walked out, leaving the door open.

'That bloody family of yours,' barked my father, still seething with hurt pride. 'They're nothing but a bunch of scum!'

'At least they're honest,' countered my mother. 'Not hypocrites like yours!'

My father's face, still white, now reddened. Eyes cold with anger, he advanced on my mother. She flew to the hearth, her fingers trying frantically to pluck the poker from the middle of the ornamental companion set by the range. His hard hands grappled for a hold of her fleecy yellow cardigan and as they cursed, panting, I glimpsed through the letter-box slot of his pyjama bottoms his willy dancing curiously in its jungle. Seeing my chance, I headed toward the open door.

Though located only one floor up, the stairs to our flat were broad and many. Their bare grey concrete was cold and sharp at the edges with wear. I know this because I had the opportunity to inspect each one at close quarters as I rolled and bumped, striking my still soft cranium on a considerable number, en route to the bottom. Crawling down a flight of stairs is a difficult enough skill for an adult to master, as I have many times subsequently discovered: for a six-month-old child it is well-nigh impossible. I lay on my back enjoying the warm snack of blood in my mouth and the cosy interior glow that was growing inside my forehead. I wondered who Bobo might be. An air of exoticism already shimmered around his unknown presence. As the pain hit I stopped wondering and instead did quite a bit of howling.

*

When I woke, my mother was sitting on my bed, blubbing messily. Dr Lenco stood, snorting with disapproval behind his grey moustache.

'Obviously a wilful child,' he said, giving me a beady look.

'How long should I keep the bandages on, Doctor?'

'Till he heals,' said Lenco, drily.

'And the one on his head, what about that?'

'Longer. I fancy that one will ooze,' he said, pressing the lint dressing on my head, a little firmly, as if to abet his own prognosis, 'for a long, long time.'

My mother whimpered in alarm and bit her lip. 'When you say "ooze", Doctor, what is it that comes out?'

'I won't baffle you with jargon, Mrs Nesbitt,' said the healer, 'but "badness" is as good a word as any.'

'Oh my!' wailed my mother.

They both looked at me. 'A wilful child,' repeated Dr Lenco, as if free will was an antisocial disease born of self-indulgence.

Dr Lenco was of Polish extraction, though too much Pole had been extracted and the cavity filled with standard-issue dour Calvinism so that his position among the sickly poor was as rigid and sour as a rhubarb stalk thrust into a bag of sugar, a fittingly Scottish confection.

He picked up his bag. 'I'd knock that out of him before he comes to a sticky end.'

I attempted some plucky insolence but all that emerged from my mouth was a parched gurgle.

'But he's only six months old,' pleaded my mother.

'Mrs Nesbitt, I'm a GP not God. I can't be around for every mother that leaves a front door carelessly open.'

'I know, I'm sorry,' said my mother, chastened.

The doctor softened, becoming almost sentimental. 'Pull yourself together, woman! We lose enough of the herd round here to nature, what with cancer, heart disease, strokes, polio, scarlet fever and the rest of it, without me having to stamp on an infant's death certificate: *Cause of Demise: Took swallow dive downstairs while parents were battering each other senseless with ornaments.* The horrors of nature I can stomach, Mrs Nesbitt, the horrors of humanity are quite a different thing. They're avoidable, woman, avoidable.' To ensure the message had sunk home he repeated: 'I cannot be God, Mrs Nesbitt.'

My mother smiled, surprised. The very notion. 'Och, I know that fine well,' she said, 'you're only human, like the rest of us.'

Nevertheless as she helped him into his coat, I saw her sneak a touch at the hem, just for luck.

*

I lay in my crib for some weeks recovering from my injuries. As I lounged, scoffing chocolate drops with as much restraint and pathos as greed would allow, my parents would rage and bicker as to which of them had been responsible for my accident. My father rebuked my mother for being slatternly and forgetful. My mother would retaliate by upbraiding my father for being domineering and pernickety. I, of course, was excused giving evidence on grounds of diminished vocabulary. All the same, should I have been required to chortle under oath, the worm of guilt would have lain coiled around my utterances. In Scotland even Protestants suffer from Catholic guilt, since both faiths view existence itself as a form of showing off and therefore punishable by the eternal flames of damnation. Catholics solve the problem by affording magical powers to superstitious eejits in black

13

suits who sit behind a velvet curtain, flicking through *Playboy* while dispensing easy forgiveness for the price of a few Hail Marys. I may have missed the odd theological nuance but this seems the main tenet. Protestants, on the other hand, are fundamentally different. They afford magical powers to superstitious eejits in black suits who poke the grey intricacy of human fallibility with a stick before stoving its head in with the mighty cross of Jesus. A vague distinction to the doubting mind but an unbridgeable chasm to the soul of the true believer. The difference in approach is best expressed in the respective hymns of praise. Protestant hymns are militaristic, 'Soldiers of Christ' being urged, constantly, to 'put your armour on' and 'Stand up, stand up for Jesus!' Catholic hymns resemble Country and Western ballads, damaged souls seeking tentatively for the small light in the permanently dark corner. These are songs of consolation, their message being best summed up in the sentiment 'Help me make it through the night.'

Complex philosophical musings such as these lay far ahead, however, as I gradually regained my strength. Once mobile again, I sought a change of image. After experiments with tottering, hopping and falling over, I decided on walking upright as my favoured means of propulsion. I changed my dress code, too, eschewing the casual charm of the polka-dot all-in-one with matching bobble hat and bootees for the more robust and manly appeal of yellow Tricel breeks with crossover straps and mitten ties. I was growing older. Only forty more years and I'd be hairless and living on milky drinks for my ulcer.

'Look at that face,' chirped my mother, thrusting my arms into a set of leather reins that had little tin bells lined along the front, 'always frowning.'

'I'll be too old to die young,' I thought, morosely, 'and

I hardly know what lies outside the front door.' Apart from stairs, of course. 'Where are we going?' I asked.

'We're going to visit your auntie Ginny, remember her?'

'No.'

'Aye you do. She put a Caramac bar in your pram, remember, and you ate the paper and threw away the chocolate.'

'Oh yes,' I recalled. I didn't like Caramac. It seemed too adult a treat, like a digestive biscuit.

'And who knows,' said my mother, 'you might even meet your uncle Bobo.'

My ears pricked up. Just who was this Bobo?

* * *

Aunt Ginny lived in the next street, Burndyke Street. In later life I've been called, amongst other things, a cynic. But what is a cynic but a disillusioned idealist? When of an evening I lie jaked to the nines in the gutter, discussing weighty matters of state with like-minded friends, one of our number, perhaps heady with fellow-feeling or lighter fuel, might posit the possibility of world peace. It's then, with regret, rather than through any sense of misanthropy, I find myself citing what I refer to as 'The Burndyke Street Question'. It goes like this. How can there ever be world peace when, ahem, East hates West, North hates South, Arab hates Jew, Jew hates Arab, Arab hates infidel, black infidel hates white infidel, rich white infidel hates poor white infidel, poor white Protestant infidel hates poor white Catholic infidel, Serbs hate Everybody, Everybody hates Americans, Paisley hates Glasgow, sober Glasgow hates drunken Glasgow, and, most damning of all, the people in Logie Street hate the people in Burndyke Street? For, as the Bible puts it, 'If a man loveth not his own neighbour, how can he love distant buggers in turbans who ride bikes without tyres and talk a lot of gibberish?' I'm paraphrasing but you grasp my point. True, the configuration of these allegiances might occasionally alter if given a rough enough shake within the kaleidoscope of world events, but the parameters of prejudice remain always, upon threat, ancient and unyielding. No, forget love, the best we can hope to mould, given the poor Play-Doh of humankind, is a capacity for tolerance. This is achievable since tolerance is little more than indifference with a Dulux coat of manners. Surely we can manage that? Call me a dreamer but I can see a world where people of all races, creeds and colours will live together in harmony because they don't give a toss about each other. Where if some crazed-eyed zealot asked you how you felt about the dreadlocked cross-dressing lesbian Sikh next door you'd say, 'Who gives a f—, as long as she keeps her music down.' Gleaming groups of neo-idealistic multiracial kids will gather together to sing the revised Pepsi anthem 'I'd like to teach the world to shrug'. But that's a long way from Burndyke Street.

'This isn't a nice street, son,' said my mother, through pursed lips. She had plonked me on a litter bin while she negotiated the task of furrowing out discarded chips from the ridges of my shoe with a kirby grip. A little heap of the offending articles lay scattered near the bin. A garnish of crusted vomit dressed the side. A smeared puddle of blood close by told a story she didn't need to be Joe Friday to work out.

'Drunk men,' sneered my mother, grimly. 'You'll not drink, will you, son?'

I shook my head. It was an easy judgement call if 'drink' made you sling away your food, throw up and start battering your head against the kerb. 'Who's that, Mammy?' I asked, pointing up at a window.

My mother looked. An attractive woman with dark hair

was waving to us. My mother waved back. 'That's your auntie Ginny, son. Mammy's sister. Do you not think she looks just like Mammy?'

I compared the two faces. They were similar, except that one was lively, vibrant and twinkling. The other, my mother's, looked like the Turin shroud without the beard. Something told me to nod. I nodded. My mother looked pleased. 'Let's meet your cousins,' she said.

Auntie Ginny's flat was no bigger than our own. When we entered she was performing a limbo dance under two chairs and a mop pole to the song 'Bandit of Brazil'. One of her breasts hung free and a newborn child in a half-open dressing-table drawer wailed in a small doll-like voice for food. 'I'll be with you in a minute,' called Auntie Ginny, 'I couldn't miss my turn.' Children of assorted sizes clapped rhythmically as she completed, successfully, her manoeuvre. Small people scuttled to and fro. Auntie Ginny had children it seemed, the way we had mice.

'Look at me,' cried a small upside-down face suspended from the light flex.

'Get down!' scolded Ginny, prodding her with the limbo pole. The face dropped onto the chair and came to rest with its legs in the air and its head on the seat, and began chewing the stem of a liquorice pipe.

'Would you like some tea?' asked Auntie Ginny. My mother nodded. 'So would I, it's a bugger, isn't it? But I've got no tea nor coffee.'

'Nor sugar nor milk,' added the pipe-eater, not at all concerned.

'The tap still works,' said a blonde girl in the corner, working with a crayon at the wallpaper.

'If you like brown water,' sneered yet another sister. A small noisy scuffle broke out between the two.

'Honest to God, Issy, I'm rooked,' said Aunt Ginny, intervening with the mop pole.

My mother bit her lip. Her bony fingers clicked and unclicked the clasp of her purse – as they always did, I'd noticed, in times of financial pressure. Tentatively, she yielded. I saw a folded red ten-shilling note slip regretfully from donor to recipient. This was the housekeeping money. Mother's private stash that she kept stuffed at the toe of her shoe was evidently bare.

'Are you sure?' offered Aunt Ginny. It was patently obvious to me that Mother was anything but. She nodded anyway.

'Gonny do me a wee favour, Ginny? The wean . . .' Mother's voice trailed off. Aunt Ginny looked at her, then at me and at the bare breast I was eyeing with curiosity.

'A chest man,' smiled Ginny, folding away the offending article.

'Like his father,' said my mother.

'And his uncle,' said my aunt.

They looked at each other. 'Oh, Issy,' said Ginny.

'Oh, Ginny,' said Issy. And they fell into each other's arms, wailing.

Not for the first time I remarked the startling mood swings of the poor, the grimy froth of gaiety that rose from the dark chaotic torrents of despair. To cheer things up, I pissed myself. A child was despatched to the sideboard and emerged with a torn pair of pants of dubious cleanliness. A volunteer was sought to run to the corner shop for provisions, a bribe of threepence being offered. Many hands smote the air. The eldest, Maureen, was charged with the task. 'Can I take the wean?' she asked, looking at me. My mother nodded and pulled the pants up, the elastic stopping just south of my nipples. A wad of grey adult underpant hung maturely from a leg of my frivolous yellow shorts. I felt oddly pleased and assured, like one who has just taken membership of a club, which of course I had, since I now looked like a fully paid-up subscriber to that most ancient of bodies, the poor.

Cousin Maureen led me through the drab dirt of the communal back court. 'This is a short cut,' she said, tugging my hand.

A hunchbacked beggar in a long coat sleek with grime sang up at the closed windows, eyeing us as he did so. 'I get no kick from champagne, mere alcohol doesn't thrill me at all . . .' he lied, melodically. 'I have the gift of irony,' he called in a rasping voice.

'Try the gift of soap, ya clatty midden,' countered Maureen.

The beggar, stuck for a witty riposte, tottered a few steps forward. 'Show us your knickers!' he barked.

Maureen squealed and quickened her pace to a brisk trot, dragging me behind her. The beggar laughed. A window opened. A thrown penny plopped into a dark puddle. He fished for it. 'Many thanks,' he called up, employing his gift of irony. We made the safety of a closemouth, Maureen giggling, me gasping and whining.

'You all right?' she asked.

'No,' I whinged.

'Just stand there,' she instructed. She craned her neck, listening for activity in the close and, finding none, turned back to me.

'Look at this,' she said matter-of-factly, lifting her dress. I looked.

'Right, that's your lot,' she said, lowering it again. 'Tell anybody and your dead.' She showed me a fist. I cried. We shook hands. 'Right, let's get the tea.' As we emerged from the close Maureen let out a scream. She began waving hysterically to a broad, dark-suited figure across the street. The figure, wavy-haired and good-looking, made a calming gesture with his hands and put a finger to his lips. Maureen stopped shrieking and pulled me hurriedly onward. She was impatient and excited.

'Who was that?' I asked.

'My da,' she replied.

'Uncle Bobo?'

She nodded. I turned to look but the broad figure had already disappeared.

'Let's hurry up,' I urged.

'OK,' she said, and we ran the rest of the way.

The two policemen stood sternly in the middle of the room, surrounded by a ring of Aunt Ginny's children. A queue at the corner shop had delayed us. One had a notebook open, for effect, evidently, since he made no entries. I recognized them as Blunt and Rude, the same pair who had visited on the day of my escape attempt. My mother sat, tight-lipped and pale with intimidation. My aunt Ginny didn't.

'We know he's out,' said Blunt, 'and living in a safe house.'

'Well, this one's none too safe if a pair of bams like you can break in,' said Ginny.

'Open the door and we won't need to kick it in,' said Rude.

'If I opened the door you'd get the impression you were welcome,' said Ginny. A draught of wind billowed the thin curtains. Aunt Ginny closed the window. 'Is that all?' she asked with a defiant air.

'Fine example you're setting your kids,' said Blunt, shutting his notebook. He knew he was getting nowhere. 'We're getting nowhere.'

Rude nodded. 'We'll send a joiner round to fix the door.'

'You sent a plumber last time.'

'You were less cooperative last time,' said Blunt with what he thought was a winning smile as they left.

My aunt Ginny exhaled. 'Close call.'

'Say that again,' said my mother, trembling. 'I don't know how you can live like this.'

'It beats working,' said Ginny. There was a rapping sound from outside the window. We looked up. The broad man with the wavy dark hair squatted, smiling, on the ledge. Maureen opened the window. Uncle Bobo peeked in.

'All right?' he said. He gazed around the room. He stopped gazing when he came to me. 'Who's that big boy,' he said, 'wearing his uncle's pants?'

I struggled to quench a glow of pride. 'Being poor is fun,' I thought.

*

Yes, being poor is fun. Compared, that is, to being destitute. As I approach death, or middle age as it is known in Govan, I have made the journey, on foot, between both conditions, calling at all stations in between, and can attest to the luxury of poverty. Destitute people aspire to poverty. Poor folk fret over trifles, like holes in shoes, while the destitute crave only the security of an approximate pair, being content to escape the curse of hopping. True, I myself have walked the streets of Glasgow barefoot many times, usually in the small hours when the police, as is their sporting custom, throw open the overnight cells at 5 a.m., and hurtle the occupants footwear-free into the streets. The Glasgow police may one day open a shoe repository, a sort of black and tan museum, for they must house a larger, if less savoury, collection of footwear than Pied à Terre and Dolcis combined, much of it mine. But at the end of all my damp and huddled walks, no matter how miserable, has lain the prospect of a warm though sagging bed, alongside a warm though sagging wife. In the hierarchy of scum society a roof is the demarcation line that separates the hard-core professional waster from the merely gifted amateur like myself. To the remainder of society I may appear a roaming random beast, but within the parameters of my own world I'm as bourgeois as a town hall clock. In this, I am my father's son.

My father once banned a mantelpiece clock because he deemed its tick 'too rowdy'. With a proper clock, that is to say a proper Scottish clock, only two sounds are permitted, namely 'tick' and 'tock'. Anything additional, say some echoing reverberation deep down in the mechanism, as in this case, is deemed extraneous and as anything extraneous is a form of showing off such a clock is given short shrift in respectable, which is to say unhappy, Scottish homes. Of which we were one. When I enquired as to the fate of the clock my mother informed me tenderly that it had found a new home with some laughing tinkers, where its delinquency could enjoy full rein. However, I digress.

*

I was becoming a small boy. The carefree days of toddlerdom were behind me and ahead lay the weighty responsibilities of small-boyness. Henceforth a gauntlet of character tests and initiation rites would be thrown down and picked up daily, or ignored at my peril. Out of cowardice I chose the path of bravery, having no wish to risk the scorn of my fellows, for fellows there now were.

A small boy's life is one of curiosity and disobedience. Each morning I would rise and test, diligently, the parameters of my condition. Electrical sockets were duly probed with knitting needles, cheek administered to sundry adults, wallpaper daubed with crayon and small sums of cash conscientiously pilfered from purse and pocket. I savoured the thrill of illicitly breaking rules. It was like discovering a torrent of dark lava flowing underneath a church.

The back court was our playground. To describe a back court is simple. Picture Hampton Court. Now take a stout rag and wipe that image from your mind. Picture instead a rectangle of black dirt, flanked on all sides by soot-stained four-storey tenements. Add some battered grey bins in a pillbox structure from which scabby cats leap, discomfited, on the intrusion of hot ash or rummaging vagabonds, and you have the accurate likeness in your head.

I was squatting on the ground, accompanied by some like-minded friends, digging at the dirt with a bent soup spoon when my colleague Angus burst suddenly into tears.

'What's the matter, Gus?' I enquired.

Gus shook his head, causing the bell on his Noddy hat to ring dully. 'Nothing,' he said. 'I find I get like this sometimes, these overwhelming panic attacks.' He looked at us, sheepishly. 'I know it's not manly.'

Drew and I exchanged a glance.

'That's allowed being as we're only four,' said Drew. His parents were divorced, which made Drew something of a celebrity in our street. In the fifties only film stars divorced.

I offered Gus some bubblegum. It was second-hand, of course but there was still some flavour left, if you sucked really hard. Gus declined and lit up a Kensitas. I watched his hand tremble as it held the match. Drew gave a little cough. He had bad lungs but the concept of passive smoking was still just a glint in the eye of some sadistic bureaucrat who wanted the poor to live longer. Drew and I feared for Gus. We knew that compulsory conscription into infant school was only days away and we doubted whether he had enough lack of imagination and innate stupidity to survive the rigours of the state education system. He offered me a draw and as I took the fag I could see the fear in his eyes. Sure the kid had flair, talent, sensitivity but how was he on sneering or dumb insolence?

And could he sleep with his eyes open for the next ten years while some menopausal drudge in a tweed skirt droned on about parsing or the principal exports of Ceylon? I doubted it. The smart money said Gus would take a rap on the knuckles with a ruler on day one and be carted off gibbering to a special needs school somewhere safe behind enemy lines.

The cigarette passed back and forth in silence. Then Drew said, 'Ever wonder what this is all about? I mean the patronizing voices, the Big Ears braces, the endless mind-numbing obedience?'

'It's best not to talk,' said Gus nervously. 'It's best just to try and get through it.'

He was only parroting what I'd said myself many times, 'Just get through it.' But we all knew it wasn't that easy. We were inquisitive live-wire four-year-olds, we lacked the practised docility of the hard-core institutionalized adult. Ahead of us lay the no-man's-land of Religious Instruction, followed by a mindless charge across the years, disappearing into the foggy confusion of arithmetic and English grammar, urged on by a plimsoll-wielding PE zealot till we staggered dazed and altered into the eerie self-conscious calm of pubescence. No wonder we were scared.

*

Dull and early on Monday morning, we marshalled in the playground, baffled and apprehensive, waiting to be conscripted. Our mothers massed outside the railings, looking fraught or stoic according to temperament. The air resounded with the click-clack of imaginary scissors, trying to hack at steely apron strings. Our mothers looked more panicked than us children, as if they knew something we didn't, which of course they did. They knew that not all of us would show grace under fire, that our private whines and snivellings would henceforth be on public display, each budding weakness of character exposed and frozen under the harsh glare of authoritarian scrutiny. And let's face it, Govan mothers were a macho breed. Who wanted to have given birth to a pansy? Consequently we were instructed to be 'good wee soldiers', 'big boys', and to keep our disquiet as noiseless as possible. My mother pointed out Edward Doak as a model of taciturn resilience. Doak stood tall, straight and silent, his grey flannel shorts flapping in the breeze. 'Look at that big boy,' she encouraged me, 'he's not worried.' I took my lead from Doak and was silent. Doakie, I learned, never said anything, either in class or out of it. When, six months later, he dropped stone dead from a brain tumour I began to question his value as a role model.

A middle-aged ball of wool called Miss Rimmer tolled a hand bell. A prostrate drunk at the school gates, mistaking the sound for a police car, spreadeagled himself dazedly against the school wall, awaiting a frisk that never came. We marched in twos through the cloakroom, our noses thick with the stink of damp gaberdine, past the janitor eyeing us dourly over his *Daily Record*, into the bare drill hall to begin our wondrous voyage of education with a short prayer of grovelling thanks to the Lord.

'See you at playtime!' called waving mothers, plaintively.

'Fuck off, wee cunts!' called the drunk, flicking the V's. This was, after all, Govan.

*

'What did you learn in school today?' asked my father, flossing gristle from his teeth with black thread from which a bobbin dangled.

'Arithmetic,' I said.

'Pythagoras?' he asked, raising a hopeful eyebrow.

'No, two times table.'

'Give him a chance,' pleaded my mother, 'he's only young.'

'He's no prodigy,' sniffed my father, tugging at the bobbin till a gum bled, 'he'll never match his cousin Donald.'

Mother rallied to my defence. 'Donald's had every chance in life. He's at a fee-paying school.'

'Yes,' I thought, 'and I bet the bastard's got a wooden pencil case and a blazer that fits.' I surveyed my trailing hemline. 'A generous fit,' the salesman had said. So generous my arms could now be crossed and the empty bits of sleeve pinned behind my back like a straitjacket.

'Never you mind, son,' said my mother, 'you're as good as they are any day.'

I was puzzled. 'Who's they?'

My mother frowned. 'Other people,' she said, 'you know, toffs. Office workers.'

It had never dawned on me that my mother suffered from an inferiority complex. This would explain why whenever she tried to be uplifting I'd feel gloom descend on me like a damp wet coat. She was trying now.

'When I was your age, I was near the foot of the bottom section. But I worked hard and guess what, one day I made it to the middle section, you know, the mediocres. And that's not all, when I left school I got a job in a pie shop. Handling money and everything. So what do you think about that?'

I looked up at my mother's drawn face as it tried to beam, confidently. 'My God,' I thought, 'even her inferiority complex is substandard.'

My father prodded me in the school badge with the stiff peak of his cap. My father's cap peak was straight, as per standard issue. Most discerning bus conductors bent them almost double, like SS men. He gave me a hard look.

'If your mother hadn't fallen pregnant with you, we could still have been in Millport. I'd still have been at sea.'

My parents had lived on the Isle of Cumbrae. My father had commanded the ferry that ran ten-minute trips to the mainland. My parents' landlady disliked children and they'd been forced to quit their digs and move to Glasgow. My father was determined to allow this circumstance to scar his life. We'd stroll to the Elder Park and my father would gaze out wistfully at the boating pond as if it was the mighty Pacific. He'd speak of shore leave and of roistering in the pubs and ice-cream parlours of Largs where he and his fellow seamen would sing heart-rending songs about being far away from home, even though the lights of those homes could be seen, clearly, twinkling across the bay.

'Never forget the price I've paid,' said my father, leaving. As soon as he was out of the room, I forgot the price my father had paid.

'Ignore him, son, he's only angry with life,' said my mother.

'Only because it's beaten him,' I said.

My mother considered her loyalties. She gave me a skelp on the cheek. Afterwards she felt guilty and offered me a laddered stocking into which I pushed a bald tennis ball and chucked it around the back court, like a hammer thrower, imagining it held my father's head – which, I admit, was unprofessional in an athlete.

*   *   *

Miss Rimmer was our form teacher. She was round, plain and smiley, seemingly at ease with life in a way that so many of the other staff, mostly women, were not. On our first morning Miss Rimmer ordered the classroom curtains drawn so that we could be given a slide show. I have no memory of what the slide show comprised, possibly 'Drizzle through the Ages' or something equally Glaswegian. What has lodged in my memory, however, is that Stig Foley cried. As darkness descended and the black drapes closed on their squeaky runners, Stig sobbed and implored repeatedly, 'What are you going to do, Miss?' Note the absence of colloquialism, no 'whit' or 'dae' but scrupulous standard English. The dominion of adult tyranny over Stig was so comprehensive that he had instinctively served up his rawest fears on his finest linguistic teaset. When, in later life, Stig became a named hooligan and respected sociopath, I could never take him seriously in his new incarnation. When I'd picture him in the basement of some scabby club poised to extract miscellaneous teeth from the head of some sweating debtor, I'd see those drapes close, the pliers drop to the floor and the intended victim rise, sportingly, from his chair to offer Stig a consoling hug, shitbag to shitbag, as he whimpered, 'But what are you going to do, Miss?' This privileged insight into the budding psyche of a crazed nincompoop was to cause me some consternation during a small drinking adventure many years hence, a tale I shall recount in due course.

*

I was a brightish student, surprisingly, early on, duly occupying the semi-coveted position of second back row of the class, we pupils being graded from back to front, according to performance. The Back were invariably pale creatures in enviably spotless uniforms who looked as though they'd been bred in captivity and nurtured in dark rooms, like veal. The Top never daydreamed in class and would sob inconsolably if they scored less than eight out of ten for spelling. To my row, second from rear, eight out of ten was a bragworthy credit, a comfortable academic cruising speed, the pursuit of perfection seeming vulgar and excessive beside the complacent grace of middling achievement.

The front row were wretched beings, usually the poorest amongst us. They'd sit, paralysed by dimness and self-consciousness, and if asked a question would allow slow seconds of tedious silence to crawl past before whispering some dismal response, which they'd be invited impatiently to repeat. The weary ritual would begin again and again until the answer was delivered in sufficient volume to be heard, comfortably, by tribesmen crouched with an ear to the ground in the Kalahari bush. It was, needless to say, always wrong. To the rest of us the front row were both a source of genial amusement and stupefying exasperation – how could the capital of Belgium be seven-eighths, as Grant Ferrier once posited – as well as being a handy lightning conductor for the random rage of our teachers. I had no way of foretelling that in a few short years circumstance would deposit me on the front row and that I'd know, first-hand, the twin mortifications of threadbare poverty and dozy ignorance.

But for the moment all I recognized was the proposition that extremes met. The very bright and the very stupid were granted, by dint of their unique but differing capabilities, that most lusted-after commodity in the eyes of a child, attention. The others, average, like myself, who occupied the academic equivalent of no-man's-land, could rely only on the odd stray parcel-drop of basic hard-tack flattery and bully beef encouragement to sustain our efforts and assure us of our importance. Consequently, in an attempt to enhance my esteem in the eyes of the education system, I decided to become stupid, judging that, on balance, this would be easier to attain than intelligence. My plan involved a deliberate and wilful mangling of the laws of arithmetic as well as some grotesque yet inventive grammatical diversions and misspellings during the writing of essays. I took to the task with a will. Perhaps too much of a will, for my efforts, with hindsight, were overstated to the point of pantomime. I realized this when, after setting down my pencil and settling back to savour the full impact of the decimation of my solid mediocrity on Miss Rimmer, she failed to summon me before her. Instead she calmly read aloud our marks to us, adding, as usual, the occasional 'Well done,' or 'Tch, tch, should have done better.' My own test mark, a gratifyingly poor one, passed without comment. Miss Rimmer simply set the bundle of papers aside and spoke, in general terms, of our performance. I fidgeted at my desk, outraged and perplexed. How could she have failed to spontaneously combust, or at the very least be stretchered from the room in shock? Only at the end of her summary did she allude, tangentially, to my efforts. 'Oh yes,' she said in the tone of an afterthought, 'and someone, I can't remember who, spelt the word "through" as "throo".' She allowed a slight customary pause for licensed mirth, then a slight snicker herself by way of closing the subject.

She produced a geographical manual from her desk drawer and opened it, smoothing out the spine with the sleeve of her cardigan. 'Now,' she began, 'who can tell me the principal export of Canada?'

Hands smote the air to cries of 'Me,' 'Me,' 'Me, Miss.'

My moment had come and gone. I sat silently, stunned and broken. 'Someone, I can't remember who . . .' The words echoed in my head, cruelly. Even my stupidity was too bland to be memorable. Or so it seemed to me then. With hindsight it may of course have been the case that Miss Rimmer knew more of the egotistical workings of the childish mind than she indicated and that dismissing my subversive efforts was nothing other than a tactic by which she sought to outmanoeuvre me. If so, she was right, for I never repeated the ploy. Though in subsequent tests I was to prove spectacularly ignorant this could be ascribed to honest limitation rather than wilful corruption.

Indeed on only one subsequent occasion was I to draw attention to myself academically, in fact to distinguish myself, albeit fleetingly, and here the motivating factor, appropriately enough for a fat bastard in the making, was hunger.

A brother, Gash, had appeared and then a sister, Rena. These arrivals necessitated a move across the landing to a larger and therefore more expensive flat. The cumulative effect of these changes was to gouge a bottomless hole in Father's tiny, unskilled worker's wage packet. These added burdens of responsibility meant that he was now obliged to work interminable overtime in a job he detested for what, to him, must have seemed no measurable improvement in circumstance. The result of which was that Father's frustration turned to bitterness and his bitterness to drink. He would sit in his armchair after a shift, his shirt removed for comfort, the red chafe marks of his collar like a chain around his neck, his badged cap still perched on his head. Beer would be sipped from a stolen pub glass, or whisky, when he could afford it, from one of a cheap set of ornamental vessels in the display cabinet, each depicting an oafish piper in tartan drag engaged in full soundless blow.

'I married the wrong woman,' my father would opine, affecting an ugly twist of the lips in an attempt to heighten the dramatic effect of his utterance. In the early days, Mother would wince at this unkind remark, wounded to the core. Gradually, however, the core toughened and Father's barbs were deflected harmlessly outwards from Mother's sensitive soul. She rarely struck back, though once I did hear her emit a weary 'You're telling me,' when Father held forth with his familiar refrain. Only when he threatened violence did she grow wary. She was a thin neurotic reed of a woman, and a couple of clumps from an oafish fist would have been enough to inflict substantial damage. As we were all to discover.

As money grew ever more scarce so staples like breakfast or supper became haphazard treats and our appetites hostages to fortune. So it was that on one nourishment-free morning when Miss Rimmer produced a large shiny green apple and offered it as a prize to the essayist displaying the neatest handwriting, I resolved to win. We were given forty minutes to complete our essay, scarcely enough time to assemble one's thoughts let alone render them in one's finest copperplate. I reasoned, sensibly enough, that style on this occasion was of greater value than content, particularly since time was of the essence. Eschewing all linguistic complexity along with the occasional full stop or semi-colon, I embarked on a stream of semi-conscious tosh under the given subject heading, 'My Life as a Sixpence'. Our requirement was to fill both sides of a foolscap sheet. Cunning born of necessity told me that Rimmer would in all probability peruse only the top page of each essay since sense was a purely secondary consideration and that it would therefore be worthy, at best, of only the most perfunctory glance. At the call of 'Time up,' I handed in my essay. On one side, a conscientious example of the schoolboy calligrapher's art, on the other a hastily scrawled pig's ear.

'And the winner is . . .' Tension. Pencils chewed, desks gripped till knuckles whiten. 'Robert Nesbitt.' Relief. Euphoria. A curious inner certainty that alongside Granny Smith's was written my name. I rose, walked to the front, turning inner cartwheels, face set in scowl, collected my prize. Miss Rimmer made a gracious presentation, putting me at my ease as my feet fidgeted on the unknown terrain of Successland. 'Well done,' she said with a smile, academic to academic, handing me Granny's plump round form, to have and to hold. And to munch. Which I did, in the playground, later, surrounded by a ring of envious watchers, eager to swim in the slipstream of my unexpected celebrity. As I crunched, I watched a boy with the unmistakable awkward gait of the new initiate make his way, flanked by two unsightly heaps of clothing which I took to be parents, toward the interior of the school building.

'Who's that guy?' I asked my temporary acolytes.

'Him?' said Gus. 'He's moved into the next close to me.'

The boy was grimy, shifty and sly-looking. He carried an army-surplus haversack for his school books, which was de rigueur at the time. I disliked him on sight. This impression has never changed though that same boy has been my closest friend for nigh on forty years.

'His name's Jamesie Cotter,' said Gus.

*

At home I told my mother about the apple.

'That's marvellous, son. Where is it?'

'I ate it,' I confessed.

My mother looked at my father. My father looked at me. He clumped me behind the ear. 'Liar,' he said and returned his attention to the *Exchange and Mart*. 'Here's one,' he said, prodding the page with a laden fork.

'One what?' I enquired.

'A television set?' ventured my mother, hopefully.

'No,' said Father, giving her a look. 'A radio transmitter!' He left a small pause into which we failed to insert the required token of glee. So he continued.

'With one of these I can transmit messages everywhere, all around the world!'

'What kind of messages?' I asked.

'All kinds!' shouted Father, sternly, proffering volume in lieu of detail.

'Will you be able to compare bus fares from all around the globe, Da?' Skilfully, I'd kept the hint of contempt from my tone, leaving Father floundering. His half-closed fist hovered, uncertainly, unable to decide whether a secondary slap was warranted. He relented, picked up a pencil and ringed the advert. 'I'm going to view this piece of equipment.'

'Are you sure, Rab, it's awful expensive,' counselled my mother.

'Just to view,' assured Father. But he tapped Mother for a pound, just in case. He turned to me. 'Do you want to come?' he said. 'It's in Balornock.' He was trying to make it sound like an adventure. It was not.

'Do I have to?' I asked.

'Yes,' said Father, divesting himself of the slap that had been brewing for some minutes. 'You might learn something.'

And I did. I learnt that standing in drizzle for thirty minutes waiting for a bus to the north of Glasgow was an experience to be savoured by only the most ardent yea-sayer to life. Similarly I learnt that a transmitter when lugged down three flights of tenement stairs loses mystique in direct proportion to the weight it gathers during descent.

'This transmitter will be the making of you,' promised Father as we staggered toiling through the dank close. And it was. It made me indifferent to transmitters, broadening the gulf still further between Father and myself.

*

My father, essentially, was a man of discipline, whereas I, essentially, was a boy of sloth. Having acquired the barest rudiments of reading, writing and arithmetic I'd concluded to my own satisfaction that further refinement of these tools would be excessive and unhealthy. Already blessed with the curse of a melancholic temperament I could find myself in the street engaged with my friends in a routine game of Kick the Can, spy a cloud passing the sun to cast a long chimney shadow at my feet and be transported instantly to some distant land of unspecified regret like an ancient libertine lamenting lost loves and forgotten pleasures.

Forgivable perhaps in a roué of sixty, inconvenient in a boy of eight. Even in those days my principal expression was a frown. Adults would ruffle my hair and with grisly smiles exhort me to 'stop carrying the world on my shoulders'. Why? If they wouldn't do it, I reasoned, the task fell to me. Yes, it was left to me, Moses Nesbitt, the Last of the Just plc, e-mail Job@woe.glasgow. All around me I saw trapped souls, offering their grotesque existences as role models for us, their children. 'Get a trade at your fingertips,' counselled my mother. 'Get fingertips,' rued Gus's father, who'd lost seven digits to an over-zealous lathe. But I was without ambition. What was the dismal lifetime's grovelling for two-bob bits beside the sweet heartbreaking riddle of existence? Well, quite a lot actually, at least in the real world which was where I was obliged to locate myself. Nevertheless, even in those tender formative years romanticism provided a handy pose, lending a kindly spiritual glow to my bankrupt indolence.

Father was in his element with the transmitter. On rainy Sundays afternoons after dinner, sex and weeping he would pull a side chair over to the food cabinet, open the lower half which contained his equipment and spend the remaining hours of dim daylight conversing, via the banal magic of Morse code, with battered Eastern European cargo vessels as they sloughed through obscure British shipping channels. In a determined sharing effort he wrote down the code for me on a page of Basildon Bond, hoping its charismatic delight might touch some as yet undiscovered mutual joy gene. Not a fucking hope. I stared blankly at the handset when invited to repeat the alphabet, in dots and dashes. I watched my father then, mentally, pack away his suitcase full of genetic free offers and move away if not on. In his eyes I was a hopeless cause. But not quite. Sometimes, when his back was turned, I'd tap out random SOS messages, hoping to initiate a modest tanker collision or full-scale RAF sea search, anything to provide a diversion from the teatime radio ritual of George Mitchell and his dismal Minstrels. Neither did my father ever realize that I'd managed to master, in Polish, the words 'Fuck off, Da.' However this simple pungent message proved an ineffective conversational lure to exotic foreign receivers.

*

One day I was seated at my desk parsing a short dull sentence when I became aware of a steamy presence next to me and a clammy hand on my knee. I looked. 'Shush!' said the boy. 'Pass that on to her.' I looked again. Margaret Cogan sat across the narrow aisle, parsing diligently. 'Aye, her,' urged the boy, sensing my hesitation, 'it's a private joke, she'll know what it means.' I nodded. Leaning across, I placed my hand uncertainly upon her bare knee and made ready what I hoped was a wry smile of twinkling anticipation. Margaret Cogan shrieked, fit to wake the dead, if not the front row. Miss Rimmer was alerted, instantly. Before I could recover, a blackboard duster came hurtling towards me, striking me on the forehead and raising a small cloud of chalk. 'Nesbitt! Out here!' screamed the teacher.

I protested, limply. 'Please, Miss . . . it wasn't me. I was doing it for him. He told me.'

'Who told you?'

'Him, Miss.' I pointed at the sudden fetid gap where Jamesie Cotter had been. I scanned the room with a sweeping glance. Cotter had his head down and a faraway look in his eye, like a man deeply engrossed in the mystery of subordinate clauses.

'Him, Miss,' I repeated, hopelessly, 'Jamesie Cotter.'

'Cotter!' yelled Miss Rimmer. 'Is this true?'

Cotter looked up. Bewilderment dissolved to horror then genteel indignation. 'No, Miss. I don't even know what he's . . .' The voice trailed off, expertly.

'He's good,' I thought, 'he's very good.' It was like watching Sidney Carton appraise the barbarous horde. I knew I was done for.

'Out, Nesbitt.'

I climbed mentally into my tumbril and made my way down the aisle to name-calling and indignant looks.

I received, from Miss Rimmer, three strokes of the belt and was made to apologize to Margaret Cogan. Smarting with shame and eager for revenge I returned to my seat and challenged Cotter to a duel, or fight at playtime, the schoolboy equivalent, in the traditional manner by glaring at my enemy silently and showing him a fist. The smirk fell from Cotter's face. He reached down, picked it up and restuck it. But it was crooked now and gave him, to my satisfaction, a queasy look.

At playtime, I took my place in the ring of Madison Square Gardens, just behind the toilet block, and awaited my opponent. Word had spread and the ritual chant of 'Fight!' ran round the playground. Unfortunately some older subversives drifted down from the music room. Bent on amusement they struck up an alternative rhythmic chant, incorporating the stylistic innovation of hand-clapping. My peers listened, liked what they heard and adopted it. I stood, keen-jawed and menacing, shirt tail dangling from the bottom of my shorts, a hard man not to be trifled with, while the crowd chanted, 'If Doh, Me and Soh are in spaces the High Doh is two lines above Soh!' Clap, clap,

clap. 'If Doh, Me and Soh are in spaces, then . . .' Still no Cotter. To buy time, I squatted down and gouged dirt from between the flagstones with a lollipop stick, an old pugilist trick. Five minutes later most of the crowd had drifted away. After ten, I looked up to see the stern faces of the headmaster and Miss Rimmer flanking Cotter. He was whimpering. I noticed he had a sock rolled down and was leaning heavily to one side, feigning polio.

The Headie, Mr Perry, grabbed me by the jumper and yanked me to my feet. 'I'll have no bullying in my school,' he said and tugged me towards his office for three further strokes. Miss Rimmer swung the handbell signifying the end of break. As I turned, I saw Cotter, smirk repaired, flicking me the V's. I'd tried not to turn but he knew I would and was ready. You had to admire him. Or despise him. Either way he got under your skin like a tic.

*

'What happened to your good jumper?' my mother moaned at the tea table. 'Look at his good jumper.'

'There's gristle in this stew,' said my father, picking his teeth.

'It's a cow, isn't it, there's got to be gristle otherwise it would flop around like jelly.'

'That's enough, young lady,' warned Father.

I nudged Rena with my knee, urging her to continue with her plain person's guide to bovine anatomy.

'Does anybody know what sweetbreads are?'

'I said enough!'

'Rab, will you look at his jumper.'

'What about his jumper?' He looked at my jumper. 'What happened to your jumper?' he said.

'He was in a fight,' volunteered Rena, sensing greater entertainment value with a switch of allegiance.

'A fight, is it,' grimaced Father. 'Who won?'

'Well, it wasn't him,' said Rena, 'the crowd sang him to death then he got carted off by the Headie.'

My father's lips uncurled half a degree, signifying mirth.

Mother, sensing lost ground, ordered me to remove the jumper. 'See?' she said. 'That's a big darning job. And that jumper's not only to do him, Gash'll have to wear it next year.'

We all turned, as one, to stare at Gash. Cursed with the burden of intelligence, he sat fragile and alone, perusing an atlas.

'What's the capital of Venezuela?' barked Father.

'Caracas,' murmured Gash.

'Louder!'

'Caracas,' I said.

'Nobody asked you!' Father jabbed my hand with a fork. 'Go to your room!'

We all looked at each other. 'He can't go to his room, Rab,' said Mother.

'Why not?'

'This is my room,' I said. 'I'm in it. I sleep here, remember?'

'The kids are getting up, Rab,' coaxed Mother, with the deft terror of a bomb-disposal expert, 'we could do with a bigger flat.'

'This abode is adequate,' declared Father. 'We need plenty of other things yet before another house.'

'Like a television set?' ventured Rena, hopefully.

'Like a motor car,' said Father, propping his *Exchange and Mart* on some prearranged condiment vessels. Mother sat heavily and rubbed her forehead.

'Why don't you read the *Daily Worker* any more, Da?' I asked, moving the subject a further stealthy step from the jumper.

'I disagreed with its political stance over Stalin. So I stopped taking it.'

'Where do you get your politics from now,' asked Rena, 'the *Exchange and Mart?*'

Father gave her a condescending look, lowbrow to cretin. 'The *Daily Express,*' he said. 'That's the paper of the management classes. Befitting of a Glasgow tram inspector.'

Mother glanced up. 'Tram inspector? You mean you've got . . .'

Father shifted in his seat. 'Well no,' he confessed. 'But as good as. As good as.'

He swallowed his lump of stew, gristle and all, and ringed an ad confidently. I struggled to peek. I could make out the words 'Ford Popular'. I looked at mother. Her face was forlorn, the sleeves of my jumper draped uselessly across her legs. I felt a pang of dutiful sympathy. Soon she would be carrying a motor car on her back. She should have quit while she was ahead.

'Caracas,' said Gash, loudly.

CHAPTER TWO

GOVAN is a magic realist state, only without the magic.

Some background:

The name Govan was formed by joining two Gaelic words, 'Go' meaning 'stop' and 'Van', 'to be without tax or insurance'. The focal point of Govan is Govan Cross, because there is nothing to see there, whereas to look in any other direction is to view something that offends the eye and may induce weeping or blackouts. The township was formed in the early eighteenth century as a weaving community. No one knows what they wove, or why, as the community are all dead now and don't talk much. It is known, however, that they sang weaving songs, fragments of which still remain. 'We are weavers, weavers are we, see how we weave', etc. Strong drink was introduced to the area soon afterwards. As shipbuilding took over so the weaving industry died out as cloth boats were viewed to be unsound. Nowadays shipbuilding on the Clyde is in a perilous state but happily new industries are springing up, like unemployment and car theft.

The unemployment industry provides work for thousands, from small clerks to government ministers, all busily engaged in fiddling the register and devising bright new methods of tidying away the area's troublesome long-term mouth-breathers. Govan has always been a vibrant community and as the streets once rang to the calls of travelling vendors, ragmen and coal merchants, so the quaint cries of the community's drug dealers have continued the tradition. Shouts of 'ten-pound deal' and 'you're striped, ya cunt' are proof of a bustling black economy as well as providing gaiety and colour for the passing tourist.

It is often asserted that in the past this sense of community was so strong that one could 'leave one's door wide open'. This is true. Many people did leave their doors open, but in the main these were elderly or stupid people and when they'd wake in the morning to find their furniture gone they would be led away, gurgling, to sheltered housing.

Another familiar assertion is that forty years ago standards of sexual morality were higher. People will point out that there were 'none of these paedophiles back then'. This also is true. In the fifties there were no paedophiles. There were only simple honest-to-goodness child-molesters.

*

Ice-cream van drivers made popular molesters, being generally young and jocular. For the price of a fumble an amenable young lad might enjoy generous access to the magical world of Mivvies and Double Nougats. Sunshine Alex was our local molester. He wore grey flannels and had a permanent smile. His demands were modest and his allowances handsome. Boys jostled to be abused by Alex; indeed it became almost a rite of passage. 'Well, son, you can swim, ride a bike, time now to be groped by the ice-cream man.' I was saddened some years ago when I read he'd been jailed for rampaging naked round a school playground with a butterfly net.

Just as there were no paedophiles so no one was 'mentally disadvantaged'. They were only 'a bit slow'. 'A bit slow' people tended to live with parents who looked more like grandparents. Because their powers of assertion were often less than robust, 'a bit slow' boys were often condemned to dress sensibly, like their fathers, ergo they looked like grandfathers. I can still recall, at the height of frenzied Beatlemania, the tragic sight of an 'a bit slow' teenaged boy standing at the gates of Elder Park dressed in a car coat and tweed bunnet carrying a set of bowls in a string bag. The look in his eye said that he was dimly aware that something was wrong with his life but that he couldn't quite work out what. A pretty girl in a miniskirt walked past. Something stirred. He looked down at the front of his trousers and was about to hang the set of bowls from it when his father appeared, in identical car coat and bunnet, and gave him a skite across the head.

'Any more of that,' he said, 'and you'll get no *Gardeners' Question Time.*'

*

Govan men, as I have said, worked in shipyards. They spat a lot and wore ancient boiler suits that had no buttons and a ragged arse that would hang just south of the Cheviots.

In hot weather they'd fold down the top half of the suits and tie the arms around their waists showing deep sweat stains in the OXTEROS of their SEMMITAS.

In those days a man was judged by the size of his stain. Big Eldo the caulker burner had the largest stains and sometimes, if he was in a good mood, would throw his arms up and show us the two prized damp rings, the size of dinner plates, on the armpits of his shirt.

'And this is me wearing a semmit underneath,' he would boast, 'you should see them in July when I climb out of the bulkheads!' And with that he would throw back his mighty head and laugh. Or even throw it forward and laugh, according to whim.

'My father too has stains,' said Shuch, the decorator's son, 'when he stands up you can see turps marks on the seat of his chair.'

'And mine,' enthused Stobo, whose father was a welder, 'when he blows his nose, his hanky fills up with black mucus.'

Eldo grinned and hugged the boys to him. 'You are both fine young men,' he said 'and when you are older we will drink Lanliq together and stagger about a lot and tap the wife for a pound on Saturday nights.' And they all threw back their heads and laughed. Finally, his eye fell on me.

'And you,' he said, 'what does your father do?'

'Sir,' I replied, 'he's a bus conductor.'

Eldo's eyes narrowed. He stroked his stubbly chin. 'And has he stains?' He asked, slowly.

'No, sir, no stains. For in our family we set great store by personal hygiene and place cleanliness next only to godliness in the great scheme of things, except of course on laundrette days when Mother gives it a slight precedence.'

'His mother puts down newspapers to stop the light from fading the linoleum!' sneered Shuch.

'And his father won't use brilliantine on his hair because it soils the pillowcases,' added Stobo with glee.

'One of them, eh?'

I hung my head in shame. For yes, it was true. My father, indeed my whole family, were strangely devoid of grime. Only that morning I had gone through our laundry basket in a desperate search for some symbol, a crispy shirt or a blackened shirt collar, that would have brought the certainty I craved, the reassurance that we were as fallible as these other poor creatures and not, as I feared, perfect. But there was nothing, not even a skid mark. In the Blessed Church of Our Lady's Undressed Rivet Burn I had craved the indulgence of Father Antony and sought his guidance. The old priest had listened to me with much kindness and forbearance until he discovered I was a Protestant and ejected me.

'You Proddies,' he had screamed, 'you think yourselves so superior! Just because we're superstitious and take a lot of holidays! Well, the Pope could give your Queen a tanking any day, sonny, no messing!' As an afterthought he began playing an imaginary set of spoons and jigging straight armed, by the font.

As if he had been reading my thoughts, Big Eldo stood up and thrust his arms back into his boiler suit.

'I never trust a man I can't smell,' he said. And with that he took out a florin and sent my two friends running to the Tally's for ten Bristols, adding that he'd time them to see if they could break a hundred. Then he picked up his chip poke and resumed eating, slowly and deliberately, without offering me one, which was considered a very great insult in our community.

That night I related what had happened to Rena, my dear sister. Though younger than I, Rena wore a white patch on her specs so was possessed, by the blessing of infirmity, of superior insight.

'Look on the bright side,' she counselled. 'He's more than likely another fat diddy who'll probably die one day of a heart attack.'

Satisfied, we picked up our shirt pins and spent a happy hour scraping dandruff from the teeth of Father's combs.

*   *   *

Mother's lack of money and Father's thirst for status continued to produce tension. This they attempted to quell in the traditional scum way. Mam called the child Freak. At last, it seemed, Father had set aside his quest for a motor car. Or so we thought. Until one day, during my Mexican phase, an incident occurred. I remember it well. It was a warm summer evening in our village and once again I was working on the land. Resting my hoe against the window sill of our humble hacienda, I pushed aside my poncho, a folded-out double page of the *Daily Express* with a hole cut for the head, and picked up a handful of moist virgin earth. 'This is good land,' I said to myself, 'truly a man could be happy here.'

I tipped back my sombrero, which was imaginary, so was seldom troubled by the wind. From within I could hear the raised voices of my mother and dear sister, Rena. Now of 'a certain age' Rena's behaviour could be unpredictable. Earlier that day Mother had caused great mortification by paying a child's fare for her on the bus, so that consequently Rena now felt unloved.

'You hate me, you hate me,' she was screaming, 'just because I wasn't born a boy!'

Mother gave a chortle of contempt. 'You really think I'd want another bampot in the family?'

I frowned and returned to my hoeing. Mother still hadn't forgiven my sin of the previous week when, through devilment, I'd visited an inferior butcher so that once again we'd had to endure the anguish of gristle in the mince.

'Robert!' shouted my mother.

I ignored her. She gave an impatient yap and tried again.

'Ramone!' This time I answered. In those days I answered only to the name of Ramone.

'I am here, Mother,' I called back, 'working in the fields. The maize looks good this year. Truly, we will have a fine harvest.'

'Why are you speaking in the Welsh accent?'

'It's Mexican.'

Mother looked at me. 'Your tea's out,' she said coldly and shut the window.

'He is an imbecile,' Father had said over the mince scandal. He'd arranged the rubbery granules neatly around the rim of his plate. 'He must get it from your side of the family.'

'Rubbish,' Mother had countered. 'There's brains on my side. I've a cousin who's a clerkess at Littlewoods.' Then she'd fled to the sink to run her fingers over the cheese grater. Rena, meanwhile, had run from the table in tears, slighted by the implication she could be blood-tied to a galoot.

'Honk! Honk!'

I turned from my reverie to see a heap of mobile scrap creeping noisily round the corner. Father was at the wheel.

A cluster of snottery brats ran behind, jeering and pointing. The scrap wheezed to a halt. Father got out and stood, wiping his hands on a piece of semmit.

'A Ford Popular,' he said, grimacing with pride. 'The motor car of the people.'

'Yes,' I agreed. I walked around it, dazed, half expecting to find a patent number scratched on the wing. The children of the people too, were unimpressed. Some had begun whistling the theme to *Laurel and Hardy*. On the grime of the bonnet one had inscribed the word 'poor-mobile'. Seeing this, Father lashed out with a rolled-up *Evening Times* and our persecutors withdrew.

'Come,' he said. 'After tea we'll have a run.'

After tea Mother was led, weeping openly, into the front passenger seat of the Poormobile. Rena asked where she might sit. 'Anywhere,' answered Father. So she climbed into the boot, with Gash.

I myself waited till I heard the engine fire then made a quick dash from the closemouth wearing headgear and a large bandanna I'd improvised from a tea towel.

'Snobs,' sneered Father. 'Does it matter what it looks like, so long as it gets us from A to B?'

'Where is B, Father?' called Rena from the boot.

Father said nothing. He steered the car to the bottom of the road, turned sedately into Elder Street and came to a halt close by Mac's Restaurant. There he got out and stretched himself. 'Driver fatigue,' he mumbled. Then he crossed the street briskly and entered the Fairfield Bar.

*

That evening Mother opened her heart to us. A shy girl, she'd met Father at a Boys' Brigade display and been seduced by the glamour of his uniform. Released into Civvy Street, Father's anchor had not held. Now, as an extension of his virility, he'd bought a Poormobile.

At a late hour a key turned in the lock and we hushed, silent. The living-room door opened and Father stood, looking grave and defiant, his affectation of stainless sobriety spoiled only by the small damp patch to the left of his fly.

'I've brung chips,' he announced. He stepped forward, placed the steaming token on the table before us, then withdrew, like a statesman laying a wreath to the fallen.

'Stick your chips,' said Mother, unimpressed. 'We wouldn't lower ourselves.'

But we did, of course. As soon as his back was turned. Just to spite his bastard motor.

*

Despite the fact that it was old, infirm and was made to sit outside without food, in all weathers, never to be invited in to share our warm hearth, the Poormobile never elicited our sympathy so failed to become our friend. Like a black-sheep uncle, it was a shaming reminder of how far our family had failed to climb rather than, as Father perversely thought, a symbol of how far we'd come. Worst of all, it couldn't be trusted. Times without number Father would rise, spot a faint ray of sun smearing the evening sky and suggest 'a run'. Dutifully, so as not to rouse his temper, we'd wash, dress, assemble ourselves and strap on smiles of eager anticipation for our transport of delights. Once in the car Father would fire the engine and it would 'phut', exhaustedly. He'd crank the starting handle till his face glowed like a stuck 'stop' light but to no avail. Our disappointment would give way to impatience and then, most dangerous of all, to mirth. For mirth in this case was ridicule and Father could not bear to be laughed at. We'd sit in the car looking gravely ahead, biting our cheeks to suppress hysteria as Father toiled, cursing, with his useless jalopy. On one such occasion I spotted Mother sobbing, tears of desolation running freely down her face. Later she confessed she'd had to slap to life the ancient memory of her own mother's funeral, otherwise, as she put it, 'I'd have been saying hello to a severe doing.' For she knew only too well how mercurial Father's moods could be.

A hasty word or an overprotracted silence could be enough to send a household ornament or item of footwear raging through the air. Once, I narrowly missed being speared by an airborne set of coal tongs when I described Father, recklessly, as being 'a rickshaw driver in a serge suit'. Though he seldom laid hands on us, his children, violently, or for that matter tenderly, we nevertheless lived in an ongoing state of wariness over Father's moods. Nowadays, with the great white elephant of hindsight, I see Father hardly at all as the uniquely deranged psychotic I once thought him but as a basically decent intelligent man trapped by circumstance in poverty's cage and goaded till he howled by the sharp stick of missed opportunity.

Years later, when I began to read of militant women who demanded 'equality' and envied men their 'careers', I'd think of Father with his twelve-hour staggered shifts and three pounds ten shillings a week less stoppages and 'shorts' (a bus conductor is responsible through his own pocket for any shortfall between ticket sales and cash taken) and be baffled. Who would ever want equality with him? In fact the more I looked at, say, Germaine Greer, the more I'd fancy equality with *her*. Liberal doses of guilt-free sex, a university education and a big mouth that landed her regular spots on trendy TV chat shows, rather than in jail as mine often did. But when middle-class women speak of 'equality' they don't have working-class bus conductors in mind. Working-class men exist only to the middle classes as occupations: the plumber, the gas man, the mugger or the joyrider. Even when we'd try to assert ourselves we'd still be collectivized into the shirkers, the strikers, the hotheads or the great unwashed. In 1968 we unwashed watched, with interest, from the bar of Brechin's in Burleigh Street the Paris riots in full cry. To the left and right of me, wheezing welders and gravel-voiced caulker burners eyed the pitched battles in the burning streets with less sense of political expectation than we'd now watch a Nationwide Division One game on Sky Sports. Like James Bond, we were shaken but not stirred. Not a wage slave or shirker amongst us doubted that when rich-boy student rhetoric came face to face for dialogue with wage-slave Benidorm worker idealism, rather like the engine on Father's Poormobile, would go 'phut'. And so it proved. Rich kids have rich parents who spread golden safety nets for their cherished offspring to fall into. The only fallback position for a worker scumball is on his ass as it hits the street. Of course, then, as now, I could not be classed as a worker scumball. True, I was 'available' for work, in much the same way as the Waldorf Astoria is 'available' to a Bowery alcoholic, but even by that stage I didn't want the jobs and the jobs, most decidedly, didn't want me. In today's parlance I was, and remain, ambition-ally challenged.

*

I have never understood opposition to my chosen position in life as a waster. Surely, by now, it is clear that full employment is as distant a dream as the Yellow Brick Road and that consequently it follows that there will be a shortfall between the available jobs and eager souls waiting to fill them. Since most people actually prefer to work, should it not also follow that positions on the unemployment register should be reserved for those whose talents are best suited to idleness? As an unemployed waster I break few laws, cause little fuss, and go on no indignant 'right to work' weekend rambles. As a responsible citizen, I spend my meagre Giro benefit on high-duty items like cigarettes and spirits so that most of the money the government allows me is ploughed straight back into its own coffers. The remainder I spread like a thin fertilizer over the parched hard-pressed land of small businesses – corner shops, pizza parlours and low-grade supermarkets. Even, God help them, those 'worse off than myself' get a look-in since what few clothes I own are provided by jumble sales and charity shops. Furthermore, when I die, I shall leave no burgeoning bank account. Whatever may pass through the hands of a waster remains permanently in circulation since he has neither the means nor the predisposition to save. In effect, a congenital waster is as lean, fit and economically viable as the most stringently run software corporation. But, I hear you protest, no matter what you say at bottom, you're just a parasite. And I'd agree. Though I'd quibble with the word 'just'. For even sharks need parasites and by the defining shape of our society have we not agreed that parasites are necessary? Do I still detect the odd rumble of suppressed outrage? All right, then, I'll take a job. Give me one, that one over there, that'll do. It'll mean getting rid of the happy old lackey with the shit shovel in hand since it's his job but what does it matter if we take a contented worker and turn him into a burnt-out statistic, hooked on Prozac because he can't feed his own family, so long as justice is seen to be done and we can all sleep soundly because the scroungers are off the dole and our society is working? No, face it, if somebody's got to be unemployed, it might as well be them that like it.

Ne'er-do-wells, too, have had an unfairly one-sided press in Britain. As any sane person knows, it's only the drugs market and the black economy that stave off the possibility of Yahoo revolution in our country. Governments, of course, are well aware of this benefit and in true British style adopt a laissez-faire attitude to drug crime. Apart from the odd spectacular seaport swoop for show, it's much more convenient to have pinpricked emaciated nuisances stoving in your car window to steal your Berghaus anorak than to have them inconveniently politicized and organized into hurling bricks at the First Minister's Rennie Mackintosh windows. Indeed there's a strong, if perverse, argument for maintaining that our leading drugs barons should feature in the New Year's Honours Lists collecting baubles in the same way as fat-arsed over-cushioned civil servants do at present. And at the lower end of the scale who could fail to admire the degree of market penetration today's diligent and inventive young drug-pushers have achieved? Ecstasy, crack, speed. I've heard of those drugs and I'm from the generation whose pharmaceutical experiments begin and end with Night Nurse.

And yet what is the marketing budget of your average young drug dealer? A scabby Alsatian dog and a spyhole for his tenement door. These promising young kids should be coaxed into Labour's New Deal. Get them into the breweries. Big breweries spend millions on marketing yet what names do they dream up for their products? Bitter. Heavy. And if you really want to shoot for the sun ... mild. Get the kids in there, they'd liven things up. In no time at all we'd all be walking into pubs saying, 'Right, barman, did you get that? That's three pints of Orgasm, two double Velvet Shudders, and a half-pint of God's Spunk for my granny.' Just one note of censure for today's young drug dealers. Don't rule out my generation as a possible market. If my wife was to say to me, 'Rab, what do you want with your chips tonight, ecstasy or speed?' I'd say, 'Depends, which one fries the best?' This is an important marketing tip to any enterprising young drug pusher. If you want to tap the wrinkly generation, put a wee bit of batter round the drugs. A little touch of crackling in with the cocaine, we're elderly, we'd appreciate it.

The trouble is that nowadays there's a lot more self-esteem to be had for a kid in pushing drugs than serving burgers in some joint. 'Enjoy your meal, sir.' I hate it when somebody says that to me. I always give it, 'You're on three twenty an hour, what the fuck do you care if I enjoy my meal or not?' Enforced servility makes my flesh crawl.

*

Owning a Poormobile, had we but known it, was the high-water mark of Nesbitt dynastic achievement. Once we managed a day out to the Nesbitt family seat at Millport without us having to carry the Poormobile on a stretcher with a breathing mask. Predictably, Father's first stop was the pub, where he intended looking up some old friends. Instead he found only enemies and stepped back out desolate, condemned to spending quality time with us, his family. For once the sun shone. We went to the park, picnicked on Irn Bru and cinnamon sticks, laughed and yes, frolicked. At one point on the drive home I caught myself humming a tune and felt guilty. I suppose I was happy or sunstroked or something. We stopped at a cafe in Dalry and Father, grandly, ordered chips for all. I had just noticed a young attractive girl rise from her chair showing a patch of cotton triangle, a detail I'd squirrelled eagerly away with salacious intent for a private moment later, when a strange thing occurred. Father, in the middle of a tediously bombastic racist ramble on the relative merits of the ethnic races, suddenly stopped talking.

'What's that?' he asked.

I listened. Someone had put a record on the juke box. A rich brutal magnificent voice filled the fetid room. 'That's the Animals,' I said. ' "House of the Rising Sun".'

Father snickered routinely at the outlandish name. But he remained silent, enthralled, and listened to the end. Some moments passed before he spoke. 'So the black races will always remain inferior to the white races because . . .' But his heart was no longer in his rant. Something had jolted him, moved him at the core. Unique for a man whose musical tastes had ossified with 'Maisie Dotes and Dosie Dotes'.

I rose and went to the toilet. There I expressed my glee by pissing all round the walls.

*

At first, we only saw Father hit Mother by accident, whenever one or both had neglected to shut the door before assuming their respective roles as bully and victim. But later that night we all saw Father lash out with a short jab to the ribs that drew a soft startled sigh from Mother before she slid down the wall. Rena started to cry. Gash rose silently and enclosed himself in the cupboard under the sink and began, in a crazed voice, to conjugate Latin verbs. I said nothing, continuing to read my *Beezer*. But I was aware of Mother's tearful fearful reproachful eye watching me as she lay, girning, her nose bubbling snot. 'You're the oldest, you should do something,' accused Rena with trembling voice. I glared back at her and turned my page to Colonel Blink. Though silent, I now knew, without reservation, that one day I would have to kill Father. Probably with an axe or a knife. And probably soon. But not now. Father sat primed in his chair, sipping cold tea. We were all aware that a wrong word would see the teapot hurled, charged with hate, through the tense air, so remained silent. The Colonel was in particularly striking form, I recall. But it was an unfortunate incident, spoiling what had been an otherwise enchanting day.

The following afternoon I returned from school to find Mother deep in conversation with Aunt Ginny. It was a tacit understanding between the two of them that in the event of either of them having 'taen a beating', i.e. suffered physically at the hands of a spouse, the other would appear to offer comfort and support. Advice was not required since advice implied action and the parameters of choice for an impoverished mother in those days were even more stringent than now. Cousin Maureen was in attendance. I noticed she was filling out nicely. She noticed me noticing and gave a haughty sneer. Maureen and I were instructed to go and sit at a table whilst Mother lifted her blouse to reveal a bulky strapping at her side. Maureen and I faked polite conversation while we eavesdropped.

'Did you ask for it?' asked Aunt Ginny.

'No,' said Mother, 'I don't think so.'

'Sometimes I ask for it,' said Ginny, 'and that's when I tend to get it most.' They nodded together like hardened veterans. Aunt Ginny continued, 'Of course sometimes I don't need to say a word. Sometimes a look is enough. What did you do wrong?'

'I blame myself,' said Mother, mournfully. 'I was visible.'

And they both chortled, Mother gingerly, for fear of her ribs, one of which was cracked.

*

Wife-beating was both popular and fashionable in the fifties and remained so until around the late sixties when it gave way to free love, velour pants and its chicer cousin mental cruelty. Dark glasses on females in deepest November were a common sight and owed less to the pursuit of style than the desire to hide a pair of 'keekers' from the nosy world. Had we but known it, however, all the old certainties on which our community was founded were about to crack and break asunder. Within a decade hairy-arsed welders would be pushing shopping trolleys round supermarkets looking confused and outflanked. Within a further decade those same welders would become ex-welders, their trade decimated by unemployment, standing outside those same supermarkets begging change for cans of Tennents Super. Women would enter the jobs market and gradually inch towards equality. Soon they, too, would be drinking to excess, having affairs, going to strip shows, and in short declaring as liberating all those excesses they'd hitherto perceived as degenerate vices in men. Unless of course they were scumball women. In which case they did all those things then came home to clean the house and get the tea on.

'Maureen, do you think you'll ever have children?' I asked my cousin.

'Probably. You get a lot of attention when your legs are in stirrups. Round here it's the nearest thing to being a film star.'

'What if your husband gave you baitings?'

'Who says I'd be married?'

'All right,' I persisted, 'what if your man gave you baitings?'

'I'd cut his cock off while he slept and shove it up his arse.'

Yes, things were changing. But not now. Not yet.

*

One day Cotter and I were walking home from school. I was getting up my maddy sufficiently to ask him a personal question.

'Jamesie,' I said at last, 'you're my best pal. Tell me something, does your father bait your mother?'

He looked at me, blinking incredulously. 'Of course,' he said.

I felt a great weight fall from my shoulders.

He continued. 'And I'll tell you something else, an' all.'

'What's that?'

'Sometimes, so do I.'

I picked up the weight and put it back on my shoulders.

'Come home with me,' said Cotter urgently, his slit eyes glittering with conspiracy, 'I want to show you something.'

Cotter lived in Wine Alley, an estate some distance off, but due to a complicated covering of fiscal tracks his address was always given as Huckle Street, same as me.

On Wine Alley the ground-floor flats enjoyed small gardens which were fertilized, inexpertly, with old bed-steads and bits of rusty motorbike, thus failing to maximize their bucolic possibilities. Cotter stood me by a long trench in his garden. It measured about four feet deep and six feet long. It looked uncommonly like a grave. 'What is it?' I asked.

'It's a grave,' said Cotter.

'Who for?'

'Who do you think?' He pointed to a near window. Behind a crack that lunged across the glass like a bolt of lightning I discerned a crone, clutching a cup with both hands and trembling.

'Is that your granny?' I asked.

Cotter shook his head. 'My mother,' he said. He flicked the V's to assure the crone's attention then began jabbing his forefinger downward, pointing to the grave. 'Die, die, die,' he chanted. The crone shuddered. She must have been about thirty-five. 'That's for you,' shouted Cotter, unnecessarily, 'once I turn sixteen and join the army!'

'Are you joining the army?' I expressed surprise.

57

'Once I turn sixteen. Oh, I won't go looking for trouble,' he assured me. 'But let's face it, they give you a gun, so you're sure to find it, aren't you?' And we laughed. I don't know why, for I felt out of my depth and was still troubled by the grave.

'Do you want to stay for your tea?' invited Cotter.

I shook my head. 'I can't,' I said, 'it's Thursday. The man with the grindstone will be coming round our street.'

'What's a grindstone?' asked Cotter.

'It's a thing for sharpening knives,' I answered, as blithely as possible. 'See you.'

*　*　*

The next evening, before he left for work, Father did a dastardly thing: he bought us all ice creams. We stood confused, holding our blobs of frozen vanilla, clutching our hatred like unwanted umbrellas, unsure where to find a stand.

'What does it mean?' asked Gash, fearful and suspicious.

'Just eat it before he changes his mind,' said Rena, ever the pragmatist.

Melting vanilla ran down my wrist and up my cuff. I was a sensitive youth. I couldn't take ice cream from a man I intended to murder, especially my father. I said as much to Rena. 'I'll have yours, then,' she said, through stuffed cheeks, reaching out a podgy grabbing hand. A backhand flick to the lower jaw dissuaded her. 'Not that bloody sensitive then, are you?' said Rena, rubbing her gob. I assured her I was and demonstrated the fact by eating my cone in a meditative manner, too preoccupied even to snap off the tip and dip it to form another smaller bonus cone, true measure indeed of moral gravity.

'What'll we do now?' asked Gash, unhelpfully.

'What's the capital of Uruguay?'

'Montevideo.'

'Go there.'

'I was only asking,' said Gash.

Unlike the rest of us, Gash was seldom tempted by the low gratification of a justified sulk. Instead he bruised, easily and constantly.

Father emerged from the kitchen looking flushed and manic. 'Oh well, folks,' he announced theatrically, like a woodcutter in some children's tale from Finland, 'that's me off to my work.' He straightened his tie, plonked on and adjusted his cap, then left. Mother followed in from the kitchen, looking grim and dishevelled. She was holding a wilting 99 with one hand and zipping up her skirt with the other.

'Is that your father away?' she asked.

'Aye,' said Rena, 'and he was in a good mood. What's up?'

'They're giving him the job today. He expects to go from temporary inspector to staff inspector.'

Mother waited for a reaction. We waited for her to stop waiting. 'It's a great honour,' she continued, hoping to clinch the deal.

Nobody spoke. Finally I said, 'Excuse us. But might we be permitted not to give a fuck?'

Mother looked shocked. But only on the surface. Underneath she looked exhausted and in great pain. She shuffled back into the kitchen to lie down, still clutching the 99.

*

That night we were awakened by a loud knocking at the door.

'The police?' ventured Gash.

'Father?' guessed Rena.

'Neither,' I said and rose to let in Dr Lenco. Two hours

earlier Mother had shaken me awake and I'd run in blazer and pyjamas to the phone box at the corner of Elder Street.

'I'm sorry to be dragging you out at this hour, Doctor,' said Mother sheepishly.

'If I'd a pound for every time I'd heard that,' said the doctor, chuckling in jovial fashion, not quite convincingly. 'What seems to be the trouble? I take it it's serious?'

'Oh, I hope so, Doctor. I wouldn't want to waste your time. It's . . .' Mother noticed my quizzical beadies. 'Robert,' she said, 'away and put the kettle on, son.' I obliged but continued to squint. I looked for the plastic basin. Perhaps Gash had requisitioned it for under his side of the bed. I could hear the ancient healer cranking up his bedside manner.

'A busted rib can be a nuisance. But it's nothing that rest and a good firm—'

'Oh, it's not so much the ribs, Doctor. They're helluva sore, right enough, but they'll heal. Only you remember my condition? I'm, you know . . .'

'Oh, yes, of course,' recalled the doctor, 'and how is that coming along?'

'Well, that's the thing, Doctor. At the minute I don't know. You see it's coming along like this.' Mother pulled away a Bonnie Scotland dish towel like a nervous conjurer about to bungle a trick. 'What do you think?'

I risked a full peek. The doctor was gazing at a tub of frothing dark blood. So that's where the basin had gone. I wondered, grimly, what sort of affliction could cause such a lurid discharge. Dr Lenco gave a satisfied snort and rose quickly, like a man about to snap into decisive action.

'With something like this,' he said, 'we should get you into hospital straight away.'

So that's what was ailing Mother. 'Something like this.' Just as well it wasn't this itself or she'd be done for.

'On the other hand,' he continued, 'it's raining and the nearest phone's at the far end of Shaw Street.'

'Elder Street,' I corrected, 'near end.'

'Elder Street,' repeated the doctor, affecting an air of vague and lofty academe. He allowed himself a moment of austere reflection. 'No,' he said firmly, 'we'd better get you in straight away. That way I'm covered if anything should go wrong.'

'I'm sure I could hang on till the morning,' said Mother, obligingly. 'I wouldn't want to give you any more trouble.'

'You're a bit late for that,' said the doctor, making a scoffing noise that was supposed to be jolly. He lifted the basin and carried it over to the sink. 'I've been out of my bed for over an hour now.' He tipped the gunge into the sink. It drenched the cups I had been considering washing. The kettle started to whistle. We both looked into the small porcelain abattoir. Dr Lenco frowned.

Will you be wanting any tea, then?'

'No thank you,' he said.

*   *   *

An ambulance arrived in the small hours and took Mother to Duke Street hospital. Disappointingly, due to the lateness of the hour no crowd gathered at the closemouth. Normally an ambulance, a police car or a hearse could be relied upon to confer a status of temporary celebrity. Instead, we watched from the window as Mother, looking tiny and perishable, was ushered into the gaping yellow mouth of the ambulance. Afterwards, in a state of wretchedness and hysteria, we bounced on the chairs and ransacked the house for food. Rena donned Mother's high heels and clacked about smoking her cigarettes one after another while I slapped Gash, benignly, to bring him out of his panic attack. Freak sauntered over idly to help. I jabbed him in the chest and he pivoted away to return to the *Dandy*.

'Something's going to happen,' Gash kept repeating in his spittly, whiney voice.

'Nothing's going to happen,' I assured him irritably, 'we're Nesbitts, a kick in the arse off being dead.'

Some hours later we heard Father's key in the lock. Rena rushed gleefully to convey the terrible news. 'Dad, Mother's had an internal haemorrhage, can I stay off school tomorrow?'

'Who told you that?' said Father.

'Gash,' said Rena, pointing.

'Did Gash tell you to smoke your mother's fags as well?' demanded Father, wafting the air theatrically. He removed a nip from behind Rena's ear.

'I'm in distress,' she whined.

'We're all in distress,' said Father. 'I've just come from the hospital. They phoned me up at work. After I'd finished the Balornock run they let me go.' Father seemed far away, his voice mechanical. He stared into the far-off horizon of the fireplace. Gash was first to speak.

'And what about Mammy?' he asked, hesitantly.

Father roused himself from his distraction. 'Hmm? Oh aye, fine. A few days and she'll be as right as rain.' He fell silent again. We looked at each other. Something didn't make sense. Then it did.

'I didn't get the job,' blurted Father. His lips were tight and he fixed us with a steely gaze. 'I didn't get the bloody job.'

'What job?' I asked.

'The inspector's job. What in hell job do you think?' He swept his cap from the table with a petulant brush of the hand. It landed in the fireplace. I rose. 'Leave it,' barked Father. I sat. Father continued. 'There's to be a two-year experiment with one-man buses,' he said. 'It means twenty redundancies.' His voice trembled as he said, 'I'm one of them.'

We looked at him not knowing what to say. 'Da,' said Gash, gently, 'your hat's melting.' In the grate, brazed by glowing embers, the skip of Father's cherished cap buckled crazily. This time I rose and grabbed it.

'You should have left it there,' said Father, bitterly, 'I'll be handing it back into Stores soon enough.'

I nodded sympathetically, for show. But my hands were eagerly working the pliable plastic before it cooled hard. Whilst Father agonized, I studied my handiwork discreetly, hidden by the tabletop. There. At last. The Nazi peak and bend. Gash leaned in close. 'You see?' he whispered.

'You were right,' I conceded, 'you said something was going to happen.'

Gash smiled, ethereally. 'Oh no,' he said, 'I don't think it's happened yet.'

I looked at him and gave his face a slap, this time unbenign. I didn't like it when he turned spooky.

*

In Mother's absence Father soon assumed mastery of the kitchen.

'Where are the eggs?' he'd demand.

'In the cupboard.'

He'd look round impatiently. 'And where's the cupboard?'

'On the wall,' Rena would drawl, sarcastically, eliciting a smack with a spatula across her fire-tartanned knees.

Father's culinary repertoire was small but unique. 'Scrambled eggs in mustard sauce' was an early presentation, a sample of which sent us retching to the sink. 'Mince in grated cheese' drew a similar response for its appearance alone, a brown fibrous mass that could have grouted the bathroom, if we'd had a bathroom.

'How can this meat be burnt yet it's still pink?' queried Rena, reasonably, one teatime. Father blustered about Continental cooking and how the best chefs were almost always men.

'Men, yes,' conceded Rena, 'bus conductors, no.'

'Ex-bus conductors,' qualified Gash, helpfully. Father glowered and out of revenge forced us to eat. But the next night we were despatched to Mac's Restaurant for Hot Pea Specials. Father followed on behind, having some business to attend to.

'How much did you get for it?' asked Rena, without ceremony.

Father muttered the modest truth.

'For a motor?' exclaimed Rena, loudly.

Father flushed, sat and ordered mince on toast. But he didn't eat. Instead he rose, paid the bill and headed across the street to the Fairfield Arms. Seizing the opportunity for anarchy, we wandered the streets of Govan for hours.

When we returned, Father was sprawled asleep in his armchair snoring heavily.

'Drunken bastard,' said Rena. 'And with Mammy in hospital too,'

'What's that got to do with it?' I countered. I was moved. Now and again, when he slept, Father looked like a human being.

'Listen to you, sticking up for him,' said Rena, huffily. 'You were the one that wanted to kill him.'

'We all wanted to kill him,' I corrected. 'And we will.' We gazed down at Father, starting to feel resolute.

'Look,' said Gash in a startled voice. We looked. A

clean tea towel had been folded neatly over the draining board. On top of it sat a battered-looking television set. Rena squealed. Father woke up.

'Oh, you saw it,' he said gruffly, shambling himself awake. 'I bought it off a bloke in the pub.'

'Does it work?' asked Gash.

'Of course it works,' said Father. To prove it he switched on the set. We watched a small white dot in the centre of the screen swell majestically into a large blank off-white blur. We gasped. 'There's nothing on at the minute,' explained Father, 'it's too late. But first thing tomorrow afternoon, you'll see.' Gash felt for Father's hand. We stood transfixed by the flickering screen. Outside a small fault in the endlessly rolling fabric of the Govan cloud allowed the moon to peep in. Life indeed could be rich and mysterious when one's emotions were teased into trust. I felt proud of Father and his reckless senseless dodgy purchase. I sneaked the bread knife in my pocket back into the drawer by the sink. At that moment I didn't want to be reminded, particularly, of why I'd put it there.

*

When Mother returned from hospital she told us all about the lost baby. It had been a boy and she had intended calling it Graham.

'Just as well it croaked, then, eh?' I volunteered perkily, misjudging the moment. Mother's eyes filled up.

'There'll be other sprogs,' counselled Father kindly, clamping a gruff hand on Mother's shoulder.

'I'd have loved a wee brother,' sobbed Rena, not to be outdone.

'You've got us,' said Gash, referring to himself and Freak.

'But the novelty wore off you pair pretty sharpish,' said

Rena. 'Every time I looked in your pram you were either having a fit or being wormed. What fun's that to a nurturing lassie?'

It was the first time I'd heard Rena refer, even fleetingly, to her femaleness. It made me feel squeamish. Boys at school made reference to their sexual experimentation with their sisters, Doctors and Nurses and such. But I could never envisage being a doctor to Rena's nurse unless it involved giving her a mercy killing.

Mother was not to be easily consoled. 'Every time I think of that poor wee lost soul,' she trembled, 'I can't help but think why? Why?'

Lost for words, I looked away to Freak. He sat jammy of face, gleefully reading the *Dandy*. When he saw me looking he glowered, shyly. I marvelled at the depth of Mother's grief. How could anyone bemoan the loss of another one like him? Or me, for that matter?

'Never mind,' said Father at last, 'we might have lost a son, but at least we've gained a television set.' He gave the top of the set a paternal brush with his sleeve. 'The Lord giveth and the Lord taketh away.'

Mother seemed unconvinced by the theological wisdom of Father's stance but for the rest of us it more or less covered the subject.

*

I was growing closer to Father. Unemployment had induced in him a mood of passive despair with which I empathized. As his desire for activity diminished so his capacity for reflective thought grew. Which is not to say his moods became any the less unpredictable. Once, on a bus trip to the seaside, he attempted to unravel for me the mysteries of man's place in the universe, or, if not the universe, then Saltcoats putting green.

'Play through, play through!' called Father imperiously to the tut-tutting anoraked family behind us.

'We can't,' protested the father.

'Why not?'

'Because there's a beer bottle sticking out of the hole where the pin should be.'

'Ah yes,' agreed Father. He had filled the cup with sea water and placed a McEwan's Pale Ale in it both 'to cool' and to 'focus my aim'. I ran and retrieved the bottle, my face ablaze with adolescent shame. The Anoraks' daughter was around my age, freckled, amused and pretty. As Father flopped down by the short sixth and broke wind noisily, I knew she would never be mine. 'Stability is an illusion,' Father was explaining. 'All things change, therefore Communism, which is a state of shared custodianship, is man's natural condition. But you see, we only sense these things in our higher moments when, let's say for argument's sake, we're pished and can rise above the fray.' Father took a long glug from the screwtop. I felt uncomfortable. Other families had appeared and were putting around us as if we were a bunker or, to be more accurate, bits of rough. Children giggled, trustingly, assuming Father was some sort of friendly, cursing municipal giant installed for their increased entertainment. He flicked away a stray ball with his sandshoe and rolled over to face me. 'Don't disrespect the drink, son. The drink is our ally. It blots out our sense of reality while simultaneously increasing it.' He looked at me fiercely, tears of noble self-pity welling up in his veiny eyes. 'How else would an unemployed bus conductor aspire to a higher moment, other than through the miracle of drink? Can you answer me that?' I shook my head. I couldn't answer him that.

I was conscious of a bunch of lank-haired older guys in combat jackets teeing off at the long fifth. For a giggle they were ignoring the designated target and had begun attempting chip shots instead at Father's head. Golf balls like hailstones began raining around us. When one knocked loudly at Father's temple, he stepped down mentally from his Olympian height and addressed his assailants.

'Who did that? Which of you terrorist Arnold Palmers putted that ball?'

'Be careful, Da,' I warned. 'There's a lot of them.'

'I did,' one of the bunch called back. They all shuffled forward, then stopped. 'You going to do something about it?'

Father stood, breathing heavily, contemplating his options.

The bunch shuffled forward some more. Father considered a forward step, hesitated and instead began pawing the ground with his sandshoe. I picked up his putter and handed it to him. Assuming, for camouflage, the knock-kneed stance of the serious putting player, I gripped my own club two-handed and began taking delicate practice wafts. I'd noted one with yellow buck teeth. He was going to get it in the gob, I decided, before we died.

The families had stopped playing and timorous fathers were escorting children floridly to conveniently placed ice-cream vans. 'Well,' came another call, 'it's your shout, big mouth.'

I glanced to Father for leadership. He in turn glanced to the sanctuary of the cheap coloured lightbulbs lining the amusement arcade across the road.

'Do you fancy a game of bingo, son?' he asked. Without waiting for an answer he turned and walked away. Catcalls and derision followed.

At the bingo my eye was in. I quickly won a tea towel and a bedside lamp. To mollify Father I gave him the tea towel but he threw it to the floor. On the bus journey home he said little. At Govan Cross, disheartened, I gave my table lamp to a drunk who lay prone in a doorway. 'Thanks, son,' he called, 'all I need now's a house to put round it.' I turned to convey this witticism to Father. But he was gone, already steaming heavily through the soft winking lights of the streets, his knuckles large with rage, bunnet jutting forward like a masthead, ploughing headlong through the tempests of despair toward the small fragile port of home. I ran behind him crying and shouting. I was afraid.

*

Though he never, to my knowledge, underwent a sex-change operation, Father was, nonetheless, a cunt. I was reminded of this at his funeral during the minister's customary eulogy. 'Robert was a fine parent.' 'Robert was a fine husband.' 'Robert will be sadly missed by his adoring children.' What complacent pish our men of God talk. Other than the odd grunted street politeness our minister had no dealings whatever with my father, otherwise he would have known that in his entire lifetime no one of his acquaintance called him anything other than Rab. To sanitize Father's name was to attempt to sanitize his life. To spread a thick and hasty sheen of forgiveness over that which had never been acknowledged, far less understood. Hope for scum lies in exposure not concealment. Thus do countless thousands of twisted agonized suffering Roberts go to their graves with their sins forgiven before they have even been recognized. I said as much at the funeral, though admittedly in fewer words. Unable further to restrain myself in the teeth of some unctuous drivel about doves and clouds I jumped to my feet and shouted, 'Da was a cunt!' at the top of my voice.

As you might expect this drew a startled pause that was not altogether approving. The minister, in an attempt at ecclesiastical suaveness, continued with his text. Unfazed, I added, 'And you're a cunt too, and if God doesn't know it then so is he a cunt!' This did the trick and, I'm gratified to recall, the man of peace threw down his Bible and started to cut up rough. Bundling ensued, more shouting and threats of police action. The minister reached for a phone and, bypassing Jehovah with his doves and clouds, went straight for the hot line to Orkney Street nick. Only on Mother's tearful intervention did the minister relent and hang up. Flustered, he banished me from the graveside service then, remembering we'd already buried Father, withdrew the punishment.

Father's relatives, whom we rarely saw, were present. From their expressions I could see confirmation that they thought my conduct conclusive proof that Father had 'married low'. Only cousins Donald and Edna seemed quizzical but not judgemental. Mother, inevitably, was mortified but allowed herself to be soothed by Aunt Ginny's kind if solitary reassurances, Uncle Bobo having been unfortunately detained by drinking business. My sister Rena, lipsticked, sobbed noisily while looking around for talent. Freak dreamed. My brother Gash was absent. Yes, things were changing.

*

Sometimes people say to me, 'Rab, are you religious?' And I answer, 'Yes, in the past I've found the Church a great comfort.' This is true. For after Father's death nothing would bring me greater comfort than leaning out of the window to take pot shots with an air rifle at sanctimonious old gits as they entered the church at the corner of Huckle Street. Their checked tweed coats with buttons as big as Frisbees provided excellent targets. Blam! I could pick off a Christian, especially an arthritic one, quite deftly. The more agile worshippers would dive behind motors and present more of a challenge. This could be tricky on dark mornings but like a skilled hunter I'd just listen for the telltale squeaks of the lace-up Clark's granny shoes as they tried to make a break for it towards God's bungalow. This always illustrated to me the fundamental dichotomy under-pinning life and Christianity. They'd be forever howling their dirgelike hymns about how happy they'd be to find peace in heaven but the instant I'd point a wee high-velocity rifle at them to help them on their way they'd be off so fast they'd leave friction burns on the pavement. Being no sadist, I'd aim, of course, for the fleshy areas. Apart from which I'd no intention of creating any uninten-tional martyrs.

In my opinion this is where Pontius Pilate made his crucial error. He turned Jesus into a martyr. The Glasgow police would have handled the matter with more expedi-ency: take him down the cells, give him a doing, up before the beak, fifty-shekel fine, on your way you hippy bastard. Post on his sandals second class. From the Pilate perspec-tive ridicule would have proved a better weapon. If I'd been Lord Provost of Jerusalem I'd have stuck Jesus on that cross the other way round. Blam! Slug up the arse. Theologically unorthodox, I grant you, but it's hard to make a religious icon out of some guy rubbing his bahookey while turning round to give you the viccy. Slug up the arse, send him on his way, I guarantee within six months he'd have been on a Restart programme as a plumber down Galilee and you'd never have heard of him again.

But that's the trouble with Christianity today, it just doesn't cut it with us scum. When a scumball turns on *Songs of Praise* he sees three hundred quantity surveyors warbling about 'my Lord in heaven' and he knows his name's not on the guest list. Religion needs again to touch the masses. Here television could help. If I were Prelate of BBC Television I know what my centrepiece would be for Christmas Night. Forget *ET*, let's show a crucifixion, live from Wembley. Stick some disposable zealot, John Selwyn Gummer or some such, up on a cross in a paper hat. Have Carol Smillie and Jamie Theakston on a couch below, poking him with a spear from time to time in between Slade records and poignant shots of Kosovans staggering about with their settees on their backs. O ye of little faith you may doubt my word but I bet it would tan the arse off *The Generation Game*. And think of the commercial possibilities. Little Speedo logo on the loincloth, Cuprinol to sponsor the cross, Reebok sandals, Nike crown of thorns, the lot. Get Cadbury's to lay on a telethon, make the bastards work for their Easter Egg concession. I know, call me a dreamer . . .

*

One thing about television, it teaches you how to sleep with your eyes open. When I dream of Govan, which I usually do incidentally while I'm walking through the place as a means of avoiding it, I can only see it as it used to be, not as it stands today. And I'm walking through it now. I'm in the Elder Park at the end of Huckle Street, with its flower beds, immaculate bowling green and quaint cottage toilet where Gus and I were groped by a prowling workman on the fag end of his dinner break. Now I'm at the disused railway line at Govan Cross that you could walk along kicking rusting hulks of goods carts till the Wine Alley gang chased you up to Bellahouston. Now I swoop down to Langlands Road with its feast of small shops, Galls Wool, Stewart the Butcher, the Modern Book Shop (still extant) and alas, for I remember it well, Woolworths. Thousands of pained eulogies have been written about the demise of Govan's shipyards, Stephen's, Fairfield's, not to mention their stunted cousins Thermotank and Blairs. But never a word about Woolies. This is because a shipyard is to a Scottish writer what a concentration camp is to a Jewish one. The decline of our industry is the strongest emotional hook they can muster on which to hang our identity. That's why, by comparison, our literature is tight and insular; we're a small people in a tiny country to whom wee things happen. It's one of the reasons our writers swear a lot in print, they're peeved because they've never been persecuted. The cunts. Until recently they tried to be Russian, which was understandable. After all, we've got the melancholy and the drink. But what good are these without a vast turbulent geographical landscape to pose against? Having painted ourselves into a Communist corner we then had no choice but to mythologize our boilermakers as worker heroes. As a result the poor bastards were overelevated to the point of ridicule; keys of the Hillman Imp in one hand, thermos flask in the other, pointing out boldly towards the bright new dawn of a Beazer home in Riddrie. Yes, our writers wept buckets for Govan's shipyards but nobody doffed a respectful cap for the quiet passing of F. W. Woolworth, Govan's Mother Teresa. Recently, I read an article on the plight of Scottish seabirds. Huge numbers of them are dying because the fish shoals have moved away. I know how they feel, we were the same in Govan when Woolies shut down. Fucked our ecosystem right up. It was a terrible time. Decent men, who'd never missed a day's thieving in their lives, suddenly thrown onto the scrapheap. Shoplifting was a way of life to us scum. There were heartrending tales of husbands and fathers, too proud to admit the truth, who'd go out every morning and pretend to go shoplifting rather than own up to the stigma of being unemployed. Make no mistake, a Woolworths-trained shoplifter was the finest in the world.

I know, I served my apprenticeship there myself, And Woolies, as public benefactors, did their best to spread their bounty. Why the hell else would they leave a two-inch gap between the glass panels on the sweetie counter? Beats me how they ever made any money. F. W. Woolworth – the F. W. must have stood for Fucking Wankers.

And as we all know, a major implication of unemployment was that crime started to bite. Nowadays, we in Govan, like anywhere else, are terrified of being burgled. Some burglars are vermin, they're no better than, well, currency speculators – there, I've said it. But in Govan I'm proud to say that some of the old standards of burgling decency have remained. A Govan burglar will only blag your house around September. This is chivalrous as it means you get the cheque off the insurance in time for Christmas. Several times I've been through the familiar routine with the man from the Pru, Mary and me sitting there with the holes in the elbows and the sag-arsed tracky bottoms trying to look distraught. 'Yes, they got clean away with my wife's pearl necklace and her Fabergé egg, not to mention our brand-new Antler suitcase.'

'Was there anything in the suitcase?'

'Yes, our MG sports car.'

*

I'm still walking through Govan. But I've stopped now by a hole in the street where the Ibrox House used to be. After Father's funeral we went there for a ham purvey. The minister didn't come, citing a heavy workload, I don't know, a logjam of prayers to Jehovah perhaps. Mother offered to buy a round of drinks but people demurred, for show, until they'd finished their chips. Uncle Bobo pitched up from the Ants Club, swaying benignly. 'Sorry I missed the funeral,' he said solicitously to Mother. She murmured her forgiveness through wretched lips. Bobo looked around the table. 'Still, at least there'll be no gristle in the mince in heaven, eh?' People laughed, free from the corsets of decorum. The drinking cannon inaudibly roared. Someone produced a mouth organ. A fellow mourner snatched up a pair of soup spoons and drummed them, wheeching, against his thigh. During a lull in her weeping my father's sister, Aunt Alice, stole over for a discreet word. Cousins Donald and Edna sidled across and stood awkwardly by her side. 'Hello,' I said. 'Hello,' they said, shouting over the din. It was over five years since I'd last seen them. Good clothes and education suited them. They looked like finer chiselled versions of me.

I'm glad Father was buried, it made his death more definite. With a cremation there's always the paranoid fear of jiggery pokery. Let's face it, once that little velvet curtain twitches shut it's all hearsay. Since none of us ever actually see the coffin lobbed into the Gas Miser we've got to take the finale on trust. For all we know the deceased could have a bike waiting out the back and be pedalling away like buggery down the Govan Road while we're all still warbling the second verse of 'Rock of Ages'. Though I'm an atheist, I regard myself as a Catholic atheist rather than a Protestant one. Protestants, being stifled emotionally, don't know how to behave around death. If a Prod had his da's corpse in his front room he'd start shifting it around like a sideboard from IKEA. Once he'd given it a quick once-over with a feather duster and polished its specs with Windolene he'd start getting irritated because it was block-ing his view of the telly. In no time the da would be carted out to the garden shed and stuck among the plywood offcuts till cremation time. Catholics are more relaxed around death. Often the corpse will play a functional role at his own wake and willing hands can often be found to help him jig around the room to Wolftone records. Corpses can be huge fun at parties and with assistance can make great limbo dancers and win many free pints. Drunks too admire stiffs, frequently mistaking death for quiet intelligence, and will often come away from a conversation with a corpse muttering, 'By God, he's a deep one, that.'

But in life we add the soundtrack with hindsight. It's what softens history, making it possible for us to look back on some screamingly ugly event so that with luck and skilful self-delusion we can even infuse it with a little grace. Like my 'Saltcoats Symphony' in Rab C Minor, which I began composing the night I stabbed Father but didn't complete till I was a married man with two children and a bad back. It opens in pastoral mood, with a mother feeding chips to her young on a mild spring evening. Soon a darker mood descends and an ominous note is struck as an ugly bastard in a tweed bunnet with dubious stains on his flannels glowers into the room. At first the mother is playful and coquettish. She scolds her man for his lateness whilst performing a series of charming pirouettes around the table. However a solid thump to the belly soon knocks that shite out of her and she is quickly reduced to a squalid heap of limbs on the floor. The children, trained in the beautifully spare choreography of domestic mayhem, retire to the corner and wail a touching lament to Freefone the Govan God of Adoption. The harsh timpani of a boot to the mother's jaw freezes our tableau momentarily. At once the father's features soften, his eyes gazing skywards and his fists opening out like the first trusting blooms of spring. Has he seen God? Heard the distant call of a celestial horn beckoning him to glory? Well, possibly. On the other hand it could be that his eldest son's just stuck him in the back with a bread knife.

*

I dug him below the shoulder just to the right of the spine. I used both hands since I'd no idea how much force you needed to stab a guy in the back. The front I was more sure about; a one-handed thrust to the gut area I figured ought to just about do it. The front was option one, offering a nice soft target, but of course the big drawback was the high possibility of the chib being seen coming. After all, unless you've advertised in the Yellow Pages under 'Smiling Psychopaths', chances are you're going to look pretty obvious as you come hurtling toward your intended victim, Hovis loaf in one hand, bread knife in the other. It sort of gives the game away so the chances of evasive action are high. The back, on the other hand, or 'Coward's Dartboard' as I'd come to think of it, and believe me I had come to think about it, offered the advantage of surprise but the huge disadvantage of clunking into some large unhelpful chunk of bone before I was even halfway through my 'banzai!' warrior cry. An increased, or indeed any, knowledge of elementary anatomy would have told me that a confident lunge to the kidney or liver vicinity would in all probability produce the desired result but, like most beginners in the art of stabbery, I'd set my sights higher, equating death only with a nice safe instantaneous jab to the bandbox.

I'd discussed the matter with Gash previously. We'd agreed the heart was the safest option. Such was my vague sense of its topography I'd made Gash draw a detailed sketch of the human body, locating its various vital organs. If the heart was out of bounds then it was to be the liver, big and locatable without a compass, followed as a reluctant third option by the smaller and more elusive kidneys. Trouble was, not being a big offal man, I'd kept getting the sides mixed up. For added certainty I'd asked Gash to draw me a life-size cut-out I could hastily pin to Father in the event of an advantageous stabbing situation arising. Gash agreed that this was an interesting idea but also cretinous as it would give Father time to roll up the cut-out before beating the shit out of us. Eventually we agreed on a stab to the heart but via the back door. Only I'd missed the target.

As Mother lay unconscious on the floor, Father staggered, grunting and gasping, around the room, trying to reach the handle that was embedded in his back. His eyes were glassy and he was dripping a lot of blood.

Rena was whimpering, 'If he gets hold of that knife, we're dead.' As if it really helps to state the obvious.

'Shut up!' I told her.

'It's not in deep enough,' said Gash.

'I know, I know,' I said.

Father made a lunge for me but crashed into the table, sending crockery flying.

'He'll kill us!' screamed Rena.

I grabbed the frying pan. 'Help me,' I said. I jumped round behind Father and gave the knife handle a bash with the pan.

Father glowered over his shoulder. He looked let down. 'You ungrateful bastard,' he said.

'Help me,' I shouted again. I threw two saucepans to Gash and Rena. 'If he comes at you,' I told them, 'whack him in the back.'

Every time Father made a drunken lunge toward us we'd nip behind and give him a dunt on the handle. But because he was on the move we couldn't negotiate the leverage we needed. Our chance came when Father made a grab for Rena, pinning her by the arms against the wall. Gash was nearer than me. 'Hit him!' I shouted. He looked at me, frozen. Being intelligent doesn't help in these situations. Smart people can't help seeing the overview of hideousness which in turn tends to cramp the happy-go-lucky homicidal urge. 'Do it!' I yelled again. But Gash just stood panting, staring at me. I waded through the debris, steadied the frying pan and gave the handle a solid thump, catching it satisfyingly square. Father didn't even moan this time, just collapsed at Rena's feet. We all stood breathing hard, looking at each other. Somebody said, 'Mother?' We looked around the room. She was gone.

'Is he dead?' said Rena.

Gash checked. 'No,' he said, 'still breathing.'

Beery methane filled our nostrils. 'Through both ends,' said Rena. We heard voices in the hallway. Mother entered, flanked by two policemen.

'What happened here?' asked one. We all looked at each other.

'He fell,' said Mother, hesitantly. 'He fell onto his knife.'

The policemen looked at the plastic handle jutting out from below Father's shoulder blade. 'Backwards?' said the other.

We were, as they say, at a loss. It looked like the proverbial fair cop. But help was to come from an unexpected source. 'Aye, backwards,' said Father in an impatient gurgle from the floor. 'I was teaching them how to hang up a coat while you're still in it, comes in handy when you're . . .' We awaited the punchline but Father had passed out. There was a further clump of feet on the lobby lino and two ambulancemen appeared. They surveyed Father's stricken frame.

'Fight?' asked one.

'Nah,' said a policeman, 'domestic.' He looked at Mother. 'Most accidents happen in the home, eh, dear?'

Mother's shoulders slumped in relief. Through the burst plums of her lips she smiled her unspoken thanks. We were a family again.

*

For light relief while Father was in hospital, I'd visit Cotter in his garden to find out how his mother's grave was coming along. We'd sip Tizer and eat Merrill's while dangling our legs over the hole. Cotter had struck the equivalent of writer's block with his enterprise, having four feet down encountered a bulky sewage pipe. Daunted by the prospect of starting over in another spot he'd allowed the project to languish. This reprieve had perked up his mother and I noticed she'd dyed her hair a sparkling new colour, 'Traffic Light Amber' I guessed to be the shade.

'How come I never see your da?' I asked Cotter one day.

'Because he's always in his room,' he said.

'In his room? What's he do there?'

'Nobody knows, but sometimes I hear shouts and, well, sobbing.'

'Sobbing?' I queried. Cotter nodded. I took the question mark out of my voice and replaced it with three meditative dots. 'Sobbing . . .' I repeated.

Cotter offered me a slug from the Tizer bottle. 'Have you ever wondered what it would be like,' he said, 'if we could tear down the dividing walls of every house in the street? If we could see folk the way they really are after they stop talking their crappy garbage about the weather and go in and shut the door? Have you ever wondered that?'

'I have,' I said, 'I've often wondered that.' I cleared a globule of second-hand Merrill from the neck of the bottle. As I did so I felt that nauseous momentary mental scene-shifting that occurs when some lurking amorphous notion is about to be dragged centre stage and spotlit into an unshakeable conviction. I imagine Galileo felt something similar on discovering his theory of gravitational accelera-tion or Vidal Sassoon on formulating a shampoo that could wash and condition at the same time. As I struggled to clothe this newborn prince of insights in the silken shawl of language I found that Cotter had nicked round first to Paddy's Market and given it a quick low-life kit-out. 'If you ask me,' he said, 'every bastard's half mental.' Inner wheels clicked and whirred. Lights flashed on complicated panels as this data was processed and evaluated. I took a long slug of the Tizer and belched. 'Confirm,' said the microchip in my cerebellum.

'What'll you do about the grave?' I asked, seeing the walking fright that was Mrs Cotter manifest itself at the window.

'She thinks she's off the hook,' said Cotter, treating his mother to a sarcastic wave. 'But she's not, I've got plans.' He lay full length by the hole and mimed a prim corpse. His mother snapped shut the curtains. Cotter sat back up again. 'I can't wait for the school dance, can you? I'm dying for a ride.'

I grinned, feigning enthusiasm. Secretly, I was worried. I hadn't the clothes for it and, worse, the third dance on the card was a ladies' excuse-me and I was having nightmares about being unchosen.

Cotter was rubbing his crotch. 'Is it not time you were off well?' he said. I nodded, taking the hint. At the gate I turned back in time to catch him slinking into the grave. By the time I was at Elder Street he'd be scraping the telltale flaky bits off his shirt front with a kirby grip. It was all very well murdering your mother but as long as she washed the underpants she still held the whip hand.

*

Things were never the same after we stabbed Father. About a week after the event he returned home in a taxi looking pale and shaken. Anticipating a wedding, kids clustered round the car shouting, 'Scramble! Scramble!'

'I've been stabbed,' Father told them peevishly, 'you don't get a scramble for a stabbing.' When they still refused to disperse, Father, in frustration, threw a handful of small change into the air and staggered to the close. We watched warily from the window, not knowing what to expect. But when he entered all Father said was, 'Bloody kids. Any tea?'

Father was thinner and quieter now and would sit for long hours in his chair thinking and smoking. The knife had pierced a lung, condemning him to half bellow. With every fag he lit he anticipated the imminent delivery of a terminal growth courtesy of Intercancer. He was wary of me now, his confidence having been reduced while mine had grown. I still felt, deep down, that he could take me in a square go but neither of us was eager to put the matter to the test, though I also felt that the test would one day surely come. I was in my second year now at Metalwork High having narrowly scraped the C pass that would segregate me from the mouth-breathers and mountain men of Grade D whose hairlines started at their eyebrows. Every week I'd measure myself against a mark on the cloakroom wall, checking for signs of thrusting development that would ensure victory in the test to come.

'I haven't grown a single inch this year,' I complained one day to Rena.

'Maybe not up the way,' she corrected, 'but if you were to start drawing those lines at gut level you'd wear out a pencil every week.'

I aimed a boot at her arse in lieu of a witty riposte but the observation was well founded. With the school dance looming, a rapid trauma diet seemed my only hope of achieving svelte attractiveness. I was gazing idly out of the window wondering how I might catch a helpful bout of malaria when the ping of a ruler to the knuckles commanded my attention.

'What were you doing, boy?' demanded Mr Crieff, the maths master.

'Thinking about my algebra, sir.'

'Unhelpful,' said Mr Crieff, 'we're doing geometry.' The

knee-jerk guffaw flattered him into letting me off the hook. 'Proceed at once to Miss Greer's English class. An incident has occurred with your brother and some urine.' He primed himself for another chortle. It disappointed. People knew Gash and anyone could see he was a misfit.

I rose dutifully and walked down the aisle. This time spasmodic sniggering grew in ripples as I passed. I looked about, grinning inanely, as the laughter swelled into mass hysteria. 'Maybe it's just me,' I reassured myself, 'maybe I'm just a funny guy.'

My face was starting to hurt from seeing the funny side of nothing. Even the no-hope creeps at the front were having a desk-pounder at my expense. I let my smile clunk to the floor and was about to turn ugly when Mr Crieff grabbed me by the head and twisted my neck round and down as far as it would go. 'Making any sense now?' He smirked. And yes, I had to admit it made sense now. A frayed patch of cheek I'd kept hidden with my blazer hem had given up the ghost and split to reveal a sizeable spread of arse. I didn't know whether it helped or hindered my embarrassment that I wasn't wearing Y's, my one pair having that week been boiled to such shreds that stepping into them was like donning a centipede's leotard. I stood at a loss, stuck, as it were, for a face-saving note to play. 'P. J. Proby,' said Arthur Quince, the stupidest boy in Christendom, and got the one and only laugh of his life, save for fifteen years later when the dinner siren sounded at Fairfields and he stepped out of the cockpit of his crane forgetting he was still a hundred feet in the air.

I felt the ominous prickly heat around the eyes but before humiliation found its natural conclusion, Crieff stepped compassionately in. 'Go get your blazer from the back of your chair,' he instructed. I did.

'One day I'll have money,' I told myself as I clumped defiantly back up the aisle. 'No, one day I won't,' I told myself as I trudged disconsolately back down again, the overlong blazer pinned tight by a discreet hand. One day, I told myself finally, is much like any other day.

'Go and get your brother.'

'Yes, sir,' I said.

Gash had pissed himself. He was always pissing himself. That hadn't mattered so much at primary school where occasional seizures, howlings and general inadvertent grossness were pretty much par for the pre-pubescent course. In high school, however, the stakes were raised. There was status to be conferred, girls to be impressed, sideburns to be cultivated, all of which hard-won advancements were wiped out at a stroke by an unruly bodily function. One could be as witty as Wilde, as intelligent as Einstein, but leave just one errant puddle under a chair and that's all you'd be remembered for from now till Judgement Day. Worse, the spray, so to speak, hit other members of the family. One was guilty by association. He stinks therefore I am.

As luck would have it, the interval bell sounded seconds before I reached Miss Greer's classroom. Gash was in Prep A. He'd do six months there then be assessed and streamed into an A, B, C or D strand. I'd no doubt whatever he'd be a glittering A. I waited while the Preppers, still docile with intimidation from being the youngest and smallest herd in the school, shuffled out, muttering and packing jotters into haversacks and briefcases. Miss Greer beckoned me in. Gash sat a far corner desk, snivelling.

'Go and speak to him,' she said, 'tell him it's all right.' Nervousness made her concern sound shrill.

'Yes, Miss,' I said. Gash didn't even look up as I sat beside him. Watching him give those catchy-breath sobs like stricken people do, I found I couldn't think what to say. Maybe Cotter's father would know. They could meet and sit together speaking the hidden language of sobbery.

I asked myself how a top London child psychologist might handle the situation. Finding nothing in the drawer marked 'experience' I then asked myself how the average Scottish school nurse might approach the matter. This time when I tugged at the drawer thick sheaves of dark dog-eared print cascaded to the floor.

'What d'you keep pissing yourself for, you dirty bastard?' I said.

'I can't help it,' said Gash, voice gurgling with snot. 'It just comes over me.'

'Well, it's not a smart move,' I told him. 'You might think it's an attention-grabber but birds hate it, you'll never get your hole at this rate.'

'I don't want my hole,' Gash protested, 'it's you that wants your hole.'

I resented this unhelpful remark on the grounds that it was true. I pressed on. 'But you haven't pissed yourself once since you came to high school, this is the first time. Why now?'

'I think he was a wee bitty stressed.'

We looked up. Miss Greer was standing over us, fiddling with her engagement ring. I could smell her body heat and perfume. I would dedicate a private hymn of thanks for her loveliness in the toilets later. 'Gash has extremely good grades,' she continued. 'Now as you know assessment comes up soon. There are a couple of assisted places up for grabs at the James Logie School in Paisley. Gash could possibly manage one of those.'

I considered. 'The Logie. That's fee-paying, isn't it?'

'Yes, but as I say it's assisted. Your parents need only pay a percentage, perhaps a half or even a quarter of the annual fees. I think you should ask them at least, don't you? It can't do any harm.' I wondered. 'I've written a letter for Gash to take to his father.' I saw an envelope poking out from his blazer pocket. Miss Greer continued,

'With Gash's grades and a lot of hard work he might even go on to university.' She gripped the desk for emphasis and leaned in. 'Will you at least ask him?' she said. She was in earnest.

Gash and I looked at each other. There was no choice. 'We'll ask him,' I said.

And we did. We asked him. Though none of us expected the answer we were given. It changed everything. Neither Gash nor I was to know this as we walked home from school that evening.

'When should I ask him?' said Gash.

'You've got all week,' I said, 'you won't see Greer again till then.'

'But that's not when,' Gash insisted, 'when?'

'I don't know,' I said. I was irritated, bound up with the school dance and the prospect of that hideous excuse-me. For dance practice I'd been coupled with Anne Doak, Edward's sister, but she was proving more silent and uncoordinated than her dead brother, so clumping around the gym together to the St Bernard's Waltz was a twice a week agony of tangled scuffling. Nevertheless I prayed wholeheartedly to the Lord of the School Dance that this pigtailed heffer would, at the appointed moment, save me from the public agony of rejection. In the weeks leading up to the dance I'd attempted to manipulate her using smiling and flattery but, as one of nature's wildebeest, she was alert to all angles of approach and had quickly scented beneath my solicitous attentions the cold sweat of craven expediency.

'I'm not dancing with you come the night,' she said one afternoon as we Gay Gordoned dismally up and down the straining floor.

'I never asked you to,' I'd replied, trying to look astonished and amused by the very suggestion.

'Well, that's all right, then,' she said, terminating the

exchange. I hated the cow, I hated her for seeing through me. More than that I hated that she was punishing me for what life had done to her. After all it was in both our interests, surely, as also-rans in the great Beauty Steeplechase of Life, that we should share the culpability of failure by cantering home together.

As the night had approached and desperation grown I said as much to her as we changed out of our plimsolls. 'Look here,' I said, 'you're a dog and I'm not much better, it makes sense that us hounds should stick together, if only to take the bad look off each other.' She flushed but made no reply.

'Ah well,' I thought, 'at least I tried.' And now the night was almost upon us. Every time I thought of it I'd feel my bowels melt.

'Well,' said Gash, 'should I ask him tonight?'

'Why tonight?' I asked, feigning interest.

'It's dole night, he'll be in a good mood.'

'Nah,' I said, 'against that if he says no, you'll have a full week to live with it before you see Greer. Best sit on it till the night before.'

'You sure?' said Gash.

'Uh huh.'

'That's the night of the school dance.'

'So what?' I said.

*

I will never know but I still wonder if that was the single worst piece of advice I ever gave. If I'd let Gash follow his instincts maybe all would have been well. Some would say it depends whether or not you believe in fate. But that's the illusion of free will. To me what really matters is whether fate believes in you.

Time limped on slowly and tortuously, then, like a shuffling mummy in a horror film, leapt on its fleeing victim. It was the night of the school dance. I stood in front of the wardrobe mirror and assessed my sartorial effect. 'Looking pretty good,' I said to the clownish figure in the cracked glass. I was wearing my father's one white shirt, with a shrunken jumper on top to disguise the overlarge dimensions, cracked shoes that through age had achieved a fortuitous crocodile or dried-up river basin effect and a pair of canvas jeans belonging to Gash that I had contrived, more or less successfully, to cram myself into, barring of course, the zip, the two sides of which now strained like a warring couple to part themselves. A gnarled snake belt provided a modicum of insurance against that unfortunate eventuality and just in case I carried a large safety pin with which I proposed to pin the front of the jumper to the bottom of the fly in the event of a conclusive decree nisi for the zipper couple. This would have the unfortunate side effect of rendering me bent double for the remainder of the festivities since, as I've said, the jumper had shrunk violently in the wash, as if to withdraw to a finer world. 'Looking pretty good,' I said again, 'if it was a coming-out ball for the Turd of the Year.'

I met Cotter for pre-ball cocktails at the fashionably unfashionable Lyceum Café on Govan Road. Here we enjoyed our favoured aperitif, Vimto, which we discreetly spliced with aspirins. This acted exactly like alcohol except that one went directly from sobriety to hangover without that time-consuming feel-good part in between. Cotter eyed my ensemble. I sensed trouble. 'Do you have a wasting disease,' he asked, 'or is that your father's shirt?' He slid down furtively in his chair and trickled a slow white line of aspirin sludge onto his tongue.

'Neither,' I said. My neck rattled around inside the collar like a straw in a Coke bottle. 'It's my shirt, I just keep it for special occasions, that's all.'

'Special occasions,' mocked Cotter. 'When the fuck did

you ever have a special occasion?' It was a stupid answer.
I regretted it. 'It's your father's jumper, though, right?'

I nodded. I'd concede the jumper. It could be dismissed
as a nonchalant afterthought, as something my valet,
Nesbitt, had pressed upon me as I'd been about to leave
the family seat to select a horse from my stables. 'Here,
young Master Rab, don't catch cold.'

'You're such a fusspot, Nesbitt,' I'd replied, as I saddled
up my trusty steed. 'When this damn war is over,' I told
him, 'I'll make sure you and your dear loyal wife are
granted your freedom.' I can see them now, falling prostrate at my feet. 'Oh, Master Rab, we don't want no
freedom, all we desire is to serve your every need, don't
we, Mother?'

'We surely do,' said Mother with trembling voice, 'do
dah, do dah, deh.'

'Then so you shall,' I quoth, laying my kingly hands
upon them, 'and when—'

'What the hell are you doing in my good shirt?' Father
had barked, as I'd slunk toward the door. I couldn't work
out what had alerted him

'Did somebody lob a tear gas canister in here,' said
Rena, 'or is it just your aftershave?'

'A dab of spice,' I mumbled.

'Aftershave,' boomed the doltish beast that was my
father, 'are you not supposed to shave first before you put
on aftershave?' They all guffawed, dutifully, including
Mother. They were buttering Father up for later when
Gash and Mother would spring Miss Greer's letter on him.
Father took a closer look.

'And is that my good jumper too?'

'There's nothing good about it,' I protested, 'you really
think I'd wear this effort unless I had to? Here,' I said,
'have it back.' I started to unpeel the jumper, half-
heartedly.

'Oh, shut up,' said Father. He steered me into the lobby away from prying eyes. I sensed a bung so played bewildered innocence. Sure enough the hand of plenty rummaged in his pocket. 'Here,' he said, giving me five bob, 'buy some razor blades for that five o'clock shadow of yours.' He opened the door for me.

'Thanks, Da,' I said, and meant it.

'Cheerio, son,' he said, 'have a good night.'

The door shut. I stood on the landing. 'He called me son,' I thought, as I pocketed the two half-crowns. Curious. Maybe God, in his mercy, had afflicted him with a little light softening of the brain. If so, he might yet prove susceptible to the wheedlings of Gash and Mother. Maybe the evening would be a less than complete disaster after all.

*

'Are you ready?' said Cotter.

I drained my aspirin sludge and nodded. 'I feel sick,' I said, trying to rise.

'Good,' said Cotter, 'that means it's working.' White-faced, swaying, we headed for the door. 'Man, what a high,' slurred Cotter. We'd read about highs but, being Scottish, had never met anyone who'd had a high, far less experienced one ourselves. Consequently we interpreted any self-induced state that deviated from our daily norm of anguished boredom as 'a high'. With hindsight, of course, I realize that what we were celebrating was not a 'high' but a 'low'. We were ill. Brilliant. Let's go dancing.

*

The school assembly hall was decked in streamers and balloons. It made for an incongruous, squeamish effect, like watching an undertaker do the Hucklebuck. On the raised stage where the Headie daily thumped and ranted about the mercy of God, two collections of elderly bones, lightly clad in parchment skin and kilts, were playing accordion and fiddle, occasionally pausing for an asthmatic 'hooch'. As we entered they were just finishing 'The Mucking O' Geordie's Byre'. 'Any requests?' beamed the accordionist. 'Twist and Shout,' called Cotter. At the top table the Headie shot to his feet, reaching instinctively under the shoulder of his jacket for his strap until his wife's hand on his arm calmed him and his deputy proffered cheese as a diversion. Girls in frilly droopy party frocks lined the far wall.

'See anything you fancy?' asked Cotter. I shook my head. I couldn't speak for nerves. I scanned the room for Anne Doak. Yes, there she was in the Ugly Corner with the rest of the Rejects trying to slink an upgrade into Borderline. She had her hair piled high and I could tell from the way she was nibbling her crisps she thought this made her the goods. But it didn't make her the goods, it just made her ugly in a more spectacular way. I could only hope that tonight my prayers would be answered; that Anne Doak would realize that what I'd been telling her so passionately was true, that she and I were truly hideous and that our hideousness was made to find true union on this magical night of unforgettable horror.

'If Anne Doak doesn't pick me for the excuse-me,' I vowed, 'I'll have no choice but to kill myself.' The accordionist, polished professional, rapped the mike with a gnarled knuckle and cleared his chest via the PA to seduce our attention. I heard him utter the dread words, 'Will you all please take the floor for . . .' My heart pounded. The ordeal had begun.

Up until that moment I had never held a corset with a woman in it. We danced with teachers, touching them as equals. And they liked being touched, some of them, you could tell. Not for the sex of it, for we were untried boys and they plump women, well, yes, for the sex of it, for the frisk and tremor of strange hands on curvy places, heat on heat, yet fully licensed, bits of boys with thrilling hands, not the dour dead hands of dull husbands, any hands but those hands. And our young safe hands would do very nicely, thank you. And your name is? Thank you, Rab. Thank you, Miss Peacock. Only one dance down and already a potential wank squirrelled away for a rainy one. That knuckle on the mike. 'Ladies and gents, will you remain on the floor please for . . .' That pounding in the chest, louder than the thump of the fiddler's boot. Stay up, easier to hide, find some low-level grunter, someone my status. 'Hello, Anne, would you like to dance?' Keep the eye twinkling, that gob grinning, don't die now die later, there's a battle going on, all hands to the rumps. And she hesitates, this odious bag, the cheek of it, waiting for a better offer. 'Um . . .' The accordion wails. That pre-skip intro. Too late. And we're off, stripping the willow, and I'm all teeth and smiles and nicey nice chat though in future she can strip her own willow, I wouldn't touch it with a willow stripper, this ungrateful hound. 'Are you enjoying yourself, Anne? Which is your favourite dance, Anne? Lovely frock, Anne. Who did your hair, Anne?' And even, wretchedly, 'We're a good team, aren't we?' She glares at me. 'No, we are not.' The music stops. She about turns away. That thumping heart, now in my mouth. 'And the next dance is . . .' My heart stops. Four faults for a refusal. 'A ladies' excuse-me.' A frisson of chatter. Get off the floor. Feet glued. Get off the floor. Sit down. Head down. Study your hands. Fine hands. Manly hands. Wanker's hands. Unchosen hands. Oh, the pain of it. All around the party skirts swishing. Giggling. Alone. This, boy, is your place in life. That thumping chest, slowing to sad certainty, when . . . A pale blue party dress from the corner of my eye. A hand outstretched, a little hanky in it, a bangled wrist quite close, then closer. Can it be? No doubt about it. That hand is reaching for me. Look up, you fool, look up! The fool looks up. Before my eyes reach her face I'm in love through sheer gratitude. And what a face. Will you look at that. Not even a grunter. I love you, I love you, whoever you are. Who are you? It doesn't matter, let's dance. We take the floor. Please don't ever start the music. Look everybody, I'm chosen, I exist. That little blue dress. That dark bobbed hair. And the nerve of her. Sweet bashful nerve. Just hovered, then touched. Her fingers, my wrist. Up I got. No words. Hardly even a look, not either of us. Too shy. I got up, her chosen one. And by the way, did I say, thank you, thank you, thank you God? Or whoever. For my heart which bursts with pleasure. And relief. For the exotic country which shows me at last how it feels not to be me. I am alive.

And dreaming. Even in Govan. Thank you. For this miracle called girl.

*

'And did you dip her?' asked Cotter. It was raining. Dirty water puddles squelching our feet. We wore paper head-gear, *Evening Citizen* for him, *Daily Mirror* for me, that, folded out, made drooping roofs for vain nappers. I shook my head.

'No dip?' he said, amazed. 'How about the finger, let me smell.' He grabbed my hand, sniffed the digits. 'Not a hint of minge. So what did you do?'

I shrugged. 'Just danced.'

'Just danced?'

'That's it.'

'Must've been some dance.'

'It was,' I said.

At Drive Road we protected our chips, climbed the railings and dropped into Elder Park. On the other side he offered me a bit of battered fish. I broke him off a shred of mutton pie.

'I never got my hole,' he said.

'Me neither,' I said.

'But you'd think you did, the way you're carrying on.' He scrutinized me closely. 'Are you sure,' he said, 'are you sure you didn't get your hole?'

'No,' I said, 'I'd have noticed. I never got my hole.' He made me promise that I hadn't got my hole. I did, on the lives of assorted close relatives. He was relieved.

'I'd hate it if you got your hole before me,' he said, 'I think I'd have to rape my mother.'

'A waste,' I said, all waggish, 'she's a disappointment.' At the boating pond we pished in silence, savouring the deep plonk of our arcs on the dark water. Before us, the tethered beasts of Fairfield's cranes.

'I'm not going into the yards, are you?' said Cotter, giving it a shake. In less than two years we'd be fifteen, time to leave. No chance, being dim, of our being cajoled into staying on for Os or As. 'Bring a wage into the home,' the standard order in every dim household.

'No,' I said, 'I'm not going into the yards.'

'What'll we do, then?'

'I thought you were for the army?'

He shook his head. 'They send you to Aden with Mad Mitch. A guy in Neptune Street lost both legs. You'd never get your hole with no legs,' he said, 'so basically, fuck the army.'

'We'll think of something.'

'You're awful chirpy,' he said.

'Fuck off,' I scowled. But inside I was grinning like a lobotomized Jesus Freak. We were at the granite memorial, corner of Govan Road and Elderpark Street. We climbed the railings, kicked each other's arse by way of cheerios. At last, the wondrous elation of seeing him go, free now to romp in the clover of my love. I trudged down Fairfield Street, the rain still belting. Not just any rain, that V.S.O.P. Scottish rain that seeps through the skin to peel the wallpaper from the living room of your soul.

*

'Take my soul, what care I for it, being a man by love o'erwhelmed?' Curious, how fancying a woman gave you an urge to invert your syntax. I took out my key and went into the house. 'At least he didn't suffer,' said Cousin Edna at the send-off. Well, if you call having no money, a lousy job, a hungry family and a drink problem a state of unsullied Brahma then yes, I suppose that's true.

'Stop,' shouted Mother but Father wouldn't stop. He had Gash by the throat and was slapping him.

'Where've you been?' said Rena.

'You know where I've been,' I said, 'the school dance.'

'Well, you're needed here,' said Freak, 'please do something.'

I looked at Freak. It must be serious. Nobody said please in Govan. Difficult to take in. Moonlight and love to a family doing, full human gamut with a turn of a key. 'What's up with the da?' I asked.

'Gash laughed,' said Rena.

'Laughed?' I said.

'Sniggered,' said Freak, 'Da was in a mood and Gash sniggered.'

'You know what he's like,' said Rena, 'a bag of nerves, he couldn't help it.'

'What about the letter?' I asked, remembering.

'That letter?' said Freak. He pointed, I looked. A flap of Basildon Bond poked from the corner of Gash's mouth.

'Stop it, Rab, stop it,' yelled Mother. She risked a grab at Father's jumper. He threw her off with a shove. Still a big bloke, powerful, when angry. Then the first dull thump of Gash's head against the wall. Three porcelain swallows flying upward from the rammy.

'Jesus Christ,' said Rena. She looked at me.

'What can I do?'

'Something,' she said. Her pleading look hovered on the cusp of contempt.

'It's you,' said Freak, 'you're the oldest.'

For improved leverage, Father now had Gash's face in his big hand and was crumping it against the wall. Years later Rena and I would debate the quality of that sound. For me it was a coconut, hard but hollow, for her, something softer, almost soft fruit, a mushing sound, the blows perhaps cushioned by the hair. Mother's sound we both remember as a wailing, it chilled, all tribal and bereft. To me it was a dog whistle and the next thing I've got the bread knife in my hand and I'm screaming at the da. 'Come on then, ya big bastard, you want another taste?' Da releases Gash, who slips down the wall into a squat. Shouting and mental as I am, I'm relieved to see there's no blood on the wall from Gash's cracked nut. And Father turns his attention to me. I know he's lost it, all animal now, no man left, the 'Here's five bob and have a good night' ripped off like a too-tight suit to reveal Beastman bursting from his Poormobile.

'Put that down, kid,' he says.

I flash teeth, all showy defiance. 'Not so smart now, you big dickbrain, are you?' I give him a warning jab with the bread knife. Only it's not the bread knife, it's a whisk, a member of the same plastic-handled family, true, but less comforting in battle than its lethal cousin.

'Put it down, kid,' he repeats, keeping the volume low for added menace. 'Don't make me step across that floor to you,' he says, 'because if I've got to step across that floor, I'll . . . I'll . . .'

A hiatus. To fill in I swish the whisk like a rapier. 'It's OK,' I say, 'I'll wait till you think of something.'

His face hardens. He takes a couple of steps toward me. I know I'm going to lose. But maybe he does too. If so, that's all he knows. Because now he's on the floor at my feet and I haven't even touched him. He's lying on his side, arm upstretched like he's signalling for a foul or something, which in a way he is because he's dead. Rena's trying his pulse but we know a dead body when we see one even if we've never seen one and this is such a thing. A carcass at our feet that a moment ago was a living breathing man, our father, in full red-eyed cry hurtling, now cut down.

'I think he's had a heart attack,' says Rena.

'Well, let's hear it for Cookeen,' says Freak. We're looking down at our father. A moment ago we were in fear of our lives. Soon we'll be hunting through the Peek Frean tins for the policies that'll take care of his disposal. Already I'm thinking in the future tense and the poor bastard isn't even cold yet.

They look to me for a response. I realize what I'm still holding. 'As well for him,' I say, 'or I'd have whisked the shite out of him.'

We notice something's missing. Mother's voice. 'Gash,' she's saying. An urgency, pleading, fearful. Oh yes, Gash, we all recall, as one, the guy who got us into this. Just wait till we . . . But something's wrong. Mother's on her knees shaking Gash by the shoulders. 'Look at his eyes,' Mother's saying, 'look at my wean's eyes.' And we do, we look at his eyes. And he's perfect, our brother is perfect in every way. Except for his eyes, which have a broken look, like a doll that's been dropped on its head from a window. Which is a very apt analogy, as it happens, because just as I'm thinking this Gash says, 'Mama.' Which becomes an historic utterance in the Nesbitt family since it marks the transition, for Gash, from intelligent boy to mental cripple.

*

Gash didn't attend Father's funeral. He was already in a Tweedledum unit, struggling to grasp the finer principles of finger painting. He was in a hospital on the semi-rural outskirts of the south side of Glasgow. I'd gone already on the three-bus trek with Mother to visit him. The patients were encouraged to pour tea and hand round digestives to their visitors but Gash wasn't up to it. They'd stun him with medication then tip him out from a wheelchair into an armchair in a cunning bid to try and make him look casual and relaxed. This effect was undermined by the rubber neck on which Gash's head now rolled like an egg on a spoon and a tongue the sole function of which was to act as a doorstop that kept his mouth a permanently gaping fly trap. His trousers were damp and I noticed a rubber sheet on the cushion. 'Look, Ma,' I said, trying to turn it into a plus, 'business as usual, that's something.'

It was a virtual two-hour each way trip for nothing as Gash didn't know who he was let alone anyone else. He had suffered some kind of brain rupture and they wouldn't know how badly he'd been affected until the swelling was gone. Some degree of permanence was implicitly assumed but how much they just couldn't tell. We broke off bits of biscuit and tried to feed him but we might as well have tried feeding the Scott Monument in George Square, the bits just fell out of his uncompliant mouth and rolled into a crumb repository in the damp V of his legs on the chair. 'What's the capital of Bolivia?' I asked him suddenly, like he was playing some sort of 'let's pretend I'm a basket case' game and I could trick him out of it. He didn't even flicker. Leaving him yanked the guts from Mother. We'd head for the door and he'd sit there drooling and lolling, a broken shell where intelligent life used to be, and vital bonds, once precious, now severed and forgotten. He was beyond all of us now, even saying his name, Gash, felt like you were picking up something he'd discarded.

So as I've said, I went a little apeshit at my father's funeral just to give the comfy ecclesiastical cunt a bad half-hour he'd be forced to remember. At the service I accosted the minister, at the purvey I punched my cousin on the mouth and later, alone in the closemouth, I raged in the silence of the dunny, a bottle of Lanliq in my fist, sliding for the first time into comprehensive drunkenness. I have a dim memory of crawling along the pavement and passing Cotter slithering in the opposite direction.

'Another cold one,' he said.

'They say it'll brighten up tomorrow,' I seem to remember replying, before crawling on.

'By the way,' he called back, 'did you ever see that bird again?'

'What bird?'

'The school dance, remember?'

Ah yes, the school dance. How many stained lifetimes ago was that? 'No,' I said, 'I don't think I'll be seeing her again. I've too much on at the minute.'

'Pity,' said Cotter, 'she was a good-looker. Still, you know best.'

'I do,' I said, raising my head from freshly served soup of pungent vomit, thankfully my own, 'I know best.'

'What was her name again?'

He was asking me to think. I put in a distress call to emergency services. The last sober chromosome in my body leapt out of bed, donned rescue equipment and potholed through a hundred bat-filled caves to reach the lost world of boyish fancy. I had aged thirty years in fewer days. He wants the name, let him have it, as sure as I'm alive I'll never see her again. I fought to get my tongue around the words as they slithered like mossy stones. 'Mary.'

'What?' he said, leaning in close.

'Mary,' I said, louder. 'Mary Regan.' I crawled on. It was hard work, this crawling lark. Especially if you didn't know where you were crawling to. A man could crawl all his life without realizing he had arrived the moment he'd started. It was a sobering thought. But who was in the mood for thinking?

CHAPTER THREE

WHEN A BOY is bored with Glasgow he is ready to live. The Beatles had chased Harold Macmillan from the front page of the *Daily Mirror* and Harold Wilson, heeding the lesson, was all but doing the Funky Chicken to woo the voters of Britain. An interim stage had been discovered between being your father's son and turning into him and it was called 'teenager'. I was a teenager. Unfortunately, I was also a poor teenager, which meant always being slightly behind the times. When jeans came in, I was in khaki shorts. When Mod suits came in, I was in jeans. When kaftans came in, I was in a Mod suit. By the time I experimented with a kaftan, psychosis was in and I was duffed up at a bus stop by the Govan Team, narrowly escaping with my karma intact.

We'd hung around the Lyceum Café in that awkward era between Frank Ifield and the Rolling Stones, waiting for the sixties to reach Glasgow. The routine was simple, the collective noun for two or more teenagers being a vacuum. You'd slouch in, play the three most raucous records you could find on the juke box, order a Coke, then sling the money over, casually. The ecosystem of the average teenager is precarious, however, and one night when Coke went up a penny we were each obliged to sign IOUs promising to stump up the extra copper next night. Alcohol was a sporadic delight and on the odd occasions when resources permitted, a compliant adult could always be found who'd purchase the necessary on our behalf from an offy. Right from the start I loved drink, adoring everything about it except the taste. One glug of cheap wine could change reality. Everything became heightened and even Govan seemed interesting. It was worth the back court vomit afterwards in order to have touched Nirvana.

Of course we were innocent in those times. Nowadays kids of twelve are hooked on Thunderbird and Buckfast. I say let them drink it. What else are they going to wash their Ecstasy down with? Nowadays the planet is drug crazy. Opium has become the opiate of the masses. In those days only poofs, i.e. students, took drugs. Other poofs included Society Men (insurance money collectors) and any man who could say 'I love you' to a woman.

*

My time to leave school was approaching and everyone, including me, realized it would be a waste of time all round attempting to educate me any further. Careers Guidance in those days consisted of a visit from a grey middle-aged soldier who exhorted us to join the army then a grey middle-aged sailor who told us to join the navy. Anyone who failed to be mopped up by the services was instructed to visit the Careers Officer who asked everyone the same question: 'Do you prefer to work with your hands or with your brain?' Legend had it that no matter how this question was answered the resultant response would always be the same: 'They're taking on folk at Stoddard's Carpet Mill.' When the question was put to me I answered, out of perversity, 'Brain.' The Careers Officer pretended to peruse a sheaf of exciting opportunities. Finally he said, 'There's nothing in the brain line at the moment but they're taking on folk at Stod—' I stood up. He asked me where I was going.

'I don't want to work up the carpet field,' I said.

'But you're not qualified for anything else,' he said. I

shrugged. 'All right, then,' he said, 'ideally what sort of job would you like to do?'

I looked aimlessly around the office. Fitted carpet, two radiators, pert little typist next door with prim knees enticingly locked. I said, 'No offence, but your job looks a piece of piss.'

He made a sort of surprised snickering sound. He didn't throw me out but instead reached into a desk drawer, slowly. 'The other man's grass,' he said, 'always looks greener.' He laid a shiny mouth organ carefully across his desk blotting paper. 'Each of us,' he said, 'has our secret sadness. The dream that never was.' He picked up the moothie and squeaked out a simple tune. Next door the typist rose quietly and shut the door. As I eased myself into the corridor he'd wheezed into the opening bars of 'Summertime'.

As a child in Miss Rimmer's class, we'd once been asked to draw a picture of what we expected to be when we grew up. I drew a man in a cage surrounded by black walls. 'Very good,' said Miss Rimmer, 'a miner.' I looked at her. I didn't even know what a miner was. Sensing a faltering first step on my career ladder Mother extended feelers to selected relatives in the hope that one of them might be persuaded to 'speak for me' at their place of employment. Despite the occasional encouraging noise, blanks were, to my relief, drawn in every case. I had no idea what I wanted to be, only what I didn't want to be and that was another boiler-suited drone in a dead-start, dead-middle, dead-end job ticking off the weeks to the grave, or retirement as it was also known, on an oil-stained girlie calendar. 'To live, to live, to have erections' as Flaubert, or was it Vera Lynn, once put it. I had the erections all right but work was the opposite of living.

In a final act of desperation Mother sent word to Aunt

Alice, their first contact since the funeral. Aunt Alice worked for a firm of tweed consultants, I'd no idea what they did but I assumed, vaguely, that any worries the public might have about tweed, they could enter Tweed House and consult with a tweed expert who would allay their fears and send them off unburdened, no longer living in terror of being mauled by a length of Harris. My hopes were dashed when Aunt Alice promised, graciously, to help. I was scrubbed up, given a clean shirt and despatched to be interrogated.

'So you're a relative of Mrs Nesbitt,' bawled the Master of Tweed, leading me through a work floor where rolls of rough cloth were batted bewilderingly to and fro on rackety looms. 'A very fine employee.' He had red hair, wore a fibrous suit and looked like an inhabitant of a strange country of which I knew little, probably Scotland. In his office he asked me all about myself and as I told him he sat, shaking his head and muttering 'No, no, no,' until I'd finished. In the Scottish custom he corrected me on the details of my life then set about adjusting my perceptions impatiently, like they were a fuzzy picture on a television set for which he'd paid good licence money. 'Come this way,' he instructed and we zigzagged through baffling corridors with walled prints showing Tweed Awards and ancient pictures of Belsen-eyed weavers forcing cheery smiles as they shaved their thumbs at primitive looms. 'In here.' He opened a door. About thirty middle-aged clerks looked up from school desks. 'Mrs Nesbitt?' He called. Aunt Alice, somewhere in the middle, smiled and waved diffidently. She looked small and washed-out in her oatmeal cardigan, no longer the prim custodian of family honour and respect, just another lowly clerk, presided over by a watching supervisor, demeaned among the servile cluster.

'This is Robert, everyone. He'll be starting on Monday.' There was a light ironic cheer and a spatter of applause, to show how free and easy they were, before the heads dipped dutifully once more. 'I hope you'll be a credit to the firm,' said the Tweedsman, 'and to your aunt.' I nodded, mumbling thanks, deep gratitude.

Free on the streets, I breathed out at last. That was it then, the future. Head down in silence, twenty quid a week top whack till you fall off the chair or retire. Brain or hand, it's the same crap deal. The harsh din of traffic, the impatient to and fro of suited worker ants as I stand floundering, getting in the way. What am I for? What is the point of me? Across the street the harsh good news of an ancient dosser with widow's peak and newspaper underwear seated calm as Buddha in the gutter, quaffing from a flask-sized Eldorado. Walk with me, brother, for I am alone and sore confused. But not that confused.

'What d'you mean, you're not taking the job?' shouts Mother, shocked to the core.

'The job, taking it, am not I,' I say smart-arsedly taking, appropriately, a skite on the cheek for my cheek. 'It doesn't suit me,' I elaborate in more sober fashion.

'Doesn't suit you? It's a fucking job, not silk pyjamas,' contributes Rena, helpfully.

'Shut it, lady,' says Mother, showing a warning finger, then, to me, 'I can't believe it.' She shakes her head and clasps a hand to her brow to verify that, indeed, she can't believe it. I stand, shuffling but unbudgeable. Defeated, Mother finally asks, 'Well, if you're not going to do that, what are you going to do?'

I shrug. 'I don't know,' I say, 'I'll think of something.'

'Well, make it fast,' says Mother, 'it's time you started bringing some money into this house.'

I open my mouth to protest. 'I mean real money,' says Mother, beating me to it, 'not those pennies and halfpennies you bring in from God knows where.'

'My paper round,' I say unconvincingly.

'Paper round my arse,' says Rena.

'Fair enough,' I offer, 'but I'll need ten rolls and scaffolding.'

'If he doesn't want the job, I'll have it,' says Freak, easing himself ingratiatingly into the slipstream of my disfavour.

'You're too young, Freak, son,' says Mother.

'And too thick, and too ugly,' adds Rena, winning back some lost self-esteem.

'And that's not the worst of it,' frets Mother, 'what am I going to tell your auntie Alice?'

'Tell her anything,' I say, suddenly irritated by it all, 'tell her I'm an ungrateful bastard, tell her hanging's too good for me.' I grab my jacket and flee. I did good fleeing in those days, with plenty of indignation.

*

We sat in Cotter's living room, watching regional news at micro-volume while his father ate his tea. Cotter's mother was reading the *Govan Press*, which made more noise than the telly since her hands shook uncontrollably. I could make out the earth-shattering headline 'Dandruff in Govan Butcher's Mince Shock' between shakes. On telly the lead story was of an old crofter and his dog who'd perished on a loch when his rowing boat had overturned. The cold and rain were hampering the search for bodies. It was July.

Only country folk got to 'perish'. Gangsters were 'slain', pensioners 'passed away' and scum either plain 'died' or, on special occasions, were 'killed outright' when the cars they'd nick would batter into lampposts. No one in Govan ever 'perished' in an unfortunate hatchet incident. I was saying as much to Cotter when his father interjected.

'Shut that door,' he said, without turning.

'We haven't opened it yet,' protested Cotter.

'No, but you're about to.'

We took the hint and went upstairs. On Cotter's bed-room walls discrimination had set in. The Merseybeats and Pinkerton's Assorted Colours had been succeeded by The Temptations and The Four Tops, both of whom had been awarded the four thumb-tack accolade. The Rolling Stones and Yardbirds, having fallen from favour, now merited only used strips of Christmas Sellotape. Cotter pro-duced a well-thumbed copy of *Parade* and we took it in turns to use the bathroom. We were becoming desperate men. I'd lately read of a woman, trapped in an unhappy marriage, who slept with her car keys under her pillow. This I understood. Sometimes the idea of escape was enough of a consolation to defuse the necessity of seeing it through. Cotter and I had a similar mental bolt hole and we'd retreat to it whenever the crushing weight of Scottish-ness grew too heavy to bear. It had a name and we tingled when we spoke it.

'What about it, Cotter? It's time.'

'Time for what?'

'London.'

Tingle. Frisson. Thrill. We laugh. We look around the walls at the other posters. Lennon, Jagger, Relf. A *Rave* magazine pull-out guide to the clubs where they go. Scotch of St James, Whisky a Gogo, Bag O'Nails, Marquee.

'It'll cost money,' says Cotter.

'We can get money,' I say.

'How?' he says. He knows how, he just wants me to initiate the dirty deed.

Two nights later we're in the walled back yard where Cardoma's Cafés keep their ice-cream vans. The vans are loaded by the girls from the cafe at the arse end of their day shift and there's a one-hour gap before the drivers appear for work. We clamber in through the sliding win-dows and fill our jerkins with as many fags and half ounces of rolling tobacco as we can find, helping ourselves to the loose float change in the drawers as a bonus. Fags and tobacco can be sold door to door without any problem, even honest people being unable to resist the temptation of half-price smokes. Having disposed of the last twenty, inevitably Craven A, the 'healthy' fag, we buy a bottle of Lanliq and – Cotter and I sharing a shameful predilection – a box of Farley's Rusks. We sit in the drizzle of Elder Park counting our winnings and dunking rusks into the neck of the bottle.

'How much?' says Cotter.

'Twenty-one pound eight and fivepence,' I tell him, very deliberately, 'not of course counting the sleekit fiver you've got stowed away in your back pocket.'

Cotter tuts and hands it over. 'How did you know?' he asks.

'I didn't,' I tell him. 'I know you, though.'

He looks a bit sick but attempts a roguish chuckle to take the bad look off it. If he was Japanese he'd offer me his pinkie out of shame, but being a scumball I know he'll just work more diligently at his slyness.

*

To me London was the centre of the universe and Glasgow merely a piss-stained bus shelter where you queued to be taken there. If that seems harsh it's because Glasgow brought us up to make harsh judgements. In Govan vocabulary there are only three adjectives: crap, shite and, on the odd glorious occasion, say the Second Coming or the eradication of world poverty, not bad. The terms 'please' and 'thank you' are deemed superfluous and when used by a male are an admission of certain poofery, or, worse, an Anglified affectation. In those days, to avoid boredom, the population fought a lot, forming themselves for this purpose into two broad gangs, Protestants and Catholics. It's important to remember, however, that one great unifying factor binds us all, and that's that we're all arseholes. The most visible assertion of Scottishness, even today, crystallizes at Old Firm matches between Rangers, the Protestants, and Celtic, the Catholics. Rangers fans pay homage to their Scottish roots by singing the English anthem while celebrating the victory of an ancient Dutch monarch on a dreary Irish battlefield. Meanwhile the Celtic fans are belting out songs of Fenian nationalism. Then both sides strike up chants about the Pope who, at the time of writing, is Polish and lives in Italy. Very Scottish. Only people who don't know who they are fight over identity. And you can bet we'll still be fighting as we separate from the UK, because our contradictions are internal not external. I don't see the point of a Scottish Parliament or of breaking up the UK. In twenty years we're going to be Europe plc anyway, with Britain as a regional office, so what's the point of Scotland breaking away to form our own broom cupboard? That long streak of overeducated piss Orwell got it wrong, there won't be three national superpowers running the world, just three immense belching business conglomerates of which nation governments will form the PR departments. They'll have private armies to fight price wars and our grandchildren will be exhorted through their controlled press to sign up and lay down their lives so that future generations will have a better warranty deal on their fridge freezers. And you won't need a letter from the battle front, you'll be able to watch the whole thing live on the twenty-four-hour War Channel, provided, of course, it's not a big midweek conflagration, in which case we're talking strictly Pay per View. Do we really think a legal separation from England is going to stop that?

I can identify with England these days, know why? England's like the drunk tumbling home from the pub on a Friday night and we're the nagging wife.

'Hey, Percy, where's the pay packet?'

Fumbles in the Union Jack boiler suit. 'Here it is.'

She opens it. 'What's this? Forty billion pound? Expect me to run a regional infrastructure on that? Your fancy women next door gets twice that.'

'Ireland? She's off her head.'

'Exactly, Ireland's yer exciting flame-haired mistress, I'm just the boring wife.'

Six months later England's down the singles club. 'Yeah, I was married, but it didn't work out. What's it they say, one in three democracies these days winds up in the divorce court. Just never thought it would happen to us, that's all. Give's another one, will you, love? What's your name, anyway? Europe? That's a lovely name. Can I buy you a drink . . . ?'

And that's how the love story will end. Either that or they'll bomb the shit out of us for the oil.

Because the thing is, under all the ill manners and the lard, we're actually quite an outgoing lot. You can see us at airports, ready for holiday action, all in designer gear. Daddy Billboard, Mammy Billboard, wee boy and lassie Billboard, fighting. 'Reebok, stop that!' 'Ellesse, sit on your arse!' Sportsmen get paid thousands for advertising shit like that but scum works overtime to be allowed the privilege to buy it. Da standing there in his Nike V-neck and white loafers. Walked past Shelly's shoe shop in Argyle Street forty times, doing battle with his conscience. 'Get them, Alec, they're not too young. After all, you married the wrong woman, don't you at least deserve the right pair of shoes?' Family standing at the departure gate, waiting for Grandpa. He bowls up in wheelchair being pushed by a stewardess. He's bent double with arthritis but wearing a full Fiorentina strip. BATISTUTA on the back. Family knows he's going to croak soon but they're taking him on holiday so they can fight off the guilt pangs when they're rummaging under his living-room carpet for his policies in six months' time. Father goes, 'C'mere, Pop, you're sitting with me, you'll take the bad look off my shoes.'

Course when you're from Govan strange things happen to you when you go abroad. The sun to us is like a blowtorch. We stand under it, next thing you know there's a big pile of shale at our feet. Welding slag, soot, scabs, fag ash. You give a wee cough and this grey dust puffs out from when they sandblasted the tenements. You look at your gleaming new fresh pink forearm and you discover a tattoo you'd forgotten all about. 'Right to Work March 1980.' And you start to think, 'I thought I was Glasgow but I'm not. I'm me, whoever that is . . .'

*

I stole the tartan holdall my mother used as a laundry basket and met Cotter at Govan Cross Underground. 'How long do you think it'll take us to hitch-hike?' I asked him.

Cotter did 'pull on my chin and look thoughtful' acting even though he'd never hitched in his puff before. 'I'd say, oh, ten hours. Twelve hours tops,' he said.

'You sure?'

'Positive,' said Cotter, 'absolute max.'

Fourteen hours later we crawled out of a hedgerow in Lanarkshire, shivering and soaked. We'd covered twenty miles. 'We could go back,' I said, testing his resolve as we pissed down a rabbit hole to brighten the day.

He thought for a minute and shrugged. 'To what?' he said. We were committed.

We scored lifts to Scotch Corner then to Doncaster. Every time I looked to the horizon it seemed I could hear those Bow bells calling out to me. 'Turn again, Nesbitt,' they were saying, 'Whittington's fucked off.'

Outside a motorway service station near Nottingham we were reminded of how young and green we were. We were standing, bags at our feet, dithering at the cafe entrance when two men appeared out of nowhere. 'Where are you headed?' said one. He was old, not just comparatively to my young eyes but sixty-odd maybe and slightly shrunken through age. The other was much younger, early thirties perhaps, daunting looking, very powerfully built and tall. He was dark with thick eyebrows and he looked at me intently.

'London,' we said, eager for a lift.

The old one spoke. 'We're going for a cup of tea,' he said. 'Our car's over there, can you see it? We're going to London too, we'll take you.'

'Great,' I said. The dark one laughed. I couldn't see why but I smiled anyway.

'Yes,' said the old one again, as if trying to reassure us, 'we're going all the way to London, we'll meet you by the car in five minutes, OK?'

'OK,' we said. They went in to the cafeteria.

'That's fantastic, isn't it?' said Cotter.

'Brilliant,' I agreed, 'can't believe our luck, can you?'

'No,' said Cotter. We stood for a few minutes, silent, shuffling our feet. Then Cotter spoke. 'Rab?'

'What?'

'Let's just leave it, eh?' I nodded. We dodged around the back into a separate lorry park and were lucky enough to catch a quick hurl in a furniture van. It was empty and we lay flat out on a big pile of dust sheets, kicking our feet in the air and laughing hysterically. 'I didn't fancy that,' said Cotter, 'did you?'

'No,' I said. But I was uneasy. I'd have gone along with it if Cotter hadn't spoken up. And quite possibly neither of us would be around today. After all, what's two more lost runaways to the world?

As the lorry rumbled along the motorway I thought of Mother. I'd left a note on the kitchen table telling her that though I had no job, nowhere to live and hardly any money, I was off to London and not to worry. A little jab up the conscience wouldn't do her any harm. I hadn't wanted to tell her to her face in case she argued with me to stay. Equally I didn't want to tell her to her face in case she didn't argue with me to stay. I wanted at least one bridge left unburned. Money was a biting issue and I hadn't been bringing much in; the few bob from knocking out of Woolies or the occasional lucky blag from an ice-cream van was not going far. In addition I was a fat bastard who ate more than his share and couldn't help it. So London seemed the best solution all round. It had to be better than Glasgow.

In Glasgow you walked around like a schizophrenic, bored stiff yet at the same time at constant red alert in case you were jumped on at any moment and cleavered. Sundays were the worst. You'd read the football in the *Sunday Mail*, have a wank to the obligatory negligéed tart who'd tempted this week's innocent fat priest in the *News of the Screws* then go for a walk before you went mad with despair. Outside, free from the lethargic tobacco fug, the very air would seem starched and raw, chafing at your soul like a too stiff collar. Last night's vomit would have shrivelled on the pavements, the drizzle would be wearing the bounce from your Beatle cut and the church bells would hammer at your head like fucking nails. At around four o'clock, the Lyceum Cinema in Govan Road would prop open its doors to show its regulation Lana Turner double bill, *Madame X* and *Imitation of Life*. There'd be a picture of John Saxon, all square jawed, tweed jacket and pipe, looking like no cunt who ever drew breath in Govan, but the old biddies and widowers would already be making their way in ones and, if they were lucky, twos, to the pay desk.

When you got home your mother would be drying clothes in front of the fire and every so often the safety pin that held the fireguard together would burst open, sending a damp vest or torn pair of Y's into the sooty grate. At five past six the opening dirgelike bars of the George Mitchell Minstrels would drone from the radio, a coffin would open somewhere in Broadcasting House and a zombied clone of Henry Hall would say, 'We invite you to Sing Something Simple.' You'd cover your ears and scream at your mother, 'For fuck's sake turn that off!' But she'd accuse you of being dramatic and instead turn it up to drown out the racket of the young couple next door screaming, yelling at each other to be quiet because the other one's shouting was frightening the kid. Fuck that, I'd seen the kid, mutant bastard, it frightened me. 'What else can you do,' the old biddies would say, 'you've just got to get on with it.' That was the mantra by which we lived. 'I hate Sundays,' said Tony Hancock, 'ruins me Saturdays thinking of Sunday.' And your heart would gladden momentarily because, despite all, you were not alone.

Of course Govan has changed radically now. These days you can be just as desolate and bored on Sundays, but you get to eat a burger while you're going through it. So you'd lie in your bed and dream about London. You'd seen the Wednesday Play, you'd bought *Melody Maker*, you knew London was teeming with sassy but ordinary guys who looked like Ray Brooks and said wry things in a soulful way and stunning blonde debutantes who zoomed straight out of Swiss finishing schools directly into Hackney squats and who would only drop them for hip and horny no-nonsense lumps of working-class mulch-parcels like moi. 'After all,' you'd reason, 'Michael Caine and Albert Finney are working class and they're fighting off the quim.' The fact that both these guys were additionally rich, handsome and film stars tended not to impinge on this sustaining fantasy.

I'd floated the idea of London past Mother before and

she'd always issued the same dire warning: 'In London cafes they drop dope into your coffee when your back's turned.' For years the absurdity of this assertion never struck me. Some impoverished junkie, desperate and gasping for a score, was going to go out and sell his meat on the Piccadilly rack, buy pills, head for the nearest Wimpy Bar, drop them into my coffee cup then rock back and forward in ecstasy, clutching his forehead going, 'Oh man, look at that sucker slurp his Nescaff, what a fucking high!'

*

The furniture van dropped us off near Luton and a guy in a Morris Traveller obliged a while later. 'What do you want to go to London for?' he said, as road signs started to yield intoxicating messages like 'Hatfield 15' and 'London 25'. 'It's nothing but a great big sleazy den.' We said nothing. He got the message. 'Of course,' he said, 'I almost forgot, I was young myself once.' He stopped the car at Wood Green and we got out, planting our first steps gingerly as though these soft southern pavements might be made of marshmallow. 'Do you know where you're going?' he asked.

'Oh yes,' said Cotter, 'a hiking friend recommended a cheap yet clean youth-hostelling establishment.'

'Really, whereabouts?'

'Soho,' said Cotter, a tad sheepishly.

The driver gave a rueful laugh and pointed across the street to a tube station. 'Piccadilly Line,' he said, 'good luck.' He drove off and we stood, waving soberly till he was out of sight, then we began jumping up and down the pavement, yelling, like the hick idiots we were.

*

When you first arrive in London as a pale-faced lump of Scottish veal, bred in darkness and suffering from acute glamour deficiency, the mesmerizing whirl of the capital grips and dazzles your senses. Time spent doing anything other than drifting around the streets gawping becomes quickly regarded as time wasted: you came here for adventure, remember, and adventure doesn't happen in dingy bedsits or depressing factories, that's real life and you can get all that at home. No, the tingle is on the streets and you daren't leave the streets, you might miss something. The West End streets are a free twenty-four-hour nonstop floor show and if you're homeless you've got front-row season tickets. Which isn't to say we were completely irresponsible.

We left our bags at Victoria Station, disappeared into a hole in the ground and surfaced from another one at Piccadilly Circus. In a Leicester Square bierkeller called, appropriately enough, the Wunderbar, we devised a careful strategy.

'How much have you got?' asked Cotter.

I assembled my crumpled ball of wealth and assorted loose coinage on the table.

'About a tenner,' I said.

'Me too,' said Cotter, 'so why don't we do this. Have a wee drink tonight then find a job and digs tomorrow, eh?'

I nodded. Glee welled up within me. 'Excuse me, Heidi, two more supersteins, bitte. You've got beautiful eyes, by the way . . .'

We woke on a bench by the Embankment around ten hours later. My limbs were stiff with cold and the contents of my cranium had been subjected to a small controlled explosion. Cotter stood creakily upright, shivering from head to toe. 'Dying for a pish,' he said. We found a cafe a short stiff stagger away in Villiers Street and over a wholesome breakfast of hot chocolate and Rolos appraised our situation. 'Three quid down, man,' said Cotter, 'fuck sake, in Glesga you can get drunk for a pound.' I felt a creeping sense of alarm. Even in those days I knew I could fairly estimate my financial condition the morning after a binge according to how severe was the limp I had acquired when I attempted to walk. The more pronounced the greater the volume of small change I had accumulated through the buying of rounds. I unburdened my leg onto the tabletop and counted. Five quid down. Jesus H. 'Oh aye,' admitted Cotter on interrogation, 'you bought an extra round. Or two. And chips.' I dug into my pocket, took out a packet. 'Oh, and fags,' said Cotter, helping himself to a Black Sobranie, the kind of fancy shit you buy when you're drunk, stupid and trying to impress a girl.

'We'll have to get a grip,' I said.

'Absolutely,' agreed Cotter, 'the honeymoon's over.' He shook his head gravely, doing self-disgust acting. Minutes later, bodies still hunched in an early morning crouch as we shuffled, purposefully, to nowhere, I spotted a card in the window of a Lyons Tearoom. *Dishwashers Wanted. No Exp. Nec.*

'That's it,' I said to Cotter, 'we're laughing.'

We tried the door. Locked. What time do they open. Eight a.m. What time is it now. Six. Jesus, two hours to kill. Still, this is it, salvation. I felt Cotter tug at my elbow. 'Let's go for a walk,' he was saying. 'we can come back.' I didn't want to go anywhere. I wanted to stay and hug the door to make sure it didn't go away. 'I ask you, man,' repeated Cotter, 'two hours. We'll come back.' He tugged me again. I let myself be tugged. We drifted away from Lyons Tearoom like survivors from a lifeboat.

How was I to know Cotter had his own private rescue plan tucked slyly away? 'A walk' drew us back inevitably to the streets of Soho. Excitement. Swarthy Maltese hard men. Strip clubs, deadbeats, misfits and mental cases, the Amalgamated Union of Runaway Kids, hanging around corners waiting for night so they could hang around corners waiting for day. We walked down Wardour Street.

'See that lane?' said Cotter. 'The boxer Freddie Mills, he was shot in that lane.' Excellent, a dead celebrity, this is what we came to London for. We walked down the lane nosing in doorways for a blue plaque or gold lamé bloodstain or other tribute. 'Makes you think,' said Cotter at the other end. 'It does,' I agreed. Between us we hadn't a thought in our head, we were so tired. Soho was full of lanes. You could get lost. We got lost. In Golden Square we lay down and slept, pretending to sunbathe in the grey afternoon for the benefit of passing policemen.

'How much have we got left?' asked Cotter.

'Don't keep asking that,' I told him. We were in a pub somewhere. It was late afternoon. I was beginning to get ratty with Cotter, which surprised me, him being my best pal. 'We should have gone back to that tearoom, what's it called, Lyons.'

Cotter struck a martyred pose. 'And it's my fault we didn't, is that what you're saying?'

I shook my head, suddenly anxious not to fall out. After all, we were a long way from home and we only had each other. 'It was my fault too,' I said, 'it was stupid of us to lose track. It can't be that far away, I mean we haven't walked that far, wouldn't you say?'

Cotter looked at his empty glass. 'There'll be other jobs,' he said.

'Of course there will,' I said, taking the hint, 'I'll get them in.'

Six pints later we were sitting, swaying on the stone steps of the Eros statue. Groups of hippies gathered there to sing wistful songs of gentle love that made you want to thump their lights out. We were drawn by the girls and the faint hope that a spot of universal love might manifest itself in the form of a sympathy poke down the crypt of St Martin. A pretty girl was sitting next to me. She had braided blonde hair and the sort of pert winsome face that should be looking down at you from a tumbril on her way to the guillotine.

Cotter nudged me. 'Speak to her,' he muttered.

I spoke to her. What I'd intended to say went along the lines of 'Excuse me, you are extremely beautiful and I should like to devote my life to worshipping at the altar of your being.' Instead what came out sounded like 'Hullorerr, we're fee Glesga, pished oot wur boxes, steamin' since we goat here, perra fuckin diddies, nae kiddin', doll,' which translates approximately as 'Greetings. We are two drunken idiots from Glasgow.' I offered her a cheery smile, Brother Sun to Sister Moon, but she looked at me, blinking. 'I'm sorry,' she said, 'I don't understand what you're saying.' I tried again, feeling my face redden to an attractive shade of crimson. She shook her head this time, briskly, eager to disentangle herself and return to a finer world of grandad vests and flat guitars. As a deal clincher Cotter leaned in, breathing beer. 'How much is your free love, doll?' he enquired, wittily. She rose. She left. 'Another pint, Rab?' said Cotter.

The police allowed you to hang around the steps till midnight then council workers would appear from a truck and hose the place down to budge the hordes. By this time you were desperately tired having tramped around all day. We spent part of a night in a shop doorway in Brewer Street, munching bruised fruit from the gutters of Berwick Market, till two policemen appeared. It was important to avoid policemen, not only would they move you on, they could also take you in and despatch you back where you came from if you hadn't a roof or the means to support yourself. We walked to Paddington which was an area less teeming with policemen and slept unmolested till the early morning porters shook us awake. 'Haven't you got homes to go to?' seemed a rather pointless enquiry and we invited them to work it out for themselves before leaving the station, briskly. We queued for six hours in a National Assistance office near New Oxford Street. They gave us an Emergency Payment each of twelve shillings and sixpence (sixty-two and a half pence) and recommended, to our amusement, that we apply for work at the zoo. We walked to Regent's Park where a man feeding monkeys told us we were wasting our time. 'It'd be different if you were students,' he said, 'now if you were students we could take you on.' That night we spent at a Salvation Army hostel. It cost more than we'd expected and the hard-core crazies and jakies terrified us. We followed their example by placing our shoes under the legs of the bedhead to prevent them being stolen and fell asleep wearing our jackets and hugging our holdalls. We each woke about five minutes later and spent the remainder of the night hoping not to be shagged or eaten.

Things were getting desperate. Something had to give. It did. We stole a few hours' sleep in the toilet cubicles at Piccadilly Underground, the traffic in human arses by day being so brisk that an attendant, unless in vigilant mode, would be hard put to tell which cisterns had remained unflushed for suspiciously long periods.

We sat in a cafe in Charing Cross Road, where Cotter insisted on buying me a rum baba.

'What's this for?' I asked.

'For being you, Rab,' he said. He put a finger to my lips. 'Don't thank me.' We held another in-depth strategy discussion.

'How much money have you left?' I asked.

Cotter shrugged. 'No idea,' he said.

I was surprised. 'I'm surprised,' I said, 'you always know how much dosh you've got, right down to the last bit of pocket fluff.'

He shrugged again. 'Two pound? Two pound ten, who knows. What's the plan, Rab?' I showed him an ad in an old *Evening Standard*. He read it aloud. 'Labourers wanted.' He looked at me. 'And?' he said.

'And? And all we have to do,' I said, 'is find this agency in Marchmont Street, wherever that is.' I couldn't believe how casual he was being. 'You do still want to find jobs, don't you?'

He nodded. 'Natch,' he said. He stood up. 'Come on,' he said, 'time to get help.'

We walked back to Piccadilly. Eros Island was the point from which we took all our bearings. It was late afternoon and the place thronged, as always, with tourists and dead-beats. 'What d'you reckon?' I said.

Cotter bit his lip. 'Wait here,' he said, 'I'll go and ask that polis.'

I watched him walk towards the policeman, who was about twenty yards away. I mention this in some detail because even now, more than thirty years down the track, what happened next still takes my breath away. Maybe you're way ahead of me, dumpling that I am, perhaps I was born gullible. You'll say I should've seen it coming. Put simply, when I looked back, he wasn't there. He was gone, the policeman too. He'd done a bunk, bailed out, given me the hipsway, surrendered himself to the forces of justice, whatever. All I know is, one minute I'm making plans for the future with my best pal and the next he's malkied me in the back, left me on my ownio and well-nigh penniless in a strange city miles from home. Not a word of warning, nothing. Don't get me wrong, I knew he was low, it's just that with Cotter, whenever you think he's led you to the basement, you turn around to find another set of steps leading down.

*

You'll understand of course that all this was a long time ago, a long time ago. And that nowadays I see better with my eyes shut. What I like to do now, I'll pull a chair out from under the kitchen table, pamp it by the front of the close and watch the worlds go by, the inner and the outer. If I've been up to the Southern General for my treatment, I'll rest on a bench at Linthouse, by the bookies'. Folk say the Health Service has gone down the stank but if you use the noddle you can get by. For instance I'm not short-sighted any more. I just sit here and school weans going by on the bus shine laser pens into my eyes, cured me in no time. That daft bastard Richard Branson paid twelve grand for the same treatment off BUPA, he could've stood outside Govan High School at playtime, he'd have got it done for Jack Shit. Sometimes I see guys from the old days go past on their way up the hospital for treatment or therapy. The odd one's normal but most are walking car wrecks by the time they hit fifty. I'm not good with names but I can put an ailment to a face almost instantly. Breakdown, TB, prostate, bankruptcy, heart, kidneys, alcoholism, show me a face and I'll put a catastrophe to it. Besides, we don't need names in Govan, everyone's called the same thing, 'that cunt'.

People say to me, 'Rab, you don't have a job, what do you do all day?'

I go, 'Well in the mornings I work on a cure for cancer, in the afternoons an irrigation scheme for Namibia, then . . .' What the hell do they think I do, sleep for eight hours, watch telly for eight hours, like everybody else, that just leaves a third of the day that's any different from theirs. I think they expect tales of nonstop anarchy and madness and they're disappointed if they don't get them, like that's what they'd be doing if only they didn't have to work. My arse, most of them would drop dead through fright within a week if they didn't have some suit with an arsehole at both ends telling them what to do.

I do try to avoid daytime telly. I think it's cruel keeping people artificially alive like that and denying them a dignified end. I walk instead. They gave me a stick up the Southern but I only use it if I have to. Down Wine Alley, all gone, up Govan Road, along past the craters where the works used to be. Sentimental times. I can remember when all this was junkie shooting galleries. Shuffle past the shopping centre and that white-faced prick of a mime artist, trying to ingratiate himself by doing welders and one-man ship launches, let him mime a drive-by shooting or a joyrider wrapping his napper round a lamppost and I might salute his contemporary fucking bravura with twenty pence in the Kangol bunnet. Useless wanky bams, I'd slaughter the lot of them.

It's true, you get mellower as you get older. Not because you're a nicer person. It's because you've begun the slow retreat to a place where niceness doesn't matter a fuck, you get in anyway. Am I scared? Believe it, even my tears of panic are shitting themselves. Where was I? Oh yes . . .

*

It's one a.m. at Waterloo Station and I'm fighting sleep. I've got my holdall at my feet to validate my traveller status but it makes no difference. As soon as you shut your eyes the police shake you awake and ask you where you're headed. 'Basingstoke, missed my train,' you mumble, hoping to hell they don't ask you where Basingstoke is. 'You're not allowed to sleep in the station,' they warn you. The polis are more human down here, in Glasgow they're straight in with the do you want to cop a lift attitude before you've even opened your hole. The net result's the same though, do as you're told or else.

Beside me an elderly couple fidget under a tartan rug. They look like genuine passengers but I notice they've no luggage. Homeless people don't always conform to type. Last night I slept by the Arches and at 6 a.m. alarm clocks were going off and I even heard a whistling kettle. I feel

123

myself drop off again and a hand wakes me up. When I look this middle-aged guy is smiling down at me. 'Are you looking for a place to stay?' He's wearing a suit, a collar and tie. On closer inspection the collar's so frayed Buffalo Bill could use it as a fringe and his suit's so grimy a flea landing on it would skid and break its ankle. He's got some leaflets in his paw to try and make him look official. 'No,' I say. I'm more wide now, you only have to clock that predatory look once and you don't forget it. 'I've been on a stag night,' I tell him, 'I'm just waiting for my other friends to meet me, then we'll find some dirty fucker to kick the shit out of for a laugh.' He doesn't believe me but he knows I've got him taped, so either way he's lost. 'I'll take a leaflet anyway,' I say.

He slings one at me and hurries off. I glance at it. *Looking to trade in your old gas cooker? Why not come to* . . . Tosser. I crumple it up, rise. Can't sleep here. Can't sleep anywhere. Please let me sleep, I dream of being able to sleep.

I half open one eye. A face next to mine says, 'Morning.' I yelp, am on my feet, my brain having pressed the panic button before it's even opened the shutters for business. I'm in a shop doorway. A guy with an Elvis haircut is looking up at me. 'All right?' he asks. Another bout of panic. 'Relax,' he says, 'your bag's here.' He nudges my holdall forward. 'Bet there's nowt in it but old socks and shite anyway.' Liverpool accent. Vague Teddy Boy allegiance. One of those leftovers the Merseybeat hoover must have missed. 'How long you been skippering?' I tell him about a week. 'Got a job?' I tell him no, you can't get a job without an address. He looks at me like I've got learning difficulties. 'Oh, yes, you can,' he says.

An hour later I've got my head in an oven gouging great curly slivers of grease off the sides with a wallpaper scraper. 'When you've finished that,' says Reya, the Spanish head chef, 'you can clean out the lift shaft.' I grunt from inside the oven. 'Say yes, Chef,' he commands. 'Yes, Chef.' I'm in the sprawling tiled-floor kitchen of a restaurant near the Haymarket. Scouse – 'me name's Tony but I prefer Scouse' got us both in for a 'casual'. This means queuing at the back door in a straggly line of other deadbeats and misfits hoping to be picked for a day's work as a counter hand or kitchen porter. If you'll work 'a doubler' you get preferential treatment. A doubler means sixteen hours on the bounce, 8 a.m. till midnight with two half-hour breaks. The money's crap but the enticement is you get paid cash in hand.

'Is he experienced?' asks Pepe the Underchef.

'Oh yes,' says Scouse, 'trained him meself.'

'What's his name?'

Scouse looks at him like he looked at me earlier. 'Jock, what else.'

The oven's clean of grease, as it should be, since most of it is now sticking to me, and Pepe leads me over to a small lift by the door that has a wooden shelf in the middle. This, I learn, is called a dumb waiter. There's a bit broken off the corner of the shelf so that when the thing is hoisted and lowered on its rope pulley dishes fall off and smash on the lift floor. Pepe hands me a broom. I lower the lift down to the basement, lift the detachable floor on the dumb waiter and drop down into the empty shaft, my feet crashing onto a thick slippery carpet of gunge and crockery. It's pitch black. They've given me a pair of rubber gloves and I fill handfuls of anything I can into a series of plastic bin bags. When I finish, about forty minutes later, I climb out into the glaring light and frenzy of the kitchen.

Scouse is looking at me. 'All right?' he says.

'Aye,' I say, 'but I wouldn't want to be doing that every day.'

'Won't need to,' he says, 'I've been here nine months and it's the first time I've seen it cleaned.'

I absorb this news, realizing I've been made a chump. It's not every day they get a gullible young fool through their doors.

Scouse looks a bit queasy. 'I'd clean up, if I were you.' I look. Maggots are sticking to my clothes and skin, writhing sickeningly on a gluey film of oven grease. I feel my face. Jesus, they're in my hair, in my ears, I can smell their mealy odour. I freak out, hauling off my jacket and shaking it. Everybody yells, starts stamping. Pepe runs me into the staff toilet for delousing. When I come out, Reya hands me a bottle of Coke. 'All right, Jock?' he says. I'm accepted.

*

I was a somebody. I was Jock the Maggot Shoveller. Reya offered me a full-time job at the restaurant. I told him I could only take it if I could find an address. He went upstairs to the manager's office and had a secretary draft a letter establishing me as a bona fide employee. I was honoured. The building blocks of an independent life were starting to be put in place.

I'd never lived in a bedsit before. I found one in Ferndale Road in north Clapham. It was small. If the walls had been quilted it could have doubled as a coffin. For six days a week I worked sixteen hours a day clearing shit and on the seventh day I rested. When I rested I felt lonely so I stopped resting and usually surrendered my day off to overtime.

The Irish are Paddies, the Welsh Taffs and the Scots Jocks but there is no collective dismissive epithet for the English, only regional ones – Geordie, Tyke, Brummy, etc. I didn't like being called Jock. It made me feel responsible for the nation. If I was in a bad mood it was because Jocks were grumpy. If I did something wrong it was because Jocks were stupid. In retaliation I started calling the Spanish staff Pedro and the English Percy. This arrangement worked quite well until, in a rare burst of international harmony, two Pedros and a Percy got together and shoved my head in an oven for cheek, an incident that cost me both eyebrows and a lovingly cultivated sideburn.

Anyone who works in catering is struck by the contrast between the public and private faces of a restaurant. I was no exception. I watched in puzzled fascination as our customers, many of whom were well-dressed, comfortably off members of the professional classes, out for a pre-theatre bite, aimed tastefully laden forkfuls of food from white plates into well-bred mouths. If I positioned myself by the waitresses' arch, I could observe simultaneously the well-fed customer faces and the unwashed dossers prised from shop doorways who, minutes earlier, were washing those same plates in scum-filled sinks and polishing that cutlery with scraps of kitchen roll and gasps of fetid breath. If only they were to look up and wonder, those customers might realize that the swarthy man in the white coat cutting gateau was one hour earlier waking up on the floor of a public toilet cubicle.

Soon puzzlement gave way to amusement as I learned that glamour is a paper-thin confidence trick relying on the gullibility of the audience and the skilled hypocrisy of the performer. But amusement came with a price. To see through an illusion is to be free, therefore freedom equals disillusionment, but what are illusions but buffers against the bleakness of existence?

A lot of the staff were middle-aged lost souls, ex-army types who couldn't adapt. One such, a dapper little guy called Sidney, taught me the art of drying a wine glass at high speed without shattering it into smithereens in my ham-fisted Govan paws. Sidney had a gentle manner, a slight air of refinement, and he didn't, when the same thing happened for the third time, berate me as a 'fucking useless cunt' as would doubtless have occurred in Glasgow. Instead he demonstrated the technique quietly, yet again, with the result that to this day, alcoholic fuckwit that I am, I can dry a wine glass with the gossamer touch of an angel with a celestial hair dryer. True, this skill has grown somewhat redundant as I've tended to eschew my fine crystal in favour of the bottle neck.

The basement of the restaurant housed a bar and a new strip club, which was why I'd been charged with the task of clearing the lift shaft. One of the strippers was an alcoholic and Scouse informed me that for a large Smirnoff she would permit 'a rub at me tits' in the corridor. A barman called Dean would, additionally, administer blow jobs at five bob a throw. Did he avail himself, I asked Scouse. His reply has lodged in my memory. 'Of course,' he said, 'after all, mouth's a mouth, isn't it?' Sex was a common way of supplementing income as well as injecting a little excitement into slavish lives.

One day Sidney approached me while I was drying cutlery. He looked flushed and produced a silver pocket watch on a chain and showed it to me. 'Jock,' he said, 'give me ten bob for it.' He was trembling and breathing hard like a man about to have a seizure. I didn't know what to say. I was fifteen, what did I want with a pocket watch? 'Here, hold it.' His name was inscribed on the lid. Not nicked, then. Probably a retirement present from the services. 'Please, Jock, please.' He was pleading, this middle-aged man I respected, demeaning himself for the sake of a few bob, what need I wondered could be so urgent? Out of guilt and embarrassment I'd started fumbling in my pockets when Scouse appeared and steered Sidney into the corridor. He reappeared minutes later with Sidney's pocket watch. 'Gave him ten bob for it,' he said, twirling it on its chain, 'but it'll cost him a pound to get it back.'

'I don't get it,' I said, 'why'd he need the money so fast?'

I always felt slow on the uptake with Scouse. He took me by the elbow and gave me a gentle shove. 'Have a look for yourself.'

I peered into the corridor. Sophie, a plump, permanently tipsy young Irish waitress, gazed back at me in the dingy light. Her overall was pulled up over her hips and I could make out the hunched dark figure of a man pumping away at her. With a shock I made out his sagging bare white arse. Sophie's arms were thrown languidly over the man's shoulders and a glowing cigarette tip bobbed between her fingers to his rhythm. She held up her hand and flashed it at me twice. 'It's ten bob,' she mouthed. Sidney's grey drawers flapped at his ankles. I could discern his face, thin and desperate, wheezing between the mounds of Sophie's greasy black overall. I made a mental note to cut my cock off if I ever reached fifty-five.

*

You met a lot of guys like Scouse in London, flotsam on the vast shifting sea of the homeless and the drifters. I'd ask him about his background but would receive only reluctant one-word answers. 'Birkenhead . . . one sister, somewhere . . . Navy,' then he'd veer the conversation sharply away on to a different topic, usually pubs. Together we visited many, cider houses mostly. One near Waterloo Station was a virtual cave in a wall, held no tables or chairs 'to discourage vagrants' and had a sign above the bar which read 'Any customer who falls down will be ejected.' Another in a basement under a railway bridge was run by two drag queens who hated each other. The night we were there they ended up having a catfight, scratching lumps out of each other on the chipped tile floor, wigs askew, fish nets and Y-fronts flashing, the lot. I didn't like cider and I hated being ruinously drunk on it, with every day off I'd feel there must be something better I could be doing but loneliness would drive me into Flanagans at Piccadilly where I knew I'd find Scouse or some of the other Brits, hanging about for the noise and the illusion of company. None of the other nationalities were keen on drinking, as soon as the floor was mopped, off would come the tall hats and they'd disappear home to their families. The rest of us were the loose-enders, outsiders and misfits in our own country.

On one day off I drifted into town and for once, finding no one, took the Northern Line train gloomily back home. It was raining. At a loss I stood in my room feeling as flat and inanimate as my utility wardrobe. It occurred to me I still hadn't written home. I pulled my holdall out from under the bed, blew the stoor off it and looked inside. No pen. No paper. Just my old copy of *White Fang*. Cousin Donald had given it to me years ago. It was still unread. I picked it up, flicked through it, lay back on my bed. When I looked up again it was early evening. I had an anvil on the back of my neck and a cement mixer rumbling in my stomach. I couldn't believe it. So that's what it was like to read a book? Why hadn't anybody told me? I shut the book and stared at it incredulously. I was still dazed by the wonder of what I'd found inside, this dull-looking little object with its drab covers, hiding its dazzling secret. 'Jeez oh,' I kept repeating to no one, 'Jeez oh.' Finally I stood up and the magic drained down out of my head and disappeared out of my shoes to wherever it goes. What time is it? Five o'clock, Smiths will still be open. Maybe I could try another one? I was hooked.

*

White Fang led to *The Call of the Wild*, before I stumbled on *The People of the Abyss*. That book was about the hideous conditions of the East Enders of London. I was in London. The Mile End Road that Jack London walked along in order to visit a sweatshop in 1902 was probably seven or eight miles from where I was sitting. I could go there. I went there. The East End didn't look so bad to me. It seemed to me that Govan folk would go to Whitechapel for holidays. That's when it dawned on me that I was one of those that London was writing about, 'the submerged tenth', though recent makeovers have seen us reinvented as 'the underclass' and 'the socially excluded'. I prefer my own term, of course – 'scum'. I want to hear those hard unpleasant words ripped from mealy New Labour mouths. I don't want my image freshened with fabric softener.

London wrote his way from the working class to the middle class and had a morbid fear of sinking back where he came from. This taught me something else: the view from the middle was indeed better than the view from the bottom, if only because you could see where you had been. Up until then I'd bought the myth of Christianity sold to us by the middle classes that said because Jesus was poor poverty equalled virtue. Consequently it followed that unemployment and outside toilets were verification that we were indeed God's chosen people. 'God loves you, he made you poor like his son.' So how come churchgoing account-ants and quantity surveyors weren't casting aside their Volvos and bungalows and running to Possilpark to catch ringworm and live like Jesus? How gullible can you get?

Through London, via a chance mention in a magazine article, I discovered Orwell, himself a Jack London admirer. Like London, Orwell prowled the streets of the East End sniffing, touching and taking notes. Though an Old Etonian, Orwell was unknown and living in genuine poverty when he made his forays, consequently he passed my priggish credibility test. I devoured the novels first, then a book of essays. When I came to *Down and Out in Paris and London* I felt weirdly sure that with each turned page the next names I'd encounter would be Scouse or Reya. His life was my life. Our lives, however poor, could be the stuff of literature. Fuck me. Books lifted the dust sheet off life and showed me the furniture underneath. An empty life could be revealed to have hidden meaning, such was the power of the writer's art. Equally of course, an apparently busy life could still be empty

I stole a day off work and went to Portobello Road then Canonbury Square, following the arc of Orwell's rising star through his improved addresses. Writers became my earthly gods. Day to day you'd intuit a poetry raging from certain individuals, something underneath the curses and the dull mechanics of the day, some subtle current that made them who they were but which, without a sympathetic eye to record and preserve, became as wasted as a comet shower over an empty desert. I needed more of this. September came around and I joined an evening class in literature in Brixton College.

The teacher was young, attractive and married. She let us call her Gina. We acted out Wesker's *Chips With Everything*. I got to play the sergeant role because I could shout with conviction. Darling, I fucking adored it. Afterwards one or two people came up and congratulated me. One of them had rich auburn hair and a pretty smile. Her name was Sarah. Afterwards, with some skilful engineering, I was able to induce a coincidental meeting. She lived in Brixton but had recently come to London from Oxfordshire. Hers was the next village to Sutton Courtenay, where Orwell was buried, her mother could remember the funeral. The cinema? Why yes, she'd like that very much, what about Sunday, Sunday evenings are so drab, although they're not so bad in London, are they?

I walked home to Clapham on a silver cloud that covered a round trip via Stockwell, Kennington and Nirvana. I couldn't have gone home before I'd walked myself out, if I'd sat in an armchair I'd have spontaneously combusted. That night, lying in bed, post-wank, gazing up at the tree shadows playing on the ceiling, I looked upon my improving life and saw that it was good. I decided I'd stay in London. I decided London was a great city. Scotland, I decided, wasn't great at anything. 'Scots Lead World In . . .' How many times in my life had I read those half-assed lying headlines that assured us the rest of the world bowed down in awe before us. Bollocks. Tarmacadam, penicillin, the White Heather Club, then forget it. We probably weren't even the best Scotland in the world. Scenery? Canada does it just as well and has more of it. Tartan? Canada does it just as well and has more of it. Moaning-faced gits? Canada does them just as well and has more . . . No, tell a lie, I think we do lead the planet there.

I thought of what they'd be doing at home. Ten o'clock. We'd be listening to the drongo through the wall battering his wife's head in with a chip pan. My mother would be turning up the wireless going, 'I wish he'd chuck it, I can't hear Moira Anderson singing "My Old Heiland Hame".' I thought of Oxfordshire, the forthcoming Nesbitt country seat. Of course Sarah's parents would have to approve of me. No problem. I'd integrate quickly and win her mother over by dressing up as a Morris dancer and slapping her traditionally about the head and knees. And her father? Well, with a daughter called Sarah, he'd bound to be middle class, so I'd chat to him about malt whisky or, if not malts, then the nearest approximations on which I could speak with authority, Thunderbird and gassed milk.

I was considering these cherished fancies next day as I cleaned the women's toilets. What you learn about women through toilet cleaning is that they'll try and flush anything. Old tights, dumped boyfriends, snapped stilettos, broken hearts, name it. I was about to tip my dirty bucket down the drain when policemen appeared. Two of them. Reya, the head chef, was with them. He looked apologetic.

'Are you Robert Nesbitt?'

I nodded.

'In that case, sorry, Jock,' said the other one, 'but it's time to go home.'

'What's up?' I wanted to know. They wouldn't tell me.

'We'll give you a lift to pick up your kit.'

I looked at Reya. 'What's going on, Reya?'

He was keeping out of it, looking innocent, playing the 'I from España' card. 'The police . . . I donno . . . they say me . . .' Fly git. When it came to putting on a bet he had the fluidity of an auctioneer.

Scouse gave me a supportive slap on the back. 'Never mind, kid,' he said, 'we'll have a wet later on.'

'Yes,' I said, 'later on.' I put down my mop and bucket. I'd like to think they're still standing there, as a tribute. There was no later on. I couldn't even ring Sarah, not having her number. Like Peter O'Toole's Bedouin guide in *Lawrence of Arabia*, I wondered about Oxfordshire.

I was driven to Clapham, allowed to pick up my things and to deposit my keys with the old Polish couple who lived upstairs and rented me the place. Then I was driven to West End Central nick where two Strathclyde plods with standard-issue beer bellies and corned-beef faces signed for me and steered me out the door. It was odd to be confronted again with the dour familiarity of those accents. Outside, they went through my holdall looking for God knows what. Meaty fingers rummaged through my crispy socks and dirty underwear. Serves them right. They flicked through a few books and shook them, I don't know why, maybe they expected a stolen Ford Capri to fall out. Really they were just pissing on me like dogs against a lamppost to reassert their authority. They hadn't looked too confident sitting in the interview room with their teacups on their knees like two village idiots down to see a musical. Now they were getting their own back.

'Books, is it?' said a big tartan sausage-fingered McPlod. 'Who the hell do you think you are?'

I didn't have an answer. I looked out the window of the cop car as we sped toward Kings Cross. Marylebone, Holborn, Bloomsbury, Euston. If I'd had a bit more time down here to find out, maybe I could have told him. 'Still,' I thought, 'I've got my whole life in front of me. Like I said to Scouse, I'll be back.' Footfalls echo in the memory. Toward the mop and bucket we never emptied. Into the rose garden.

*

On the train journey back to Glasgow I asked the plods how they'd found me. Turns out if I hadn't dropped a picture postcard to Mother out of duty they'd never have tracked me down. I tried utilizing the last vestiges of my innocent youth to glean more information. 'So is that why you've come to collect me, officer, because I'm a runaway?' The one with the fingers made a snorting noise and snapped a KitKat breadthwise, against the grain. The Met would never have permitted that. 'You're a runaway all right, fuck face, a runaway from a crime scene.' He filled his mouth with biscuit, looking pleased with himself. You could see him embroidering the exchange into the fantasy of how he'd fucked those London diddies. The other one glared, being more sussed, he didn't want to give out even that much. I thought of dredging up some cheek to pass the time but our wives are ugly and our pleasures small, their tight little faces seemed to say, and if you give us even half an excuse we'll wallop you with our great big sticks, so instead I looked out the window at the cows and sheep. Something further up the track had obviously gone wrong. As usual I'd a fair idea of where to lay the blame.

CHAPTER FOUR

'AWRIGHT, RAB?' Cotter greeted me like I'd just slipped out five minutes earlier for a packet of fags.

'What do you think?' I said. I gave him a stare that aspired to be menacing. I'd been fantasizing over this moment for months, of how I'd give him a fair hearing before cutting off his head and presenting it to his mother as a door knocker. We were in the interview room at Orkney Street. True to form Cotter had held out on four hundred fags from the ice-cream van raids and tried to peddle them in a pub. The fact that he'd chosen to approach two off-duty plods couldn't be put down to misfortune as if I stood up I could see the pub directly across the street. Generally there were more cops in the public bar than in the nick itself. This confirmed to me that Cotter was a unique combination of slyness, cunning and utter prickery. The plods, he maintained, had browbeaten him into owning up. Probably threatened him with a bath and a good shampooing. More damningly they'd matched prints from the till drawers to Cotter's. And mine. We were doomed.

'Just tell me why you did it,' I said. 'And I don't mean the fags,' I said, 'just tell me why you buggered off and left me in London.'

He gave me the trembling lip. 'Rab, I had to,' he said, 'your moaning was doing my head in.'

I was stunned. The bastard. He'd stop at nothing to save himself, no manoeuvre was too slimy, no tactic too low. Now he was even resorting to honesty. It worked.

Mentally, I put away my machete. Nevertheless I vowed never to speak to him again for the rest of my life, or his, whichever was shorter.

*

Having suffered the bad luck to have turned sixteen, I now qualified as a Young Offender. We were sent to the YO Unit at Barlinnie. It was the height of the swinging sixties, so called because hanging was still popular. Especially, I discovered, among the idealistic young. One minute you'd be chewing the fat with some harmless schizo about football, the next you'd be talking to his bootlaces as he dangled like a Crombie from some makeshift coathook.

Violence was frowned upon and anyone caught raising his fists would be subjected to a heavy beating from the Unit staff. These took place in the office of the principal while he sat and watched, ensuring fair play. The regime was strict, with an emphasis placed on physical training. This worked wonderfully well and succeeded in taking thousands of unfit young criminals and turning them into fit young criminals.

The gangs of the day commandeered the tables in the dining hall according to ferocity. Being without tribe Cotter and I were forced to share with the shoplifters. Some of these were highly skilled individuals. Once I dropped my spoon and when I resurfaced the soup had vanished from my bowl. I sat back and applauded. You had to be dedicated to steal soup.

It was largely two per cell and I requested not to share with Cotter. He was a liar and a scumball, I explained, and if we were placed in close proximity I would probably kill him. The principal listened sympathetically then shoved me in with him. The screws, sensing sport, would gather at our cell door, placing bets and taunting us. When

I succumbed to pressure and beat up Cotter they burst in and beat me up for fighting. On another occasion when I refused to beat him up they burst in and did me over for insolence. It was strange beating up a guy you weren't speaking to. I heard every ouch and oyah in an exaggerated way that heightened the absurdity of the act. I felt ridiculous, like Harpo Marx going six rounds with the guy who signs for the deaf on *Scotland Today*. This taught me another invaluable lesson. In future I'd always make sure I was on good terms with someone before I beat them up. Sometimes I'd even offer fruit before I'd thump their melt in.

*

At the Govan Team's table sat a thrusting young psychopath who was making an impressive name for himself on the exciting career ladder of headbangery. It was Stig Foley. We recognized one another immediately and, in the true Govan spirit of friendship, ignored each other for weeks. Finally, trapped together one day at the urinals, we were compelled to exchange pleasantries.

'Awright, ya fat cunt?' said Stig.

'Hunky-dory, Stig,' I told him. 'Yourself?'

He looked me over. For a moment I thought I was about to become the proud owner of a brand-new facial stripe but he relented and I felt my sphincter twitter in relief. 'What you sitting with them daft bams for, come ower and sit with us.'

So for the remaining months of my sentence I shared a table with the cream of Govan's rising scum. In those days young neds assumed nicknames that made them sound as cute as Teletubbies – Bimbo, Tojo, Teaser, Bunny; in fact it was almost an axiom that the fluffier the appendage the more lethal the ned. If you're ever introduced in a Glasgow pub to anyone called Zebedee or Tinky Winky, run like fuck – the cunt's a killer.

Stig grew to trust me and in time confided his plans for the future. One day in the exercise yard as we trained for the future by leaning against a wall and spitting he opened up.

'For the last couple of years,' he confessed, 'I've been involved in meaningless violence. But I spoke to the chaplain and he's persuaded me to give that up.'

I waited for the punchline. It didn't come. 'Oh, aye?' I said.

'Aye,' said Stig, 'from now on it's meaningful violence only for me.'

I gathered up some spit and lobbed a neat ten-footer. A line judge ran forward with a tape measure and confirmed my estimate. 'What's the difference?' I asked.

'Meaningful pays better.' He cleared his lungs and threw down the gauntlet of a mighty twelve-footer. He was a fine competitor. 'What's the point of giving someone a good going-over for free?' he went on. 'That way the doee gets a first-rate tanking at no charge which means there's nothing in it for the doer apart from a measly sexual thrill second only to committing murder.'

I nodded. I saw his point. It was either that or walking down to the boiler room, opening the furnace door, and stepping in. 'I see your point,' I said.

'Good,' said Stig, 'then come and work for me, me and my team are going to start hitting the betting shops and pubs for protection dosh. Not only them but – get this – the churches and chapels too.'

I was surprised. This was an audacious business innovation.

'They can afford it,' Stig explained eagerly, 'no pay no pray, it's a dawdle, the minister just passes two plates around at collection time instead of one. What d'you think, smart, eh?'

I looked at him.

'Well, say something,' he pressed.

I said something. I said, 'How do I get to the boiler room from here?'

*

Mother was overjoyed to see me home. 'What do you want?' she said. 'I don't like jailbirds in my home.' Jailbirds. Those courting years watching George Raft movies had finally come in handy.

'Awright, Rab?' said Freak, suddenly gangly and gawky with bones too big for his skin.

'Don't call me Rab, call me Lefty.' It was a little nudge at Mother but half serious, I wouldn't have minded becoming Lefty Nesbitt. 'It's a handle the other hoods gave me inside,' I said.

'Inside what,' said Rena from behind a *Titbits*, 'inside the blanket when you were having a wank in the dark?'

Mother pretended not to know what a wank was, thereby sparing us all an embarrassing scene.

'Get you,' I told Rena, 'you were spotted in a dunny last night with Shuch Munton, that's what I call having a wank in the dark.' This was a satisfying double dunt, smearing both Rena and my old persecutor from infant school days.

'That's despicable,' protested Rena, 'all we were doing was eating chips.'

'Aye, but what was he dipping them in for vinegar, ya clatty midden?'

This was a pleasantry too far for Rena. She caught me with the edge of a soup pot on the forehead. It cost me five stitches. One way or another I was having a lot of trouble with soup.

Despite this, it was nice to be back in a house. I admired my returned eyebrows in the mirror. They sat oddly below my near bald head. In YO, when they forced us to cut our hair, I insisted on a savage rump, down to the wood as a form of protest. So much of power is dressed in fashion. Back then kids were being sent home from school for having their hair too long, nowadays they can be sent home for having shaved heads. Back then teachers belted the life out of children and magistrates pined for corporal punishment, birching like on the Isle of Man. Now physical punishment is deemed to be damaging to a child and those same magistrates are happily fining adults for whacking their kids. Fashion, all is fashion, the iron fist in the velvet Nike.

*

Every day had felt like a holiday in London, with no time to think. Thinking exposed limitations, and limitations dragged down my spirits. In Glasgow you didn't need extra help for that, there were always plenty of people who'd do it for you. Years ago my brother Freak told me of an incident that summed this attitude up. Miraculously, one Christmas when he was about six, Freak woke to find that Santa, by dint of working double shifts on Glasgow Corporation buses, had for once left him exactly what he'd asked for, a Manchester United strip. Freak had immediately donned it and in a fit of magical goodwill had run out to play in the street. Watching him kick an imaginary ball around were two grown men, probably around Father's age. As Freak careered around, lost in his private Dingly Dell, mimicking crowd, commentator and all twenty-two players plus ball boys simultaneously, the spell was broken by an utterance from one of the men to the other. 'Eddie, get a load of that cunt.' The bubble burst around Freak: he was disillusioned at six, punished for committing that most heinous of Scottish offences, showing off.

I knew London wasn't perfect, its bigotries might be different but they were as prevalent. In Scotland, the first thing strangers ask of you is what school you attended, so they can work out if you're Catholic or Protestant. In London they were just as quick off the mark with the same question but in this case the purpose was to establish whether or not you were middle class. Not that there was much doubt in my case, you might suppose, but these were the sixties, remember, when shabbiness was de rigueur and until a mouth was opened it couldn't be damned or categorized.

Thoughts like these made me pine for Sarah. Scottish girls, having little confidence of their own, liked to chip away at yours, then when they'd brought your spirits crashing down to their level would turn chirpy, fall mysteriously pregnant and just happen to know about a lovely wee room and kitchen that had fallen vacant round the corner from their mother. Not that I had anything against marriage, I just wanted it to be a means to an end, not an end in itself. It was simple, then. All I had to do was return to London and sweep Sarah off her feet. No bother to a penniless louse from Govan. 'Are the Mars Bars to your liking, darling?' 'I love the way the moonlight dapples the Jakies' wine bottles down the midden, don't you?' So first I had to lay hands on some money. But how to do that?

*

It was becoming hard to avoid Cotter, Govan being a tiny culture. In addition, my life was so crummy that the gratification I gained from cutting him dead was becoming outweighed by the inconvenience of having lost a friend. In a spirit of self-interested magnanimity I turned up at his door one day, bringing a bottle of Lanliq, Govan champagne, to celebrate our anticipated reunion.

His mother opened the door. She was poised now on the brink of fashion since she trembled like a junkie. I waited for her to invite me in. She didn't. Instead she shouted Cotter down from his bedroom.

'Awright, Rab?' He looked more inconvenienced, I detected, than perplexed by the sight of me. I launched into my prepared speech. 'No point carrying grudges . . . You're a shit but I accept that . . . Look to the future . . .' All tried and tested clichés from the *Boy's Own Book of Manly Behaviour*. Cotter listened, fidgeting. When I'd finished and felt as noble as the Boy Brutus he said, 'Aye, very good, pal, no bother, but if you don't mind I've a wee mate waiting upstairs.'

I was narked. 'I'm narked,' I said. 'I've made a big effort here, the least you could do is humour me.'

He looked at me, rummaging in his foul being for one last vestige of decent behaviour. 'I'll give you a knock tomorrow,' he said at last and shut the door.

I was bemused and stunned. Then somewhere inside I heard the echoing clunk of a penny dropping and I was only stunned. Probably I loitered around two hours in the bus shelter down the street from Cotter's house, though it felt like four. I'd drunk a good half bottle of the Lanliq to kill the time and I was feeling decidedly woozy. At last the door opened. Cotter stepped out first, zipping up a Fred Perry golf jacket, which sent my envy off and running. Jealousy soon leapt to its feet, gave chase and roared in a blur over the horizon when Mary Regan followed him. Mary. Her hair was tousled and she was smoothing the knees of her navy crimplene ski pants *as if they had recently been pulled down*. I felt that melancholy lover's wrench at my gut and the telltale nip of tears. With Cotter! How could she? Mary, the only pure sweet decent thing in my life apart, admittedly, from Sarah. There was only one thing for it. I'd have to kill them both. Why not? Provided I had the decency to top myself afterwards this was an entirely acceptable course of action. But how to murder two people? It would have to be quick. A gun, then. But where to find a gun and learn to use it without blowing your own head off? And how to afford one? Yes, that was it. I'd get a part-time job to afford the gun, meanwhile enrolling at night school to learn Firearm Use and Maintenance. Why, in six months, maybe a year, I'd have all the qualifications I needed to commit a spontaneous crime of passion. But what if they had split up by then? Best hold my fire. I watched them disappear, arm in arm, down Broomloan Road. Innocent fools. They'd never know they'd only been an employment vacancy, firearms certificate and Adult Education course away from being gunned down in their prime. Lucky for them I was the ice-cool, calculating type.

*

Cotter duly knocked on my door next day. Being the aforementioned ice-cool dude at arms, I'd decided not to mention the subject of Mary, lest his own guilt and awkwardness blunder him into confessing. Meanwhile I'd recline, smiling enigmatically, cruelly even, gently stroking my imaginary white cat.

'Awright, Rab?' He stood, drookit in the pouring rain, drawstring pulled tight on parka hood, a square of face, white as Mother's Pride, peeking out, all in all looking not quite the supreme sexual conquistador.

'Awright, my arse! You never told me you were going out with Mary Regan!' My voice was high and squeaky and shook with pain. My white cat leapt from my lap and went searching for a more worthy master.

Rain dribbled from Cotter's eyebrows. 'Can I come in?' he said.

Mother was out. I took him into the living room and we glugged yesterday's remaining wine from tea mugs. My cool blown, I tackled the subject head-on. 'You knew I fancied Mary Regan. You knew she fancied me. You just nipped in there for badness.'

He didn't protest. He didn't shout. I wanted him to protest and shout.

'I can understand why you're upset,' he said with maddening restraint, 'but let's face it, you were in London and Mary and me were up here. You never exactly bombarded her with rose petals, did you?'

I had to concede that all forms of tribute, including floral, had indeed been in regrettably short supply, vis-à-vis myself and love object. I speculated aloud whether this was in fact the true reason for Cotter's treacherous behaviour in London, so that he could sneak off home to conduct an affair with Mary. He denied this and cited once more the real reason for his abrupt departure, my 'pain in the arse crabbiness'. Then he said the thing which seemed to settle the issue for all time.

'Of course you know Mary and me are going to get married?'

I informed him that I did not know. I informed him that he was an arse. I pointed out that he was only sixteen. He nodded.

'Exactly,' he said, 'most of the guys we knew at school are fathers already, we've had a good run at the single life.'

'Fathers?' I said. I steadied myself. 'And when are you getting married?'

'Oh, soon enough,' said Cotter, 'as soon as we can afford the pram.'

I ransacked my being for the *Coolness under Pressure* handbook. 'I see,' I said. I realized I was holding a vase of plastic tulips. Daz were giving them away free at the time. I put it down. 'Well, that'll be that, then.'

'Aye, looks like it.' He rose. 'I hope we can still be pals,' he said.

He offered me his hand. I took it. The right one, the one that had fumbled down Mary's blouse and . . .

'I wish you both all the best,' I said.

'Rab,' he said. He made a big show of hugging me even though there was no one to see it. 'You're a big man,' he said. I hung limp in his pincer grasp like an elderly patient being restrained in a rest home. I didn't feel like a big man. I didn't feel like a man at all. I had to change that.

*

I met Stig and his team at Pirie Park. They were playing five-a-side football prior to an evening's mayhem and invited me to participate. Stig liked football, but as a career move. He explained his logic to me. 'Successful gangsters play golf. No golf club'll touch me because I've only got the one club and that's a putter I half-inched out the public park. So until I turn successful fitba is my golf. After I'm successful golf will be my golf.' With that he fired a starting pistol in the air and the game began. We all ran about swearing, chasing as a pack after the ball. Our centre half wore a sword in a scabbard, which hampered his mobility somewhat. After an opponent scored, however, he drew the sword and promised to behead him if he repeated the achievement. This had a dampening effect on the opponent's scoring potency and he was seldom a threat thereafter. Eventually Stig brought the game to a halt by puncturing the ball with the pistol and we gathered in a circle to hear the plans for the evening's activities.

Two hours later we were gathered outside Wilson's

Bar at Govan Cross. Everyone was tooled up, except me. It had occurred to me to bring a whisk following the dramatic effect the last one had had on Father.

'Are we right?' said Stig.

I put up my hand.

'What's up?'

'I've no chib,' I said.

'You were told to come chibbed up,' Stig yelled.

'I know,' I said, 'but when I got home my mother was chopping carrots with it.' They looked at me. 'She's making a pot of soup, you see,' I continued limply.

Stig looked impatiently around his team. 'Teaser, you got a spare chib?'

Teaser rummaged in his Commando jacket. He pulled out a sherbet lemon, a Chicklet, and an awesome looking broad-bladed hunting knife with a serrated edge. 'Here,' he said, thrusting it at me, 'it's a German Panzergrenadier knife, don't lose it, I'm still paying it off my Granma's catalogue.'

I nodded.

Stig was seething at the hold-up. 'In future there'll be penalties for any team member who fails to provide his own chib prior to a rampage. There will be on-the-spot fines, payable to the club secretary, OK, Crazy Horse?' The gang secretary, Crazy Horse, nodded and waved a ledger. We were all nervous, eager to get on with it. Stig let out a sudden cry. 'Young Team, ya bass!' We roared in response and steamed into the pub. After all the infuriating technical hiccups we were at last open for business.

We steamed every pub from Govan Cross to Linthouse, encountering no opposition along the way. Most landlords were keen at all costs to avoid any reputation for trouble that might just put their licence at risk. As long as the demands were affordable, most were more or less happy to comply. Not that it was all plain sailing. On the return leg we bombed into a dour-looking man's pub near Harmony Row. There were about half a dozen customers, mostly emaciated-looking old labourer types. Two or three had sad, scabby dogs at their feet that gave us the 'poor me' eyes as we walked in. I've no time for dogs. Any creature that'll take orders from a dumber looking bastard than itself, all for a plastic plateful of marrowbone jelly, deserves all that's coming to it, in my opinion. An elderly woman stood, wiping the bar counter. It looked easy-peasy as Stig walked up and laid his hatchet on the bar.

'You in charge here?' he asked.

'Go fuck yourself,' said the elderly woman, without looking up.

Stig pressed on. 'I'm looking for the manager. I think it might be in his interests if you run and get him.'

She lifted Stig's hatchet and dropped it in the wastepaper basket on the other side of the bar. 'You deaf?' she said. 'I thought I told you to fuck yourself.'

Crazy Horse took over. 'We want to look after this gaff, you know what I'm saying? Give us dosh and nothing'll happen to it, understand?'

She was unimpressed. 'Nothing's going to happen to it anyway,' she said. 'This pub's known a lot harder cocks than yours. Now are you going to fuck off or what?'

Tojo thumped a knife into the well-tended mahogany of the bar counter. 'We're not going anywhere till we get paid. Now open the till.'

The woman looked at him. 'Not a chance, ya fucking ballerina. But I'll tell you what I'll do. The manager'll be back in a couple of hours. You can ask him. If he decides to pay you, I'll open the till, deal?'

We looked at each other. 'Deal,' said Stig.

'Good,' said the biddy, 'now are you going to buy a drink while you're waiting, this is a pub not a fucking bus terminus.'

We went into a huddle. Stig turned back to her. 'Five pints of lager, two heavy, a rum and Coke and a shandy top.'

'Coming up,' she said. She started pulling on a pump. 'Is it cold out?'

Stig shuffled uneasily. 'Not too bad,' he mumbled.

We took our drinks to the tables and sat down. Three hours later the manager still hadn't put in an appearance. At closing time the biddy gave Stig his hatchet back and we staggered out, having blown a sizeable hole in our extortion capital. Outside, swaying on the pavement, I strained to read above the door the tiny gold-painted name of the pub licensee. 'Betty McCrindle. Licensed to sell . . .' Small wonder the manager hadn't shown up, she *was* him. This proved a valuable business lesson to us all.

'Fucking publicans,' said Stig, 'bunch of bastarding gangsters. C'mon, let's get chips . . .'

*

I enjoyed little about running with a gang, except the hours. A typical day might pan out like this. Ten a.m., rise. Ten till twelve a.m., practise looking psychotic in wardrobe mirror. Twelve till two, intimidation of passers-by. Two till five, arguing and spitting. Five till six, rest. Six till seven, spitting and arguing. Seven till eleven, extortion. The money was welcome and I was able to buy Mother little luxuries like expectorant and a ceiling fan that kept the cigarette smoke circulating and prevented smog from forming over the kitchen table.

On Sundays we'd gather to hit the churches. Most thugs being superstitious, I was delegated to undertake this duty on the grounds that, as an atheist, I was the nearest thing we had to a religious expert. We'd target randomly to evade the police. Most ministers complied, being as pragmatic as the publicans, and provided we were humble, coded our threats with care and helped to hand out hymn books, we were allowed to extort modest amounts with the Lord's blessing. As usual, of course, there was always the unexpected, for which any extortionist, however diligent, could not prepare. Once, seated with three henchmen in the front pews of a church in Duntocher, I gripped the minister's elbow for the customary quiet word as he headed for the lectern. Disconcertingly, he fainted into my arms. The flock, assuming me to be some sort of church elder, urged me to continue with the service. It was a memorial service for a small-time rivet manufacturer and they'd all left babysitters on Sunday rates and were eager to stick within budget.

Their spokesman made a persuasive plea but I wasn't keen. 'I'm an extortionist,' I protested, 'I don't know anything about the dead guy.'

The spokesman persisted. 'Just read from the notes on the lectern,' he urged. He started to sweeten the deal. 'Look, I promise you, whatever you'd hoped to extort today, I will personally double it.' I looked around at the hopeful pleading faces. Who was I to deny them the joy of worship?

'OK,' I said, 'but I want the dosh up front.' The spokesman agreed, we passed plates around and I conducted the service. I was nervous at first but I started to enjoy it. I laid it on thick about the guy's achievements – how he'd always loved rivets, sometimes even filling his briefcase with them to work on in the evenings at home, how he loved his family and wanted them all to be welded together in the family crypt when they died. To close, I got them to rise and sing 'Twist and Shout' since I didn't know any hymns all the way through. Afterwards I stood at the church door, shaking hands like a real minister and blessing my flock as they left. It was all going fine till an old woman spotted the chib head sticking out from under my jacket.

'Reverend, what's that for?' she said, tapping it.

I had to think fast. 'Oh, this,' I said, 'this is for the kiddies' pageant later on, when Abraham gets his ear bent by that big sadistic bam Jehovah, telling him to stove in the napper of his wee boy Isaac.'

She looked at the chib, doubtfully. 'With a claw hammer?' she said.

I treated her to an unctuous smile while I fumbled briskly in my mind. 'Verily, Abe was no mug,' I said, 'a gun would mean eternal life, but with a hammer there's always the chance of a reduced charge to manslaughter.' She nodded and bade me good morning, I waved. I like to think she went away a better person.

*

My career as a hooligan was all-consuming and left little time for my other interests, sleeping and moping. We were much too busy protecting small businessmen by extorting their money and lying around the parks drinking and boasting. They must have slept easily at night knowing we were on the case.

Sometimes we'd have to repel invaders who'd try to usurp our territory. These occasions unnerved Stig, not because of the violence, which he cherished, but because of the rousing pre-battle speeches tradition called upon him to make. Like most Glaswegians, Stig was a doer not a talker. Because he'd seen me thieving a book once he assumed I was an intellectual and appointed me his speech writer. This was an unenviable task. He once rejected the phrase 'get stuck into these wanks' on the grounds it was 'too flowery'.

Success in Govan saw us seek to extend our empire by

crossing the Clyde into Partick. Team-handed, we rolled a few pubs in Dumbarton Road in the accustomed style. Money was handed over reluctantly and in an ungrateful manner. Most landlords expected to be touched at some point but resented extortionists coming in from outside when they had plenty of unemployed local extortionists of their own. We knew we were pushing our luck and it was no surprise when Stig received an invitation from the Maryhill Fleet, who regarded Partick as their sovereign territory, to join them for an afternoon of coffee and violence. This was an exciting career opportunity for Stig as the Fleet enjoyed a reputation as a stylish and witty bunch of thugs and a successful engagement on his part might lead to further bookings with perhaps, who knows, the ultimate accolade of an invitation to be pacified on television by his Royal Highness Frankie Vaughn. Naturally, Stig was more than usually nervous and demanded that I come up with a speech befitting the importance of the occasion. To encourage me he pulled out a carpet cutter and pressed it against my ear. I pictured my face, trimmed and squared, fitting snugly against a door frame. I set to work.

We'd arranged to do battle in the old pedestrian tunnel under the Clyde but, the weather being unexpectedly delightful, the venue had been changed to Glasgow Green. The Fleet, being both elegant and long-established, arrived on scooters wearing matching fishtail parkas. These bore their own club crest on blazer badges, two crossed syringes with the words *Semper Desperandum* stitched in fine French silk underneath. The Govan Team, being poor, provided a refreshing contrast. We breathed through the mouth and bore a pot pourri of simple rustic weaponry, including chair legs with nails through them. The Leader of the Fleet unsheathed his sword, knelt, and held it toward heaven.

Stig nutted a tree. 'Have you got my speech?' he asked.

I gave him my handwritten page of Basildon Bond. As the Fleet formed battle lines, Stig addressed his troops, reading haltingly from the page. 'Methinks I am a prophet new inspired . . .' He looked at me for reassurance. I nodded vigorous encouragement. He continued. 'This royal throne of bams, this heap of shite, this other Eden, this happy breed of psychos, this . . .' He looked to me for help. I mouthed 'precious'. He resumed. 'This precious midden set in the silver slag, this fucking hole, this dirt, this germ, this . . .' He stopped as an arrow hit him in the eye. He sank to his knees. 'This Govan,' he muttered.

*

It was a bloody battle. Both sides played four four two, which spoiled it as a spectacle, though the tackling was fierce and both teams lost men to bite wounds. The Fleet were the more technically accomplished side but the up and at them aggression and spirit of the Govan Team gradually wore them down and they retreated after suffering several serious injuries to their suits. Our victory, however, had come at a cost. Teaser lost a hand and Tojo half a nose. We scoured the battlefield and found the hand but when Teaser tried it on it was the wrong type, being a left instead of a right. We kept it anyway and zoomed him along to the Western, figuring that two left hands, however ungainly, would be preferable to a solitary right. Sadly the operation couldn't take place as apparently there hadn't been enough advances in medical science. We hung around for an hour or two in case an advance turned up but when it didn't we threw the hand in a wheelie bin and decided to go for chips. It was then that someone noticed a fresh new addition to my profile. It seemed the long handle of a steel comb was sticking into, or indeed out of, depending on your point of view, my back. I hadn't been aware of the pain owing to the adrenaline rush but now that the matter had been brought to my attention I did the sensible thing and fainted clean out.

When I awoke I was in a hospital bed. I thought I was dying. This impression was reinforced by the sight of a priest standing over me, giving me the last rites. A doctor took him by the elbow and shooed him away. 'Wrong bed, Father, next door,' he said. He turned to me. 'He's a bastard, he only does that to the Proddies to wind them up.'

I felt weak. 'How do you feel?' said the doctor.

'Weak,' I said. 'What's wrong with me?'

'We dug this out of your back,' said the doctor. I remembered the steel comb. 'Quarter of an inch more and you'd have punctured a lung.'

I looked at the sharpened handle. 'Just as well I smoke,' I said, 'my lungs have shrunk to kippers otherwise it'd have popped like a balloon.'

The doctor looked unamused. 'You've a quaint sense of anatomy,' he said. He wrote something on my chart. Possibly 'stupid prick thinks he's funny'. I asked him when I could leave. 'Couple of days,' he said, 'you've lost a lot of blood.' He added, 'Have you somewhere quiet to convalesce?'

I pictured our room and kitchen. The only quiet place was the coal bunker and that was where we stored Gash's raffia work. 'No,' I said.

*

Mother wept when she saw me lying forlorn and pale in my hospital bed. Naturally I laid it on thick when she came in, having made myself suitably wan in advance of her visit by imagining what it would be like to eat human tripes. I judged she deserved that much of an emotional dunt and was gratified to see the old lip tremble. When I mentioned the convalescence she boxed on the retreat for a few rounds till it was established I'd be paying and she started to perk up. She said Millport but I held out for Rothesay, I didn't fancy the ghost of Da drifting behind me, clinking his empties and calling me an arse for getting myself stabbed. The wound was healing nicely though in truth I was more concerned about catching pneumonia with the amount of times I was obliged to howk up my T-shirt to let every bastard and his granny have a swatch at it. A stab wound looks like it's been applied by the make-up department of the Little Theatre of Mull the year after its grant was cut. Mine was a small squalid-looking puncture mark below the shoulder blade that from a yard away looked like a pink leech was grabbing a quick half-pint before heading home for its tea. The doctor, being well attuned to the cast of mind of the average west of Scotland youth, assured me that in his experience stab wounds on a corpse look no more glamorous than mine so I wasn't missing out. I took his little rub that I'd been a lucky fellow and that perhaps I should count my blessings and retire gratefully to some Twilight Home for Disabled Hooligans.

A week later Mother, Freak, Rena and I took a self-catering room and kitchen near the castle. It was good to get out of the mean constant rain of Glasgow and into the mean constant rain of Rothesay. Freak and I had brought a football and every morning we'd hurry to the window to see if the elements had relented sufficiently to permit us a kickabout. Fat chance. Scotland is a green place because the sky is a watering can that never empties. The cloud sits over us like a blanket over a budgie cage, defying good cheer. The only diversions were bingo and the buying of chips. The front was awash with defeated Glaswegians in soggy straw hats carrying Prize Bingo table lamps into joyless boarding houses. 'Are you enjoying yourself?' asked Rena one afternoon as we sat in a bus shelter waiting for the squall to abate so we could return to the flat and the relative joy of dry misery. She burst into tears.

But the very next day a small miracle happened. Rumours of a film show had swept the island and we were hanging around the jetty awaiting firm news of this temporary oblivion when the *Waverley* steamer pulled in from Glasgow. Freak approached a dungareed man at the pier's edge who was casting from a hand-held reel for crabs. 'Excuse me, Mister, do you know anything about the film show that's supposed to be here today?'

The man gave the rude laugh of the local who knows the mysterious workings of the Island. 'There's no film show,' he said, 'it's just a cruel hoax put out by the bingo owners so you'll gather down here then hit the stalls in disappointment when you find out there's bugger all else happening.'

'How do you know that?' asked Freak.

'Because,' said the man, crossing his legs with glee, 'I own that bingo stall across the street.' He laughed so hard he had to adjust his cap. Freak, never robust mentally, had proved a simple conquest.

I sidled over. 'I bet you wish the crabs would bite as easy as him,' I said, flexing my new hard man status, 'you crabless fucker.' His smile froze and he made a little feint towards me. When I didn't flicker, he muttered something neutral in a caustic tone and turned back to face the sea.

Another day squelching around in the wet haze looked imminent until Rena spoke. 'Look,' she said, 'isn't that Uncle Bobo and Auntie Ginny?' We looked. It was. They leaned over the deck rail, as glamorous as film stars.

'Bloody hell,' I said.

Rena looked at me, beaming. 'I know,' she said, 'great, isn't it?' And it was, it was great. But that wasn't what had taken me aback, welcome sight though it was. To the left of Bobo, about six drookit dewdrop-nosed passengers away, her black handbag resting askew on a lifebuoy like the cap of a jaunty hanging judge, stood Mary Regan.

*

Who among us can account for the contrariness of the human heart? No takers? Then permit me to take a whack at it. When Mary stepped tentatively down the gangway and, flanked by her parents, Death and Pestilence, passed within brief steps of where I stood, we did what any lovers, young or old, rich or poor, would have done in the circumstances; we ignored each other. 'All right, kid?' said Bobo. I nodded. Bobo was in no mood for supplementary questions. 'Good. See you later,' he said and veered in the direction of the nearest pub. Auntie Ginny embraced Rena. It was strange to see her with her tits in.

'We thought we'd take a wee run down,' she said, 'is that all right?' It was, of course, more than all right. It was a rope ladder straight to heaven from the seeping pit of Bute and Argyll. 'Bobo took some persuading,' she continued, 'he said the only good thing you can say about Rothesay is that at least it's not Dunoon.' We all shuddered at the mention of the D-word. Dunoon. Even saying the name felt like drizzle on the roof of your mouth.

'Come on home and get a wee cup of tea,' said Rena.

'Is there somewhere we can sleep?' asked Ginny.

'Och, we'll think of something,' said Rena, airily.

The airing cupboard was deep but narrow. I crouched in my favourite foetal position and considered the erratic tapestry of my existence. Through the wall my bed creaked and wheezed under the strain of Bobo's slumbering bulk. Occasionally, there would be breaking of wind and mumbling. I prayed there would be no lovemaking. Once he cried out 'Cel-tic' in his sleep. Another time I heard him plead, 'Time to pay, Your Honour.' I got up and went into the kitchen for a mug of water. On the fold-down couch in the living room Mother had fallen asleep with her mouth agape. As I rustled past she muttered, 'Is that you, Hamish?' 'Yes,' I said, 'it's me, Hamish.' Whoever the fuck Hamish was, I was him. Rena, on her side, slumbered next to Mother. I shook her, roughly. 'You awake?' She mumbled something with the word 'kill' in it. Under an alcove, Freak, oblivious, slept with thumb tucked into palm as he had done since childhood. Freak's waking dream was to be a labourer in the shipyards. In pursuit of this ambition, he had ruthlessly stripped away all distractions such as literacy and numeracy. He twitched wildly as he slept, no doubt avoiding the careless flight of hot rivets or a scalding slurp from an imaginary billycan. I considered my people. We were a touching, desperate bunch, no freer in night dream than in waking day. If there was such a thing as a collective human unconscious I had little doubt that, once upon a Great Time, it had stopped at Gretna Green, peeked over the Cheviots at the natives in their duffel coats guzzling Mad Dog, shuddered, turned on its winged heel and flown off home to Esher. I climbed back into the airing cupboard. Before me I felt the future slip away as dimly as the past. Scouse. Eros. Sarah. My mop and bucket. Eros, eros, eros . . .

*

Having successfully snubbed Mary once, I now took to trudging round the town seeking her out, hoping for fresh opportunities to do it again. After two fruitless days, I saw her enter a souvenir shop and stood outside for long minutes, negotiating prams and aged pairs of crones in Rainmates talking in cracked voices about death and scones. When she came out, I brushed past Mary hurriedly, muttering a tight-lipped, 'Hello, can't stop,' and bustled on, very much the keen-jawed young dynamo with pressing things to do. Actually, the only pressing thing I had to do was hurtle round the corner and come to a dead stop by a tobacconist's window, gazing blindly in while my heart crashed down through the gears back to boredom speed. *Everything for the Smoker* read an embossed crescent sign on the glass. My focusing eyes perused the display but saw no clean lungs for sale among the pipes and tins. Someone tapped me on the shoulder. I turned. Mary stood, looking pretty, flushed and feminine. Her dark eyes glistened with what I took to be impish humour until she clumped me on the cheek with the meat of her fist.

Women know no restraint when they hit a man. They've been brought up on that 'Her puny fists bounced harmlessly off his manly chest as Lars laughed scornfully' pish, so they assume they can batter away with impunity. Mary was the same height as me and no feather. My jaw made a crunching sound and I could hear ringing in my ears. I tried to be Lars and laughed scornfully.

'Don't you ever, *ever*, ignore me in the street, do you hear?' Lars nodded scornfully. 'Your nostril's bleeding,' she said.

Once a nostril decides to bleed you can't stop it. Nostril blood doesn't get out much and if you give it the opportunity it'll rush like a madman down your chin and romp, hatless, in the clover of your shirt until you can harry it back safely to its cell. Mary gave me a paper tissue with little pink teddies on it. Lars plugged his nose with it, scornfully of course, and went for a Horlicks at the XL cafe with the woman who would one day become his wife.

'I thought you were marrying Cotter?' I said, expertly disguising my bitterness. 'I heard you were desperate to have his ugly swivel-eyed little brats.'

'Who told you that?' said Mary.

'Well . . .'

'Cotter? Natch. Quite gullible, aren't you?' She skimmed

off some froth with her spoon and swallowed it. Yes, I had been gulled, here, beside the seaside.

'So, I mean, you're saying there's nothing between you and him?'

She shrugged. 'He paid me attention, that's all. When you were in London. I suppose I was flattered.'

London. The devious bastard. Get me down there, dump me and nab my woman. He was despicable, you had to admire him.

'Why are you asking, are you jealous?'

Lars laughed, scornfully. 'Me? No. Just curious.'

She hid her hands under the table. Being from Govan we found distaste in all intimacies other than carnal. 'It's you I fancy, not him, remember?'

I remembered. The school dance. Her blue dress. My brother's trousers. The way the safety pin binding my flies buckled when we waltzed. No, they can't take that away from me. Not without heavy medication, anyway.

'I hear you're running with a gang now,' she said, trying to sound disapproving. I shrugged and gave her a wry smile. She took it, flicked the wry off it and handed it back. 'There's nothing smart about that, only bampots run with gangs.' She wasn't playing at it, she was disapproving. I tried to reclaim some lost ground by howking up my shirt and showing her my wound. She eyed the whitening scar like it was spit on the street. 'Stabbed?' she said. 'With a comb?'

'A steel comb,' I qualified, reddening, 'and sharpened.'

No respite. 'That shows you the mentality of these numpties, what do they use to comb their hair, bread knives?' I chuckled, appreciatively. 'You're a total prick,' she said. I stopped chuckling. I should have – there and then – I should have thrown down some change on the table, winked and said, 'See you around, doll.' But I didn't. For a kick-off I had no change, just a single note, and I was fucked if I was paying a pound for two Horlicks. In addition her taunt had rankled. I needed to prove to her that I wasn't a total prick, just a partial one like everybody else. If I'd stood up and gone, my whole life might have turned out differently. But I stayed. Did I lack the strength to leave or had I found the strength to remain? Decide for yourself.

*

The upshot was that Mary and I became inseparable for whole hours, then separable again. We'd sit in the bingo stalls talking of the future. I was nervous about any signs of commitment. Once she won a table lamp. As she turned to show me it I was back in the airing cupboard with the curtains drawn before my stool had stopped spinning. I wasn't ready to be tamed, having just started to be wild. Women were a trial. Already she had me walking around frowning like a cuckold and I hadn't even dipped her yet.

One afternoon Bobo rose early, having being disturbed by a bluebottle. I was standing, in troubled mode, by the sink, attempting the difficult trick of making a spoon (soup) hover, supported by the fulcrum of its stem, on a flooded porridge pot. I am unclear as to why I was doing this. Perhaps, at the time, I had ambitions to become an aeronautical engineer and, lacking any knowledge of engineering, or aeronautics, thought the old soup spoon on the porridge pot stunt might impress potential employers in the absence of more formal qualifications. The others sat in torpor round the table, watching the three o'clock dullness gather. Bobo pulled back the window netting and eyed the rain. 'Away for a pint,' he said. We nodded defeated acquiescence. Bobo pulled on his jacket. 'Nobody going out?' We shook our heads. Freak drew the word 'pish' with a thick finger on the window condensation. Mother was in too deep a lethargic mire to rebuke him.

'What's the matter?' said Bobo.

'What do you think,' sighed Rena, 'we're bored and it's pouring.'

Bobo sat down at the table. He poured himself a stewed tea from the lukewarm pot. When I was a boy, I'd once asked Bobo what he did for a living. 'Son,' he'd said, 'I'm with the police.' It was only in later years that I was to reflect on the delicate wording of his job description. Truly, Bobo was often with the police. Sometimes he was under them, other times on top. Usually, after a few mutually energetic turns of the boot and fist, he was their overnight guest, reclining with bruised ribs while drawing on a furtive dog end.

Both Bobo and my father had poured their lives into large glasses and jumped in. But each sipped from a different side of the rim. Father turned to drink as an escape from the misery of unemployment, Bobo as an escape from the horror of employment. Bobo hated work, feeling that it robbed him of his dignity. He was born to prop up a bar somewhere, his elbow lodged in its own groove on the mahogany counter, entertaining gaggles of tawdry wasters and semi-derelicts with tales of drunken mayhem and mischief. A staggering minstrel he, a dispenser of instant good cheer and piquant oral memoir.

'Has anybody here heard of the Farquhar brothers?' he asked us generally, putting down his cup. We shook our heads. Bobo told us of Finn and Billy Farquhar from Govan, how Finn would wear cardboard shoes which he'd dry off in the oven, then paint over the cracks and pretend they were crocodile skin. The Farquhars could do versatile things with a tin of paint. With the same black gloss Billy Farquhar painted over the bald spot on his dome then used the rest on his bike frame. Their mother, Babette, would pour tinned custard over their mince and tatties on the basis that it was all going to slop together in their bellies anyway so what was the point in dirtying an extra set of plates. After Babette's funeral, legend had it that Billy, free at last from the yoke of maternal oppression, visited the decorating department of Woolworth's, swiped a tin of Dulux Sandalwood and painted his hair blond in celebration. Bobo told us of the Latta sisters, Agnes and Mette, from Golspie Street, who'd harpooned their father, an amorous Norwegian seaman, and hung him from the pulley like a salmon when he'd got fresh one Saturday night after the pub. Bobo told these tales with restrained relish, not as examples of low-life urban horror but as quaint manifestations of the essential daftness of the human condition. Bobo said that when he died he wanted his ashes scattered on the floor of Brechin's bar, so that he might provide a foothold for unknown generations of wasters yet to come. His good looks, storytelling gift and ability to coax humorous poetry out of the stark dross of Govan life had both empowered Bobo and ensnared him. He was popular and his presence sought out, drinks would be bought, sometimes even unwanted ones, and in return he'd hold court for an hour, a day or a lost weekend, according to the dictate of the moment.

Had he known what he wanted to achieve with his life, he might have escaped Govan. Instead Bobo knew only what he was good at and it had never occurred to him to marry the two. As a result, much as I liked and admired Bobo, I also pitied him. His feet were stuck fast to the sticky bar mat of Glasgow pub life and I flattered myself I was lighter on my toes than he. Govan would never keep me. I was John Lennon, Jimi Hendrix and Steve McQueen. I was a winner. Put another way, I was eighteen.

*

One afternoon Mary and I went walking in the Skioch woods above the town. The wind was blustery and raw but I took my jerkin off, complaining of the heat, and threw it across my shoulder. I was keen to demonstrate to Mary that garments could be shed without serious loss of body heat, even in a Scottish July. On the contrary, I hoped to demonstrate, with luck, that there could even be a gain. I loosened my shirt collar and offered to carry her raincoat. 'Maybe later,' she said. I took this to be a hopeful sign and steered her upwards toward sheep country, along a narrower path and through the thick of the trees. 'We'd better not go too far,' she said, a remark which I chose to believe was sheathed in metaphor. Halfway up the hill we began to smell smoke. Close by we could hear the low grumble of voices and the occasional startled laugh, the crackle of twigs in an open fire.

Mary saw him first. 'Isn't that your uncle?' she said. In a clearing, a patch of sky visible above, the meandering funnel of black smoke, sat a ring of tinkers playing cards. Four occupied a battered settee, two a one-armed armchair. Small coins clinked onto the broken glass top of a three-legged coffee table. A wine bottle was being passed from hand to hand.

Bobo stopped dealing long enough to call out to me. 'All right, kid?'

I gave a horrified nod. I gripped Mary's hand and urged her to stroll with all speed.

Bobo didn't even lift his head. 'Have you finished,' he said, 'or are you looking for some place to start?' Sensing lewd sport, the couch dwellers added their own clumsy tease.

'There's a hiker's bothy at the top of the brae,' suggested one, helpfully.

'She's got a nice wee arse,' volunteered another.

For Bobo this was a drool too far. 'And she wouldn't use it to shit on you,' he said to the man. I thought there might be a fight but in the split second it takes an offended party to assess a likely outcome the man had shrugged and returned to his cards. 'You're a good boy,' said Bobo, over his shoulder.

'Thanks, Uncle Bobo,' I said. My ardour had not only cooled but had vanished part way up my colon, through funk.

'How does he know these people?' asked Mary.

I struggled to answer. 'He knows everybody,' I said, 'people are drawn to Bobo.'

Mary glanced back at him. 'Is that a fact?' she said. We negotiated our way back down through the packed clumps of dank stagnant leaves. 'Promise me something,' said Mary, 'promise me you'll never end up like him.'

I slipped my hand between the buttons of her blouse. 'I won't,' I said, 'I'm different.'

I am different. I grew up in the enchanted shipyard forest, I bevvied, fought in gangs, was unemployed, had been in clink and would nick anything that wasn't strapped to its owner's back. The only thing different about me was the growing horror that I was the same as everyone else. I was blessed with the curse of introspection. Self-awareness is a hair shirt to a waster, robbing us of the easy spontaneity of the mindless act of stupidity. Conscience became a moral hangover the only cure for which was a hair of the dog.

Mary walked me to the *Waverley* ferry at the holiday's end. 'It's all right for you,' she said, 'I've another week with Death and Pestilence. It'll be purgatory.'

'It'll soon pass, sweetheart,' I told her, cranking up a loving smile, 'then we'll be together.'

Mary shivered. 'Don't smile like that,' she said, 'you look like an undertaker.' We stood on the cusp of one of those black hole silences that all couples know and dread. I didn't want to be together, I wanted to scuttle away, I could feel the future closing in on me. Before I left, Mary

165

gave me the traditional female parting gift of a jab to the heart to keep me company during our separation.

'Jamesie wants me to marry him,' she said.

I looked at her. 'I thought you said he made that up?'

She shook her head. 'No,' she said, 'I made it up that he made it up. He's given me to the end of the summer to decide.'

I was upset. I wasn't sure I wanted her but I was positive I didn't want Cotter to have her. I was also puzzled. 'Why wait till the end of the summer?'

'I don't know,' said Mary, 'I think he saw it in a Tab Hunter film. He's a very romantic guy.'

I was unconvinced. 'No,' I corrected, 'he's a pervy bastard.'

'Whatever,' said Mary, tossing back her hair, 'you say potato . . .'

Rena shouted from the rail of the *Waverley* to hurry up. I looked up to issue some light abuse by way of acknowledgement. When I turned back, Mary was already gone, heading up the pier to join Pestilence, her mother. I knew what she was doing, putting the squeeze on me, but like I say, it's one thing knowing and another having the will to do something about it. The crew cast off and the big paddles thrashed the water, angling to turn. Minutes later we were in open firth. I sat in the cafeteria having a mutton pie and a fag. I felt low. I was ready to hang up my dick and join a monastery. After three pints of magic in the bar, however, I'd decided on a different plan.

*

I knocked on the door and waited for Cotter to appear. Glasgow was cold, grey and unwelcoming. It was good to be back. Anything was preferable, I'd decided, to the isolating misery of wet afternoons in a Rothesay flat through which experience I'd glimpsed the true hell of exile. I pitied poor Napoleon on his double banishment, condemned to endless solitary games of crazy golf on Elba, with nothing to cheer him but the occasional paltry win at prize bingo, damned to dreams of conquering Europe, whilst stoating up and down on a bouncy castle. This was no fate for warriors such as he and I.

These thoughts were in my mind as Cotter opened the door. 'Sacré bleu, ya bass,' I shouted and thumped him with a chair leg. He grabbed my arms in fright and we grappled to the ground. We rolled untidily around the front garden but, by a skilful use of steerage, I was able to roll us untidily toward the back garden away from prying eyes. Cotter picked up a rusting shovel and hit me with the flat of it, catching me on the hip. He rearranged his grip to swing edge first but I rapped him on the knuckles with the chair leg and he yelped. We returned to grappling with just the odd punch slapping teeth and bone. I rationed my blows trying to aim for nose and side of mouth. Fingers are fragile things and a lot of fights end prematurely with a digit cracking against the bony mass of jaw or noggin. Cotter began to weaken, concentrating his efforts on covering up to defend, lashing out with only the occasional flailing blow. His nose was bleeding.

When I tried to speak I realized mine was too. 'I told you to keep away from my bird.'

The words gurgled out from the back of my throat. Still on the ground he caught me with a stamping kick in the general ball park of, well, the balls. 'You crazy bastard,' he yelled, 'you've got the wrong end of the stick.'

Initiating phase two of my battle strategy, I rolled him into his own overgrown grave. 'So have you,' I said, letting him have it once more with the chair leg. He groaned, holding his head. I picked up the rusty shovel he'd hit me with and worked at the packed hillock of weedy earth that surrounded the grave. With shovel and foot I scraped chunks of crunchy dirt into the grave over him.

'What are you doing?' he said, trying to rise. I wielded the shovel like an axe. He lay back down. The earth under the crusty top layer was surprisingly loose and moist and I worked at it, quickly. Cotter resorted to pleading. 'Rab, let's be sensible, let's not you and me fall out over a woman.'

I told him to button it. 'Shut your eyes,' I said, 'I'm going to cover your face.'

He made a Cotterish whimpering sound. 'Rab,' he said, 'you don't understand, things have changed.'

I bashed some of the earth smooth on top of him with the flat of the shovel. Gardening was satisfying work. I began to see the appeal of it. 'Rab!' A heaped shovelful shut him up. He began to cough and gag. 'I've had enough of you,' I shouted, at what I could see of his face.

'Yes,' he gasped, choking, 'I can see that.' I was running out of earth. I began to cave in the sides of the grave with my foot and the shovel, collapsing the hole so that it looked like a badly risen sponge cake. A foot and a chunk of forehead were the only visible signs of Cotter. I leaned on the shovel, breathing hard. An arm forced its way up through the soil. It held a crumpled banknote. Cotter's gasping mouth loomed out of the earth.

'A pound, Rab. A pound if you don't garden me to death!'

'Keep your pound,' I said, taking it. I worked with renewed vigour at the hole.

'But you've got me all wrong,' insisted Cotter, craning his scrawny grey neck to breathe.

'Do you mean it?'

'I promise you, Rab,' he gasped, 'on my mother's life.'

I remembered his mother. I remembered her life. I saw a dustbin lid by a broken clothes pole and, clutching the handle like a shield, pushed the hollow down over his simpering gob. He continued to plead, his dusty muffled words clanging around inside the lid. 'Shut it,' I said, pressing down hard against what I hoped was his nose, 'you've had this coming.' I was aware of a presence. A light feminine cough distracted my attention. I looked up from inside the hole. A straw-blonde with black-furrowed tractor roots gazed coldly down at me. She showed no hint of concern or alarm. Her skirt was short, her legs white, tinged only by a blush of fire tartan to the wing of one calf. She had the face of a hurriedly hewn puppet with a letter-box mouth that looked like it demanded a ceaseless diet of poison-pen missives to keep its own biliousness from revolt.

'I take it that's Jamesie you're burying?' she asked without qualm. I nodded. Cotter forced the bin lid from his face and with a great heave sat upright, cascading earth from ears, mouth and hair.

'Rab,' he said, 'I'd like you to meet my new girlfriend.'

My brain fuzzed. What new girlfriend? What fresh treachery was this? 'Pleased to meet you,' I said to the girl.

'This is Rab,' said Cotter, now on his feet and bowing his legs, allowing more earth to escape from his trouser bottoms. 'Rab, say hello.'

'Hello,' I said, as instructed.

The Letter Box looked me over. 'Cheerio,' she said and led Jamesie away by the hand.

'I told you, Rab,' he called back, 'I told you things had changed.'

I felt thwarted, like he had wriggled off a hook. I decided to put him back on it again. 'You told Mary you wanted to marry her. You said she had till the end of the summer to decide.'

The girl stopped. She dropped Cotter's hand. 'Is that true?'

I could hear the alarm bells ring in Cotter's head. Sincerity mode was adopted instantly and seamlessly.

'No,' he protested, 'strike me down on the spot if I tell a lie.'

She let him wriggle for a few moments. 'Looks like I'd need to get in the queue for that,' she said. She yanked his arm. 'Come on,' she said. She led him out of the back garden, slamming the papery lattice gate behind them.

At the Cotters' bedroom window, the punch-drunk stick insect that was wife and mother gazed inscrutably out. If she now felt relief that the grave her son had dug with such enthusiasm would never be filled by her, no trace showed on her dough-white countenance. Perhaps she thought she'd cheated one lurid fate only to find another. She'd met the Letter Box. Its name was Ella. One day she'd be her daughter-in-law.

*

When Mary discovered she no longer had Cotter as an option she became more temperate in her approach to the question of me. I, in turn, sensing the new reality, became, well, cocky. I'd started getting the tit on a regular basis, not just as a holiday treat. The quim came later, I admit, how much later I cannot exactly recollect but I think I could state safely, on oath, that I first put my hand down Mary's drawers without encountering a slap or the threat of arrest some time between the assassination of Robert Kennedy and the break-up of Dave Dee, Dozy, Beaky, Mick and Tich. I retain a memory of having confronted her on both these occasions, achieving the tit on the former but full drawer exploration only with the latter as Mary, never rigorous in her musical tastes, grieved openly for the demise of these giants of pygmy pop. I was taken to meet her parents, Death and Pestilence. The occasion was a great success and I only dozed off twice during the entire evening. Nevertheless, I was aware of having been drawn closer to what I saw as the marriage fly-trap. This prospect alarmed me further when, after tea and Tunnocks, Pestilence rose from her gasping armchair, smoothed her Hall of Mirrors figure with meaty hands and attempted a catwalk twirl for my instruction. 'Just think,' she said, sending out a waft of beefy roll-on and knocking over several small ornaments from the glass coffee table with the great rose-petalled parachute of her hem, 'in twenty years Mary will look just like me.' As I ingested this appalling prospect, I heard my mouth say, 'Only if I'm very lucky.' Death, reading the obituary notices in the *Evening Times* over his Caramel Log, gave the deftest dog-whistle snort of contempt that only a wretched prospective son-in-law can detect. As far as I can judge the only difference between the married and the dead is that the married get to watch *Stars in their Eyes* from a slouching position whereas the dead are contractually obliged to be horizontal. I knew the time would come when Mary and I would reach the end, would sit together without frisson or interest, unable to dredge up a single word worthy of speaking to each other. Then, being scum, it would be time for us to marry. In the meanwhile, the only proposal I was determined to make was that I would put up a stout fight before the end.

Stig welcomed me back with open arms. True, they were not his arms, they belonged to Bimbo who, in my absence, had become Stig's most trusted cohort. I was up against a wall in a pub toilet being frisked for weapons, prior to reacceptance into the fold. 'Are you chibbed up or clean?' asked Stig. 'Clean,' I said. Stig muttered an instruction and Bimbo booted me in the balls. I fell to the floor feeling surprised and sick. 'You were told always to report chibbed up,' said Stig, 'it's your own fault.' Justice dispensed, we entered the bar where Stig sat at the head of the table, chairing the Annual General Meeting of the

Govan Team. Using beer and a fingertip, he drew an awkward graph on the formica tabletop and reprised briefly the year's peaks and troughs.

'It's been a good year for stabs,' he began. 'I can report a dozen confirmed serious stab assaults and a gross of slashings for the fiscal year ended March thirty-first. As we know, slashings are the bread and butter of gang violence but it's a good high-profile stabbing that enhances the profile of a team and puts us in poll position for a British League of Mentalness which I predict will surely come, though maybe not within my chairmanship.' Glasses were drummed on the tabletop in traditional fashion at this hint that Stig might not lead our team into the new decade. Stig smiled modestly at our gesture of support. 'Cheers, you ugly bastards,' he said, briefly moved. The highlights dealt with, Stig delved into the shaky ruin of the Team's financial structure. 'Mentalness is an enjoyable business, but a business nonetheless. Our traditional trading methods such as hitting folk over the head and running away with their wallets are becoming outmoded. These days there are too many crooks chasing too few marks. Last week, at Govan Cross, three gangs engaged in an embarrassing pitched battle for the right to blag one rent man. Clearly, we have to diversify.' Stig outlined a future world in which unemployment payments would be delivered direct to homes and credit availability broadened to include trash though not, unfortunately, scum. In Future World, credit cards would be delivered by postmen. It followed, therefore, that it would be infinitely more resource-effective for a team of headcases to boot the shit out of a solitary Royal Mail Santa than a hundred random civilians. As a result of this change in social habit, Stig predicted that by 1984 postmen would be armed and carry tear gas and would make their deliveries by Panzer tank. As we now know, he was totally wrong in this judgement, except for certain parts of Paisley.

In conclusion, Stig outlined his proposals for the coming year: quarterly dances and raffles so that sufficient funds might be generated, enabling the Govan Team to buy its own Sunshine Coach to shuttle us to and from battle; an education scheme, incorporating tours of Sheffield cutlery manufacturers so that we might develop an appreciation of the chib-maker's art; fact-finding visits to high-security prisons to sit at the feet of the nation's top psychos, absorbing handy hints that might help us overcome what he referred to as 'the sanity barrier'. Finally, almost casually, he announced the most urgent target our sales team had to meet in the coming year. A murder. A good malky, he assured us, would guarantee the position of the Govan Team in the premier elite of mayhem. He paused for effect before looking around for volunteers. Most of us fidgeted and looked away, including me. 'Call yourselves Govan men?' derided Stig. 'Is there not a madman amongst you?' Inevitably, his gaze rested on me, as I'd suspected it might. I was fresh back from holiday and had arrived unchibbed, therefore my commitment to mayhem must, in Stig's eyes, be reaffirmed.

'Nissie,' he said to me, 'you were at the last square go, that Leader Off of the Maryhill Fleet needs tobering, why don't you oblige us?'

The rest of the team, now off the hook, lined up enthusiastically behind Stig. 'Aye, Nissie,' urged Teazer, 'they chibbed you, why not grab some back backers?' The team grunted its self-righteous approval.

'Unless maybe you've not got the balls,' urged Stig, baiting the hook.

Cornered, I fumbled in my mind for escape. From the cowboy boot of racial memory I pulled a derringer and cocked the trigger. 'Balls, is it,' I said, 'it wasn't me that was bubbling the first day of school when Miss Rimmer drew the curtains.'

I looked at Stig. The team looked at Stig looking at me. He seemed to pale before my eyes. He pulled a cleaver from his parka pocket. Now it was my turn to pale before him. Stig had lost face and if I wasn't careful I was about to lose some too. 'You calling me a shitebag, Nissie?'

Squirmingly, I assured him that no, I did not regard him as being a suitable receptacle for effluent. 'Just as well,' he said, 'or that barman there would be throwing sawdust over your spilt brains.' His angry eyes darted around the table. 'Is there not one of you that's up for this?' Silence. No takers. 'All right, you pishwipes,' he said, 'I'll do it myself.'

This was soothing chamber music to our wounded ears. Mentally, I reclined on a soft divan and draped a cool flannel over my fretting forehead.

'Nissie,' said Stig, 'you'll come with me.'

I threw off my flannel and silenced the Bach. 'I thought you were doing it yourself?'

Stig looked at me like I was sane. 'What, walk into their boozer on my jack? There's dozens of them, I widnae stand a chance. You must see that, surely?'

I nodded, to all appearances swayed by Stig's military acumen. Inside, I thought he should be sedated and have his shoelaces removed. Two enemies, trapped on hostile turf and outnumbered, absurdly. We were dead men.

Stig seemed cheered by the imminent prospect of futile oblivion. He grabbed my shoulders and shook them. 'What'd you say, Nissie boy? Two of us. We'll be fucking legends!'

I smiled, wanly. I was nineteen. There was plenty of time to die young, anything up to twenty years, twenty-five if I dyed my hair. No, I decided, if it was to be curtains once more for Stig, then again he would cry alone.

*

Stig chose a Sunday night for the murder, on the grounds that Sundays were depressing and it would give us something to look forward to. I entertained some sympathy for this rationale but left to my own devices would have preferred the softer option of the cinema or a hand of whist as an alternative to carnage and suicide. In addition, the selected date clashed with an invitation for tea at Mary's parents' house. Having no alternative but to accommodate both commitments, I duly arrived for tea proffering a box of After Eight mints with a hatchet tucked down my waistband for the later soiree. Throughout my visit, I kept my jacket buttoned and I became conscious of the admiring glances drawn by both parents to the shaft of the hatchet tucked, impressively, down my trouser leg. After a while, it occurred to me that I might have tucked a second hatchet down the other leg and presented an indelible portrait of a young man of substance. Throughout the meal I eyed the clock nervously and, on the stroke of six, arose and made my excuses. Pestilence urged me to stay, pressing homemade tipsy cake upon me, and when I steadfastly demurred, insisted on wrapping some in greaseproof paper to take home. At the living-room door, Death gave me a vigorous handshake of the man-to-man variety and I marvelled at how a short length of oak down the strides could induce such a pleasant reappraisal of attitude. Mary was disturbed that I was leaving so early and at the door, as we kissed, she put her tongue in my mouth and wiggled it about. I knew instinctively that sex would now soon follow, all I had to do was remain alive and, preferably, avoid disfigurement. As my hand lingered on her drawers, I knew that if I didn't get that axe out of my underpants pronto, the first concern would prove easier than the second.

In these days, pubs remained closed on Sundays. Drinkers were forced to root out sympathetic hotels, these being subject to less restrictive by-laws. The Leader Off of the Fleet was known to frequent the Aberfoyle, a humdrum tartan carpet and brasses establishment in primly suburban Milngavie. Three buses, two excruciating waits and a bag of chips later, the Govan Task Force in the shape of Stig and myself stood on the gravel driveway of the hotel. A solitary adorned scooter in the car park told us that the enemy was camped within. 'We're in luck,' said Stig, drawing his cleaver, 'he's on his jack.' I pulled the hatchet out of my trousers. Instantly, my inconvenienced leg succumbed to the numbness of pins and needles. 'Come on,' said Stig. We walked up the gravel path, my afflicted leg wobbling in a rubbery fashion, compromising my fierceness. 'Fucking walk normal,' demanded Stig, 'we look like Tarzan and Cheetah.' He broke into a purposeful trot. I struggled to keep up. At the bar door, he paused and wished me luck. 'Die good, you bastard, or else,' he said. He then gave a fierce cry, threw open the door and dashed in, waving his cleaver. I followed, a few prudent steps behind, my own fierce cry a more muted, self-conscious effort. In the middle of the room, Stig halted and looked around. The place was harshly lit and deserted. Two old men playing dominoes looked up, blinking. 'I think maybe you want the lounge,' said one. We thanked them, resumed our fierce cries and dashed back out again. The lounge door was to the left of the main entrance. We laid down our fierce cries while Stig negotiated the ornate wrought-iron door handle. Succeeding, we picked up our fierce cries once more and again followed tentatively as Stig surged headlong into the lounge.

On a raised stage at the far end of the room stood the Leader Off of the Fleet. He was receiving a rolled diploma from an older man who had a long scar on his forehead. They looked surprised to see Stig. Around the room sat parkaed hordes, watching the diploma presentation. Above the stage, a banner proclaimed *Maryhill Fleet Tenth Anniversary Reunion*. Outside the window, at the rear of the car park, I could discern a sleek, single-decker coach with a sign reading *Fleet OK* in the passenger window.

'Gentlemen, we have a guest,' said the scarred diploma-giver. Around a hundred parkas rose, as one.

'Govan Team,' cried Stig, a tad limply, I felt. My plan was simple and not at all honourable. Judging, correctly, that all attention would be on the first crazed fool to charge into the room, that left the second, myself, free to locate the bar flap at the counter, crawl under it and crouch in a non-military but expedient foetal position, pending the expected messy conclusion of events. I saw no glory for Govan in two ridiculous deaths when one would surely suffice. With attention diverted, I lay low on the cleaning shelf, next the Dettol and the Jeyes Fluid, awaiting the inevitable.

'Come ahead, you bastards!' I heard Stig shout. I assume the enemy then did as instructed for he shouted no more. I heard the rough scrape and fall of furniture then harsh laughter, followed by the grunting exertion of boots against bone and flesh. I was aware myself of a sharp pain in the ribs and squinted fearfully up to see a ginger-haired barman jabbing me with an upturned mop handle.

'Don't, pal,' I pleaded, 'they'll kill me.' For a moment, he seemed to consider my plea for clemency before looking me in my cornered eyes.

'There's another one in here,' he shouted, showing broken buck teeth.

'Shitbag,' I said. I was dragged from the cleaning shelf by flailing hands and thrown onto the floor. I couldn't see Stig. I imagined, luridly, that already scooter riders were being despatched to all corners of the country bearing parcelled quarters of his body as a terrible warning against interrupting the Annual Dinner Dance of the Maryhill

Fleet. I remember friction burns on my palms from the tartan carpet and being aware of the freshly spilled stickiness of beer or blood. I remember looking up to see a horde of feather-cut hooligans clustering curiously around me. I remember the first boot to the back of my left knee. I remember hands going through my pockets. And voices. 'What's that, ya prick, a block of hash?'

'No, it's tipsy cake.'

I remember opening my eyes, and a dimly familiar figure in a white coat peering down at me.

'You again,' said the doctor who had so recently tended my stab wound. 'We just can't keep you away, can we?'

Two broken ribs, a fractured kneecap and concussion. Apparently, I was lucky. My beating had been cut short when a Tamla Motown tribute band, the Four Screw Tops, hired to entertain the Fleet, had complained at the delay to their performance. Rather than incur a penalty payment, the Fleet's Treasurer had decreed that I be ejected from the building, pointed in the direction of a nearby taxi rank and ordered to crawl. The rest, as they say, is mystery.

Mary came to visit me. Rather than admit to gang allegiance, I invented a fiction about having been worked over by devout Christians when I'd walked into their church and invited them to let doubt enter their lives. No, I couldn't remember which church because they'd chloroformed me and driven me by fast car to another, sleazier church, down by the docks, where the attack had taken place. This lie remained unbelieved but it served the useful function of drawing Mary's fire, leaving her only to speculate on the real reasons for my incapacitated state.

'If there's any more of this,' she warned, 'you're chucked.'

I promised her faithfully I'd seen the error of my ways. I'd laid down the flaming torch of agnosticism, I said, let some poor other sucker carry it. I was bitter and disillusioned, I said, you try to bring a little darkness into people's lives, you try to make them question their contentment and what thanks do you get? They beat you up while singing 'Jesus wants me for a sunbeam', that's what. She should be proud, I said, I was a martyr to doubt. One day they'd nail me to a cross shaped like a question mark.

I enquired about Stig. He'd been less fortunate than I, they said, a bit guardedly. When I pressed the doctor, he'd only tell me that Stig was in a different hospital. On my discharge, I went to see him. Not only was he in a different hospital, he was on a different planet. When I saw him, he was sitting in a wheelchair being pushed around the gardens by a bored male nurse. Someone had given him a Biggles book, which seemed ambitious to me – he couldn't have read it when he was normal, why should he be able to now? When the male nurse slunk off for a fag, my brother Gash took over wheelchair duties. I walked around the cinder path with them, not too fast, the hospital having given me a stick while my knee healed.

'Do you like it here?' I asked Gash.

'Geneva,' he said.

I nodded agreement. We walked on in silence. After all these years, the class softy was getting to push around the school hard man. Life was a funny business. I wanted to share the joke with Gash but he'd only have said 'Geneva.' And he'd have been right.

He was always the smart one.

CHAPTER FIVE

THE HUMAN SOUL is defined by its absence. I walk through Govan, I see the half-finished estates, the cratered streets, the fly-by-night shops on the old landmark sites, the wizened thirties faces in millennium Reeboks, the quaint urchin cries of, 'What are you looking at, ya fuckin prick,' and a thing, suddenly alert, flickers uneasily within. It's only age, of course. I grow old, I grow old, I shall wear the bottoms of my combats rolled. Do I dare to ring my nose? I believe in the soul, that thing inside. I believe hunger keeps it alive. Indeed I do. Do I really? No, I don't, I believe in nothing. I hereby found my own Church, Our Lady of the Sacred Fuck-All. I'm feart, of course. Scared of dying. There, I've said it, I feel a great burden lifted. And dropped on me from a greater height. There is no escape from the worn-out slum of the self. You're getting it all now. No make-up, no tediously plucky indomitable spirit, just Rab C. in the raw, you might say, divested.

It's afternoon, midweek. After a scan at the *South Govan*, I shuffle into nearby Rattray's, just for a change, and order a pint. Two chefs are on the telly with some flossed-up fat bint in Armani egging them on to outsalad each other. They know fine well only scum like me watch telly in the afternoon and we wouldn't recognize a salad if one was in an ID parade with six fish suppers. Which is why they're trying to educate us, of course, through the wonderful medium of middle-class condescension, showing us pictures of sprouts and stuff, hoping we'll hop on-message and lift our snouts out the sherbet fountains.

These jabs fuzz my napper. Last week, or was it thirty years ago, I saw a lettuce in a box outside the mini-mart. A dog was pissing on it. Which seemed like a valid critical judgement to me. Round here we've got a drug crisis, a job crisis, a housing crisis, a crime crisis. What's the solution? Show them a vegetable, let the scummy bastards live longer, it'll serve them right. I hate a telly in a pub, you've got to watch it. Even if you turn your back to it all you see is forty sad bastards with vacant expressions looking over your shoulder.

All in all, I'm not in the best of moods as I put the pint to my gob in readiness for the first sacred sip. That's when I hear, at my back, a voice I seem to recognize. I can't think why, I don't use this pub, it's too piss cute, with its baseball artefacts on the walls and its designer bar staff forever running their hands through their hair like any minute now those smug cunts from *Friends* will run in and they'll all have a big bonding hug. Bears like me, it still goes against the grain for us to call a pub a 'bar' and I'd sooner cut my paw off than high five anybody. Anyhow, I hear this voice and I'm alarmed, it's a well-spoken voice so I assume I must have encountered it in unfortunate circumstances and it's some magistrate or snoop about to lurch out of the hideous past. So I sneak a little peek. And straight away I recognize Cousin Donald. He looks well dressed and prosperous, by my standards anyway, these things being relative. He's lost a lot of hair and what's left is grey but he looks sleek, the jammy bastard, and I guess he's still the same waist size he was when I last saw him. He's with a smart dark-haired woman. She's ages with him and wearing one of these no-nonsense tweedy two-piece suits that look like they've got moths in the pockets who've never eaten out since the fifties. I guess this is Mrs Donald. They've got their coats and brollies spread out over about an acre of chairs in that middle-class 'we'll pitch base camp here' sort of way. As he lifts his Highland Spring, I see a smart silver watch strap dangle loosely on his wrist and that snuffs any lingering notion I had about strolling over and saying hello. She's talking intently at him, he looks distracted, worried about something maybe. I'm gratified. In my mind, it evens things up that he's getting a bit of earache. All the same I don't feel comfortable.

I look myself over, mentally. Prune effect shoes, all clenched and wrinkled, curled at the toes like jester boots, suit you wouldn't cut up for dusters, on top of that my illness. I don't want to speak to him looking poor and ill, there's nothing more depressing than a chirpy loser. And if you start telling people the truth, well, they leave friction burns. I sip my pint at last but it might as well be tap water, I can't enjoy it now. I want out. The thing is, I can't avoid them, they're by the door. I'm just going to have to risk it. If he looks up, I'll give him my 'busy scumball ducking and diving' knowing look and keep walking. It's pig-ignorant but better than the alternative. I head for the door and a funny thing happens, the thing I hadn't bargained for in my fevered imaginings. He does look up. He catches my eye, deep and square. Only he looks away quickly and starts jawing again, suddenly all engrossed, with Mrs Donald. In his split-second glance, I don't even get the chance to begin my lie, to mouth the H in hello, far less to reach into my pocket for my imaginary ducker and diver's mobile. I feel hurt and angry, the five-year-old in me demanding the spoilt brat's right to cry on demand. But I don't do that. I hit the cold street feeling sad, and hard done by. I try to rationalize, his wife was with him, he was having a private conversation about courgettes or something and didn't want to be interrupted and let's face it, after all these years you just can't get away with a simple 'hello', can you? No, of course not. There, you see, I can be adult. And I almost persuade myself. Though I know it's not the truth. The fact is, he didn't speak to me because my poverty embarrassed him. Simple as that. And why not? After all, it embarrassed me too, didn't it?

I shuffle down Govan Road towards home then, on a whim, wheel into Elderpark Street, heading for the library and a free warm and squint at the papers. 'Flames of Hatred', screams the *Daily Mail* in its usual menopausal fashion. There's anarchist rioting in London. All the papers are full of it. The Stock Exchange twitters and falls a couple of dozen points. There are images of young folk in balaclavas giving single-finger salutes, overturning police vans and torching them, riot polis boxing on the retreat. I wouldn't worry about it. Everything is grist to the capitalist system, including protests against it. In a few months' time you can guarantee those same images will be turning up on billboards with a Nike logo and 'Just do it' underneath. The ringleaders will turn up as guest panellists on *Have I Got News For You*, and any average-looking bird anarchist with decent tits will be fronting her own gardening show. All the same, it's refreshing to see a bunch of idealistic young people indulging in a spot of homespun political carnage. It's dangerous for our kiddies to believe that bad behaviour begins and ends with Liam Gallagher spitting beer on a stage floor. The news fair cheers me up. I sit back, enjoying the pish-scented library fug, still marvelling at the fact that I'm a grown-up now and have inherited the inalienable right to walk into a library without having my hands inspected for grime. A female assistant approaches, bearing the afternoon edition of the *Evening Times*. I watch her place it on a perspex shelf between the *Exchange and Mart* and the *Scottish Field*. A couple of cardiganed pensioners are in edgy competition but thanks to relative youth and my superior will, I saunter over at high cruising speed and snatch the prize before their swollen-knuckled mitts can sweep it up to their watery eyes. I don't like touching anything after a library pensioner. You know exactly where their hands have been.

The top story is a typically Scottish tale of lurid triumph. A Britain-wide national survey has revealed that Shettleston in the east end of Glasgow is the poorest district in the country. Infant mortality, premature death, name it and Shettleston leads the nation. With five other neighbouring districts, this cluster forms six of the all-Britain top twelve. I scan the list hungrily. No mention of Govan. We've slipped out of the super league. We'll never get a theme park if we're not seen to be hopeless cases. At least I'm doing my bit, disease-riddled bastard that I am, to restore us to our rightful position in the dominant elite of national penury and affliction. With any luck a few close friends and relatives will perform a similar civic service and keel over with something poor and despicable before the next published results. Ask not what poverty can do for you, ask instead what you can do for poverty. I bask in the warm glow of renewed purpose. In Scotland, even an own goal is better than no goal.

'We are more European than British', declares page two of the same paper, totally ignoring its own front page. 'Sure,' I think, rising tetchily to my soggy feet, 'when Giorgio Armani opens a branch in Shettleston, then I'll believe we're European.' Only, the trouble is, I haven't thought it. Instead, I've crossed the first threshold of senility, I'm talking aloud to myself in the library. I pull out my pill bottle, rattling it theatrically in a craven attempt at mitigation. The mad and the old look at me blankly. Time to go, I decide, before an assistant leads me away by the wrist.

*　*　*

With Stig laid low by his brain injury, a vicious power struggle ensued within the Govan Team. We resorted to any means, fair or foul, to avoid becoming leader. Daunted by Stig's suicidal example, nobody fancied the job. As a result, nobody got the job. Instead, everybody did. It was resolved by committee that we'd each assume the leadership for six-month stretches apiece, until Stig's hoped-for return. While I was up at the bar, ordering a round, skulduggery ensued. A hasty vote was convened and I returned to find I'd been nominated for first go. When I protested, I was informed that the decision was a democratic one and that if I didn't like it they'd all take me outside and kick the shit out of me. I was not surprised by this turn of events, it's my experience that all institutions, more or less, adhere to similar guidelines. How else is democracy to be upheld and avoided unless by collusive treachery? I suppose, in much the same fashion, Frank Dobson was sent out for crisps by Tony Blair at a cabinet meeting and on his return found he'd been nominated to be Mayor of London. 'You bastards,' Frank would have said, as I did. 'Shut up, Santa, or we'll give you a kicking,' the cabinet would have replied collectively, after a focus-group meeting. That's what happened to me. I was Dobsoned.

Of course my new status was to introduce further difficulties into my relationship with Mary. After all, for some time I'd been struggling to convince her I wasn't even in a gang, far less the leader of one. As a useful cover for my increased absences, I informed Mary I'd joined a scripture group. I explained how I and like-minded friends would meet of an evening to ponder the words of the prophets, sing hymns and engage in energetic debate which, yes, might on occasion require the use of a hatchet 'for emphasis'. In short, I paid Mary the compliment of lying to her.

When nearby teams learned of Stig's incapacitation, they invariably used the upheaval as an opportunity to usurp our turf. One of these, the Wild Young Bogle from Renfrew, issued us with a direct challenge by tying Tojo to a back court clothes pole and stealing what was left of his nose. The Bogle's Leader Off was a grade three mid-table mouth-breather called Shango. All our imaginative psychos, including Tojo, ended their nicknames in 'o', calculating that the introduction of an exotic vowel would somehow imbue them with a vaguely gangsterish connotation. We responded by hunting down Shango's mother and pinning a message to her Rainmate stating that unless the nose was returned by noon prompt the forthcoming Saturday, a state of war would exist between Govan and Renfrew. The Bogle's was an impudent slur to our reputation and I was resolved to act with the utmost vigour. Apart from which, watching Tojo trying to sink a pint without his conk was giving us all the boak. In the end, we tied a crisp bag round the hole to muffle his slobberings.

On the appointed day, we lined up on waste ground near the Prince's dry dock and awaited our enemy. We favoured this venue for its amenities, regarding it as our home ground, since it was within staggering distance of the Southern General and boasted an excellent pie shop close by that helped fill in the tedious hours spent waiting in casualty. The hour came and went with still no sign of the Wild Young Bogle. As paranoia crept in, we began to wonder if we'd been set up and formed a defensive circle. When Bimbo mistook shipyard workers over by Shieldhall Road for Bogle, we regrouped hastily into a triangle. Unfortunately, the guys who formed points felt exposed by this new formation and after discussion we adopted the Roman defensive square. This model too was short-lived when the centurions facing east complained of having their arses tickled by less professional colleagues at their rear. Finally, it started to rain and we all ran into a bus shelter.

We'd been there a couple of minutes when a bald man in a combat jacket appeared walking a whippet. He stopped by the shelter and looked at us. 'Youse the Govan Team?' he said. We improvised a collective tough nod. 'Good,' he said, 'Shango said to give you this.' He fished in an inside pocket and pulled out a crumpled white hanky. 'Who's your Leader Off?'

'I am,' I said, not entirely without swagger.

'Right,' he said and opened up the hanky. 'Here y'are.'

A shrivelled dark object dropped into my open palm. I remained steely. 'Tojo,' I said, 'can you identify this as your nose?'

Tojo forced his way to the front, took a look and burst into tears. Some of the team led him away in the direction of the pie shop, where it was hoped the splendid mince savouries on view would help compensate for his lost sensory apparatus.

'Fair do's, then?' asked the man in the combat jacket. 'After all, you've got it back.'

I nodded, not knowing what else to do. 'Fair do's,' I said.

The remainder of the team, realizing the day was to end in anti-climax, had begun drifting away. Me and the man stood looking at each other. I sensed he wanted to ask me something. 'Was there anything else?' I said.

He rubbed his chin. 'See that nose,' he said, 'that nose'll be no use to man nor beast now, will it?'

'I suppose not,' I agreed.

'Then I don't suppose I could . . .' He let his voice wind down. Something in his tone alerted the whippet. The vacant look vanished from its eyes and its ears pricked up.

I got the point. At a loss as to what else I might do with

it, I dropped the nose. The dog pounced on it, gripped it between its teeth, flicked it back and forth in its jaws until satisfied with its grip, then let it drop, whole, down its throat. Treat over, it licked its lips once, then let the same gaunt stare of defeat settle over its bony features. 'Waste not, want not,' said the man in the combat jacket, 'mind, he'll still be wanting his tea though. There wasn't much eating in that, most of it was nostril.'

*

Soon afterwards, Mary fell pregnant. I asked her if it was mine. She slapped my face. I pointed out this was a reasonable question, given that she and I had never actually had sex. She slapped me again. She reminded me that, two months earlier, she had bathed my wounds after a scripture class and that, being a Govan girl, the sight of clotting had aroused her and we had been intimate on her parents' sofa. I admitted that I could recall, through a haze of pain and alcohol, a brief writhing fumble on cold plastic sheeting, which we had diligently sponged down afterwards. Mary confirmed that this was, indeed, the occasion of our mutual ecstasy and that now, as a result, we were to be blessed with issue. Naturally enough, being scum, we did not discuss the matter in these precise terms. As I recall, the conversation went this way.

MARY
Rab, darling, I have something to tell you.
ME
What is it, my sweet?
MARY
I am up the duff.
ME
I see, that's wonderful news. Do you want a gin bath and a knitting needle?

MARY

No, thank you.

ME

Well, that's that, then. I suppose we're Donald Ducked.

In this way do the poor celebrate the miracle of conception. Pestilence, to forestall shame, insisted on railroading us into a speedy legal union. When I resisted, a plague of huffiness was instantly visited upon me. For weeks I was offered, instead of a Jammy Dodger, a frozen stare with my tea. Death kept out of it, busying himself with sudden urgent household chores whenever I called round. Having snickered in the early days over my craven hypocrisy, he could hardly now himself be seen to engage in behaviour of a dual-countenanced nature, particularly as his own miserable existence, swinging wretchedly from the marital gibbet, served as such as stark warning to a prospective husband. Sometimes, for spite, I'd twist him on his rope by seeking advice of a fatherly nature concerning life and love. Queries like, 'Tell me, what's the secret of a happy marriage,' would have him scrabbling in the dank cellar of his soul for some mildewed platitude about the need for compromise. This, and others like it, I would dismiss. Any fool, and I flattered myself I was one, knew that compromise was marital code for the woman getting her own way. I resolved that if I succumbed to marriage as, it seemed, succumb I must, then Mary would never adorn a display cabinet with my balls the way Pestilence had with her father's. With that foundation stone of marital understanding firmly, if resentfully, in place, the mansion of our future happiness could now be completed, and in the early autumn of the year, Mary and I were duly married.

*

The ceremony took place in Martha Street Register Office. A reception, courtesy of Mary's parents, was provided in the 'Banqueting Suite' of a one-star bed and breakfast in Tradeston. My mother, eager to keep the Nesbitt family end up, proffered a dowry of sixty fags. The occasion was not without colour or incident. By virtue of my status, the Govan Team felt obliged to honour our union, and when Mary and I emerged, blinking into the afternoon light, as man and wife, a protective archway of thuggish hooligans holding chair legs and meat cleavers awaited us. Their presence was not entirely ceremonial, as representatives of both the Bogie and the Fleet offered their good wishes by launching shite grenades (excrement of generic origin, marinated in warm urine garnished with glass shards and sealed for flavour freshness in plastic Asda bags) onto the smiling clusters of guests and well-wishers – 'Govan Confetti', as it is sometimes also known. My brother Gash, whom we had signed out for the day to share in the nuptials, pined openly for the humdrum safety of his low-security psychiatric unit. Stig too, out of politics, had been offered an invitation. However, I was not sad to learn he was now straitjacketed and in a secure cell.

At the reception, Mary's father made a tedious speech which, judging my side to be as close to the animal kingdom as it's possible for a biped to be, he'd pitched at the faintly ribald. His efforts were received with polite good humour, the well-mannered trade-off being that since he had paid for the scran it would be seemly to laugh at the poor gink's jokes. I had no best man, merely, as usual, a witness. Nonetheless Cotter, fuelled by drink and a wish to impress available females, felt it incumbent upon himself to state a case for my defence. To this end, he warmly praised my choice of wife, assuring the assembled company of Mary's many talents as a sexual partner. A hushed and reverential room heard how her 'clinker funnel' was, remarkably, only marginally more snug as a penis receptacle than her 'front privet'. To approving silence, he attested that I should, in fact, 'walk proud' since every orifice in my new wife's body was 'tighter than a paper cut'. He continued with a note of personal chivalry to myself, assuring me that it was now quite safe to engage in congress with my wife since the antibiotics she'd secretly been taking had 'almost certainly' worked since he'd 'last dipped her'. He proposed a toast to the bride and groom, wishing us a 'bouncing, healthy semi-bastard', adding that if we couldn't manage healthy, could it please be covered in hair and have an extra head 'for a laugh'. He concluded by sitting down in the wrong chair and putting his hand up the bridesmaid's skirt. Since the bridesmaid was my sister Rena, the incident did not pass unnoticed and his head received a sizeable dent from an ornamental candlestick for his temerity.

Ella too, accompanying Cotter, was unimpressed. She revenged herself, we later learned, by receiving oral sex in a toilet cubicle from Tojo, after which she recommended that all men should be compelled, at birth, to undergo compulsory 'nosectomies', since the absence enabled them to 'flick and suck at the same time'.

Mary and I considered a honeymoon in Marbella. Then, when we'd stopped laughing, bought a bottle of Scotsmac, got warmly pickled and had a pleasant al fresco fuck in the bushes by the putting green in Elder Park. We started married life, inevitably, living in with Death and Pestilence since they were the only people we knew with the luxury of a spare bedroom. Close proximity and increased familiarity did not endear me any further to my new in-laws. Especially Death. Pestilence, I discovered, could be partially won round with meaningless flattery and the odd ribald remark, and provided I didn't choke on my own hypocrisy, relations between us remained tolerable. Death was a

191

different matter. He saw the way I worked his great ham of a wife and, having slaved all his life to win her respect, and been denied it for precisely that reason, he grew simultaneously to despise my presence in his house and to relish abusing his authority over me while there. If only I'd found a job and been as wretchedly miserable doing it as he was doing his, all might have been wellish. Occasionally, at tea, he'd circle likely vacancies in the evening paper and slide them over silently for my perusal, watching with reproachful eye for any response that was less than gratefully euphoric. At first I was wrong-footed by this tactic, felt uncomfortable and for a while took to eating in the bedroom. Finally, deciding to fight fire with fire, I resumed dining at the table. When next he slid the paper across, I turned to the obituaries page, took out a pen, circled a few 'suddenly at home', 'after a short illness', and 'sadly missed' fragments of eulogies to the dear departed and slid the paper back in returned silence. We glared at each other for a long moment before he folded the page over, put it away and retreated to his armchair to smoke a spiteful pipe. This was a small victory and by no means a comprehensive one.

New, more inventive ways were found to increase my discomfiture. Sitting watching television, a spade would be planted into my resting hands and a bony digit pointed in the direction of the patch of scabby earth he insisted on referring to as 'the lawn'. Similarly, aware that my knowledge of all things mechanical was, at best, sketchy, he'd engage me in tortuous conversations about car engines, knowing full well that the possibility of a valid contribution to the discussion from myself was as unlikely as it would have been unwelcome. My role was to be talked at, wriggling like a fly on a trap while he puffed himself up for the kill. Any attempts on my part to point the vehicle of the discourse toward the welcome vistas of other subjects were resisted immediately and the wheel of control wrenched with vigour from my grasp. I controlled my frustrations as best I could, recognizing that they were not exclusive to me, but inevitably a defining incident occurred.

I returned late one night from a scripture meeting, bearing a black eye, a torn jacket and a stomach swollen with consoling pints. Pestilence was routinely sniffy at my late arrival but not unduly so, drawing me a tight-lipped stare as she let me in. Mary was sitting on the sofa watching television while Death reposed on the velour throne of his armchair, fiddling with the non-functioning guts of an electric iron. 'So he's back,' he said, without looking up. I considered the third-person nature of this observation, concluded it to be insulting and made to reply. Mary gave me a warning look, however, and I desisted.

Pestilence lowered her *Weekly News* and sniffed the air. 'What's that smell?' In gentlemanly fashion I confessed to a small vomiting occurrence that had taken place prior to my return to the hearth, some unfortunate remnants of which were still located on my shirt front. Pestilence narrowed her eyes to look, found what she knew in advance would disgust her, drew her hand over her mouth and pretended to retch. I use the verb 'pretended' with confidence since, moments later, she resumed with undiminished gusto the guzzling of After Eights. Nevertheless, Death now sensed an opportunity for a little bear-baiting and seized it.

'He'll need to buck his ideas up,' he said, in the general direction of the sofa, 'if he's to go on staying in this house.'

Mary had little choice but to defend my honour. 'He's doing his best, Dad,' she protested, 'there's not much work around Govan, you know.'

Death stopped fiddling. He pointed his screwdriver like it was the Fearful Sword of Truth. 'There's always work for those that want it,' he decreed, his eyes aflame with judgement and ginger wine, 'never forget, I came through the great depression. Do you know what that made me?'

I hazarded a Puckish guess. 'Greatly depressed?'

'Determined,' he said, 'that never again would I miss a day's work in my life. And thank God, I haven't.'

The mention of Him Upstairs gave me an in which I seized with all speed. 'If you want to thank anything for your staying in work then thank your own fear of being out of it and while you're at it, thank the Yanks for building a car plant at Linwood. And Douglas Home for giving tax breaks to capitalists, what's God got to do with it?'

I knew as soon as I'd uttered the 'car' word I'd made a tactical error.

'He talks to me about cars,' said Death, showing teeth, 'he lectures me about the internal combustion engine.'

Mary attempted a loving intervention on my behalf.

'No, he didn't, Dad,' she protested, 'he just . . .'

But the protest fell on deaf ears. I heard the dread phrase, 'When I first entered the motor industry in 1957, there were . . .' and prepared myself to be flayed by an hour of browbeating instruction. I felt nauseous with the beer and the coal fire in the hearth, stifling the air. I found the combination of its cloying heat and his hectoring drone suddenly unbearable.

Without warning, my limbs found a will of their own. I heard my voice say 'Excuse me,' as I was propelled to my feet. Taking out my cock, I emptied my bladder on the cosy pile of red glowing coals in the grate. Dark clouds of pish-scented smoke wafted outwards. When I had finished, I gave my cock a prudent shake and continued from my dreamlike state, 'Do go on.'

The next morning, I was invited to leave. Mary had been permitted to stay on the strict understanding that I was never again to set foot over the family doorstep.

Reminding her parents of the inconvenient fact that I was her husband, she packed a holdall and left with me. As we were closing the garden gate, Pestilence ran after us. She pressed an envelope into Mary's hand. Face puffy from tears she said, 'That's from your Dad and me,' before clumping back, wheezing, into the house. Mary opened the envelope. She counted two hundred pounds in tens. I looked to the window. There was a gap where Death might legitimately have been standing, taking a deserved bow.

*

We used the money to rent a room and kitchen, on the first floor of a dowdy little close in Neptune Street. The factor insisted, as was the custom, on a month's rent as deposit. He also demanded the first three months up front. He knew I was out of work and looked like a hooligan, and while he was keen on the money he was prepared only to take as few risks as avarice would allow. With what we had left, Mary and I picked up a few items from news-agents' windows around Govan. *For sale. Pram. Big dent. But still goes a bumper. No shit. Apply within.* Addition-ally, we were able to acquire, from a binman friend of Bimbo, some still presentable 'luckies', all of which items, sprinkled round the room, gave a shimmering illusion of comfort. When put to any serviceable test, however, arms detached themselves from armchairs, doors from cabinets and once, whilst preening my locks, the entire glass of a wall mirror slid like snow off a roof to land with a crash at my feet. Mary explained that as the mirror had come from a good home the sudden shock of my ugliness had been too much for it.

Having no television, we'd wheel the pram into the corner of the room and sit looking, speculating for hours on what sort of small occupant would soon be filling it. Mary wanted a boy and was convinced beyond all doubt that she was carrying one. On balance, I too preferred a boy. Girls, I reasoned, though often favouring their fathers, were nonetheless demanding and manipulative. Boys were less complicated creatures; though on the debit side they usually grew to despise their fathers, this was counterbalanced by the bonus of the obligatory ten-year angry silence between father and son which would, I realized, at least ensure a lengthy respite from financial obligation. Ideally, if I could organize his contempt between the ages of six and sixteen, I'd be a free man once more whilst still in possession of relative youth.

Mother, too, was thrilled by the prospect of becoming a grandparent. She took to visiting us and would pull up most of a chair and join us for a quiet evening's pram-watching. When Rena took to joining her, bringing knitting needles and a soft cushion, I grew uneasy at the cloying domesticity and alarmed by the prospect before me. If this was them while the pram was still empty what would they be like after the birth? The endless clack of knitting needles began to sound sinister to my ears. I started to think of these dextrous fiends as a shoal of piranha fish in reverse: instead of stripping their victim to the bone, they ruthlessly dressed him. First bootees, then a romper suit with a bobble hat, then a little woolly bicycle, followed at twenty-one by a hand-crotcheted Hillman Imp, at forty-five an ulcer, at sixty a darn on his aorta and at seventy they'd knit him a coffin. Thanks then to the dull miracle of repetition, some other hapless sacrificial victim would slurp from a womb somewhere up the street, they'd move their chairs and begin the whole process anew. In fact, if Boots had only sold nappies to fit me, I'd have climbed into that pram myself and struck a cutesy pose that would make Baby Jane look like sweet baby Jesus. In a word, I was jealous.

*

The sprog arrived bang on time, three days late in the small hours of the Glasgow night. I was not present at the birth, suffering as I was from a painful case of petted lip. Arriving around tea time, I was greeted warmly by my gushing spouse.

'Pubs just shutting?'

I ignored Mary's pleasantry and squinted around the room.

'What you looking for?'

'A lump marked bundle of joy,' I said.

'It's here,' said Mary, indicating a pink runny thing in a white wrap I'd managed to overlook.

'Ah,' I said. I leaned over and peered at the Pink Thing. 'It's got your hips,' I said, out of idle flattery.

'That a fact,' said Mary, 'it's got Cotter's eyes.'

I stiffened.

She relented. 'Just kidding.' The Thing pursed its eyes and, kicking, made tiny cries.

'What's up with it?' I said.

'Just hungry.' She made soft purring sounds at it which attracted its attention. I looked at it, fascinated myself by its fascination. I couldn't believe that with one throwaway semi-fuck this complex Pink Thing had been created. 'What'll we call him,' said Mary, 'we have to decide soon.' We'd been unable to make up our minds, torn between Jim and, my favourite, Clint, Thane of Cawdor. It was squeaking again.

'What's up with it now?' I said.

Mary reached for a wipe. 'Nothing,' she said, 'he's just peed himself.'

And as I watched him wiggle about, it came to me, simple as that. 'I've got it,' I said, 'problem solved.'

Mary looked at me. 'Go on, then.'

'There's only one name for this kid,' I said. 'This kid has got to be Gash.'

'Gash?' Mary drew herself up on her elbow to get a discerning view. The Pink Thing was still wiggling and squeaking. He was helpless, wet and dribbling from both ends.

'OK,' she said, 'Gash it is, then.'

And I picked him up and together we wiped his arse.

CHAPTER SIX

THERE IS no more solemn enemy of good hooliganism than the pram in the hall. Unless, of course, it is the pram in the living room. Young Gash howled all night and most of the day. I hated him and wished him drowned in a bag. Unfortunately, the toilet being communal and we being the only couple on the landing of child-rearing age, suspicion would too readily have fallen upon us, which is to say, me.

Nothing enrages us more than seeing our own faults replicated in our children. Gash cried and cried and would not, whether coaxed, chided or ignored, shut his tiny wailing trap. Like millions before me I discovered to my horror that children were not only non-returnable but non-exchangeable for a better fit. Nevertheless, within these new constraints I still selflessly devoted myself to a life of petty crime and violence.

Stig emerged from the lunatic asylum looking fit and rested. He appeared in every way restored to his old self except that his forehead was now two inches lower. When we questioned him on this novelty he would grow sullen and turn himself into a teapot, so we tended to leave it alone. Unless, of course, we fancied a brew. He was not best pleased on learning that the leadership had become a communal, if temporary, trophy to be passed from hand to hand and he felt, perhaps rightly, that its mystique and currency had been devalued as a result. The corollary to this for all of us was that once having tasted power, we became reluctant to return obediently to the old status quo. Sensing this, Stig felt it necessary to reassert his authority.

Like a champion boxer on the comeback trail, he needed a foe who would provide a worthy challenge but one he knew he would, without dangerous exertion, lick. He chose me. We'd settle it like gentlemen, he said, with half-bricks at dawn. Unless, he added, I was yellow. I considered this insult to my reputation, I considered my standing within the gang, I considered the glory that awaited the victor. I considered yet another fortnight on a glucose drip.

'You win,' I said, 'I'm yellow.' I was sore, tired, a husband and a father. I stood up and left the table. This was necessary. This was the Govan Team's pub. From now on I'd be required to drink in another pub, a lesser pub, where the losers drank.

Cotter knew just the place. He'd been drinking in the Two Ways for years. I appraised my past life. I'd used violence as an attempted means of escape from the ghetto. I had failed. Still, the nice thing was it was now called 'the ghetto'. Up until *Shaft* came out people like me were 'slum-dwellers' in 'tenement sprawls'. Ghetto had a chic New York chime to it. Times were changing. Instead of the means test to tell us we were poor, we now had murals on gable-end walls. This was thoughtful, since otherwise we might have forgotten.

As in New York, people were using any method available to climb out of the deepest recesses of the class pit. Over there, trash of all colours and creeds were becoming magazine stars, movie stars, serial killer stars, in the case of the Manson family, all three at once. Soon we would follow. When the Tory government tried to orchestrate the closure of four Clyde shipyards, a spirited work-in ensued. Jobs were saved, pride restored and the world watched. Like Bisto Kids, the workers shut their eyes to savour the coming scent of socialism. When they opened them again, the gravy train had moved on.

One leader left for a career with the media, the other won promotion and bought a nice camel coat. We learned anew that the system always wins. If it didn't it wouldn't be a system. I remember that year well. Freak, having achieved his life's ambition of becoming a shipyard labourer, promptly fell off a crane and broke his neck. He was unlucky. If he'd landed on his head he might have lived.

Mother took it hard. But she still took it. Life goes on. And on. And on. And if you don't believe me, try and stop it.

We buried Freak as close to Father as we could manage. Which turned out to be two burghs away, in Finnieston. Just as well, really. Any closer and Father might still have reached his windpipe. I was twenty-one. When the key of the door turned, it was in a cell door in Orkney Street. I had been Huckled as drunk and disorderly. Next day, I conducted my own defence, conceding that while I was indeed drunk, I remained nonetheless orderly. For a drunk. This subtle behavioural distinction fell on unheeding ears and, in the absence of funds to pay a fine, I did a routine seven days.

While inside, I met an older man called Zap who had a foolproof plan for robbing cinemas. It seemed like easy money and I was soon beguiled by his boyish, wide-eyed enthusiasm, which I learned too late was a tragic mask which concealed congenital lunacy. Had I realized at the outset he was completely mad, I might have entertained second thoughts. Had he, however, been furnished with the knowledge of my utter incompetence, he too might have confessed to some doubts, though admittedly one struggles to guess at what tempering notions the average fully-certified Tweedledum might consider prudent. At any rate, we thought ourselves dangerous men, driven on by dreams of ticket rolls and Butterkist.

The raid went like clockwork. By which I mean the alarm sounded as soon as we stepped into the manager's office and we were caught the minute we emerged into the street. My share of the haul was eight quid in loose silver and a packet of Munchies I'd nicked from an usherette's tray. In court, I prayed the stolen items would not be recited as a list. It was. 'And a packet of Munchies . . .' bringing a snigger all round. I did six months and swore I'd change my ways. From now on nothing but After Eights would be big enough for Rab 'the Fondant' Nesbitt.

*

Mary made me look after Gash while she went out to work. She'd found a part-time job in a Home Bakery which was good for the odd stale pie or Paris bun that was usually more tooth-resistant than the Eiffel Tower. Gash and I struck up an instant rapport that has lasted all our lives. I detested him and he despised me. He cried a lot in my company. Not that I blamed him for that, I cried a lot in my company too. I could see much of his Uncle Gash in him. He embodied every frailty and character fault in my brother's handbook but was without his compensating intelligence. Don't get me wrong, I love him now, but back then I would have swapped him for a goldfish. I suppose neither of us was ready for the responsibility of childhood. I'd be sitting in my armchair, dandling him on my knee, reading him chunks out of *People of the Abyss* to cheer him up, then there'd be a furtive knock on the door. Cotter would be standing with a bag of Pale Ales and a borrowed rusk, asking if I was coming out to play. I rarely resisted. The booze never tastes better than in the stolen daylight hours and though the comedown is sharper you get used to that.

Once we went walking in the Elder Park. We lay down on the grass and drank the bevvy. We argued, had a brief demented fight about something stupid, the origins of the universe or something, then curled up in the flower beds and went to sleep. When we awoke, people were over by the pond, shouting. The parkie had donned waders and was sloughing out, hooked stick in hand, toward a toy yacht in the middle. I could just make out something small and pink clinging to the mast. I ran straight in and reached for Gash, scooping him up while the Parkie glared at me. I enjoyed a momentary benefit of the doubt as horrified parent before, smelling the drink on my breath, he admonished me in a softly spoken way. 'Try to get a grip, son,' he said, 'before something bad happens.'

Maybe that was the point, dark and unsavoury as the sludge at the bottom of the pond, maybe I wanted something bad to happen. From that day forward, I never doubted my obligation to my son. True, I ignored it, and yes, at times, resented it but his existence was now as real to me as my own limbs and organs. To my ongoing amazement and occasional horror I was forced to confront the palpable fact that something of me existed outwith myself, something bumbling and burbling that increasingly sought independence from me, its progenitor and partial self. The banal mystery of life fell open before me like a badly wrapped Christmas present. The only point of life is procreation. We exist to perpetuate our own existence, to create other superior selves, grown tall and proud on the cream of our genes, boasting a full head of teeth, an aorta that's DynoRod clean and with luck, a solid middle-class income. By this logic, a scumball father has only done his job when his child grows up to despise him for his failure. Perhaps I sensed this from the day Gash was born. Fearing rejection, I'd opted for early retaliation.

Bobo took to visiting Gash. His own children now married and scattered to distant Scotch corners of the globe, he craved a fresh, pink template to inform, if not to form, in his own image. He was middle-aged now and the portly hooligan of a certain age is a pitiful beast, condemned to roam from room to room away from the habitual wifely snap and suck of brush and vacuum hose around the ankles. Feet that once knocked heads insensible now shifted in awkward tartan-slippered obedience, hither and thither in search of food, or drink, or purpose. It is a sad thing to see a once mighty man return from Safeway all pleased because he's achieved two pence off a tin of own-brand beans. We'd go for walks with the pram, Bobo seizing opportunities to push, I still taking no liberties out of past respect and wariness. We'd sit on a bench and he'd reminisce. All his friends were dead of drink, heart attacks, or 'the old tap dancer'. All that remained were the feart ones, the bores and two-pint cardy men. Life was a perilous thing, why, he was practically stepping over corpses in the street. Turn your back and some bastard's keeled over, like as not owing you a round or a fag. He himself had suffered a mild stroke only a year since. But he wouldn't give up the drink, oh no, not while he could still sup it through a straw from the still nimble side of his phizzer.

'Wee Breda, remember her, the one that hung upside down from the light cord the first time you visited, she's a nurse now, in Auckland, I've been out once already and no messing I'm going back again. Her and me, Ginny. It's a different life down there. I like the Kiwis. They like me. Sun and that. Porches. You can put on shorts and no bastard laughs. Try that here and it's "look at that cunt". Sure, you know that.' He looked down at the pram. 'Gash, eh?' I nodded. Then he said a curious thing. 'Isn't he awful like his grandpa?'

'My father?'

'Sure, your father, how would I know any other one?'

I looked down at Gash. I saw it. Sometimes personal history slams into you like a shunt at traffic lights. I ventured a tentative enquiry. 'Did you know my old fella well?'

He looked away absently over the hood of the pram to where two jakies were arguing with a rotted willow tree. 'If you're asking me if I liked him,' he said, 'we were very different men. But we found common ground in the drink. Zebras and wildebeests, we all need a drink in the desert. And let's face it, there's a lot of desert round here.'

I considered the bittersweet sensation his words evoked. The truth about death is that time doesn't heal, it accommodates, and the further the years part us from the dead, the deeper and more mysterious is the void they leave within us, for the fact is we are growing closer to them, not further away. One day we will join those we now love but at the time couldn't abide when they were up and about roaming the earth, hogging the last of the milk, flicking ash into saucers and fouling the outhouse air. I considered my new son, tepidly alive in his battered Silver Cross pram. Children, I believed deep down, were an admission of defeat rather than a declaration of faith, a handing-on of the baton of life by those too weary to continue with the race. All fine and good if you've made your mark, if you've pissed your height in life's golden sands and can hang up your cock with quiet pride, saying, 'There, kid, if the future belongs to you, let's see you beat that.' But not to retire with a full bladder, the yellow beads dribbling down your thigh like bitter tears of frustration. I marvelled at the crude brilliance of my own poetic imagery as Bobo pushed the squeaky pram down Langlands Road, taking the long way home to prolong the outing. Inside me something stirred. I had tasted battle at all points of the globe from Carntyne in the east to Maryhill in the north, westward ho to Drumchapel and Castlemilk in the deep disturbed south. Like Alexander, I wept for fresh fields to conquer.

*

Beggars have it easy nowadays. In my time, there was a showbiz dimension to panhandling that demanded, at the least, the semblance of an effort to entertain before the squeeze could legitimately be put upon the punter. A little soft-shoe here, an epileptic seizure there, the necessary vaudeville gloss would be exhibited before the bottom line was revealed and the hat went down or round. No longer so. Nowadays some of the bastards are too lazy even to open their yaps and ask, let alone treat you to three cracked verses of 'My Way'. No, a grunt and the rattle of a paper cup, that's entertainment. While I'm all for minimalism, there's no way 'any spare change' is a substitute for an extract from *Tosca* or 'Guantanamera' played on pan pipes by two native Indians from Paisley. The laziest bastard beggar I ever saw was a stump-legged schizophrenic who used to slump in a stupor outside What Every Woman Wants in Argyle Street. Plainly, this guy was not at home to Dr Irony. He would just lie against the wall, asleep, with his hand out, absolutely no midfield play. He had two halves of a necktie knotted round his trousers to hide his stumps. He annoyed the hell out of me. One day I offered him some constructive criticism. I said he was a useless lump of midden refuse who should either rent himself out as a trampoline to a flea circus or else smarten up his scabby ideas. About many pints later, I tumbled out of the Horseshoe Bar and was promenading up the gutter when I saw a sight that restored my lack of faith in humanity.

Taking my inspirational words to heart he'd moved up in the world and was now slumped outside the House of Fraser. His trousers flapped half empty, exposing two grey runts of leg end. The necktie was now around his throat in two knots. Seeing me pass, he called out, 'You were right, big man, it's time I got a grip of myself.'

I mention this subject because my next endeavour was not, itself, far removed from wanton beggary. My growing despair was made manifest in an increasing desire and capacity for drink. By chance I discovered that bored guzzlers will pay good money for the possibility of seeing a misguided waster drink himself to the edge of death. By definition, this was a dangerous occupation. Any less than a coma and the audience felt cheated, conned into providing free drink. A vigorous kicking incident might ensue. Any more than temporary unconsciousness, of course, and oblivion was the inevitable result. Though I had cultivated a flourishing death wish, I had no intention of harvesting its solitary bloom just yet. I was twenty-two. I calculated that I could die young at anything up to thirty-nine, or forty-five in a plane crash, providing I kept my hair.

There are thirty-two nips to a bottle of whisky, thirty-five if the pub landlord taps his optic measure with a small hammer, and my record stood at thirty in a single session. Cotter acted as my agent on these occasions, for the usual percentage fee. When I say I drank thirty whiskies, three went to him on a pro rata basis. He was an enthusiastic agent. When once I was admitted unconscious to a Paisley infirmary for twenty-four hours, he negotiated it up to thirty-six and used his percentage to chat up the nurses. I challenged all comers. Usually I won. My tactic was to start slow and build up the pace gradually. Opponents would often bolt down the first few rounds, virtually assaulting their nervous systems with strong alcohol, giving the body's natural defences no opportunity to adjust. They'd be crowing at my slow progress but soon afterwards would be hurtling past me green-faced on their way to the bogs.

I found I drank better when in a sombre mood. In my opinion, drink doesn't so much alter mood as enhance the prevailing one. The trouble with starting happy is that the rush of drink will make you happier and you'll become drunk quicker because your system is already pumping with adrenaline. Start sombre, dead of mood and you stay that way, blank of visage, slow of deed. Sometimes I'd pick an argument with my opponent to pump him up before drinking commenced. A face flushed with anger was worth a five-nip lead to me. On a good night, I'd leave under my own steam, weaving white-eyed to the door, always taking care to bid a courteous farewell to all, in order to placate any pals of my retching opponent. Once outside, I'd find a doorstep to sit on while Cotter sought chips, the greasier the better. A few of these would usually render me sick as a dog and I'd throw up in a back court before retiring to my suite in the back midden to sleep it off. Cotter was well worth his ten per cent on those occasions as he was under strict instructions always to roll me onto my side before abandoning me, so that I might die, respectably, of hypothermia rather than endure the ignominy of choking on my own, or anyone else's, vomit.

Once, in Renfrew, I woke to find a rat sitting on my chest. They are surprisingly engaging creatures close up, with dainty paws, and make an intelligent squealing sound when you jump up startled, thudding their flaccid bellies with a fearful boot. The rat darted off, I recall, and a mange-ridden terrier, unsure who to menace, opted for me in preference to the rat, a value judgement that seemed less than complimentary to myself.

Competition drinker was not a career choice that endeared itself to my young wife, however, and I was not surprised, returning late one afternoon from a heavy three-day shift at the coal face of alcoholism, to find her gone. She had taken Gash with her and cleared the house of what little furniture we had managed to gather. Bare rooms, bare boards. Looking up, chagrined, I spotted a note Sellotaped to an appropriately bare bulb. Tearing it down, I squinted my eyes to read and could discern this witty message: *I've left the bulb. It'll help you brighten your ideas up.* Screwing up the note, I experienced that fleeting moment of manic glee that always precedes a prolonged living nightmare. I saw a future of cascading drink, endless parties, wall-to-wall air hostesses punctuated by the odd respite for bookish contemplation while my recovering penis lolled like a contented dog before a hearty and imaginary log fire. I looked at the room. It looked back at me. It walked around me, eyeing me up and down. 'She's gone,' it said, 'there's just you and me now, so wake up. You don't even know any bus conductresses let alone an air hostess, and even if you did, why would she want to party in an empty slum with a skint fat alcoholic – oh, pardon me, did I say unemployed? A skint fat unemployed alcoholic like you? Look in that mirror, lard-lungs, go on. No, it's not cracked, that's a dried gully of blood from where you walked into a manhole cover some council numpty had thoughtlessly placed over a manhole. You didn't do anything, it just stepped up and hit you, unprovoked. And what about those eyes? Twenty-two and already thread veins like an AA road atlas. And did I say breath? Talking to you is like potholing down an arse. No, Fatso, she's gone, now you can relax, pull up your self-pity and drink yourself into oblivion, just like you always knew you would someday.'

I didn't like the room talking to me that way. I resented

being lectured by something I'd taken the trouble to wall-paper and whose doors I'd only recently varnished. It was an ungrateful room and I told it so. When the room continued to argue back I gave it a warning uppercut to the window sash. That shut it up for a minute, then it started to gurgle, in a defiant way, through the cold-water pipe. I wasn't having any of that. I took a hatchet from the lobby coal bunker and severed the pipe at the jugular with a couple of blows. I knew the pipe was badly hurt because water pumped out in great convulsive retches before set-tling down to a steady torrent. And would you believe it, still that bastard mirror laughed. I gave it a straight right to the rose petal border, that shut it up. It slid down the wall and shattered, unconscious. The water was an inch deep on the living-room floor and heading for the lobby. I launched at it with a flying tackle and headed it off. It hovered in an uncertain pool by my midriff for a little while before slipping slyly under my flank and heading in dashing trickles for the door. From my new perspective at eye level to the doorstep, I was forced to consider that I might be encountering a problem. Referring to my range of skills as physicist and architect, I arrived at the proper solution to the problem of water. Fire. Taking a box of Swan Vestas, I lit newspaper tapers and torched the cur-tains. There, I thought, that ought to dry it out. I then took myself off to the Two Ways for a pint. Except that I never reached the Two Ways. I woke up, not for the first or second time, in hospital.

*

A uniformed policeman was sitting by my bed. I woke, took a look around and asked him hesitantly what had happened. He told me to shut up. A second policeman appeared and he stood over the bed, reading me my rights. It turned out I'd taken some sort of seizure on the pavement. I was apparently indebted to a good, or more accurately not bad, Samaritan who'd emptied out my pockets then summoned an ambulance. Alcoholic poisoning had been diagnosed. I expressed surprise.

'I only drink to pass myself in company,' I said.

'Well, keep better fucking company,' said the seated bedside angel in blue serge and clumpy boots. It was explained to me that I'd torched and flooded the flat, causing the building to be evacuated. Consequently I was to be charged with criminal damage and arson. I could expect, oh, at least a year. They confirmed with the doctor that I was well enough to be discharged. I started to dress myself. 'Oh,' added the second one, by way of a time-filler, 'the doctor says you're an alcoholic, did you know?'

'Really?' I said. 'Is it anything to do with my drinking?' I acted shocked to hide the fact that I was shocked. Among other things I was also dismayed. Having achieved my life's fulfilment at twenty-two, what would I now have to look forward to at fifty?

I received eighteen months. As I stepped toward the van, a policeman reassured me that, with good behaviour, I could be out in two years. His brother-in-law owned the flat I'd torched. In life there are said to be six degrees of separation between ourselves and any living being on the planet. In Glasgow, there is one degree. Except for certain guys in uniform, where there is no separation. If they could poke their mothers from the back while they heated up the pie and beans, they'd never bother to get married.

Mary didn't contact me. I tried everything to persuade her, not treading on the cracks on the cell floor, reading newspaper stories backwards, thought transference, all the common-sense possibilities the mature adult mind could conjure, all to no avail. Naturally, being the senior partner in the relationship, it did not occur to me to demean myself by dropping her a note and offering any hint of, for want of a better term, apology. In Scotland, men do not apologize. Instead, we grow tumours, fall over, and are buried under headstones that read *See What You've Done Now, You Bitch*. I was no exception. I would bring Mary to heel with my masterly silence. She would have expected me to bombard her with messages, begging forgiveness. Instead I would stand alone, proud and impervious, in the slop-out queue, clutching my piss pot with haughty defiance. Prisons are full of deluded fools, sitting in tiny barred cells, trying to teach people in the vast deaf whizzing world outside a lesson.

Silence built on hubris stores up repression and invariably the dam is breached. Again, I was no exception. After two months, a letter arrived, on lavender paper. The handwriting looked familiar. Little girlish posies adorned the top corners of the scented paper. The sentiments were brief and to the point.

> Dear Rab
>   I was sorry to learn you had burnt the house down. I am at present living with my parents but am going on holiday soon, to Morecombe, with Jamesie.
>
> P.S. Gash is well.

I stood paralysed, like a man whose nervous system is flooding with snake venom, rendering him helpless. With Jamesie. If I'd taken a thrombosis on the spot I would not have been surprised. I tingled from head to foot, my innards scalded and mortified. I wanted to tear down the bricks of my captivity and run rampaging and howling into the street. Instead, I gave a slight cough and sat on my bed.

'Are you all right?' asked my cellmate, 'the Warmth'.

I nodded. 'A wee touch of paranoia,' I said, 'it'll pass.'

James 'the Warmth' Munro was an ex-Church minister

who had discovered, to his cost, that Jehovah had a sense of humour. A meek and spiritual man, he had, on God's holy instructions, nailed two members of his congregation to chipboard crosses on a Beazer Homes site, only for the Supreme Being to later deny all responsibility and claim he had spoken only 'for a giggle'. Munro was horrified to find signs of cheeky-chappiness in the Lord and left the Church, his faith shattered. After his arrest, he would refer to God only as Mr Pastry and in court had even swept the Bible aside and instead swore his oath on a *Bash Street Kids Bumper Fun Book*. After sentence, his wife abandoned him. She joined an agency, in Lenzie, that specialized in finding errant priests for married women to run off with and after several ugly experiences she eventually found her Father Right.

Munro was bitter, which I like. It's the face we all hide. He kept himself to himself and was no trouble, except for Sundays when, in an effort to disrupt the chapel service, he'd run his boot along the cell bars and sing 'The Ying Tong Song' over the prayers.

In an attempt to prevent myself going mad, I sought a hobby. Many of the lifers were doing Open University courses and I enquired about these with the Guidance Officer. He looked amused and told me, in a gentle, roundabout way, not to entertain ideas above my station. OU courses, he explained, were viewed as redemptive opportunities for serious hard-core offenders and not for the likes of me. Additionally, they took several years to complete and my pifflingly short sentence provided an inadequate window for the appropriate academic endeavours. I considered this problem and offered a solution. What if I were to commit a serious crime within the prison, a heartless felony, say, a frenzied stabbing, sensitively administered, would that constitute a heinous enough offence to persuade the governors of my suitability for redemption? The Guidance Officer seemed unconvinced. He acknowledged the inventive logic of my proposal but felt unwilling, as a senior officer in the Prison Service, to encourage the inmates in homicidal acts. It might seem pedantic, he added in an attempt at rueful sympathy, but there it was.

I cursed my luck. If only I'd murdered Cotter when I had the chance, I might be a fully qualified Doctor of Philosophy by now, at the arse end of my remission. My future would have been assured. As a self-educated murderer, I would automatically marry my social worker, thereby elevating myself into the influential milieu of middle-class society. A world of book launches and dinner parties would await me. As a thrilling working-class monstrosity I'd nestle in the dining rooms of Edinburgh and Hillhead, sharing amusing memories of poverty and violence over the chilled Chablis. Remember Tojo's nose? How we all laughed! He's dead now, of course, hammered nails into his own head when he couldn't get a woman. Oh, surely not, how horrible, do go on. Oh yes, such larks, eh, Pip? And Father with the telly, and Mother with her wretched gift of fags at my wedding? If you saw it in a sitcom you wouldn't believe it. Yes, I've dragged myself up by the bootstraps, I'm proud to say, I'm not a murderer now, I'm an anecdote.

All this flashed through my wistful mind as I stood in the office. With luck, I might have been in on the dungeon floor, so to speak, of social change. Yet again, my timing was awry. Lacking sufficiently grievous credentials for the life of the mind I enquired as to what opportunities my paltry criminal damage charge might otherwise qualify me. The Guidance Officer pulled a face in an approximation of a man thinking long and hard. An intensive study of laundry might be arranged, he suggested. Or the doors of cuisine might be thrown open to me, with a special emphasis on potato peeling. I agreed to be pencilled in for the latter, the proximity of food, I reasoned, providing opportunities for gluttony by which I might undermine the penal system and help usher in the dawn of socialism. I left as I had entered, feeling worthless and alone.

*

I missed Mary. Her betrayal struck a blow to my heart and I could not think of her without tears, which circumstance obliged me to conceal. Crying in prison being unseemly, most prisoners prefer to express emotion through the accepted social avenues of violence and disruption. Outbursts of hostility were much the norm and were so ingrained within the fabric of the prison system that the weekly rosters made informal allowance, on a rota basis, for violent prisoners to enjoy 'a spontaneous act'. This might range from a humdrum assault on a fellow prisoner to the more noteworthy transgression of violence against property. On completion of his spontaneous act the prisoner would then sit sated in his cell and await, like a diner in a restaurant, the formality of the bill. This would duly arrive in the form of a kicking from the prison officers, the duration and severity of which would be determined by the degree of inconvenience ostensibly suffered by the establishment. It was an admirably British compromise, based on misery and human ignorance, with which all in the prison cheerfully complied. For my part, and somewhat to my own surprise, I did my best to avoid forfeiting self-control. Instinct told me that my sanity hung by a thread and that were I to crack, the bats might fly into my head, never to leave.

I stayed quiet and kept my own counsel. I stole Fig Rolls from the kitchen and hoarded them. Unable through constant work to crowd thoughts of Mary from my mind, I instead allowed the pain I felt to embrace me and for

215

many weeks I hung helpless in its grasp. I moved like an automaton, rising, slopping out, working and sleeping. I lived for the sanctuary of sleep. True, there were the dreams of inconsolable loss but the risk was worth taking when the respite of oblivion could prove so merciful. I did not care whether I lived or died. Sometimes I would close my eyes and hope for the ultimate release. But I did not die. Instead I regained a little strength. I awoke one morning with my heart pounding and that sense of trembling euphoria that often precedes the realization of a hangover. Except I was not hungover, I hadn't had a drink in months. I rose and stood by the cell window, lifting my head to the familiar square grey lid of Glasgow sky. A hopeful smear of milky light oozed from the blot of the sun. I felt the phrase 'green shoots of recovery' caress my suspicious soul. What could it mean?

Next day I received a letter. It was from my mother. I'd told her firmly never to write or visit as I didn't want to deal with the pained and unspoken reproach of her presence. Additionally, I didn't want her suffering the ignominy of asking for a bus ticket to Riddrie Library from a knowing driver, then walking back the two shameful stops to the prison. For her to break this agreement was significant.

Something had happened, and as I opened the envelope, my mind teemed with possibilities. 'Dear son, hope you are well . . .' I scanned the formalities, reaching for the heart of it. 'Sorry to have to tell you, Bobo died over the weekend . . .' I sat on my bed and read on. Death had occurred by natural causes. Natural, that is, if you were Bobo. He had left the pub, routinely paralytic, stating that he wished to emigrate to a sun-drenched clime. After a short search, he had fallen asleep on a traffic island, presumably mistaking it for Capri. The following morning, fuddled, and looking for his slippers in the fast lane, he had been squarely thumped by a Mercedes and killed outright. I wondered, in the welter of my confused thoughts, how Bobo himself might have regarded the manner of his own demise. With disappointment, I suspected. He was a patriot and would prefer to have been snuffed by a Jag or Roller. I lay on my bed and the green shoots of recovery caressed me no more.

After a while, Munro appeared from laundry duty and at his coaxing I explained my sombre mood. Sensing grief, his eyes lit up. 'He giveth and he taketh away,' he said, 'but usually, he taketh away.' His concern was genuine and his sympathy insane but comforting. He spoke in a low, gravelly voice about the tribulations of man. As he did so, the world seemed to contract around us, leaving a domain of silence beyond the radius of his seductive murmur. I began to understand his power as a preacher and how he could have persuaded two retired quantity surveyors from Falkirk to dangle like ornaments from a partition wall for man's sins. He asked me to speak of Bobo and I did. When I'd finished, he nodded. 'He is my shepherd,' he said, 'he maketh me to lie down in fast lanes, looking for slippers.' We were of one accord.

'Fuck Mr Pastry,' I said.

'Quite,' agreed the pastor.

*

I sought permission to attend Bobo's funeral. I was refused on the grounds that he was not a close enough relative. 'Not close enough for what?' I argued. 'To grieve for? How can you be the judge of that?' Stony faces did not trouble to blink. I returned to my cell. I paced up and down, still troubled by the memory of the green shoots. For once, I decided that the fault lay within myself. I had invested that slender feeling with the power of prophecy when really it was no more than a pleasant symptom of a gradual psychological recovery. The arrival of Mother's letter was not a blow from a hostile fate but a simple, if unfortunate, accident of timing. There was no cosmic conspiracy against me; instead, I was tangling myself up in a welter of insecurity and superstition. I felt calmer than I had done for weeks, and went to bed sad but contented, assured that my feet were now treading humbly on the ancient path of wisdom. Around two hours later I woke with an attack of the heebie-jeebies. I dreamt that Cotter, dressed as a warlock, was feeding my severed penis to a unicorn. Mary, looking fetching in a black cloak with matching warts, was copying our wedding vows in invisible ink. In case I missed the message the words 'Anxiety Attack' were spelled out above them in flashing neon bulbs. I lay awake in the dark, angered by my subconscious and its lousy Blackpool Pier imagery. What was the point of having a subconscious if it was more red-necked and slapstick than your waking mind? It was as though Freud had said to the Krankies, 'Here, you analyse this one, I'm nipping out for a fag and a Bovril.' All the same, there was no doubting the truth that was stamped on me like a brand name on a side of bacon. I still loved Mary and losing her to Cotter was like being demolished from the inside with a wrecking ball.

About a week later, I received a visitor. I'd half expected this, as I knew Mother would feel duty bound to tell me in person how Bobo's funeral had gone. She was already seated at a table when I entered the visiting room. Rainmate, message bag on the knees, belted poplin mac, the full Mother uniform. She looked old, shrunken and grey. I decided, in gentlemanly fashion, not to mention it.

'Hello,' I said and sat down.

'Hello,' she said. She took a good scrutinizing squint at

me before delivering her judgement. 'You're looking old,' she said.

The mittens were off. 'You can talk,' I said, 'you're that shrunk you should be hanging from a market stall in Borneo.'

Pleasantries out of the way, we talked in general terms of friends and events. Yes, Bobo's funeral had been a touching affair. Yes, Ginny had conducted herself with dignity, and no, since you ask, she had not hung her breasts at half-mast but tucked them both in, out of respect. In addition to family and friends, the elite of Govan's low life had turned out, adding colour to Bobo's send-off. The Methadone Kazoo Band had led the cortège, blowing a selection of airs on empty plastic syringes, and their sensitive rendition of 'Rum, Sodomy and the Lash' had brought a tear to many an eye. Some of the town's leading wasters and alcoholics had taken time out of their busy schedules to line the route. Like railway sleepers their prone forms provided a bulky track alongside which the earthly form of Bobo made its last sad journey. The Confederation of Govan Shoplifters, easily recognizable in their distinctive uniform of billowing coats, baby-free push-chairs and empty carrier bags, stood sombrely to attention till the slow train moved past, before piling into Wool-worth's to recoup lost working time. Humble drug dealers doffed their Kangols and emaciated users raised furrowed eyelids in languid salute. Govan was burying one of its own. Former Orkney Street policemen had clubbed together to offer a splendid wreath of boots which lay by the foot of the coffin. Junkie mothers held small children up to touch the hearse for luck, hoping their young, like Bobo, might attain the lofty Govan dream of having a good time with the drink, then croaking while you can still give chemotherapy the hipsway and a single-finger salute. Bobo was true scum. He never held a job, indeed no one in his family had paid tax since the Napoleonic Wars, he sponged relentlessly from the system, and he was a some-time thief and hooligan. Yet when he died, people turned out for him. To respectable middle-class eyes he was that most loathed of creatures, the much-loved popular scum-ball. In terms of profit, loss and moral probity, Bobo's case was indefensible. For myself, all I will say is that I have met sheriffs, lawyers, prison governors and other respect-able members of the middle class and I know who I would sooner have a pint with. In the eternal bleak midwinter of the frostbitten Scottish soul, he kept my spirits up. He entertained.

Mother glanced nervously around the room at the other prisoners. She was awkward and trying to negotiate an angle of entry into talking about my situation that wouldn't get my back up. Mellowed by memories of Bobo, I helped her out.

'I know what you're thinking,' I said.

She looked at me. 'What?'

'You're thinking, at least he's not pretty, so he won't end up with an arse like a wind tunnel.'

She told me I was disgusting but it broke the ice. 'How are you coping with life in here?'

I told her fine. 'In fact I wish I was in for longer, Frankie Vaughn's coming up for Christmas.'

She perked up. 'You'll be out by Christmas?'

I shrugged. 'I don't see why not,' I said, 'if I keep a clean beak. I'm sure they'd be only too glad to get rid of me, jail's like the Health Service, they need the beds.' While she was upbeat, I fluttered in a casual query that clunked onto the table between us. 'Have you seen anything of Mary?'

She tensed. It made her Rainmate rustle. 'To tell you the truth,' she said, 'I've been coming to that.'

Now I tensed. I was glad I wasn't wearing a Rainmate.

I began to mutter, offering us both an unconvincing way out. 'I mean, it's OK, if you haven't seen her.'

'No,' she said, 'I have.'

No way back, then. I looked at her. She looked at me. A coy girlish smile played across her ancient fag-tinted lips. She was drawing it out, the old bastard, tap dancing in the mean little spotlight of her power, well, from this moment on, I didn't give a shit about Mary, in fact I'd been meaning to —

'She's outside,' said the tap-dancing crone, suddenly transformed into my mother again. I looked at her, dumbly. She continued.

'Aye, she didn't know whether you'd want to see her, but in the end she thought she'd take the chance. There's somebody looking after Gash.'

Somebody. A flash of hideous lightning shook my mind. Cotter, playing hopscotch with Gash, using her wedding ring for a peever. With a mighty effort I calmed myself. This meeting was something I'd dreamed about. If I was to destroy it with an outburst of temper I was done for, I'd have to crawl into a corner of the exercise yard and spontaneously combust.

'Well?' My mother appeared to be awaiting some sort of answer.

'Well what?' I said. It was weird, I was gasping, my voice a shallow wheeze.

'Will I go and get her? She's in the waiting area.'

I felt suddenly weak, drained of strength. But I retained the power of nodding. I nodded.

'Well, don't kill yourself with enthusiasm,' said my mother, rising.

I place my head in my hands and whipped myself into calm. What did the clock say? Twenty-five to. Oh God, if only we hadn't squandered half an hour on Bobo's funeral. What am I saying? That's not me speaking. Oh, but it is.

When you get down to it, fine feelings are shite and onions, the hungry heart is the boys.

I smelt her before I saw her. The awful nostalgic ache of that cheap scent she wore for going out. If only, like Tojo, I didn't have a nose. To smell them is to want them. I raised my head slowly, to savour the moment. I wanted to remember, so summon up every bittersweet detail of love's lost countenance and expend it in a wank after cocoa.

'Hello, Rab.'

Hello, Rab, she said, sweet words from your heart's desire.

'Hello, Mary.' Hello, Mary, I thought, I hope your quim's falling off with pox from that warty Cotter cock. 'You're looking well.'

'Thanks, Rab, you too. Nice shirts they give you. If it wasn't for the arrows on your trousers I'd take you for an accountant.'

She was playing it right. First the banter, then we go hand in hand down the fathoms to where the pain lies on the ocean floor. Except I couldn't join her. My mouth wouldn't work. Words seemed the size of pyramid stones and I hadn't the strength to wrench them up and push them into line. So I looked at her. I drank in her face like it was a vitamin I'd long been denied. I'd been out to sea alone, in a small boat, without rations. Now at last, after many storms, I was in my home port and sick with scurvy.

Fearful of the clock, I took a deep breath. 'I got your letter,' I said. She made to reply but I got my long-prepared speech off my chest. 'On the one hand,' I began, 'I'm glad you told me. Truly I am. But on the other, was a face-to-face conversation too much to ask after all we've been through together?' I noticed to my relief that my voice sounded grave and hurt. At critical moments you can't tell how a voice is going to go. No matter how heartfelt the sentiments, no woman is going to take you seriously if through tension you come out sounding like Jimmy Clitheroe. But today I was positively Churchillian. Maybe that was how Winston worked up his gravitas prior to a battle, have Clementine fuck a Jamesie Cotter. Time now to grasp the thorn in my side and tug it out. 'And as a revenge tactic, don't you think humping that mobile virus Cotter makes as much sense as trying to trip up a dustcart with your foot? I mean to say . . .' Insecurity was seeping through, my voice was starting to waver. I forced myself to shut up. 'It's your turn to say something now,' I said.

She looked puzzled. 'What letter?' she said.

I was, as they say, greatly taken aback. 'What letter?' Never mind that, what kind of woman was this, who could fire off a note, announcing adultery, that puts her husband through six shades of fiery hell, then pay it such casual regard that she had forgotten she'd ever written the bloody thing? Was it me? Was I overreacting? Maybe Govan had suddenly gone sophisticated. Maybe while I was in Barlinnie they were all out at decadence lessons, turning French. Maybe Simone de Beauvoir was up the Two Ways this minute, humping a redundant welder, maybe Sartre was queuing at the ice-cream van for double nougats to impress a Juliette Greco lookalike he'd met from Thermotank. If Mary could forget that letter, anything was possible.

'What letter?' I kept repeating. She just looked at me, blankly. I reached into my shirt pocket and produced the well-thumbed evidence. The interaction alerted a screw and he let us know he was watching.

Mary looked at the letter. She opened it out warily, like it might go bang, and read it in silence. Then she said, 'I didn't write this letter.'

'You didn't?'

She shook her head. 'I never wrote you any letters. I

was really hurt when you wrecked the house. I swore I'd never speak to you again.' She shrugged and gave a limp smile. 'Anyway, Miss Iron Will, here I am. Oh, and by the way, that's not my handwriting.'

'But it's on lavender paper.'

'OK, I'll put it another way. That's not my handwriting on this lavender paper. It's similar, I grant you. Whoever wrote that letter must know me and hate you.' She adopted a dry tone. 'Wonder who that could be, eh?' It took a while but the low-powered generator in my head finally lit the lightbulb.

'Cotter?'

She applauded, ironically.

'But why?'

She stopped applauding. She gave me a look that said her next move would be to offer me plastic pants and a book on finger-painting. 'Well, let's see. Off the top of my head let's try this on: how about he fancies me and you once tried to bury him alive?'

'You really think he'd hold that against me?'

'Well, Rab, not everybody has your tolerance and easy-going nature.'

The bell sounded, signifying the end of visiting. I grabbed Mary's hand and held it. 'So you're not seeing him, is that what you're saying?'

She shrugged. 'Put it like that if you want,' she said. 'I'd say I'm not seeing anybody. I'm married to you, remember?'

'So you'll come and visit me again?'

She nodded. 'But I won't ever bring Gash. I don't want him seeing you in here.'

'What've you told him about where I am?'

'I told him you were away working,' she said. Her mouth straightened into a hard smile. 'I told him you were with the police. Ring any bells?'

224

I felt the tension lift from my shoulders for the first time in months. Thus turns the mysterious cycle of man's seasons. As one loser is hit by a truck, so another steps up to fill his shirt in Barlinnie. Truly, the wondrous cosmic wheel leaves no life uncrushed. Blessed be the name of Mr Pastry.

CHAPTER SEVEN

THE DAY I LEFT PRISON, I fell over the doorstep and landed on my chin. I wondered if this was a portent of what life held for me on the outside. Eager to grasp my second chance with Mary, I had renounced my life of crime. As soon as I'd murdered Cotter the ledger of the past could be balanced and closed. For a full year no drink had passed my lips and on my release I was two stone lighter than when I'd been arrested. None of my old clothes fitted me. I had to wear braces to keep my trousers up and if I broke into a trot they bobbed up and down like I was Coco the Clown. My own son, Gash, no longer recognized me. I was happy with this arrangement and, for a while, convinced him that I was 'kindly Uncle Tommy', home from the sea, and that his real father, a true hero, had been lost in a freak harpooning accident in Whitley Bay. Prior to my release, Mary had pleaded with the Housing Authority for a place to live. The officials, swayed by sympathy for the plight of this unemployed single mother with a two-year-old child, had allotted her a boarded-up flat on the fourteenth floor of a vandalized high-rise estate in Possilpark. Tailoring the property further to her needs, the council had ensured that it was already burnt out, no doubt to spare me the effort on arrival. A team of workmen threw up some woodchip, replaced a few boards and splashed some paint around but the smell of burning lingered on for months. Standing in a newsagent's queue, people would sniff the air and stare, as if you'd stepped in to buy fags on the way back from fighting a forest fire. It was, I agree, no more than I deserved.

In an attempt to persuade the estate dwellers of their inherent role at the heart of British Heritage, all the blocks had been named after poets: Wordsworth Court, Coleridge House, Milton Bank, etc. Our block was named after Keats. In deference to its dampness, the inhabitants had nicknamed it Consumption Cabinet. Within six months we all had recurring coughs and Gash ongoing bronchitis.

After so long in prison, I found it hard to adapt to civilian life. For a while, I couldn't make it to the shops as my feet would only walk in a twenty-five yard square, the dimensions of the exercise yard. Whenever I saw a queue, I'd join, assuming there must be food or fresh laundry at the end of it. If offered a cigarette, I'd hoard it and would later stop strangers in the street, offering to do a swap for crisps or a nude book.

Gash's cough grew worse. As Mary made friends with the neighbours, we realized he was not alone. Many of the estate's children had worse damp-related ailments and these were a source of fierce competitive honour to their parents. Several suffered from fluid in the lungs. All smoked. X-ray pictures were often framed proudly above the mantelpiece and from across the room could easily pass for 'Mist Over Loch Lomond'.

Community had yet to become a derided word in those days, and to celebrate the Queen's Jubilee the estate held a garden festival. Though no one actually had a garden we remained undeterred and, for once, turned misfortune to our advantage by cultivating assorted vegetation on our bedroom walls. Mary and I, though no horticulturists, entered into the spirit of things by nurturing a patch of mushroom-related fungus above the skirting board. I made a trellis fence out of spent matchsticks, and an oversheet of Sellotaped silver foil from fag packets helped prevent eager rodents from feasting on our crop. The Residents' Association wrote to *Gardeners' Question Time*, and though the BBC expressed no interest in our project, we nevertheless received a nice letter, informing us we were underprivileged. In a spirited effort to make a day of it, we persuaded Mr Gibbons, the principal of the local lunatic asylum, to judge the competition winner and, as he himself confessed, this was no easy matter. Indeed the day ended on a note of unfortunate controversy when a frail ground-floor pensioner, Mr Mahood, was awarded the overall accolade. Though none doubted the splendour of his verdant wall lawn, in Wembley stripes, some protested that he had held an unfair advantage, ground-floor dwellers enjoying an additional bounty from nature's storehouse in the form of rising damp. Sportingly, Mr Mahood had offered to relinquish his title but it was agreed that he be allowed to retain it on the grounds that he was in an iron lung and would soon be dead.

Moments like these, however, were but brief shafts of joyous sunlight in the grey pallor of our existence. Often our neighbours could be unkempt and rowdy. Indeed, after a few short years, the estate was to become little more than a dumping ground for released vagrants, the antisocial and the mentally infirm. In a misguided attempt at integration, the council had offered former patients jobs as handymen. This practice was abruptly terminated when some were discovered attempting to emulsion full apartments using their fingers. It was not a place to bring up a child with confidence. Strange cries could be heard through the night and there was much scuttling and muttering on the communal walkways. Once, in the small hours, I heard an unearthly rumble and rending noise and peeked out of my front door to find that two men had detached a full balcony and were removing it on a warehouse trolley. A fat woman was sitting zombie-like under a parasol, sipping a cocktail.

As she rumbled past she caught my eye and wailed out, 'Why, why?' I shut my door. I didn't have an answer.

Gash was now of school age but we dared not allow him outside to play unattended. Though the estate boasted the amenity of a playpark, this was a favoured haunt of weirdos and perverts. Indeed, sometimes the weirdos would fight running battles with the perverts to establish who controlled the kiddie park. In the end, the local paper championed a campaign to clean up the area and, like most parents, Mary and I gave a hearty cheer of relief when the franchise was finally awarded to the drug pushers. On balance, this was the least of three evils. Much less unnerving to check your child's eyes for signs of solvent abuse than to peer up his arse every night searching for anal warts.

*

Though we had made our home across the river in Possilpark, Mary and I still missed Govan. Some nights, when the wind was in the right direction, we'd scent the tangy whang from the Shieldhall sewage plant and be filled with a keen nostalgia. Though eager to return, Mary still harboured doubts. As usual, these concerned me. Though I had stood by my pledge to renounce both alcohol and crime, I had been aided by the natural barrier of the River Clyde, a broad protective arm that restrained me from the dark influences beyond its reach in the pubs and byways of my birthplace. Were we to return, could Mary trust me to behave? Could I trust myself? On the day Gash returned home from school saying that two rival teams of paedophiles had tried to sign him on an 'S' form, we decided to move on. The paedos had been insistent and enthusiastic, inviting him for trials to Blackpool, where they held a summer coaching school in the amusement arcades. Gash explained that they were eager to meet Mary and I in order

229

to put our minds at rest. From his satchel, he pulled a tiny gift of swimming trunks one of the teams had given him and showed them proudly. 'What make,' I asked, 'Speedophile?' and snatched them from him. What troubled me most was how susceptible Gash had been to their blandishments, for I knew from my own upbringing how scarce were flattery and attention in most Glasgow households and how a sudden wave of small trinkets and large compliments might sweep our son for ever from the shores of our influence. To show him he was loved, we each slapped him on the head and sent him to bed without supper.

It would not be easy to be rehoused by the authorities. The torching of flats had become such a familiar tactic that the council was now one step ahead, installing asbestos furniture and a fire hose above every mantelpiece. The worry of the situation affected Mary badly and medication was prescribed. Valium was then the wonder drug of the day for combating council estate misery. It took depressed immobile catatonics and magically transformed them into content immobile catatonics. Before Valium, Mary had been in such despair that she refused to rise from bed. Only in bed did she feel secure. After Valium she could be persuaded to take walks and go shopping and in every way returned to a normal life, except that wherever she went the mattress had to be strapped to her back. Anyone who visited a council estate in those days will recall the familiar sight of the Valium people completely normal but stunningly slow moving. Valium woman could set out to the shops for milk and by the time she returned it was Cheddar. Valium man might leave the house to place a bet and go missing. Three weeks later he'd be discovered in the lift, thin and heavily bearded. He'd been unable to get out before the doors shut. The medication placed a strain on our relationship. We argued. More than that, it placed a strain on the strain. It could take us months to finish a row. Once, in a rage, Mary threw a plate at me. I took the bus to my mother's to borrow a dustpan and was back before it hit the wall. Our sex life too was suffering. It could take a week and a half of pumping for Mary to reach orgasm. Then four days to stop moaning. Quite embarrassing when you're standing in Asda, queuing to buy mince. All things considered, it was a crazy time in which to be sane. Once, Mary ventured downstairs to the drying area to hang out towels. I went to bed for a brief nap. When I awoke, it was twilight and Gash was crying at the front door to be let in. When I peered over the balcony, I could see a dozen women below, all frozen in lethargy in the act of hanging out washing. I'd to hurry downstairs, turn Mary on her side, and carry her into the lift like a cardboard cut out.

Alarmingly, I was beginning to crack myself. Drink was starting to look good again. I'd pass an off licence and see displays of bottles lined up with the allure of Busby Berkeley chorus girls and my heart would flutter. My life was worthy but dull, like dining for ever on meat and potatoes. What fun was living without the occasional sticky pudding? Except that 'occasional' was not a permitted term in the lexicon of the recovering alcoholic. All around me, drink smiled and winked. Ads on telly, wafts from pubs, the fly quarter bottle glimpsed in a shopping bag as a purse was reached, the whole world, it seemed, was either drunk or zombied. I alone, dried-up Rab, tiptoed between the two lost worlds, dreary as parchment. Solitary, I stood on the cold peak of my drab self-respect and watched the yahooing hordes below, glorying in the shared body heat of imperfection. Young men my age were buying pints, telling jokes, eyeing sweet-smelling girls, while I perched a hundred feet above the earth, with a silent wife, a whining child and a telly blaring *Starsky and Hutch*. After prison I had been good and goodness, I now understood, was its own reward. The true reward of goodness was freedom from the risks of enjoyment. I felt old beyond my years. Too little, too young, the old scum trouble. I craved change. But from where was the miracle to appear? I had not long to wait for an answer.

*

One morning Mary stood up, yelled and, in characteristic fashion, swooned to the floor five minutes later. Alarmed, I struggled to find her pulse. No doubt it was slouched over the bean bag of a kidney, whingeing to her cerebral cortex. I ran to a phone to summon the doctor. Then, remembering I was in Possil, I ran to the doctor to summon a phone. His receptionist called an ambulance and Mary was collected then taken to the Royal for tests. I hung around the waiting room of the hospital, sweating. After a while, a nurse appeared and took me to see a female doctor.

'Your wife's condition is serious but not critical,' she told me.

'I see,' I said. 'What's she got?'

'A child, by the looks of it. She's pregnant.'

She allowed a brief pause to see if I wanted to do any 'hooray' acting or burst into tears of joy, or any of that gear, but instead I felt mildly irritated, which I could tell she found par for the course.

'One thing,' she said, 'we'll need to get her off medication, will that be difficult?'

I looked at her. 'Yes,' I said, 'we live in a high rise. It's only the medication that stops her flying out the window and making a dent in the kiddies' sandpit.'

She nodded. 'Then we'll have to see what we can do.'

Six months later we were rehoused. We'd asked for Govan and a two-room apartment had fallen vacant in

Restitution Street. When we hear a phrase like 'fallen vacant' it conjures up notions of fate clearing a magical path to facilitate youthful happiness. In this case, an old woman had opened the door to some dodgy carol singers and they'd beaten her to death with her own companion set, so if fate melts away the obstacles for some, it's not done without a measure of inconvenience to others. When we moved in there were still bits of dried brains on the grate. There were little black pellets everywhere, so we could tell the mice had been having a feast. This wasn't as bad as it might have been. If someone pegs out in the summer, they can start to liquify if they aren't found. If you're unlucky, you can be kneeling with a mop pail for days, scraping four stone of old Celia off the cushion floor with a spatula. There were rumours of a handyman in Greenock who'd pat it into blocks to sell as lard but they may have been tall tales put around by kiddies to startle social workers.

The week after we moved in I flushed the Valium down the toilet. I trusted that Mary would begin a recovery now we were back on home territory and I wanted the baby coming in to the world clean. I did this out of self-interest. Who needs a foetus around the house that's having trouble with its nerves?

Mary was still concerned that I'd slip back into my old ways. To counter my low-boredom threshold she would send me on a constant stream of small errands. Buy that, pay this, collect the other. As a tactic, it failed miserably. All it did was ensure that I was bored while on the move instead of bored sitting down. I still felt old before my time, though I kept this feeling to myself. My life was that of the discarded worker or clapped-out pensioner, hanging about, waiting to die. Sensing my ruined self-esteem, Mary did her best to make me feel valued. Occasionally, her attempts could be heavy-handed. I did not necessarily need to be applauded on coming home having bought electricity stamps.

More than once since our return I had purposely passed the Two Ways, speeding up if I saw the door swing open and darting off like a nervous fawn. One afternoon, I decided to enter. I was confident I could resist the temptation of drink, even should it be pressed upon me, and pledge my allegiance to Tizer. I had forgotten the enveloping fug of welcome in a pub that works upon the rigid spirit with the skill of some invisible masseur. I sat alone in a quiet corner, sipping my prim Tizer and perusing the Situations Vacant column of the *Evening Times*. With a fresh sprog imminent, additional income was essential. In addition to supplying this, a position might also open up fascinating doors of discovery to my enquiring nature. I started at the tolerable and worked down. This did not take long as there was nothing tolerable. Every clinical little three-line entry read to me like an epitaph. 'Bought Ledger Clerk. 9 till 6 five days. Salary T.B.A. Suddenly at home. Much missed.' Flaying the tired nag of my work ethic mercilessly, I pressed on. 'Dishwasher wanted. No Exp. Nec. 50 H.P.W. Snack lunch incl. After a short illness. Ashes to ashes, toast to toast.'

The realization hardened that I had no place in this world. Nothing for which my low social status might have qualified me afforded me the slightest interest. I considered the path of advancement. Dreary decades of grind and sacrifice while I attempted to transform myself into a pale approximation of a middle-class professional. At the end of that assembly line to emerge as another working-class arriviste, desperate to smooth his rough edges by rubbing shoulders with the better educated and bred, reclining on his deathbed with nothing to offer a new generation but his hard-won secret of how to dispose of a peach stone without your hostess reaching furtively for the scum detector. By now, I was pushing thirty. I was approaching the age beyond which fulfilment can no longer be deferred. At some point soon I would be all that I was ever going to be or, if my luck was really out, less than the nothing I was already. I folded the paper and tossed it aside.

Somewhere out there my future was forming and what it held was too potent and mysterious to be distilled down into some dead-eyed corporate elegy. I picked up my Tizer. A hand put a pint down. I looked up. A man-sized rat in a check jacket with eyes like squirming swamp life measured my reaction warily.

'Awright, Rab?' said Cotter. He left a pause, to ascertain whether I might leap up and strangle him, before sitting down. 'You still in the huff?'

I said nothing.

'Was it that letter?'

Again, I looked at him.

'It was a pure jest, Rab, and totally unforgivable, all the same you should thank me because you've not never looked back since, let's face it, fair sorted you out, when you and Mary—'

I pressed my finger against his lips, advising silence. He took this advice, though it did not suit. He fidgeted. He squirmed. He hummed tuneless bars of a self-penned nonsense song before lapsing into desolate torpor. Finally, he gave a little yap of frustration and, gambling personal injury against boredom, attempted conversation once more.

'It's a long time ago, Rab. It's all in the past, isn't it?'

'Drink your pint,' I said.

'It's not my pint,' he said, 'it's your pint. My pint's here.' He pointed out the distinction for both our benefits, mine and his, but chiefly mine.

'Word has it you've cut right back on the bevvy these days, Rab, if so I'm proud of you. Here, have a drink.'

'I've not cut it back, I've cut it out,' I said. To prove it, I took a big glug of the Tizer, spilling some down my chin. He pretended not to notice. 'I'm the happiest I've ever been,' I said, grimly.

'Me too,' said Cotter, 'I got married last year. To Ella, you remember Ella?'

An image of Robert Shaw, his body in the mouth of a mechanical shark, flashed into my mind. 'Yes,' I said, 'I remember Ella.'

'Good,' said Cotter, 'that's great. We're both happy, then.' He covered the bleakness of the moment with another fidget, then turned to me, mournfully. 'It's shite being happy, isn't it, Rab?'

I said nothing but the nerve had been tweaked. The blonde pint of lager in the middle of the table wiggled, crossed its legs and said 'Hello.'

'It's not just us, Rab, it's all our pals. Ever since they turned happy, they've been as miserable as sin.'

'Not me,' I said resolutely, 'I tell you, I'm in fucking bliss, and I'll kill any man who says I'm not.'

Cotter ignored my outburst. He pressed on. 'Andra Binnie's happy, Dodie Lang, Aiden Friel, poor Aiden's in a right state, he's on pills to battle his happiness. I'm telling you, Rab, a man pays a heavy price for his hole, regular.' He leaned forward, running anxious hands through his lank hair. 'And now you, Rab. I thought you were different. Here was a man I thought I could admire. A man with the good sense to have a death wish, to self-destruct on Planet Booze before the androids start running at him with the leather-buttoned cardies and the sponge-soled slippers.' He looked at me with sad disdain. The blonde in the glass crossed her legs once more. I picked up my Tizer and put it down again.

'Look here,' I said, 'behave yourself. We're married men now, I've another sprog due any minute. The old days have gone and it's sad and useless for us to cling on to them when there's so much out there to look forward to.'

He gave me a deserved look of incredulity. I knew I had spoken like a prick. The blonde in the glass put her fingers to her mouth and mimed throwing up. I felt like some highland vicar in Easterhouse, trying to stamp out drive-by shootings by advocating country dance.

'That's a lovely speech, Rab,' said Cotter, 'but not one I ever thought I'd hear coming from you.' He rose, lifting both pints. The blonde in the glass leapt up and took his arm. 'See you, Rab,' he said. Together they walked toward the bar. At a loss, I found myself following. I lifted the pint and drank it in two long, showy, draughts. Wiping my upper lip, I put the empty glass back down. 'See you, Jamesie,' I said, and walked from the bar.

Five dry years peeled away in a moment as the cool street air hit me. The rumble of traffic, the urgent bark of Govan voices, all seemed energized by one simple jab from Dr Carlsberg. I was pleased with myself, I had wrestled with my demon and won. Now they couldn't say that Rab Nesbitt was too scared to try a pint, he'd done it, drained his glass and walked, what a man that Rab C. Nesbitt. I was Atticus Finch in *To Kill A Mockingbird* when the redneck spits in his face, I was Will Kane in *High Noon* facing the Miller gang alone. Now I would sit back and wait for the legend to solidify. I ignored the still small voice that warned me I'd done a stupid thing. The gravelly cynicism of the Wise Hack telling me that where one pint goes others will surely follow. The taboo's been broken, he was saying, all bets are now off and it's only a matter of ticking time before normal service is resumed. No, not me, I told myself. I'm different. I've been through too much, done years in the State Pen, I know myself inside out. Around fifteen seconds had elapsed between my leaving the Two Ways and entering the newsagent's to buy Polos.

In that brief span the battle for what remained of my tawdry soul had already been won and lost.

* * *

About a month later my second son, Burney, was born in the Southern General. He was an ugly little runt with a huge head, a gummy smile and I liked him instantly. I could tell at a glance that he was going to have cheek, confidence and no brains whatsoever. He liked me too and, as soon as he discerned my looming face, proved it by having a seizure. This was not uncommon in infants, the staff nurse explained, and he would probably grow out of it. When I enquired what would happen if he didn't grow out of it, she shrugged in a 'Well, what the hell, you've got another one' sort of way and left. Under the starch and cotton the NHS is red in tooth and claw.

I was not present at the birth, having been detained on Falling Down business. After skilfully negotiating the thin end of the drinking wedge with Mary under the agreed concept of 'the occasional pint', I now strove assiduously to ensure such occasions were varied and plentiful. My drinking was not up to its old standards, however, and many doubted whether I'd ever again achieve the lofty troughs I'd scaled in my mythical past. Like a Caruso past his best I compensated in showmanship for what I now lacked in capacity. I got drunk quicker, talked louder, behaved worse. As an accident waiting to happen, I again drew a circle of admirers. When Mary queried my lack of haste in coming to first view our son, I explained that I'd been wetting the baby's head. When she enquired why this ritual had taken a full two days to complete, I replied that I'd heard he'd a bloody big head. I have no memory of making this unkind, if accurate jest, it having been reported, like many things to the habitual drunk, long after the event. Likewise the reason behind his name. My son's head was large and, in seizure, grew red, like a matchstick. As the nurses battled to douse his fiery brow, I apparently dubbed him Burney. So be it. No drunk will quarrel with legend. My son is not enamoured of his name and, from time to time, has sought to berate me for the singularity of this appellation. But as I've explained to him, it could have proved worse. A few more pints and he might have been Swan or Vesta. Or, if I'd been in a pretentious mood, he might be grappling with Phosphorous Nesbitt.

Those were the best of times. I was not yet full gone with the sauce and enjoyed pushing Burney in the same rickety pram we'd used for Gash, round the quaint drinking dens and hovels of the Govan village. He developed a taste for stout at a young age and his feeding bottle held a regular blend of Mackeson and milk. I loved to show him off and would teach him tricks. By a year he could mouth 'fuck off' to the intrusive heads of cooing pensioners and by eighteen months would proceed, unaided, to the bar for fags. He mimicked the behaviour of pub men and would scorn tissues, preferring to unblock his nose in the traditional male manner by pressing forefinger to nostril and honking. This tickled me but vexed Mary, since it often meant an ugly mess on the dinner table as he could not be persuaded to save it for the street. He could also stagger drunk to order and for a while, when Fester Rofe took a stroke, let one side of his face hang at half mast as a tribute. He was precocious and a bright future was predicted. In a Govan sense, naturally.

Burney pulsed with the full glow of life and I'd sooner see him hurtle, meteor-like, in a blaze toward oblivion than hang around with the docile herd for the slow decline into memory loss, daytime telly and pished pants.

This perception was both confirmed and confounded for me by the experience of my mother. Showing nimble footwork, she had leapt before the swinging cleaver of the Thatcher government had lopped off the choicest cuts of the council housing stock for private sale. Clambering to her feet, she had found herself in sheltered housing. For the first time in her life, she now had piped hot water and an indoor toilet and bathroom. In addition, she enjoyed the protective vigilance of the council Social Services Department. At first, this had proved disconcerting and she had suffered the occasional awkward encounter with the intercom system. Pulling the wrong chain in the toilet would result in a gruff male voice enquiring 'Are you all right?' This would send the floral drawers hurtling chin high in micro-moments. (I knew they were floral as many times, down the decades, I'd seen them toasting dry on the living-room fireguard.) She was now, officially, elderly, and adopted the role with relish. Mother took to Gash, less so to Burney. Gash was a model Scottish child, wretched, fearful and silent. In Scotland, children are guilty until proven innocent. Devoid of spirit, Gash had atoned for the crime of being young. Burney was less a child to Mother than a small pugnacious beast. Once, when we visited, Gash was given a chocolate bar and Burney a small undercooked chop. Oblivious to the subtleties of insult, he had lain on his back and attacked it with a fine masticating glee. 'I see he takes after his father,' Mother had observed. 'How can you tell,' I'd replied, 'we never saw a chop outside school dinners.' One little jab deserves another. Fragmented, as we were, by private griefs and demons, we had long ceased to be a close family. Over stewed tea and Bourbons one wet afternoon, I'd enquired, casually, about Rena. I'd expected to hear that she was buying a carpet or contemplating a change of scullery wallpaper, instead I was informed that she had emigrated to Canada.

'Emigrated?'

'Emigrated.'

'To Canada?'

'To Canada. Three weeks past. Her and Shuch.'

'I don't get it. Why didn't she tell me?'

Mother looked at me like I was wearing a joker's cap and bells. 'You know fine well why,' she said, 'Rena can't stand you.' As a leavening afterthought she added, 'It's nothing personal.' She raised the volume on the television as a signal that I should go. Having learned, painfully, to live alone, she now disliked disruptions to the routine of her days.

*

One by one, the props of my old life had disappeared. My brother Gash was now the only touchstone that linked the common heart of the family past to its brittle and divided present. And he was still a Tweedledum. Assailed one afternoon by nostalgic thoughts of lineage, I took my two sons, his two nephews, to meet him in the institution. I sat in the canteen with the boys while Gash made ready his appearance. Dozy inmates bumped to and fro, occasionally extricated from folds of curtains and offices marked 'Private' by gliding nurses. The atmosphere of induced calm was punctured periodically by an anguished howl or extraneous moan that was quickly and expertly suppressed. It was like being back in Consumption Cabinet. Nervous of the effect on my sons, I asked for their impressions. They looked at each other.

Burney voiced the consensus opinion. 'It reminds us of Granny's house,' he said. Moments later, Gash turned pale.

'What's the matter, son?'

He indicated a wraithlike form, attempting to weave its way toward us between the tables. My brother was wearing a two-piece lounge suit of doubtful cleanliness and of an age that could only be deduced by carbon-dating. From the sleeves and legs were visible full frank lengths of striped

241

pyjama. A kipper tie lent the ensemble an air of piquant ludicrousness. There appeared to be some dispute over the ownership of the pyjamas and a small round man in a nightshirt was tugging at the exposed trouser cord and yelling for the police. Some adept manhandling silenced him and he was borne by strong arms through swing doors, away to who knew what. My brother stood, beaming. I invited him to sit down and introduced him to my children. He removed a hat that did not exist, and said, 'Hello.' They looked at him like he was a rather menacing comic turn hired for their entertainment.

As usual, Burney was the first to speak. 'What the fuck is that?' he said.

Exercising keen restraint, I assumed a convivial smile. 'That's your Uncle Gash,' I told them, 'he lives here. Have you nothing to say to your own uncle?'

Silence. My elder son tugged furtively at my sleeve. 'What is it, Gash?'

'Da,' he murmured, 'can I change my name?'

It was not an auspicious introduction.

After tea and medication, we walked with Gash around the blossoming spring gardens. Apart from his invisible chapeau and distinctive dress sense, there was little about him that seemed much different from the average torn and mangled psyches I daily met around me. I pressed him gently on his memories of the past. Did he still remember school? Oh yes, he did, he'd been very happy there. On one memorable day he'd received three gold stars in his exercise books and glimpsed Miss Rimmer's knickers as she'd risen to clean the board. I was slightly disturbed by this revelation. Gentle eccentrics or not, one did not like to think of the Tweedledums running about indiscriminately poking each other. Standard-issue existential bleakness I could accommodate, a closed universe of zombied retards begetting wretched monsters of the id just outside Paisley I could not. He liked the institution, though after twenty-odd years, yes, it could get a bit samey. Yes, of course he remembered Mother and Freak and Rena and say hello to them except Freak, who'd gone to live with the angels in Tradeston. I probed a little more. 'And what about Father?' When he didn't answer, I thought he hadn't heard, and asked again. His face reddened. He stopped dead in his tracks, turned, and galloped back up the path toward the sanctuary of the tea bar.

'What's the matter with him?' laid Gash.

'Maybe his hat blew off,' said Burney, and they both sniggered.

Before we left, I wrote our address on a betting slip and gave it to Gash. 'One day you'll come and visit us,' I said. I was wrong in this. Gash came on many days to visit us, always unannounced and always without the blessing of the institution, having wandered from their keep. A simple ritual evolved. He would take tea with us, watch cartoons on television, admire the view from the kitchen window – 'Full middens are exciting' – then we'd telephone to let his carers know of his whereabouts. Once or twice he was permitted to stay the night, though this was not encouraged, on either side, as he had a propensity to patrol neglected washing lines, looking for pyjamas.

*

Despite my own blustering protestations to the contrary, I knew I was returning to my former ways. My renewed energy for drink demanded that additional sources of income be found and utilized. Cotter was again my accomplice, having urgent needs of his own. Medical tests had revealed that he and Ella would remain childless and he now used this information as a tragic backcloth before which a squalid procession of infidelities were acted out. 'It's awright for you, Rab, you know the joy of fatherhood.

I have to console myself with meaningless rampant sex.' These consolations involved trysts that required the usual trimmings of seduction, consequently his need for quick cash was almost as desperate as my own.

We considered a return to the ice-cream van racket but dismissed this on grounds of self-esteem: how humiliating to be convicted at thirty of the same crime one had committed at sixteen. The mortifying memory of 'And a packet of Munchies . . .' still had me punching the pillow some nights and I was not keen to invite fresh slights on my already dented reputation. The nation was now in deep recession, or, as the government termed it, full recovery. Even detached observers like myself and Cotter could not help noticing the droves of unemployed piling up in the streets, as other rubbish had done some years earlier during the binmen's strike. The printing of money was strictly controlled but the flutter of bills remained ever constant, so enterprising middlemen had stepped into Govan to assist with the equating of supply to demand.

Moneylending was one of the few traditional Glasgow industries that had never succumbed to decline. A lean, fit and adaptable workforce ensured that the raw material of the trade, the desperate punter, was efficiently primed, squeezed, threatened and, if necessary, harvested, to achieve maximum yield for the investor. Moneylenders were vocational employees who worked gruelling hours to deliver a high level of service to their victims. They exemplified the entrepreneurial spirit of the Thatcher era and many a government minister cast a wistful eye in their direction. If only more of the nation's businesses were to model themselves on the moneylending industry, they reasoned, Britain might one day be another Palermo. The operatives themselves were polite, well-groomed psychotics with an instilled appreciation for the value of image. Eschewing the crude class symbolism of Saatchi and

Saatchi, many had turned for instruction to American marketing gurus like Ford Coppola and Scorsese, finding inspiration in their early training films, *Godfather* and *Mean Streets*.

Cotter and I longed to join their ranks. As lifelong socialists, we were used to despising our fellow men and were confident we could exploit them with equanimity. Using our sales contacts within the crime business, we sought an interview with the industry's Mr Big. He was, we were informed, at present holidaying in the Seychelles and we were referred instead to his deputy, Mr Medium. On the day of our interview, Mr Medium was taken ill with an unexpected bullet wound and we were passed down to Mr Small. Inevitably, Mr Small, burdened by the added workloads of his absent superiors, proved too busy to see us and we were thrown down to the most menial link in the chain of command, His Worship, the Lord Provost of Glasgow. Though his Worship was unable to speak with us personally, we were informed that vacancies did exist and about a month later we were interviewed in the civic splendour of the City Chambers for the desirable positions of Finance Recovery Agents, Govan Division.

We struck incongruous figures as we queued in the huge marbled anteroom, the light-kissed droplets of the mighty chandeliers dappling our doughy faces and striping our fresh-scrubbed trainers. Feet tapped, compulsively. Overbitten nails nagged at the quick. Familiar faces drew sheepish smiles. Bimbo, Tojo, in rebuilt aluminium nose. Decent thugs, with mullet haircuts, fiddling with wedding rings on thickening fingers, they now threw themselves with desperation at the speeding Boxster of the future. Names were called. Outwardly, we wished each other luck, privately, we wished each other dead. Alphabetical, Cotter first. He was in and out in five minutes and from his perky grin, I knew he'd been rejected. We sat apart, each man fixing his eyes before his feet. Time for post-mortems later, after we'd rewritten, privately, the details of our own humiliation more or less to our satisfaction. 'Nesbitt, R. C.' I rose. 'Good luck,' said Cotter. I nodded and entered.

Jeez, a bigger room, huge, with the kind of tiled floor that will have future archaeologists marvelling over the exquisiteness of our civilization. 'Mr Nesbitt?' I looked about. Always follow the last echo. I stubbed out my Superking and trekked toward a refectory table on the far horizon where small figures sat, fiddling with spring water and pens.

'Sit down, please.' I sat down. All around the room the pigmented images of the great and good glowered down at me. Tobacco Barons, Knights of Industry, and wee fat guys in waistcoats who just fancied being painted. The Senior Officer in Charge of Recruitment and Related Forward Planning introduced himself. 'Hello,' he said, 'I'm the Senior Officer in Charge of Recruitment and Related Forward Planning.' He had no need to say this. I'd know that forehead anywhere.

'Hello, Stig,' I said, thereby terminating my interview. Allegations of croneyism were rife in the council. In order to root out the invidious practice and reassure the public, the executive had introduced a rigorous demand whereby all friends, relatives and acquaintances of the council hierarchy must pretend not to know each other prior to taking up their new positions. I had flouted this scrupulous safeguard and now must pay the price.

A man behind a desk sign that read ASSISTANT DIRECTOR OF SOCIAL SERVICES turned to Stig. 'Do you know this man?' he asked, severely. Without his feather cut and parka, I had difficulty recognizing the former Leader Off of the Fleet. Stig nodded and turned to me.

'Cheerio,' said the Senior Officer in Charge of Recruitment and Related Forward Planning.

Over pints in the Horseshoe we recounted our tales of rejection.

'My CV looked brilliant,' complained Cotter. 'Three convictions for theft and one for affray and still they turned me down.'

'What did they tell you?'

'They said they'd been swamped by applications so they were introducing more rigorous qualification requirements. The minimum was four convictions, one of which must be assault. Two serious assaults could count as one manslaughter.'

'Look,' I said, 'trust me on this. The only qualification requirement in there was that you're a pal of Stig's. Did you not notice the sleekit smiles on them bams Bimbo and Tojo?'

'Is that him with the nose?'

'Tojo hasn't got a nose.'

'That's what I mean. So you're saying it was a stitch-up?'

'From top to toe, in fine embroidery, yes.'

Bimbo and Tojo entered, looking pleased with themselves. When they saw us, they sidled round the mahogany hoof of the bar and huddled in a far fetlock. I was angry and wanted revenge. When I said as much to Cotter, he demurred.

'It's no use, Rab, I've renounced violence on principle, unless I'm absolutely sure I can win, and let's face it, them two are still big lumps of boys, lardy maybe, but game.'

'I wasn't thinking of a square go,' I said.

'No? What, then?'

We finished our pints and caught the Inner Circle back to Govan. Mary knew I'd been heading for some sort of interview as I'd put a clean Elastoplast on a Falling Down injury and she pestered me for information. Did I get the job? No, I didn't get the job.

'Never mind,' she consoled, 'it sounded rubbish anyway.'

'But you don't even know what it was.' I regretted the edge in my tone. It wasn't uninterest, she'd just been going through the wifely motions of letting me down gently. I watched her as she struggled to heave a laden washing basket onto the sideboard prior to ironing. Poor loyal beast, if only there was something I could do to lessen her burden. I'd do anything, provided it could be achieved from a sitting position while reading the paper. What if I were to shoot her to put her out of her misery? Never, what a terrible thought. Well, maybe, but wait till she does the ironing first.

'Rab, do me a favour and fill the steam iron for me. And don't bother saving the bits of limescale for the boys, they know it's not a jigsaw.'

'What am I, a pack mule?'

For the young Govan bear, domestic life is a honey barrel that in the early days is full to the brim and irresistible. As the years roll by, the barrel empties and however much he flicks and rolls his tongue around the rim, all he'll find thereafter is the occasional splinter and a taunting hint of sweetness that reminds him of what used to be. Many bears grow confused and take to their armchairs to brood over their loss in silence. It is at this point that the bear begins to die. For the price of all nostalgia is decay. As a happily married bear, which is to say one bound to his mate by fear and habit, I determined to forestall the process of decay as long as possible. Money would help. Given money, that poor drudge by the laundry basket would be a confident, alluring woman. She'd develop tastes and interests, become outgoing, perhaps acquire an education, start a career. Without it, she remains a mystery to herself, the inner bloom stillborn in the thin soil of poverty. Piteous wretch.

'Mary, darling?'

'What?'

'What would you do if you came into money?'

'Dump you.'

Bitter bitch, let her rot. A little earning is a dangerous thing.

*

The plan was simple. 'Run it past me again,' said Cotter. We were in the lounge of the Two Ways. It was worth the extra two pence on our pints to be free of the prying eyes of the bar.

'All right. We follow them while they make the collections. After the last one, we hit them with clubs and run away with the money.'

'And that's the plan?'

'What's wrong with it?'

'Nothing. It just seems a bit thin on cunning to me. I mean it's not exactly a tactical feast, is it? Hit them with sticks and run away. It's a bit route one, no midfield play, nor nothing.'

'It's as complicated as it needs to be. Are you bottling out?'

'They're big lads, Rab. Big, lardy boys.'

'We'll have surprise on our side. And baseball bats.'

'Baseball bats? Have you seen the price of baseball bats? If we could afford baseball bats we wouldn't need to go out robbing.'

'Table legs, then, with a few screws driven in for studs. Think of the money, man. What'll you do with the money?'

'Buy a baseball bat, likely, for when they get out of hospital.'

'We'll be wearing masks, man. They won't know it's us. We're talking a good few hundred here, maybe a grand apiece, who knows. Think of the fly nights out you could buy with that.'

He thought. His face paled as the blood rushed to his dick. I knew he was in. He took a sip of beer to wet his nervous lips.

'What about you, Rab? What'll you do with your end?'

I shook my head and shrugged. 'Don't know yet.' But I did know, I just didn't want to tell him. I was going to take a holiday, that's what. Mary and I had never been away, not since Millport, all those years ago, before kids and jail and drink and Provident lines. I wanted us to blossom. I wanted us both to blossom. The sun on us would make us blossom. The sea would wash us clean of soot and grime. We'd emerge, fresh and glinting, looking like new welds after the slag's been chipped away. We'd be redeemed. It would be paradise. But first, all I had to do was kill a couple of guys.

CHAPTER EIGHT

THE FINANCE RECOVERY AGENTS (Govan Division) commenced their duties with a couple of pints in the Harmony Bar before moving on to Whelan's. Here they had one more apiece, accompanied by crisps, and concluded their visit with a few quick tugs at the fruit machine. Outside, they paused in a quiet close to urinate, or possibly to make love with each other, Cotter being unable, regrettably, to ascertain which from his vantage point in the doorway of a Home Bakery across the street. Suitably relieved, they then headed for the cluster of tenemented streets that clung, barnacle-like, to the becalmed hulk of what used to be Fairfield's Shipyard.

Operating singly to allay suspicion, we had tracked them relentlessly from point to point in the early part of their rounds. Unfortunately, owing to faulty telepathy, we had lost track of each other on several occasions during our surveillance and it was only through luck that I bumped into Cotter on the dark corner of Shaw and Rosneath Street.

'Where's your chib, Jamesie?'

'Down my trousers. I got fed up kidding on it was a walking stick. I was stood at traffic lights earlier and two Life Boys helped me across the street.'

To ease the tension, I eyed the impressive bump under his jeans. 'It pays to advertise,' I said. He wouldn't be mollified.

'Get a grip,' he said, 'it's down the outside, any bird seeing that'll assume I've got a colostomy bag.'

The Recovery Agents emerged from a closemouth across Govan Road. Cotter was alarmed to see Bimbo adjust the lapel and shoulder of his jacket.

'Did you see that? Maybe he's packing a shooter.'

'Packing a shooter? Who the hell are you suddenly, Jack the Hat McVitie?'

'What d'you mean?'

'You said a shooter.'

'Rubbish, I said gun. Clean your manky ears out.'

'Anyway, that's not a shooter, Hat, more likely a big fat wallet full of scores.'

'You what? Scores?'

'Sure, what's up with scores?'

'Nothing, if you're Reggie Kray. Scores. Ooooh, get you.'

I flushed. 'Scores is legitimate petty criminal parlance,' I protested. 'Listen, I don't want to pull rank nor nothing but I've been in jug, remember? And I don't mean wee boys' jug, Remand Home, like you. I've done my time in big man's jug, with top murderers and that.'

'OK, I'm impressed, you got caught. I'm not going to argue. But to my mind even jug is a bit suspect.'

'Look, are we going to discuss slang linguistics here, or are we going to chib these two bastards?'

'Chib is good slang, chib I'm comfortable with. Let's stick to solid, honest to goodness, Queen's English slang, OK?'

'OK.'

They turned into a close in Elder Street. The close light was broken and the entrance was a thick black hole. This was our chance. We could wait in the dunny and rush them when they came back down the stairs. There was a good chance they wouldn't recognize us in the dark. My hand tightened round the taped grip of my table leg. 'This is it, Jamesie,' I said, 'best chance we'll get. You ready?'

'Wait,' he said.

I gave him a long minute while he extricated his table leg from a tangle with his underpants. 'OK,' he said at last, 'ready.'

And we crossed the silent street.

Crouching in the dark, we listened for doors and the cascading echo of voices on the stairs. 'Which flat?' said Cotter.

In the dark, no one can hear you scream. 'How the fuck should I know?' I said. 'If my calculations are correct, the flat they'll come back out of is the flat they've just been in, OK?'

'OK, OK.'

More minutes went by. Realizing we didn't need to crouch, since it was dark anyway and no one could see us, we laid our chibs down gently, stood up and stretched our aching legs. Cotter lit a cigarette. 'Put that out,' I told him, 'if they pong fag smoke in the close, they'll tipple.' He put it out, grumbling. More time passed and doubt set in. Maybe they weren't coming out. Maybe it wasn't a collect, maybe they both lived here and they'd packed up for the night. We're stuck in the close like a couple of numpties, they're upstairs munching toast in the bath. 'Let's give it five more minutes,' I said, 'then if we're—'

Cotter shushed me and clamped a carelessly aimed hand over my eyes.

'What the fuck are you—'

'Shush, Rab, listen.'

From the landing above sound voices. Crouching by the stairs, we listen intently. Female. A jingle of glass then they recede. A door slams shut. Silence. Milk bottles. False alarm. Our tense bodies slacken and mentally we're preparing to abort. A pint, chips and home in time for *The Sweeney*. Then it happens. White light floods the landing. We dither, eyeing each other, terrified, like an amateur double act thrown unprepared onto a stage. At our backs, the gruff yap of Govan Voices. It's them, in the doorway of the flat behind us. It's been a ground-floor collect, not an upstairs collect, and we've a single second left of surprise before they clock us and the fists and the blades start flying. An orgasm of fear as I fumble for my chib on the gloomy floor. I hear a voice say, 'What the fuck—' then the tug of a hand at my shoulder. The table leg is in my hand and I turn and hit a head. I'm holding the chib wrong way up and I feel a sharp stab in my fingers as heads of nails cut into me. I thrash out again and again, a thing possessed, and though I'm the one inflicting hurt it feels as though I'm fighting for my life. I'm howling with panic and I daren't stop hitting. One is staggering about and has his head tilted back like he's holding in an eye and the other is on his knees. They're both heading for the street. I don't want them out in the open where we can all be seen and I keep hitting and kicking, trying to slow them up. The one with the tilted head evades my grasp and runs, moaning and shouting out into the street. When he hits the light I see it's Tojo. Good. It's Bimbo who's got the wallet. To get it, I'm going to have to put my hand inside his jacket. I'm worried about doing this, so I give him another couple of hard batters to the head, trying to knock him out, but the bastard's got a napper like the Elgin Marbles. I'm crabbing alongside him shouting as he crawls and I'm desperate. Finally a brainwave strikes me and I ask him for the money. 'Give me the money, you bastard,' I tell him, 'hand it over or I'll fucking well kill you.' This is sheer bravado as I've all but knackered myself trying to knock him out.

'Fuck off,' he says and keeps crawling. He's starting to piss me off now and I summon up enough strength to give him a couple of dunts that would fell a sensible horse. When he starts to whimper, I know these have done the trick and he groans and mutters something. His voice is gargly with spit or blood and I can't quite catch his drift until he reaches into his inside pocket. I jump behind and give him a warning prod with the table leg, just in case he is reaching for a shooter, or gun, according to semantic taste, but he stops crawling and holds out the wallet, waving it limply, like a white flag. 'Take it,' he gasps, 'here take it.' I take it. 'I was out cold, right, you took it when I was out the game, OK?'

'When you were out the game,' I tell him, 'no problem.' What do I care?

'I know your voice, you prick, who are you?' He makes to look round.

'Gary Sobers,' I tell him and hit a sweet four off the back of his neck. 'Keep your head down till I'm away.'

'I know who you are.'

I sent the table leg rattling down the back of the close and pocketed the wallet.

Then I ran. I ran up Govan Road as far as the dry dock to work off adrenaline, then turned and walked back down the other side of the street. As I walked, I pulled out the wallet, watchfully, and inspected it. In the doorway of the TSB, half lit and half hidden by a yellow sodium street lamp, I counted a thick wad of limp, grubby notes. Each one seemed lined with the worry of its debtor but I shut out all guilt, convincing myself I was stealing from wealthy career crooks and not skint civilians. Five, ten, fifteen, twenty. Would the crooks cover their loss by forcing the civvies to pay again? Who cares, there are no friends in business. Forty, sixty, eighty, a hundred. The count finished just shy of six hundred. Not a great haul, considering the risks, during and, undoubtedly, after. I ditched the wallet in a litter bin and stuffed the folded wad into my trouser pocket. Then I went looking for Cotter.

In the heightened terror of the fight I hadn't noticed he

was missing, but as I replayed in my mind such fragmented images of the action as I could recall, his presence remained noticeable by its absence. Though I had emerged, apart from some ragging of the fingers, unscathed, it seemed wearily inevitable to me that the only real injury I sustain should be a metaphorical stab in the back from my partner. From a phone box at Govan Cross, I rang his house. He answered immediately. 'Oh, it's yourself, Rab.'

'Bloody right it's me, what the hell happened to you?'

'To me? Oh. I'm sorry I couldn't make the pub, Rab, I've been in bed all night with flu.' To verify this fiction, he gave an unconvincing sneeze.

I was puzzled. 'What's up? Is Ella there? Where did you go after the fight?'

'Fight? You mean there's been a fracas?'

For an unreal moment, I found myself wondering if I was suffering from amnesia or concussion, even checking the bottoms of my trousers to see if pyjamas protruded. Ella spoke down the phone.

'That's right, Jamesie's been at home all night. Just the three of us, me, him and the flu. He's been here with me, watching television, haven't you, Jamesie?'

'Yes, at six thirty I watched the *Regional News*, followed at seven by *This is Your Life* – the subject was a plucky lifeboat captain from Stromness. At seven thirty I watched *Coronation Street*, at eight—'

'I get the picture, Cotter,' I said, 'don't let me interrupt your viewing. If you can struggle from your sick bed long enough, you'll just catch *Late Call*. I think you'll like tonight's text, it's about Judas, your great-grandfather.'

I put the phone down. I was on my own now and scared. The words of the creeping Bimbo flashed into my mind. 'I know who you are, you bastard, who are you?' Oh fuck. I needed to urinate, badly. Hurrying into a shadowed group of shops by Water Row, I took out my cock and pissed like a rhino. I needed a plan. A respite. Somewhere to slink off to quietly till things calmed down. My voice would be running through Bimbo's head, on a loop, like a Laurie Anderson record, and I didn't want to be around if he put a name to it. On the other hand, if I could only take myself away till memory faded, drunken nights intervened, new skirmishes erupted to seize the focus, maybe then I'd be safe. I knew it was a large economy-sized maybe. In Govan terms, I was the guy who'd stiffed the mob. A childish glee gripped the pit of my stomach. The man who'd stiffed the mob was pissing down the front of his jeans. I cursed and corrected my aim, instinctively glancing about to ensure I hadn't been clocked. Where was I anyway? Coloured cards inside the window gave me the answer. *Spain. Half Board. Fourteen nights. Avail. Immed.* Maybe I couldn't piss straight but I knew a good deal when I saw one. I looked up and down Govan Road. The silence seemed as fragile as a soap bubble and if I took a step, I feared I'd pop it, bringing angry feet and slashing knives thudding into me. Breath so shallow it would not have ruffled a duvet feather, nerves stretched so tight they could be crossed on a unicycle, I moved, on the balls of silent feet, down the eggshell of the street, toward home.

*　　*　　*

'Can I offer you a complimentary drink from the bar, sir?' The air hostess stood, beaming mechanically, waiting for an answer. Mary and I stared back at her, blankly. Being scum, our brains were unable readily to assimilate the concept of free drink and there was an inevitable hiatus while thirty-five years of social conditioning strove to articulate an appropriate response. The stewardess repeated the question.

'Aye, I know,' I said, 'I heard you the first time. I just want to know, what's the catch.'

'There's no catch,' she smiled. 'You're allowed a free drink of your choice from the bar. And look, peanuts too.'

She put the nuts down. Burney seized the packet, tore it open and spat into it to deter Gash. Mary, unconvinced, sought conclusive reassurance. 'And we don't need to wash the windows, nor fly the plane nor nothing in return?'

The stewardess shook her head. 'We have people to do those things for us.'

I put my hand over Mary's mouth. I could see we were turning into an anecdote for the stewardess's collection.

'In that case spare me the compliments, hen,' I said, 'you can insult me with a whisky if you like, so long as it's a freebie.' She dished up some miniatures, with Coke for the boys, and we all cheered hysterically, startling the more seasoned travellers around us. Never having flown before we were elated and intrigued by the novelty of the experience. It was not until two young children at our backs summoned the chief steward to complain about our behaviour that Mary and I realized the display of our excitement might have become excessive. Sheepishly, my wife and I promised to stop breaking toffee by ramming it with the head rest and to refrain from running up and down the aisle with sick bags on our heads, shouting, 'We're going to crash in the mountains, we need babies who'll fit a frying pan.' On a promise of good behaviour we were given more miniatures and retook our seats, duly chastened.

Our frenzy may have been unpardonable but it was also, in the circumstances, understandable. It was only three days since I'd first sprung news of the holiday to Mary. She'd been pleasantly surprised, and once I'd placed her head between her knees and given her a glass of water she'd expressed a more detailed interest. I told her, predictably, I'd won the money on the horses and, predictably, she hadn't believed me. Nevertheless, the lure of sun-drenched foreign travel was strong and she'd allowed her doubts to be overcome sufficiently to offer her tacit approval. The unspoken quid pro quo was that so long as I attended to the mosaic-like arrangements for our trip she would kindly permit her arse to board the plane, provided it be clearly understood that her implicit moral reservations remain intact and inviolate, to be opened, like a life jacket, in case of emergency. Fearful of what the ticking clock might bring, I'd made the arrangements at sprinting speed. I'd been on the doorstep as the travel agent fumbled for his keys and had the flights confirmed and the hotel booked before he'd had time to remove his anorak. Never having been abroad before, I asked him if there was anything else I'd need. He shrugged and smiled. 'Apart from passports and pesetas, no.' I looked at him like he'd discovered the source of the Nile. It hadn't quite dawned on me that abroad meant 'not Britain' and that, selfishly, foreigners preferred their own currency and might even refuse admission entirely on failure to produce a valid document. I stood up. I bought time while I lingered by folding my receipt over and over till it was a pulp microbe that could only be reopened with watchmaker's tools.

'Was there something else?' asked the travel agent.

'I was just wondering where would I find pesetas?'

'At the bank.'

'Right. And I was just wondering, do you sell passports?'

He didn't bat an eyelid. In Govan, travel agents prefer to keep an equable temperament. This is because it's difficult to consult an Apple Mac with your head in a wastepaper basket. It took me three trips to the Passport Office before we were issued with the white emergency cards. The first time, I forgot the photographs, the second

I forgot our marriage licence and the third, I forgot my own name after being tempted by a session in McConnell's. The sight of a clock, any clock, made me panic. For the three days before departure, I lived in fear of a knock at the door. I didn't even tell the boys where they were going, for fear of word leaking out. Instead, I hijacked them from class on the day of the flight, explaining to their teachers that my Spanish father, Roberto, had been killed while dozing on a lilo in Fuengirola, after being struck by a joyrider on a pedalo. This fiction was more or less believed by the teachers, though for some years afterwards I felt obliged to fly into a flamenco routine and shout, 'Riva, riva,' if I bumped into either of them in Tesco's.

Before flying out, at the last minute, I phoned Cotter from the airport. Though I very much wanted to shut the robbery from my mind, I knew there might well be repercussions and, on balance, it was better to be forewarned of developments than to recline, in dangerous ignorance, on a Spanish beach. No, he hadn't heard anything. Though why should he, he reminded me, since he didn't know anything about any robbery anyway. Nevertheless, he assured me that if he did hear anything about the robbery to which I referred, again about which he knew nothing, he would certainly telephone my hotel to update me on the information. About the robbery. About which he knew nothing. Yes, his flu was on the mend, thanks very much for asking, you fat sarcastic bastard.

I'd put the phone down with a sense of reprieve which, with the help of several transfusions from Dr Tennent in the bar, I'd attempted to upgrade into relief. Despite our manic antics on the plane, my mood of foreboding had refused to lift, and after our ticking off from the steward I settled into a sombre silence for the remainder of the flight. Sensing my unease, Mary had attempted to cajole me into confession. This I'd stubbornly resisted and had gradually transformed her earnest probings into a snoring torpor, occasionally punctuated by song, thanks to a steady application of purchased miniatures. On landing, I kissed the tarmac and Mary kissed the steward, using tongue, for which invasive impropriety she was escorted, arms up the back, down the gangway, by two demure stewardesses who continued to smile, pleasantly. Gash and Burney walked ahead, faces crimson, while I joshed loudly over the dangers of taking too much humiliation on the first day. Nothing had readied me for the sudden wall of heat we walked into on leaving the plane. Owing to the hurried nature of our holiday arrangements, we had arrived in Spain sartorially underprepared. Sweat formed instantly on my brow and trickled down my flanks. It had been a regular June day in Glasgow, and we'd dressed accordingly. Much more of this and we'd be forced to remove our duffel coats.

*

The sun interrogated my Govan skin like a means test, flushing out hidden deposits of moles and freckles, scorching my neck like a sheriff's breath and flaying any areas of trusting unclad flesh. Though I loved the sun like a long-lost father, I could not win his approval and skulked in the shade while my family frolicked in the well-nigh scuderoony. The boys tanned in one coat, like Dulux, while my wife's pink meat, on a beach towel, grilled swiftly golden brown. For the first two days I was intimidated by the strange sounds that issued from local mouths and could not be persuaded to enter any shop. On the third day, my shyness was superseded by a wave of paranoia, and through the universal language of grunting and pointing I successfully purchased an elderly *Daily Record* from a stall vendor. Leafing through the pages hungrily, I searched out the usual tales of assault and vengeance. Finding none pertaining to myself, I resolved to discard all anxiety and embrace my new environs.

To ease this transformation of attitude, I partook of drink and made my first exploratory sortie round the town using my traditional conveyance of knees and palms. Prodded tersely in the ribs by an agitated policeman, I sat on the promenade wall and, reclining into a nonexistent head rest, toppled sedately many feet below to land with a substantial dunk on thankfully soft sand. Here I lay until the Med lapped at my visage like a salty dog. Arriving rumpled and gasping at our hotel, I was surprised to find Mary tossing our suitcase into the hold of an airport bus. I staggered up, issuing pleas and begging her not to go. A crashing of my mental gears followed when she pointed out, icily, that it was my clothes that were in the suitcase, not hers, and hadn't I better not keep the bus driver waiting? Hasty negotiations ensued during which I promised to be less selfish. If I chose to drink myself into a stupor and fall unconscious onto the beach, then in future I might have the good manners to invite my wife to share the pleasure, after all it was her holiday too. Nerves shredded by drink, I broke down into fortunate tears and the combination of those together with a generous gratuity to the driver ensured that our suitcase was surgically removed from the dark underbelly of the bus and restored, with myself, to the privileged sanctuary of our hotel bedroom.

Once there, I stripped and stood under the soothing shower head, exhausted and dreaming of sleep. My eyes fluttered open when I thought I heard the door creak but seeing nothing save the steamed-up perspex of the shower wall, I resumed my waking sleep. A moment later, my eyes blinked wide. Looking down, I saw the damp mass of Mary's hair by my groin. I gasped, as anyone might, but as much with the delight of shock as through the shock of delight. From that moment on we fucked like Lord Stiffy and Her Ladyship, the Empress Vagina.

We dined on the finest of fare, plain chips by day, crinkle cut for evening elegance. Once, for affectation, we bought a pomegranate, so we might flirt with the exotic lifestyles of social class AB Vitamin C one. The boys roamed the beach for hours, hunting for girls, each gamely determined not to return home with his hard-on. Mary and I, fired by the spirit of adventure, took the organized coach trips to bay and market, proud as frontiersmen when we'd step out at a landmark, yet secretly reassured to be herded and bunched by the tall student from Crewe, who wore his ID like a sheriff's badge and could cut the alien tongue of the swarthy natives. This inner blossoming sought outward sign. We visited an ancient church near Mijas and so moved were we by its peace and quiet dignity that we very nearly contributed to the donation box by the exit. In the end, we crossed the street to a small mall where we bought Viva España T-shirts and a naughty plastic monk. It was our way of putting something back.

I was becoming a different person. Gone was my Glasgow suspicion and defensiveness. Strangers were relaxed and friendly and I found myself responding in kind. People here wished you 'Buenos días,' especially in the daytime, I noticed. If someone in Govan wished you 'Good morning' you'd steer them into a dunny and pummel them to fuck for taking the piss. One day, gazing out at the sea, I was suddenly filled by the beauty of the universe, excluding, of course, Paisley. I became aware of why men paint, or write, or carve statues exalting humankind and its noblest aspirations. It's because they don't want to drive taxis. All around me I saw the mystery of form, the fingerprint of God the housebreaker. To gaze upon his bounty is to be filled with the joy of stolen goods. The artist is a forger, aping God's style and calling it his own. Elated by this piercing insight, I too felt a despairing need to leave my mark on this world. I thought about painting a Picasso, then realized he'd probably beaten me to it. Instead, I crossed the street to Juan's Menswear Shop and paced up and down outside in anguish. Finally, I went in and bought the white leather slip-ons with the snazzy gold chain I'd had my eye on since we'd first arrived.

One night, as we enjoyed an intimate supper in Ron's, an out-of-the-way little disco and karaoke pub we'd discovered, I told Mary I loved her. I surprised myself with the suddenness of this revelation, springing recklessly out, as it had, after a mere fifteen years of marriage. I looked at Mary for a reaction. She said nothing and continued gnawing her frankfurter. Feeling insecure, I repeated my declaration. 'Haw, you deaf bitch,' I said, 'I'm slinging you the L-word here.'

She put her fork down. 'I heard you the first time,' she said.

'Then why didn't you answer?'

She started to cry.

Now I grew agitated. 'What's up?' I said. She had a bruise on her upper arm from a wasp bite and I didn't want our fellow diners getting the idea I'd hooked her one. 'Mary, cut it out, will you?'

She wiped her eyes and spoke. 'What's up?' she said. 'I'll tell you what's up. After fifteen years, two kids, three houses and never more than twenty pence between our arse and the grubber, it takes you six pints on your first swanky holiday to admit you actually care.'

'Keep your voice down,' I growled.

'Why?'

'Because I don't want outsiders knowing I love you. That's private business between a man and wife.'

'Are you saying you're ashamed of me?'

'No, I'm not saying I'm ashamed of you. You're scum, same as me, where the hell do you get that idea?'

People were starting to look, some giving those tedious lovey smirks that say, 'We never argue, we're oh so hap-hap-happy.' Lying bastards. Every hitched man knows the law of married physics. In a nanosecond, he can go from a stroll in the clouds to the bottom of a pit of shit and ashes. All it takes is one wrong word. The L-word. Why, after all these years, had I weakened and used it? Simple. White Shoe Syndrome. I had them on, keeping my feet spread wide so I could glance at their majesty between mouthfuls of chips. They encouraged me to feel expansive and European. I'd even started casting an eye into leather-goods shops, fancying one of those smart male purse things that those big German heffers in linen suits carry about. Now I was back to feeling shabby and ridiculous. What would I keep in one of those things anyway, two Superking nips and the Family Allowance book? Feeling cold and fearful, I struggled to get our closeness back. 'How are your chips?'

'Cold,' she said. She sat there in silence. Women never meet you halfway, they want you to do all the running, all the time. No wonder the vicious bastards live longer. Oh well, time to get cute. I turned on my heartfelt voice. 'I'm sorry I said I loved you.'

Wrong-footed, she stopped honking her snout into her napkin and met my doleful gaze. 'Don't get cute,' she said. And we both laughed.

I ordered more chips to show what an attentive lover I was and another pair of drinks for a sprinkling of instant glee. We swapped a bit of banter to help crank up another frisson then toasted our union in flat Beck's. The boys arrived from trawling the amusement arcades, all breath-less and smelling of fags. Burney snatched my glass up and stole big gulps before I could slap it off him. I couldn't be arsed with their fidgety energy and tedious competitive cheek.

'Hey, Da, are you going camping?'

'No, why?'

'You've got a tent pole down the front of your strides.'

'Let's have a swatch.' To embarrass me, they rise, slurping our drinks, and stare at the front of my shorts. I'd have to despatch them. Simple enough. I looked at Mary and winked.

'That's not a tent pole, is it, Mary? Tell them.'

'No, that's not a tent pole. That's a big stick of Malaga rock that Papa's bought for Mama, eh, Papa?' She feigned a shudder.

As hoped, they retched and vacated the table, leaving Mary and me to share a wholesome family chuckle, which I extended into a prolonged guffaw for the benefit of any remaining malignant eyes around us. Once again, I defy gravity, leaping from ash pit to clouds with a single timeless bound. Standing outside myself, I watch us eating chips and sniggering. Can it really be that five minutes earlier I was planning ways to throttle this woman and feed her body, minus quim, to the crabs? How can we claim to be creatures governed by reason? We are live volcanoes in Littlewoods summerwear, liable to erupt at any time, kept in check only by fear of consequence.

'Let's take a bath together when we get back,' said Mary.

'Let's.' I smiled.

'And Rab?'

'What?'

'Thanks for what you said. Your timing was shite, and it shows you up as a shallow immature prick who can only sing when he's winning, but I accept that's who you are, and I know your heart was in the right place, although it's twisted.'

'My pleasure,' I say. Further discussion seems futile. And again we clink glasses, bashful lovers once more. She squeezes my hand and, clumsily, I squeeze hers. And though I'm beaming, benignly, I'm also thinking that it'll be a bloody long time, lady, before I hit you with the L-word again, you yellow-fanged hound of Hades. And though we entwine tender fingers, like tipsy holiday love-birds the world over, I know I'm going to poke her hard tonight, if possible up the pumper, just for badness. And from the dewy loving twinkle in her slitty sluttish eyes, it wouldn't at all surprise me if she knows that too. We finish our drinks. Raising my napkin I cleanse my gob and surrounding areas. 'Dirty bitch,' I say.

'Lucky you,' she says. 'Shall we go?'

*

Being scum, I feel like James Bond whenever I enter our hotel, except that James Bond never seems obliged to queue at reception for his key. Mary's over by the shop buying Maltesers. I used to eat them out of her, one at a time, but after the kids came along we found we could stow a decent-sized selection box up there and the practice rather fell into decline. I take the key with its huge fob you could anchor a small schooner with and slyly turn to watch Mary. She's queuing primly, purse in hand, and I'm titillating myself by picturing how she'll look in under five minutes' time. In the gulf between what we pretend to be and what we actually are lies the human comedy.

'And there's a message,' says Carlos, the desk clerk.

'What?'

He slides a folded page of A4 towards me and I open it and read this: *Please ring Jamesie. Urgent. No shit.* My stomach flips and a small explosion of fear rattles the contents of my head. I stuff the message into my pocket and tell Mary I'm feeling queasy and need a walk. She offers to come with me but I insist and to reassure her make unconvincing Terry Thomas lust noises, telling her to get ready. Ten minutes later I step out of a phone box and slide in weak instalments down the glass wall. Two days ago, Bimbo's grabbed Cotter by the scruff in the Two Ways and hauled him into the toilet. Tojo's already in there. He has a patch over one eye and is clutching a taped-up table leg. Bimbo's finally tippled to my voice and now they're after me. Any thoughts I'd entertained at having committed the perfect crime have been shattered by one tiny blemish: Bimbo's found a two-legged table by the bins outside my house. Though Cotter protests there are many two-legged tables in Govan, the remaining legs match with those discarded in the close and I'm a marked man. Despite a severe battering, Cotter refuses to disclose my whereabouts. This, translated from Cotter-speak into hard fact, means he fell to his knees on approach and told them everything. Cotter's sorry to be the bearer of bad news and trusts it hasn't spoiled my holiday.

The next few days pass in a blur. Though we swim and shag and buy trashy souvenirs, my heart's not in it because I know I'm on Death Row. Every peseta note that goes on a dodgem ride or a burger and chips I view as a kick in the chops or a bat in the ribs for me when we return. I've no doubt I'll be killed, or, worse, spend the rest of my life in a bobble cap swapping comics with the weans. After the recent closeness we've built up, Mary's hurt by my cold withdrawal. She quizzes me relentlessly, looking for reasons. 'It's nothing,' I tell her, 'just self-preservation. I'm trying not to enjoy the holiday too much or I'll be all the more depressed when I get home.' I drift alone in a pedalo, making out my will: 'To my son Burney, I leave my bad attitude. To Gash, your battered pram so you'll be the first Nesbitt with a holiday home. To my darling wife Mary, I leave my fully functioning corpse. The liver's fucked and the heart's hard to start on wet mornings but there's a decent pair of corneas and you might get a few quid for the aorta, it's at least as good as plastic though not as sound as pig.' I stick the will into an envelope and on the way back post it to our home address, just in case. It's unlikely they'd waste plane fares chasing the likes of me, but you never know. Most likely they'll just be waiting at the gate on arrival. They know I'm not going anywhere. And as I drop the will into a post box, I get a sudden glimmer of a possible way out.

*

The flight from Malaga was delayed three hours. Its new anticipated departure time was 6 a.m. I calculated with dismay that, with transfers, we'd arrive back in Glasgow at around a civilized 10 a.m. Dismay because my prospective murderers were known lazy bastards and I'd clung to the slender hope that the warmth of their beds and the earliness of the hour might defeat their anaemic will. Though my nerves jangled, I took no drink on the flight, needing my wits about me. I had set in place such meagre plans for my survival as I could; now their substance would be tested. As we approached Glasgow, I instructed Mary to make her way ahead with the boys beyond the arrival gate to the taxi rank outside, where I'd presently join them.

She gave me a cold stare. 'Either there or in the afterlife, eh, Rab?'

'What d'you mean?'

'Win on the horses, my arse. Who is it, who's waiting on you?' We were descending through drab Scottish cloud,

269

the colour of binlids, towards the airport. Mary's tone was harsh and edgy. Already warm Spanish Mary was gone; we were home, to mangled reality, once more.

'Go on,' she repeated, 'tell me who's waiting?'

'Michael Aspel and his big red book. Just do as you're fucking told, will you?'

We landed with an unpleasant thud and careered along the tarmac before wheeling and coming to a halt. Belts unclicked and luggage lockers opened.

Mary gathered up her things, cardigan, pens, straw hat, puzzle books. 'But I'll tell you something,' she said, 'I've had all I can take of this life. I mean it. I want a divorce.'

'Mary!'

She was already away, shepherding the boys down the aisle in front of her. I shut my eyes and concentrated on the job at hand. They were the first faces I saw as I tramped up the carpeted exit corridor towards the concourse. They saw me a moment later and stepped in confidently to field me at silly mid-on. Bimbo smirked, seeing the fear in my eyes. They'd been looking forward to this.

'Hello, Rab.'

'Hello, Bimbo.' Tojo was wearing an eye patch, if I got the chance I'd poke a finger in the good one, sending him blundering safely about Boots and the Sock Shop.

I'd only have Bimbo to contend with. Only. He had something tucked away in a grocery bag. I recognized the nostalgic contours of cleaver. That's all right. I had a present waiting for him. I hoped.

'Fucking robbing bastard.'

He stepped up close, pinning me by the wall next to the vacant information desk. Tojo got behind me in case I made a bolt for it back through the exit door.

'I don't know what you mean,' I said. My eyes were everywhere, looking for the cavalry.

'Just walk,' said Bimbo, gripping my elbow.

I tugged myself free. 'I'll come,' I said, 'I'll come if you tell me what I'm supposed to have done first.'

'Is he off his fucking head?'

'We know you, Nissy, and you know us,' said Tojo, reasonably. 'You know it's our job to tank you to fuck, so why don't you just behave yourself?'

'Be more than a tanking this time, Nissy,' said Bimbo, indicating the bag. 'This time, you're pork chops.'

'I hope you heard that, officer,' I called out. The two uniformed polis were zombieing about, doing that 'real cops walk slow' routine that the average west of Scotland plod thinks passes for cool. They wheeled and headed over.

'Nesbitt?'

'Hello, officer. Were you the gentleman I spoke to yesterday on the telephone?' He had small eyes and a ginger moustache. I like facial hair on a polis, it lets you know where their head's at.

'That was me,' said the other one. Tall. Small head. Big hat. 'You said if we met you here you'd have information about an unsolved murder.'

'Yes, officer, that's correct.'

'Well,' said Ginger Moustache, 'where's the body?'

'You're talking to it,' I said. I pointed to Bimbo and Tojo. Unwilling to risk running they stood, shuffling twitchily like footballers waiting for a national anthem. 'If you hadn't turned up, these two gentlemen would've driven me away and put me down a hole.'

Bimbo tried to lose the bagged cleaver in the folds of his coat.

The Tall One looked them over. 'Is this true? Were you pair going to murder him?'

'No,' said Bimbo.

The Tall One looked back to me. 'He says they weren't going to murder you. What d'you make of that?' He was enjoying himself. He'd buy crisps shortly, and they'd lie back in the motor, polishing up the anecdote. He didn't give a toss whether I was topped or not. He'd have jabbed his snotty index at the Apple Mac before coming out. He'd know I was a worthless piece of petty crim shit. It was time to crank up the stakes.

'If anything happens to me, everyone here is in serious soapy bubble,' I announced. 'As you can see, I am at this moment in the pink of condition.' I did a cocky little tap dance to show confidence. 'But I've taken the precaution of writing letters, naming names, and given them to colleagues for mailing to the tabloids in the event that my dancing days should unexpectedly end. You, the plods, have been informed that my life is in danger. These, the mouth-breathers, are the pair that propose to endanger it. To complete my portfolio of culpability, I should add that you've already been photographed together.'

They all glanced about the place, automatically. I pressed on. 'Photographed together and copies of the said snaps will of course accompany the referred to letters into the public domain, should the need arise. Which I'm sure it won't. After all, you wouldn't want to rob the world of another Lionel Blair, would you?' I did another little dance. The Tall One stayed silent, so I knew I'd unnerved him. He was worrying now about hidden tape recorders. The cops glanced at me but they looked hard at Tojo and Bimbo. The parcel had been passed and they were left holding it. I could sense sphincters twitching in uniform serge. There was a decent chance the Scottish papers would be interested in the lurid tale of some minor Govan deadbeat who'd had his napper stoved in, picturesquely. 'Ugly truth behind the poverty trap,' all that pish. Snaps of Mary and the boys by the peeling living-room wallpaper. 'Can you look sadder, please?' On the other hand all it would take was Fergie flashing half a ton of thigh getting out of a limo to spike me into oblivion. We all knew this. Mental calculations were taking place behind the looks.

Bimbo and Tojo had taken a doing. Undoubtedly, they'd be held accountable for the loss and would be obliged to restore the deficit to one of the myriad of respectable middle-management hoodlums between themselves and Mr Small. Consequently, they couldn't afford to go to jail. If they went to jail, they'd still be held accountable for the loss but would be deprived of the means to pay it back. The relentless wheels of the criminal industry would grind on regardless. New employees would be sought. Younger, fresher boneheads would seize the opportunity of an exciting career in thuggery. Tall and Ginger too wouldn't care to be smeared by any tacky story that might jeopardize promotion prospects. Inquiries would need to be held; knuckles seen to be rapped. Colleagues would express public sympathy then punch the air in the locker room in private jubilation. I was only shite, true, but the problem is, when you kick shite, it tends to stick to your shoe.

Bimbo turned and looked straight at me. 'Nobody was going to touch him,' he said.

'Aye, leprosy's contagious,' said Tojo. They did 'look of cold contempt' acting and sauntered away.

Tall stood over me looking down. 'We could charge you with wasting police time,' he said.

'You could,' I agreed, 'but wouldn't that be a waste of police time?'

Ginger loomed in, offering support. His wee eyes were screwed up in anger and concentration as he fumbled for some final damning insult.

'Fatso,' he said.

'Easy, Joe,' said Tall. Guiding Joe by the shoulder he spun him gently around. I watched them glide off sedately down the concourse, hands behind backs, in perfect step, like free-skaters warming up.

273

I felt a tap on my shoulder. I turned to see Mary standing with the boys.

'Show over?' she asked.

'I hope so,' I said.

'Good. Now get your arse in gear and help me with the bags.'

I nodded. It was a relief being told what to do again.

*

It was some months before Cotter found sufficient bravery to resume an open friendship with me. For a while we met in parks, shouting dreary platitudes to each other from bench to bench. If we took a stroll, it would be down opposite sides of the street, whereupon, if Bimbo or Tojo was spotted, he would vanish down a close and only answer his phone in fake Gaelic. The matter was only resolved one night when he saw I'd passed the pish test. Tojo and Bimbo entered the Two Ways.

Seeing them, Cotter made his obligatory scuttle to a far corner and busied himself with reading a beer mat. Exasperated, I finished my pint and headed for the toilet. If there was any lingering unfinished business, here was the traditional place in which to conclude it. I admit, I was nervous. I'd practically to prise my cock down from my bladder with tweezers. The pish came and went, uninterrupted. When I stepped back out, Bimbo and Tojo had already finished their drinks and gone. Satisfied, conclusively, Cotter sauntered over and slapped me on the back, 'Good on you, Rab,' he said. 'Mind, if they'd started anything, I'd have been right in there.'

Our life of petty crime resumed. Lead, iron, fags, money, electrical appliances large or small. We were never lucky. The video age was upon us and everybody wanted one. Seized with the Goldrush spirit, we broke into an electrical warehouse in Partick. On metal shelving by the far wall we found racks of the gold bullion, otherwise known as VCRs. Regrettably, our grasp on the available intelligence information was tenuous. We'd heard there were three systems for video recorders, one a winner, one so-so and the other an out and out turkey. But we couldn't recall which was which. You may remember Phillips VCRs. They turn up occasionally as items of scorn on curio shows, along with Squarials and the Ronco Self-Polishing Shoe Fan. I don't believe a single soul in Britain was unfortunate enough ever to buy one. Except perhaps Pete Best of the Beatles. And even then, he didn't get it from us.

I was thirty-seven. This is an awkward age for human beings. With the fifth decade looming, women attempt to thwart the menopause by squeezing out one last baby, and men escape a sense of failure by sailing around the world single-handedly, or cluttering up the drains with body parts, like Denis Nilsen. Of course this is a cynical view and we would all, one day, like to see a fairer society, where men could stay at home, rearing unnecessary children, while women went out to do the serial killing. The reprieve from death made me re-evaluate my lifestyle. A visit to the doctor about a kidney infection made me think about the level of my drinking. Having thought about it, I decided to increase it and took to long solo binges that would see me leave the house for a loaf and be delivered home by a kindly stranger, three days later, via Parcel Force. A follow-up visit to the surgery for test results revealed a damaged kidney and a liver so hard and bloated it could be used as a curling stone. To feign concern, I asked the doctor what would happen if I were to continue drinking at the same level.

'Nothing,' he said, unimpressed by my lip biting and showy wringing of hands. 'So long as you're able to live without offal, you'll be fine.'

'But I read it's possible to survive on half a kidney and a quarter of a liver.'

'I'm afraid you've been misinformed,' said the doctor.

'No kidding? I'm going to pack in that *Lancet* and go back to the *Daily Star*.'

I ignored his level-eyed warnings and kept drinking, though the binges were less frequent now and of shorter duration. For my fortieth birthday, Mary produced a cake shaped like a beer bottle. When I queried her choice, she told me to think myself lucky, next year it would be a pink elephant. If I was lucky. She steadied my hand as I attempted to cut the cake and we all laughed. 'If you live that long,' she said.

CHAPTER NINE

I NEEDED something to live for. Unable to locate it, I settled for the next best thing, nothing. At least, I reasoned, nothing was something. Duly comforted, I continued drinking. Once you realize you're never going to be a somebody, you have to kid yourself that being a nobody can still be interesting. Down and down I sank, till I came to rest on the ocean floor, among the bones and wormy skulls of wasters past and present. Down there we spoke our own language, the ancient parlance of befuddled nonsense, and invoked our own strange laws, where a man could be killed for dying at the wrong time. My memories scare me, but I cling to them because the things I don't remember scare me more. At least memory is evidence of function. Loss of function is true terror. I remember, nostalgically, the days when I had a memory. At least I think I do. When I lived in the Land of the Befuddled, my short-term memory was longer than my long-term memory and my short-term memory was, as they say, pants. Memory makes us gods of the vast kingdom between our ears. It swoops and eddies on the air, spanning decades with a beat of its mighty wings. Or it should if it's working right. If it isn't, you flay around in panic, like a man in a glass booth whose walls keep moving, relentlessly, inward.

For a surprise, on my forty-second birthday, Mary tried to have me sectioned. The surprise lay as much in that she'd managed to find me, for I'd been invited to leave the marital home some six months earlier and contact between us had all but ceased. Barred from the Two Ways following an unfortunate roughage incident, I'd drifted downmarket. As the only establishment lower down the social scale than the Two Ways was a petrol rag with some dossers around it, that is where I gravitated. My new watering hole was fashionably minimalist, lacking, as it did, walls and a ceiling. Seating consisted of an arse, which one brought with one, and plumped onto the rubbly waste ground. If, for reasons of diminishing consciousness, this body part could not be relied upon to provide an adequate fulcrum, then a back or stomach could usefully be substituted, usually, though not necessarily, one's own. Lacking funds, we drank anything. Lacking anything, we stole or begged. In my time, I imbibed several specified household cleaners and the odd tot of aftershave, all of which were unspeakable, especially the aftershave, since it was Calvin Klein. That pish smells bad enough on your face, let alone ladled down your throat.

Occasionally, my colleagues would rise above oblivion long enough to tell me of their plight. Many were ex-servicemen, many had trades, most had a broken relationship that had sent them spiralling downwards. Many of the more experienced wasters mourned the loss of status that a dosser used to enjoy. Almost all had appeared in TV documentaries or in the weekend supplements. Matty, a grizzled ex-farmhand from Ayrshire, spoke for all: 'Up till a couple of years ago, I could be sure of the odd *World In Action* or university thesis. If I went begging up the town, folk would ask for my autograph. The outsider had a place in society but not any more.' Matty had worked on a dairy farm in Ardrossan until the early sixties, but had been dismissed for his habit of fondling the farm donkeys. He explained, 'Times were less enlightened then, nowadays people take the love between a man and a quadruped for granted. If it happened now, it would be the making of me. I'd be on *Kilroy* for sure, probably *Trisha*. But it's too late now.' The alkies' collective place as renegade outsider had been usurped by the younger, more telegenically poignant, junkies. Gus, from Inchinnan, agreed. 'If you're a twenty-five-year-old junkie, that's hip and cool, daddy-o. But if you're a forty-year-old alcoholic, you're a stereotype, the media doesn't want to know. You're on the scrapheap.' He looked around, woozily. 'Where is our scrapheap, by the way?'

'Over there,' said Matty, pointing. 'The fucking junkies have pinched it.' And we all cursed and slurred at the youthful upstarts.

Fights among the derelicts were constant and could be vicious. Theft was rife. Once I awoke to find my hair missing. It had been harvested while I slept and sold as stuffing for soft toys going to Namibia. From then on, I dozed with a small brass bell taped to my forehead. Rough sleepers don't last long in Glasgow. If the rain doesn't get you, the cold does. If not those two, then it's other homeless fuckers waking you up to try and sell you the *Big Issue*. I slept in a pipe on a building site for a time, till I woke one morning to find myself part of a drainage system in Hyndland. I'd gravitate back to the waste ground where we'd pool what small coinage we had mustered and exchange it for drink. Again, this cooperation was born out of self-interest, not fellow feeling. Fifty pence buys you nothing. Ten fifty pences means a good-sized slurp from a litre bottle. It was best to find a hostel as an address meant a giro and therefore a temporary feast of drink. When supply was short, tempers would fray. Pat the Dog tapped for a week on the understanding that when his service pension cheque cleared he'd repay the debt. On the day before it was due, he took a slurp of Strongbow, fell asleep and choked on vomit. When we realized he was dead, we kicked the fuck out of him for being a selfish, careless bastard.

One day I woke to find myself blind in one eye and with my balance disturbed by an inner ear infection. I set out to find a doctor but gave up, exhausted, after spending half an hour walking in a small circle. Matty, who had some knowledge of medicine, having once strangled a sheep, sat me down and set to work, feeding me a mild sedative. When I awoke, my eyebrows were missing. Gus confided privately that they'd gone for soldier doll chest hair, but since my sight was mysteriously restored it seemed churlish to complain over the loss.

Soup was dispensed twice weekly from mobile vans in the town centre and we'd tramp over dutifully for the sustenance. The Salvation Army did a better line in scran but I could tolerate the religion less readily than most and, unless famished, would give it a miss. No matter how resolutely I was assured to the contrary, I could not make the leap of faith that would convince me Jesus wanted me for a sunbeam. By now I had lost three stone and had a beard that could have provided a fair acre of meadow for Namibian dolls. Jamesie and Ella passed me on Golspie Street once without a second glance. From a distance I looked a picture of grungy macrobiotic health but up close it was clear I would soon be dead. The eyes, as always, have it.

I was riding the tube for warmth one day when an inspector shook me awake and, after some routine questioning, threw me off the train. I climbed out of the bowels of the station and looking around dimly recognized Cessnock, a five-minute walk from my mother's house. I hadn't visited in around eighteen months and, pressing the call buzzer, wondered what sort of reception, if any, I might receive.

'Who is it?'

I had to think. Jesus, why didn't she start with an easy one? 'It's Rab,' I said.

There was a long pause, then a voice sighed. 'Come in,' it said and the entrance buzzer sounded.

She looked thin and old. 'You look thin and old,' she said to me, proffering tea, in a chipped mug, I noticed, lest I be the bearer of unspecified infection.

'I've been on a diet,' I said, 'I've lost three stone of fat.'

'There's room for more,' she said, 'you're still wearing your head.'

I don't know what I'd been expecting, but if it was Ma Joad welcoming her errant son Tommy back to the homestead with a big ole mess of chitlins I had the wrong fantasy in the video box. I realized that even maternal love was conditional and that after Rena's departure and the death of Freak, Mother had pulled up the drawbridge, leaving me on the other side of the moat. I stuck around though, as it was somewhere to go. The price of a cup of tea and a fag was listening to her report, at interminable length, some minor spat with an assistant in a wool shop, or some such, with every pause, utterance and interjection from independent witnesses recorded with tortuous relish. What happens to the human editing process after sixty-five? Is it removed, surgically, in one of those routine procedures for the elderly you hear them talk about in bus queues?

She could skim from serial killers to John Major to Toblerone in a single subordinate clause. Everything was given equal gravity, from genocide in Africa to Boy George's double chins. I learned to listen in a light doze, offering only the occasional nudge of punctuation when the flow of words becalmed itself in some stagnant cul de sac. I'd make myself useful by running errands while she made toast and put the kettle on. Modern image makers are paid to portray Glasgow as Hip City, bustling with clubs and designer shops where the breathless populace pause only to sip cappuccino before nipping to Versace for a sweater to drape lightly over their shoulders after a brisk workout at the fitness club. Wear horse blinkers and remain tethered at a ten-yard radius to a BBC radio mike in the west end and this may be partially true. Great swathes of the city remain as untouched by the finger of taste as they ever were. Point four Volvos at compass points outside Broadcasting House and just beyond the beam of each headlight lies Leper Land, home to the unsightly pensioner and to the rancid foot in the leaky trainer. No, we are not Prince Naseem nor were meant to be, some attendant lard perhaps. In Paisley Road, I can connect nothing with nothing. Battalions of pensioners creak up and down, like POWs in an exercise yard, keeping up appearances. The men have bow legs, fresh creased trousers and mysterious testicles that hang like bowling balls behind their curtain of cavalry twill. They pull tartan shopping trolleys on wheels, because the women won't, thinking it'll make them look old. In Glasgow, even the women are macho. Pensioner women shun pubs, preferring to form queues, in the drizzle, as it aids girning, or to block the pavements, exchanging tittle-tattle and games of Guess Who's Dead, before heading off to infuriate the butcher with requests for half a sausage and three-quarters of a slice of ham.

*

I think these thoughts while lingering by the sea food freezer in Iceland, where every woman dresses like my mother. If the city's image planners were really on the ball, they'd open up a store across the street called Rainmate, Message Bag and Poplin Mac Ltd., then the lepers need never leave the colony. Occasionally, she would talk about the past and my eyes would flutter half open. She'd root out her wedding photo and I'd look at the collection of impoverished half-formed beings and wonder, like Dr Mengele, how the onerous burden of procreation could be entrusted to such creatures. Mother's Lassie eyes shone trustingly out, while Father, in crumpled suit, smiled shyly, his great victory in World War Two a fading triumph, the Battle of Civvy Street already a struggle beyond his baffled powers. Bobo grinned at the back while Ginny, the bridesmaid, clutched a posy that almost hid her bump. Now forty years on, ravaged and torn, the last of the few limped toward the finishing line. One day, over tea and Tunnock's, I initiated a game. It was called Desert Island Batterings. It required Mother to select, from the rich storehouse of memory, the eight most memorable beatings she'd sustained at Father's hands.

She thought for a moment. 'Oh, that's a hard one,' she said, 'there are so many I remember, for a lot of reasons, that it's hard to narrow it down to some without being unfair to others.'

'Try,' I said.

*

When my visits had rotted down to habit, I broke the routine. I didn't want repetition to breed resentment on either part, but mainly hers. I came less frequently but stayed for longer periods, that way we didn't see too much of each other. She never asked me about my drinking and I never told her, an unspoken agreement that suited us both. Once though, I did invite a tangential response by asking her about Father's. 'The older I get,' she said, 'the fewer judgements I make. I've come to believe that everybody is some kind of asshole.' I asked where she'd picked up that expression. She showed me a video case for a film called *Blue Collar*. 'There's a stall up the Savoy Centre sells Phillips tapes,' she said, 'do you know, that video player you got me's still going strong.' I basked in the warm glow of inner satisfaction. Thanks to my tireless criminal efforts, the Nesbitt dynasty had progressed.

Mother had learned to say 'asshole'. My living had not been in vain.

I returned to the feeble hearth of the petrol rag and its bleak hospitality. On good nights, we'd pass around a bottle. On very good nights there'd be something in it. We'd have nibbles of dried shoe polish on matchsticks and we'd tell tales of our adventures on the open road. This did not take long, as few of us, with the exception of Matty, had seen the open road, let alone travelled its length. In drink, we embraced the role of free unruly spirits but in truth, we were, as I've said, lapsed institutionalists, who had passed invisibly out of the three main bulwarks of national defence, the Army, the Navy, and the Divorce Courts. When the bottle emptied and the rain sobered us the truth of our situation sank in, with the damp sending each man to retire into his private playpen of paranoia, or else go looking for a fight. On certain dangerous occasions, he might do both.

Such an occurrence took place one evening after a light supper of Chicklets and Lemon Pledge. Matty, often the butt of racist banter, being from Ayrshire, took exception to an intemperate rant from Gus. In his polemic, Gus had asserted that 'incomers' such as Matty had 'destabilized the begging community' by 'flooding into the city to steal our begging sites'. Supply had outstripped demand, Gus held, and consequently 'time-served' beggars were being undercut by the influx of cheap competitive labour. Consumers were now reluctant to part with twenty pence for a cup of tea when the beggar across the street was only charging ten. Gus urged strike action, calling for 'decent beggars everywhere' to withhold their labour. Faced with a mounting surfeit of repressed guilt, the public would surely capitulate and a 'statutory minimum beg' of thirty pence for a cup of tea could be instituted. Matty listened patiently while Gus made his case, even nodding from time to time in apparent agreement. When Gus had finished, Matty picked up a half-brick and stoved him on the head. He jumped into the midst of our startled circle, wielding the brick.

'Does anybody else want some? You snooty city beggars,' he railed, 'you all think you're streetwise, just because you've got streets. But we've got beggars in the country too, and junkies and gays. In Darvel last Easter two lesbians moved into a pie shop, so what do you think about that, you hoity-toity bastards?'

Gus groaned and made a shaky effort to rise.

Matty stood over him with the brick poised. 'Apologize, you racist pig,' he demanded.

Gus gave him an unsteady, defiant glare. 'Some of us are in the gutter,' he said, 'but we're still looking down at you, you donkey-dipping bastard.'

Matty cursed, and as he drew back the brick I threw myself on him, managing to dislodge it. One or two of the others helped me restrain him and, disarmed, he calmed himself quickly.

'I didn't take you for a racist, Nissie,' he said. I told him I wasn't a racist, some of my best friends had fucked animals, well, Cotter at least, and that he should try and be less touchy about being an in-breed from Uglyville. Again, he appeared to consider this counsel, but the glint in his eye told me that I should sleep from now on with a knife under my pillow. That night, I woke to find blood streaming from a stab wound in my neck. I made a mental note to buy a pillow.

*

As the weather worsened, finding a dry place to sleep became more difficult. When I could afford it I'd head for a hostel, but the best ones were usually fully booked, often with undercover journalists from London filing shocking indictments. You could hear them throughout the day, pretending to cough consumptively, trying to hide the pit-a-pat of their laptops. My own health was deteriorating. I caught flu while shoplifting a bottle of Scotsmac from an off licence in town. The virus descended suddenly, and I found myself running on the spot, panting heavily, while an assistant strolled towards me with pocketed hands. Sensing disaster, I struggled to uncap the bottle and sink the contents before he could collar me. My hands were shaking so much the task defeated me. 'I'd best take that before you drop it, eh?' said the assistant, kindly, letting me go. My teeth were chattering and my bones felt like they'd melted inside me. I fell to my knees, sweating heavily, shaking with cold and, by instinct, half crawled and half staggered the three miles to Mary's door in Govan. Two days later, I was fit enough to visit the doctor.

He didn't mess about. 'Your wife wants nothing more to do with you,' he said.

'She took me in,' I told him.

'Only out of pity. If you want a future there, you'll have to clean yourself up.'

'Nah,' I said, 'I'll just sling her the old boyish charm.'

He threw down his pen. His eyes danced with glee. A couple of years' less training and he'd have jumped up and down on his desk like a baboon. Instead of which, he picked up a hand mirror and held it in front of my face. 'Boyish charm?' he said. 'For God's sake, will you take a good look at yourself, man, you're dying.'

I looked. It was me all right but my face looked thinner and longer. I had acquired thread veins on my nose and cheeks and purple blotches on my neck. It was as if for an experiment Charles Darwin had stuck a vacuum pump up my arse and sucked all the life force out.

'What can I do?' I said.

'Your wife wants you sectioned.'

'She's off her head,' I said.

'Well, I agree with her, so that makes three of us. But as far as I can see you're not a violent threat to society so that could prove difficult. On the other hand, I could have you treated.'

I tried for a deep breath but had to settle for a shallow one. 'What would that involve?'

'They'd lock you up, dry you out, talk to you, then send you on your way.'

'And after that?'

'After that, it's up to you. You can either sink or swim.'

It was time to grasp the nettle. To stand on my own two feet. I asked him what he would do if he were me.

'I'd swim,' he said. I asked him why. 'Well, you've tried drowning, haven't you?' I told him yes. 'And do you like it?' I told him no. 'Well, there you are, then, that's your answer, isn't it?' He gave me a prescription for sleeping tablets, a small amount only, in case I topped myself after his dressing down and left him with a tedious dose of guilt. In the end, everything comes down to self-interest, it seems, including self-interest. My will, like an independent force, took me by the ear, slapped me on the head and made me do its bidding. At last, I had an accredited role in society and could offer a valued contribution to the human drama. I was a loony.

*

To put Mother's mind at rest, I dropped her a postcard. I told her not to worry, there were lots of other psychotics here, and that I was among like-minded people. I also pointed out how fortunate she was having two sons in the same asylum, as this would cut down on bus fares when visiting. She did not respond. Perhaps I shouldn't have added 'wish you were here'.

On arrival I was taken to a segregated wing, registered, and assigned a set of bright yellow pyjamalike apparel. 'Not bad,' I said, jokey with nerves, 'but could you widen the lapels and raise the waistband, I'll need flares if I'm to join the Commodores.'

The white-jacketed assistant looked at me, stonily. 'C'mere,' he called. I walked back. He peered at my scalp. 'You're fucking lousy,' he said, 'report to the nurse.'

I was sheared, scrubbed, disinfected and shown to a small private room. I knew it was a room and not a cell because a sign on the door assured me thus: Room Eleven, it said. Also, the walls were washed in an uncustodial primrose, almost matching my pyjamas. It occurred to me that if I wanted to escape, I'd just have to paint my face and hands yellow and slither along the corridor wall. I studied the fixtures and fittings to see how far the guests were trusted. Thick mesh over the recessed lightbulb. Private toilet with the cistern set inside the plaster of the wall. Bed a mattress on a raised concrete step, a bit like Orkney Street. Crucially, a door that locked only from the outside. Buzzer by the bed.

'If you need anything just ring.'

I say, 'Fine, I need a key.' He meant support. I say, 'How about supporting me to get a key?'

Thin smile, door gently closes, opens. 'Oh, and group is at 10 a.m., after breakfast.'

I sit and shiver. I didn't need a drink till the door closed. Need a fag, though. Always need a fag. I stand up and pace about. I feel ridiculous in these pyjamas, like Hugh Hefner under house arrest. Maybe tomorrow I'll sneak along to the cretin ward and swap them for some plasticine. With plasticine, I could make an imprint of a key. With a key, I could . . . what the hell am I talking about, this is a hospital not a jail. This is a cure, not a punishment, why would these people want to punish me? After an hour's pacing, the lights go out. I lie in the dark, clutching my willy for comfort. At least I hope it's my willy, and not some zombied Tweedledum's who's got lost searching for sugar lumps. It's a long listless night and I barely sleep a wink. As I'm finally dropping off, the buzzer sounds. In-house radio plays Tony Christie, 'Is This the Way to Amarillo?' Sure, Tony, turn left at Renfrew. What I realize now is that they won't punish me in here. They think they don't need to. They think you'll do that for yourself. Fucking amateurs.

I'm sweating in group and move in and out of concentration, like a man who's about to pass out. There are ten other hard-core gut-rot alcoholics with me, all sitting in the overheated room, in these fucking yellow pyjamas, pretending to be penitent and soulful. All the guys here, like myself, will have done group at some point, off and on, down the decades. Normally, the drill is simple. You pass a small turd of self-revelation, garnish it with a few tears, if possible, then fuck off down the pub for a sweetener. It's not that group is worthless, it's not, it's valuable, it can truly stop the rot and turn lives around. But group is ruthless, respecting only the bottom line of personality, it can help only certain people. Calling it by a name, I'd say group helps only those types with a revelation complex, who think there's something out there worth living for, some higher force. They need to feel God's keeping a personal eye on them, else they get all despondent. It doesn't help the others, like me, and those other poor bulb-nosed bastards around me. I watch them, fiddling with their leaflets, smiling and nodding, raising the occasional astonished eyebrow as some weary statistic is trotted out, knowing full well that first chance they get they'll be lying in a gutter, quietly stewing in their own pish. We come from a land far away, beyond the bottom line, in the black hole under the floorboards.

After group, it's rest break, for which I'm hanging on grimly. A man called Jack is holding us up. His eyes redden and nervy hands flutter as he tries to coax out his hideous tale of woe. There's snot, soothing words, then eventually out it tumbles. Business worries, increased drinking, has an affair, leaves wife. She attempts suicide, pills, makes a bollocks. Prangs her brain, coma, wakes up with half her face normal, the other like a landslide. He feels guilty, chucks lover, devotes life to wife's care. She nags constantly, he drinks more, and worse, he still has a stiffy for the lover. We sit, waiting for the twist in the tail, the lethal injection, the little accident with the pillow, but no, that's it, the punchline, he's consumed with guilt. Not a mention of money, we notice, definitely middle class. No violence either, no one slugged with the chip pan, probably not from round here. He ends abruptly, thanks us for listening, sniffs, wipes his eyes with his palms. I see looks of wistful envy on grizzled faces and I know what they're thinking: Jack's had his catharsis, now he's got hope. Middle-class background, family structure, support and intelligence coming out of his ears, he's laughing. Give it six months, he'll bung the wife in therapy, while she's lying there, drooling down the couch, he'll be lunching up the Corinthian, having come to a nice sophisticated European arrangement with his hard-on. Yes, for Jack the best is yet to come. He smiles earnestly and shuffles round the group, shaking hands and slapping shoulders, like we're all Billy Graham and he's saying ta for the everlasting life. It's overkill, but most likely he's working on instinct, he knows he's bailing out of here. I pump his hand and say, 'Well done.' I want to ask if his room's got a window but I save it as I don't want to put ideas into other heads. Imagine us lot all having windows to stare out of. They'd stick fountains up our arses and call us gargoyles, we'd be a listed building in no time.

Being unsuited to cold turkey, I decide to plump for tepid. Some of the guys have bribed the boilerhouse attendant to bring in some bottles of Thunderbird. We pass the sweet poison from mouth to sly mouth in the dark of the laundry store room, bonded by daring and the hardheaded self-destructiveness of the soon-to-be-dead. We feel like renegades but when the lights click on we squeal like the infants we truly are. Two security guards flank a whitecoated doctor. He looks us over, keeping his anger well doused under a thick foam of pity.

'Who are you fooling?' he asks us.

We look around for an answer. Someone puts a hand up and suggests, tentatively, 'Ourselves?'

This is a good odds-on bet as it turns up a lot in these rhetorical question sessions. 'That's right,' he says. We expect a mild rebuke, a bit of shouting, tops, but what he says startles us. 'Now could I please ask you all to be ready to leave, first thing in the morning?'

We make indignant noises. He continues.

'You each signed an agreement not to drink and now you've broken it. There's nothing more this unit can do for you.' His matter-of-factness stuns us. One or two voices start to whimper. He's unmoved, he's heard whimpering, his kids whimper, alkies whimper all the time, he's all whimpered out. He concludes: 'I'm sorry, but places on this scheme are strictly limited. Time is precious and there isn't room for deceit. There are other people out there we can more probably help. Charles, will you take names and do a head count, please?'

As the security guard steps up, I find myself crouching down instinctively behind a big pile of rubber sheets, as much to give me thinking time as anything else, it's all come as such a jolt.

One by one the transgressors file out, red-penned and rejected, processed for a quick return to filthy oblivion. I listen. The light clicks out and though the door shuts, no key turns in the lock. It seems the fuckers trust the rubber sheets more than they do us. And so they should. I've got the sweats back now the rush from the slurp has faded but I keep hidden till the small hours before stealing out, running around the building and staggering up to the night desk.

An attendant with bleached blond hair looks up from his copy of *Men's Health*. 'Why aren't you in your room?'

I tell him I was out walking in the garden and took a blackout in the shrubbery. 'I've only just come to.' I do leaning-against-the-wall-looking-poorly acting.

He peers at me over his little oblong specs. 'You're not one of the drinkers, are you?'

I shake my head, looking confused. 'What drinkers? This is the alcoholic unit, isn't it, Doctor? I am in the right ward, aren't I?' I rub my lying brow.

He sits, having a little inner conflict, then he stands up suddenly, and I follow him along the corridor.

'Thanks very much,' I say, as he opens the door of my room. He doesn't speak, just glances around looking for Semtex or orgies or something, and twirling the loop of the key on his finger. Finally, he turns to me.

'I hope you deserve this,' he says. I look puzzled. 'Don't be smart-arsed,' he says, 'just be smart.' The door closes with a little hiss and click and I hear his flip flops flop-flip back down the corridor. I'm one very relieved alcoholic. Out of his whim and my own slippery instinct, I've somehow contrived a second chance. Do I deserve it? Who cares? Do I even want it? Fuck knows. All I know is, in this life, you play the cards you're dealt.

*

After a few days, when I felt fit enough to face him, I went looking for Gash. We met in the canteen where I'd seen him as a visitor years earlier. Taking tea with a lunatic is overwhelming, it's like being locked in a broom cupboard with a mime artist – entertaining for ten seconds, then you want to choke him. His hair was greying now but he was still wearing the same jumper. He'd enhanced his repertoire of behavioural tics, I noticed, and in addition to removing his invisible hat he now placed it on an invisible hat stand along with an umbrella. When I asked him why the umbrella, he looked at me like I'd been heavily sedated and said, 'In Glasgow? Are you kidding?' In the main, his thought processes moved with the smoothness of a Rolls-Royce but every so often they'd hit a sleeping policeman from the past and everything under the bonnet would fly arse over tit. I explained why I'd been admitted and he asked how I was settling in. When I told him fine, he asked how my madness was coming along.

'The doctors are very pleased with my progress,' I told him, 'they say, all going well, I should start attacking the staff with gardening tools any day now.'

He looked edgy. 'So you're quite mad, then?'

I told him fairly.

Finally, he burped it out. 'You're not . . . madder than me, though, are you?'

When I assured him his status as top family headbanger remained unthreatened, he relaxed. I lit us a couple of imaginary cigars and we lounged back, surveying our achievement. 'Yes, we've done well for ourselves, you and I.'

'Look at us,' I said, 'matching pyjamas, three square sets of tranquillizers a day; man, we're practically civil servants. Father would have been proud.' The Roller bumped and bounced, cascading trains of thought like ticker tape. 'Don't that man please talk about again please.' When I asked him why not, he leaned his wretched face into mine.

'It's the dreams, Rab,' he said, 'every other night I dream about him, I can't help it.'

I was tempted and I fell. 'Why every second night? What about the other nights, are they better?'

He told me worse. I asked him why. 'Because that's when he dreams about me.'

Sometimes being an alkie is a tough job. I took a deep breath, flicked open my ID, and passed through the gates of Tweedledum. 'But, Gash, he's dead, how can he dream?'

Gash shrugged and sipped some tea. 'Why don't you ask him,' he said, 'he's standing right beside you.'

I hesitated but, I admit, I looked.

'Wrong side,' said Gash.

I turned my head. Mad people everywhere, rattling cups, going 'Wooooo!' and walking into cupboards. A naked man was standing in a corner, singing 'Champion, the Wonder Horse'. An old lady was squatting on a table, pretending to shit into a sugar bowl.

'Nice pyjamas,' said Gash. His voice had taken on a luscious, salivating quality. He leaned over and felt the sleeve. 'Are they real?' he said.

I stood up, quickly. 'I don't know,' I said, 'ask Father.'

*

After the casting-out of the drinkers, shunned because as alcoholics they had committed the sin of taking a drink, group was pared to a hard core of five.

Indulging my distaste for vomiting my emotions into the laps of strangers, the doctor granted me a window of absence. During group sessions I was now obliged to remain in my room, which meant I was spending upwards of fourteen hours a day within my primrose walls. I lived half in fear and half in expectation of the heebie-jeebies which, I was assured, would arrive as surely as Christmas.

This was an unfortunate image to plant in my fevered

mind, as one night, during a particularly effusive bout of the sweats, I opened my eyes in the dark to find that the dark was light. Before me, looking remarkably spry for their ages, hovered the Father, Son and Holy Spook. Lest there should be any doubts over validation, the Young Un had brought his cross and reclined, arms akimbo, after his fashion. Extra evidence for Glasgow sceptics took the form of a Strathclyde Transport All Zones Picture Pass Card that was pinned to his chest with a thorn. I was much afraid and trembling. The Pop produced a tape machine, put in a blank cassette and, using his omnipotent powers, pressed 'record'. Then he loomed over my bed and said, 'Now then, suppose you tell us what you know?' When I told him I didn't know anything, he smote me with a right to the belly and a clip with the knuckles to the ear.

'Easy, big man,' said the Spook, stepping in, 'let's keep it professional.'

God the Father grew miffed. 'That's easy for you to say, that's not your boy up there, taking a hammering because of pricks like this.'

Jesus spake, exasperated. 'Dad,' he said, 'don't do me any favours.'

God rounded on him, fiercely. 'No favours? What did I tell you, I told you don't go into social work, what did I tell you?'

'Don't go into social work.'

'No, you could've come into the building trade with me, there's a fucking universe out there that's constantly expanding, instead you're poncing about in leg-warmers trying to make dead fuckers walk, I mean that's not even social work, that's showboating, pal, that's fucking Rodney Marsh stuff, no wonder your career's in limbo.'

I watched Jesus grit his teeth, trying to remain cool. He eased a foot free of its nail and with his big toe defiantly flicked open a *Guardian* Media section.

Finding no satisfaction, God turned his angry eyes back on me. 'You see these hands?' he said. I looked at the big horny paws, all puffed and callused with work, like catcher's mitts. 'I built a fucking empire with these, six days right through, downed shovels on the seventh because I refused to pay double time. But now I look around me and I ask, "For what? For fucking what? For shit like you?"' God seized me by the windpipe and squeezed.

The Spook looked agitated. He ran to the tape. 'Terminating interview, 3.15 a.m.,' he said, and turned it off. 'Not in here, Alec,' he said, 'there's bound to be an inquiry. They'll send in the Commissioner.'

'I am the Commissioner,' said God the Father, 'now shut the fuck up.'

His fingers dug gouges in my neck, working a hold on the back of my windpipe, giving his hand a full unspeakable grip. My eyes flashed and dazzled like some sort of pissed Noah, trying to strike a welding arc on the Ark. I was shouting out, I knew I was screaming. I tried to find the door, I fought to find the door, but God the Builder had removed it and plastered up the gap with extra prim-rose. My bleeding nails scraped paint petals from the walls. My last bead of consciousness shrunk like the spot on an old turned-off television set. 'How soothing to die,' I thought. I was sliding down the wall but at the same time ascending to God's great scaffolded building site on high. My last thought brought comfort and was indicative of character. 'At least they'll get the divine big bastard,' said a voice in my head, 'he left his dabs on the light switch.'

Then there was nothing. Although I couldn't exactly say how much nothing. All I remember was coming to with a cup of tea in my hand, apologizing for having died. Two white coats were in the room. One of them told me not to worry, people died here all the time. 'You've had the heebie-jeebies,' he said, sparing me the cumbersome jargon.

I recognized the other as the unit psychologist. He leaned in, resting his hands on his knees. 'How did you find the pyjamas?' he asked, pleasantly.

My eyes narrowed. Was I still heebie-jeebying?

'And the walls, how were they?'

I fought to find sense in what he was saying. My mouth found words. 'Four,' I mumbled, 'just the number of walls I like in a room.'

'You see,' he said, 'tests have shown that bright warm colours may lessen the impact of the delirium tremens.' He leaned in again, beaming. 'What say you?' Me say nothing. Me brain no work again. His smile died. 'On the other hand,' he concluded, 'it might be just a pile of shite.'

I'd gone a fortnight without a drink. As a preliminary reintroduction to the outside world my own clothes were restored to me. Though clean and laundered, they looked harsh and impoverished after the cheery democracy of the banana republic. Nervous of leaving, I tried to stretch my stay by volunteering for clean-up duties in the gardens. When it was pointed out the hospital already employed a gardener, I offered to kill him and bury him under his own rockery. This proposal being politely declined, I sought out Gash to bid him farewell. I found him in the ward. Staff were changing bed linen and he and his fellows were running around, wearing rubber sheets as capes, pretending to be Batmen and women. I slipped him two YoYo's and a pair of pyjamas I'd liberated from the store.

'Don't worry,' I said, 'they're real.'

He looked at them, wistfully. 'Ah,' he said, 'if only I could be sure.'

I packed and re-packed my carrier bag, desperate to buy more time. I was given a hostel voucher for two nights and eight pounds to tide me over. 'Tide me over what?' I asked the same white-jacketed assistant who, two and a half weeks earlier, had issued me with kit.

'Till you become President of the Board of Trade, you useless fucker, what do you think?'

I shook hands with the remaining core of my fellow derelicts and dutifully we wished each other luck. They gave me a sad piece of information before I left. At group that morning, the Senior Care Assistant had announced the demise of Jack. Apparently, two days after leaving us, he'd hanged himself from the spiral staircase of his Swedish-style maisonette, using his old Boy's Brigade lanyard.

'A pity,' someone said, 'he was a beacon of potential achievement to us all.' We tried for a minute's silence but after a couple of seconds packed it in and instead had a good piss about laughing. The Lord giveth and the Lord taketh away. Perhaps if he'd maketh up his mind, we'd starteth to give a toss.

*

In order to minimize the chance of regression, the doctor warned me to avoid my old haunts 'if possible'. I took this advice to heart. Hostel life no longer suited me; sometimes a man feels the urge to spread out, to find some land, feel the green earth beneath his feet. Lacking a Highgrove house or a castle in Ireland, I improvised by building a den in the shrubbery of the Elder Park. Rural life wouldn't suit everyone but it was what I needed. Though it took me a while to adjust to the different pace of the countryside, I grew to love it; to pace the parameters of my acreage in the silent night knowing I was utterly free, between the hours of 8 a.m. and 10 p.m., provided I kept my dog on a lead and played no ball games, was a source of joy and calm. To feed myself, I hunted. I fashioned a spear from a supple sapling and waded through the boating pond by night, probing its slimy recesses for bottles on which deposit might be claimed. The swing park bins provided a healthy store of crisps and discarded lemon Opal Fruits, unfavoured by children, while the wide crescent of benches by the flower garden could be relied upon to yield the odd resting shopping bag from which might be deftly liberated a purse or a quarter-pound of corned beef. It is possible to survive in the wilds of the average public park provided one is adaptable. More than once I gnawed raw bacon, tearing it from the packet with my bare hands, scorning to cut along the dotted line, then washed the salty flesh down with a tin of cold alphabet soup, bashed jaggedly open with a half-brick wrenched from the prim surrounds of the flowering bulbs section. Animal is as animal does.

I was never lonely, for there is always company to be found in the hidden communication of nature; the rustle of the bushes, the creak of the trees. I savoured their conversation, though this being Glasgow we kept off football and religion. As I lay in the warm hollow of my fern-covered lair, it would occur to me that I might live there for ever. Provided Exxon were to discover no vast mineral deposits in the rainforest over by the putting green, I might live out my days in peace and freedom. The plundered world stopped at the gates of the park. Beyond its railings lay the council settlements, where the once-proud natives now ran around in Coca-Cola T-shirts, fighting fierce battles over Nike trainers and later, over tea and fags in peeling kitchenettes, recalled the Great Myth of their Origin, ten minutes earlier, in a *Brookside* omnibus. I had no wish to return to that world. I had been cleansed, mentally and physically except for the dirt, and had at last found terms for myself under which coexistence might be possible.

But coexistence implies respect, if not equality, and an ant rarely enjoys partnership with a boot heel. When, one drizzly dawn, on a routine morning's foraging, I found a sodden local newspaper proclaiming 'Wild Man Living In Park', I knew peace had lost its bounds. Alongside was an identikit picture, furnished by a bored pensioner, and underneath the caption 'He Lives on Berries'. Next day, I was competing with an uppity rodent for a discarded pizza when I spotted a posse of parkies making their way in a thin sweeping line up from the bowls pavilion by the far gate. I gathered the few clothes I wasn't wearing into a Tesco bag and scuttled, under cover of foliage, toward the railings. Once over, I crossed the street to the Vogue Bingo Hall and watched as the parkies probed and prodded in the bushes. When the inevitable yell went up and they galloped to the mouth of the den, I turned my weary back toward the traffic and walked. I had no destination in mind. Yet I was walking. For a clue, I glanced down at my feet. I looked at the street they had selected to walk upon, out of the many tempting thoroughfares on offer. I put two and two together and stopped to brush myself down. The identikit had looked too close for comfort. If Mother thought I was the Wild Man, there'd be no KitKat with my tea. She'd send me down the back green for acorns.

*

The first thing that hits you is the stink. If you can overcome that without throwing up, then you remark the emaciation and parchment skin of the doll-like figure lolling in the chair. 'Been dead for some time,' said the cop, turning off the telly. 'A matter of days, at least.' The bulb had blown on the standard lamp, which was lucky, because the fabric of the shade had discoloured with heat. It would have been a damaging blow to the Nesbitt reputation to have another house go up in smoke. Her purse was still on the table, undisturbed, and the video, micro and radio were all in their rightful places. 'Probably a heart attack,' said the cop. He asked whether Mother had been insured. I told him yes. 'Where does she keep the policies, then?'

'Where everybody else keeps them,' I said, 'under the bedroom carpet.' I trotted, dutifully, into the bedroom to retrieve the policies while he phoned Orkney Street. I think he just wanted me out of the way so he didn't have to go into sensitive mode while talking to his fellow bears. I sat down on the bed. Needing something to do with my hands, I put my head into them.

It was the flickering images of the telly from the window that had alerted me. I'd rung the buzzer for ages in case she'd dozed off. When I'd summoned the caretaker, it'd taken a while to convince him I wasn't some housebreaker on a ruse. Finally, he'd let me in. When we'd peered through the letter box, we'd caught the smell. He'd hurried to phone the cops and fetch a pass key while I tried, unsuccessfully, to kick the door in. This had alerted the neighbours. Old gits and trouts started to gather at their doorsteps, asking stupid questions. 'Is she dead?' 'Hang on,' I'd said, 'I'll check her pulse using my extraordinary fucking powers of superhearing.' Many sensed death and ran in, excitedly, to push themselves up homemade league charts, or to ring ancient relatives, urging them to badger the council for the soon-to-be-vacant flat. More police arrived and they gave the rooms a thorough going over, just in case. Finally, Mother's body was zipped into a bag and stretchered down the stairs. The Trouts oh my Godded or blessed themselves, according to taste and whim.

'Do you have somewhere to stay?' said the original cop.

'I'd been planning to stay here for a while,' I said.

He pulled a face. 'I'm not sure that's a good idea,' he said, 'no offence, but this place'll stink for days.' I didn't respond. 'I'll ring the Talbot Centre,' he said, 'see if they can't fix you up with something.'

I nodded, and we all filed out of the house. I stood by a hedge, while people in uniforms busied themselves with tasks. There was a bit of crackling on a radio and the cop came over. 'It's fixed for tonight,' he said. I nodded thanks. He hovered awkwardly for a moment, then something about a fire in a warehouse came crackling out, rescuing him, and they all piled into a car. Once they'd all fucked off, I walked round the block a few times till things had quietened down. Then I let myself back into the building with Mother's keys. In the flat, I opened all the windows, made a cup of black tea, wrapped myself in a duvet and fell asleep on the couch.

In the morning, I set about doing all the things you need to do following a croaking. Acquiring a death certificate, informing insurance companies, announcement in the evening paper, all of that. When I'd made the arrangements for the funeral, I rang the few friends and acquaintances I knew Mother had and told them the news. They knew I was a waster, so I did 'grace under pressure' acting with the odd crack in the voice thrown in, in case they put me down as a heartless bastard and used that as some kind of posthumous stick to beat her with, in that sly way people do. I hung about to a respectable hour then rang Rena in Canada. As soon as she heard my voice she had the drawbridge up. She told me she didn't have any spare money. I explained I wasn't ringing for money, I had some bad news. I could feel her panic down the line. 'Is it Gash?' she said, hopefully. When I told her it wasn't Gash, she started wailing. 'It's my mammy, isn't it, it's my mammy?'

Her use of the possessive pronoun irritated me. And Mammy made me want to vomit. 'Aye,' I said, 'it's Mother.'

Schuch took the phone and I gave him the details. 'She'll be there,' he said. When he'd left a suitable pause for gravity, he asked me how Celtic had got on in the CIS

Cup. When I told him they'd lost two one, he sighed and said, 'Bad luck hunts in packs.'

I saved whatever photographs I could find, and family effects like school reports, christening cards, that type of thing. Everything else was picked clean by a house-clearance firm I'd found in the Yellow Pages. They gave me fifty quid for the lot. I'd needed this to pay for the announcement in the paper. We buried Mother in the Craigton Cemetery between an abandoned settee and a burnt-out Ford Fiesta, this being the best spot the yield on her policy would allow. In fact if the headstone had cost any more, I'd have to have sat her in the Fiesta and scratched In Loving Memory on the wing with a pound chunk. There were hymns, of course, to which none of us knew the tune, so we mimed while the minister belted it out in compensation. 'O God Our Help in Ages Past'. No mention of now, I noticed. The spit was flying, his head was rolling, he really gave it laldy, if he'd gone down the aisle high-kicking on his way out to the hole I wouldn't have been surprised. A few of Mother's friends turned up, little shrunken women with their sad faces on. Some had been workmates in the Grey Dunn biscuit factory after the war. I recognized their names penned on the backs of photos. It was startling to see the change in them, as some, in ages past, had been good-quality rides.

After the burial I had my first chance to speak to Rena. She blamed me for Mother's death, which didn't come as any shock. 'Why didn't you look after her, you live here?' People who leave always assume the rest of us are one big family, sitting in a big warm huddle, picking each other's fleas off till the day we croak. But life's not like that any more, this is the age of communication. We're all too busy communicating to be arsed with talking to each other. She gave me a disbelieving look when I told her what I'd got for the furniture, but I decided she could please herself.

'How's Schuch?' I asked.

'He's fine. He really wanted to be here, but he's terrified of flying. Apart from that, he's secretary of the Hamilton branch of the Celtic Supporters Club and they've a dinner dance tomorrow night and he's auctioning one of John McNamee's last jerseys.'

I gave her a little incredulous look of my own, for payback. Her face reddened. 'It's for Spina fucking Bifida, OK? Honest to Christ, some people never change.' She clumped away, her wee fat thighs chafing. 'And I want my share of the photos,' she called, 'if I don't get them, Schuch'll be over to batter fuck out of you.'

'I thought he was terrified of flying?'

'He'll get the boat.'

I thanked people for coming and hugged Aunt Ginny. It's always easier, I find, to hug someone you've seen limbo dance with her tits out, rather than your own mother. I made a little joke and she laughed. Ginny liked to laugh. She wasn't built to bear much of this reality pish. I walked her to her minicab and we waved as it drove away. She hadn't asked how I was getting on because she could see how I was getting on, it was the same way Bobo had got on all those years before. No Ordnance Survey maps of the terrain were required. She herself was getting on fine, she said it helped to talk to Bobo like he was still there, though once she'd stopped for six months in a sulk after he'd scoffed at her choice of bathroom wallpaper. I walked back into the cemetery, heading for the grave, but when I saw a small van parked and two workies with shovels easing off the shored up dirt back into the hole, I turned and headed back out again. At the gate, I turned left, toward Cardonald. Then I changed my mind, or something, and turned right, toward Govan. I'm glad I changed direction, because if I hadn't, I wouldn't have spotted them, Gash and Burney, standing on the corner of Redpath

Drive, opposite, hesitating about whether to approach me. I started to cross over, clinching the deal. They met me halfway, and we all stood on a traffic island, shuffling and grinning stupidly.

'Thought you were a couple of junkies there,' I said, 'planning to roll me for my wad.'

'What wad's that,' said Burney, 'wad of cotton wool in your Prozac bottle?'

It wasn't funny, but we shared a wholesome family chortle, because we wanted to.

'We saw the announcement in the *Evening Times*,' said Gash. 'At least Maw did,' he added, shrugging.

I glanced about furtively on the reference to Mary, as if she'd be crouched behind a pillar box, or squatting in a tree fork or something.

'Is she here too?'

They looked at each other. 'No,' said Gash, 'she didn't think it was, you know, appropriate.'

I felt a pang of hostile disappointment. 'I see,' I said, 'Just tell her I understand.'

'Well, can you not just tell her yourself?' said Burney. 'She's asked you home for your tea.'

I was taken aback. 'I'm taken aback,' I said. I felt my lower lip tremble. I found myself blurting out, 'I don't drink now, you know. I've been off the swally for near enough three month.'

The grins faded. Suspicion and memory darkened faces.

'Don't go overboard,' said Burney, 'it's only your fucking tea.' He looked to Gash for support. He found it.

'Aye, big man, it's only your fucking tea, nothing special, Auntie Rena's invited too, that's how fucking ordinary it is, all right?'

'All right,' I said.

'Our whole world doesn't revolve around you, you prick,' said Burney.

'I know it doesn't, did I say it did, I said all right, didn't I, didn't I say all right?'

'As long as you know,' said Gash.

'I know,' I said, 'I know, all right?'

And we all walked down the road to Govan, for me to get my fucking tea.

EPILOGUE

WHEN I WAS sixteen I walked into a pub, when I was forty-five I stepped back out again. I'm glad I haven't wasted my life. I've seen too many decent guys piss away their youth, dreams and hopes doing dismal jobs they hated, stuck with wives they scarcely liked, scrimping and slaving for the privilege of turning their dreary, lumpen sprogs into overpriced walking billboards. Why do they continue, why don't the drones rebel? The one-word answer is fear. I'm a frightful example of what happens to those who step out of line in Scumland. 'You don't want to end up like Rab Nesbitt, do you?' 'No.' 'Well, stick that severed arm in your pocket and get back out on the assembly line.' When people talk about spongers, they forget the contribution we make to the upholding of the status quo. I am a walking, staggering cattle prod, frightening the Reeboked animals into manageable herds so that the ordered life of Western society may continue undisrupted. I am, if you will, a sort of policeman. Any year now I expect an OBE, or Lifetime Achievement Award from the DSS. So I disagree with those who claim I've wasted my time on this earth. Time is a blank canvas on which I've drawn the picture of my life. My one regret is that I've only had time to draw a single picture, that's all; I feel I have other lives left in me. What I'm saying is that, apparently, I don't want to die. I say apparently because I have little choice in the matter, it's the life force that decides, I might drive the motor but I'm not the engine. And the life force has decided I'm to pant on till it decrees otherwise. I should be dead, you see, but I'm not. I'm still pottering about, buying the morning paper, embarrassing strangers on buses and ranting about the rain. I don't look like anybody's idea of a walking fucking miracle but I am. The other day, in the paper, I saw two stories, one after the other: 'Thousands Die in Turkish Quake'. And on the next page, opposite an ad for Comfydown beds, 'Man Who Ate Knickers Lives'. Is it a wonder I've had a difficulty attaining any sense of reverence with regard to the almighty? By what process of discrimination does any self-respecting divine fucking being arrive at a result like that? Innocent Hordes nil, Knicker Nosher one. I speak not in anger but with incredulity, having been myself an unworthy recipient of the Almighty's cross-eyed logic. But I'll come to that.

*

It took a while before I was accepted back into the family fold, especially by the boys. Every time I tried to prise out and quietly dump the wedge that my drinking had caused, they'd carry it back in from the mental skip and heave it onto the kitchen table. Helpful handwritten signs reading 'Alcohol-free' or 'May contain some brain damage' would appear in the sugar bowl or on bottles of washing-up liquid. On Father's Day I received a pound of ox liver with a card suggesting I use it for a transplant. Even the sanctity of the marital bed was compromised with Burney enquiring of Mary whether the quality of the sexual fore-play had deteriorated now that my hands had stopped shaking. For my part, I turned the other cheek and kept turning. Finally, one night, having lulled the little bastard into a state of false security, I clumped him with a backhander that had him fumbling for Esther Rantzen's Childline number. When he found it, I snatched it from him and ate it. Having snapped, I was in no mood to be dallied with. 'If fucking Esther comes round here I'll clump her too, and the Social Services, I'll kill any bastard who says I've a problem with aggression!' I mustered enough spume on the lips to hint at the repressed frenzy of old and gradually an approximation of respect was restored. We sat at table, locked sullenly in our private worlds, barking our resentments between sips of sweet stewed tea, a family once more.

*

What happens to us? When we're young, time is endless and happiness may be conveniently deferred until goals, great or modest, have been achieved. In middle age, time concertinas like a pair of trousers dropped where he stood by a drunk en route to bed. These days, every dubious stain is a roundabout, every damp crease a street I used to know. I double back down the worn gusset of the decades, seeking out a black hole in the polycotton seam of time, into which I may step and magically, producing my receipt, start all over again. In my arse end is my beginning.

I said as much to cousin Donald, only a couple of months ago. We met in the waiting room of the Govan General, each due for a spot of chemo drip. He was wearing a deft old man's trilby to cover his pink dome, me a plastic Safeway bag, common rainwear in Govan and not remarkable. It's fair to say that the sight of each shocked the other. Though when I thought back to our near encounter in the pub all became clear. The gaunt, troubled face, the slipping watch band, his reluctance to engage, not, as I'd assumed, symptoms of a gathered snobbery but echoes of my own unease at dealing with the unease of others. I suppose, with the truth now as brazen as our shiny heads, we might have embraced in mutual consolation but neither of us went in much for that malarkey, and instead we gassed about the upcoming Scottish Parliament while eyeing each other furtively, trying to guess who was the more wasted. Donald was quite keen on the parliament, it turned out, and told me how he'd even motored back from an important business trip to Leeds in order to cast his vote in the referendum. He thought devolution would be a great thing 'for Scotland'. I looked at him in his McHouse of Fraser tartan tie, the *Herald* resting neatly on his lap, folded, not rolled and pocketed like my *Mirror*, and I thought: 'Whose Scotland, his or mine?'

Anyway, I had it in the belly, we established, he in the lungs. 'Serves you right for giving up smoking,' I observed and was rewarded with a wan smile.

'My first today,' he assured me.

He was called before me and we parted having arranged to meet on our 'good' day, three days after the effects of the treatment had subsided and three before the grim anticipation of the next had set in. I watched him toddle off down the corridor in his squeaky shoes and crisp, neat clothes, amazed and yes, oddly tickled, to know that this spruce upright civil servant should have an inside as raddled and disgusting as my outside. Cancer gets a bad press but, fair do's, it's a truly egalitarian illness, unlike those stuck-up bastards ME and motor neurone.

*

'You've been in the wars again, haven't you?' he'd said. I didn't believe him at first. When he told me I'd a growth I subtly suggested he might've arsed things up, him being a lowly GP and that, but he waved the specialist's letter at me. 'My opinion is neither here nor there,' he said. 'It's what Mr Crammond indicates regarding the results of your endoscopy that counts, and I'm afraid the news isn't the best.' When I asked him if that meant it was the worst he was silent.

I sort of sank back in my chair like a boxer who's just taken a mandatory eight. 'Well, that's that, then,' I thought, 'the final accolade in a glittering career dedicated to poisoning your body to death.' All the same I felt a weird sense of grievance, as if my system had failed me, if I could take the bevvy without a grumble, why couldn't it?' My body was a poof, I decided, it's what had held me back all those years. If only I'd had a different body, say, Arnold Schwarzenegger's, I might've been, well, Arnold Schwarzenegger. And I'd have been a better Arnie than him, I'd have been superior at the Arnieing, for a start I'd never have made *Last Action Hero*. After I'd got my breath back, I asked him what could have put it in there, this growth, expecting the answer 'booze'.

He didn't say that. 'I don't know,' he said, 'in many ways we still know so little.' He was doing humble acting, I decided, which was really slimy of him, using the collective 'we' to try and wriggle his ignorant tweedy butt off the hook. I sought a distinction.

'Do you mean the medical profession as a whole has reached an impasse in current knowledge, or that you personally are an ignorant pill-pusher who knows fuck-all about anything?' This was a tad unfair on my part, but you can't hand someone a wreath saying 'you're dead' and expect them to react with anything less vigorous than a one-fingered salute.

I told Mary and the boys. For a while the tea towels hung at half-mast, but then, when I didn't croak right off the bat, restlessness set in and the amusing remarks cranked up again. At breakfast, my head would be tapped with a spoon, mistaken for a boiled egg. Burney suggested that, since heroin chic was a waning fashion, I might introduce ghetto chic and strut my stuff on the catwalk, modelling surgical gowns and woolly bobble hats. 'Forty-eight and skinnier than Kate Moss, let's hear it for the King of Thin,' he said, one day, encouraging a round of applause. I don't blame them, people get pissed off respecting the feelings of others, they've feelings of their own to deal with – and let's face it, who wouldn't entertain a hint of contempt for some shabby fucker in a mouldy Beatle wig, slurping up tepid porridge through a straw? After a while they just want you to croak, so they can get it over with.

I could see Mary fighting these thoughts, trying to remind herself of the gravity of it all by playing the Last Time game. You know, this might be the last time we take a forty-five bus together or buy a tin of cling peaches from Safeway. That sort of thinking starts to affect the sufferer. He starts to engage in philosophical musings, wondering, 'What is a cling peach, anyway? Fuck me, I'm going to go to my grave without finding out who they're clinging to, or why.' And you'll have a little weep, standing there with your wire basket in the checkout queue, grieving for the lost mysterious world of tinned fruit.

'What are you crying for, Rab?'

'For the peaches.'

'What, all of them?'

'No, just the tinned ones.'

And your wife thinks, 'Fuck me, he's lost it, I hope he doesn't start mooing, or getting his dick out in this queue.'

They say stress can bring it on and that seems feasible, well, I can fease it anyway. There's a lot of stress in the life of a waster. Getting from A to B by way of D, X, and Z isn't a lifestyle that's without its shocks to the central nervous system. For me, it started with gut cramps. Simple as. I'd been out with the boys, showing them the natural wonders of the Govan Serengeti, the flower beds where I made my den, the crane Freak fell off and broke his neck, the gutter where Tojo lost his nose, I want them knowing who they are and where they come from so in forty years they can look back and have a laugh, or recoil in horror or something. When I die, I'll be skint, so all I can leave them with is the idea that Govan is a rolling pageant, with people being born and croaking and that they didn't start it all, there were others before them and, Spook willing, there'll be others after them and soon they'll be the custodians, full of youth, spunk and cheek, until they too start to wither, touch of cancer diet here, spot of brain damage there, and another generation, in turn, sprouts up to take their place. I find it painful fusing memory and imagination. The first magnifies the self, the second shrinks it, slopping out the me I know, and more or less cherish, into the mucky drains of time with the countless thousands of other anonymous turds who combine to create the gigantic illustrious Me that local history will one day know collectively as No Fucker. Memory, on the other hand, assures us we're significant. 'Come in, sir, your usual table? Have some tea and a madeleine. What? No, it's a light biscuit, sir, like a Tunnock's caramel log, only without the lockjaw.' Memory allows us the indulgence of a director's cut over our own lives or, in my case, half cut.

Anyway, that night we were sitting at home watching *Raging Bull* and guzzling Monster Munch when suddenly I pitch forward and find I'm in the ring with Jake La Motta, who's wearing lead gloves, thudding me in the belly. I put it down to food poisoning and Mary and I cast back our minds over the last day or so to consider what food we may have consumed that could be loosely termed as poisonous. We narrow it down to everything and next day, while I'm still bent double in agony, she fixes up an appointment for me to be seen. A referral is arranged at which an endoscopy is performed, until finally, as I've said, the GP gives me the final verdict. I go over and over my meeting with him in my mind in that masochistic compulsive way people do who've had a bad shock.

'What did you make of Mr Crammond?'

I suspected right away it was bad news. He had Crammond's letter sitting in front of him ready, he didn't need to rummage about in his files for it while I stood about like a failed strippergram with my strides round my ankles, like normally happens. 'He's a doddering old duffer,' I tell him.

He disagrees with this cool appraisal. 'He's an extremely experienced surgeon. He's been at South Govan for over thirty years.'

I'm unimpressed. 'Well, I wouldn't let him near me with a knife,' I say, 'his guide dog would start gnawing at my tripes.' I'm having a go because I'm in pain but I half believe it's true. Let's face it, nobody any good would snoke about Govan for thirty years, it doesn't smack of a happening cutter in demand. Basically, I'm on edge because I can sense what's coming. And it does, as I've said, in the form of silence. 'Well, that's that, then,' I thought.

He allowed me my little go at him, then he started to explain, quietly, what the trouble was. 'It appears you have a high-grade lymphoma,' he tells me.

Straight away, out of panic, I'm on with the jester cap and bells. 'Really? Well, I insisted on the high-grade variety. I thought, Rab, you only get cancer once, why not treat yourself to the best, you deserve it, ha, ha.' I'm doing my Mr Chirpy but there's a tremor in my throat. 'What's that, then?'

He goes on, using his best measured this-fucker's-going-to-croak, I'm-dreadfully-sorry high-tea voice. 'Well, basically, you have an aggressive cancer and like virtually all stomach cancers yours is inoperable.'

I heard the words, I felt them echo around in my nut like that nameless voice that calls your name on the edge of sleep, startling you awake.

'I'm sorry,' he said.

He wasn't the only one.

I sat fidgeting in the chair, not knowing if I was being dismissed or if there was some bit of regulation post-trauma stroking coming my way. 'Well, you know, what do I . . .'

He stepped into the breach, finishing the thought, as I needed him to. There's a note in the human voice that not everybody has, I don't have it, it's a simple tune played in the key of comfort you only hear at rare times, when you're deeply in trouble, and it can come from unexpected quarters. It's what used to be called compassion before the word was raped by the modernizers. It can't cure you, but it can bring acceptance, which is the next best thing. There are men who ring up the Samaritans and talk dirty, knowing the women aren't allowed to hang up. There are women who ring them too, not to talk dirty, but to drink from the compassion well, frigging themselves off on the sheer attention of a caring male voice. I could have said no to the chemo. Let's face it, as we know, most fuckers die with or without it anyway, so there's a strong case for being left in peace to croak in your own home, having one last wank to *Ibiza Uncovered*. Except that there are two compelling counter-arguments for going ahead and taking the treatment. A) There's always the chance of a miracle. B) There's always the chance of a miracle. I've omitted C, by the way, which is that it's seriously difficult to slap the pork soldier to attention anyway since chasing a little extra life through chemo is such a libido-grabbing chore you could walk through the Raymond Revuebar and not realize you'd left your cock on the bus till you needed it for a pee.

*

Cotter came to visit me at home, pretending not to be shocked by my weight loss. I don't understand the mechanics of the average malignant growth. You lose three stone in weight to feed it, yet it grows half an inch. I held out my hand for him to shake and he gave it a look of horror, touched it like it was an electric door knob, then fled to the toilet on the pretext of a piss. There was no flush though and I heard the tap running. He came back in doing ah-that's-better acting. To get my own back, I raised the subject of the afterlife. Having confirmed his belief in it, I told him that if he ever so much as dreamt of dipping Mary I'd come back ghosted up, team-handed, with some heavy ghost muscle, and we'd haunt the fuck out of him. I told him he'd know I was there by the curious smell of cigarette smoke everywhere he went. He made the not unreasonable point that that's what happened anyway in Govan. I'd to think on my feet. 'Menthol, then?' I said, in my best eerie croak, hooding my sunken eyes and extending a bony finger in an approximation of imminent death, 'I will come unto you smoking Consulate, or Berkeley Mild, whichever's on special offer in the Lord's dwelling place.'

I knew he still had his eyes on Mary. He and others had already, like foot in the door comfort salesmen, tendered bids, offering support, understanding and, by implication, cock, to help her make it through the night. Cotter, nudging ahead of the pack, had already grown desperate, informing Mary tetchily that she 'couldn't grieve for ever'. The fact that I wasn't yet dead but listening downstairs in thieved yellow pyjamas and mite-eaten Beatle wig appeared not to impinge on his conscience but instead, predictably, to inflame his desire. He'd never forgiven me for winning and wooing Mary and if he could take her now, on my deathbed, then revenge would indeed be for him a dip best savoured cold. Mary, for her part, gave him no encouragement but, being stressed, and a woman, valued the warmth of his touch on her shoulder and sometimes, under duress, thigh. I could do little but fume and rant, pissing into a bucket and vomiting into a basin. I had to concede I was not at my most alluring, sexually. At times, the pain and discomfort were intense and I was given morphine sulphate tablets together with a top-up morphine elixir which I quickly abused then discarded because they worked too well. I needed a clear head to watch the sniffing dogs around me. The prospect of shuffling around the house in witless bliss, drooling and singing 'Happy talky talking Happy Talk' while Cotter snickered and letched at my wife was one I viewed with horror and alarm. Hatred of him as much as love for her kept me going. I wanted to live, fuck it.

I met Donald at Govan Cross Station. In a shameless bid to have their franchise renewed, the gods of privatized weather, Scotdank, had laid on an hour of drizzle-free calm which we decided to celebrate by going walking. Fifteen minutes later, having arrived, panting, at a street corner fifty yards away, we settled for a cup of tea instead. The cafe in the shopping mall proved a bad mistake. Govan being the rich and fertile cancer county it is meant that we were interrupted constantly by a steady drip of emaciated fellow baldies and chemo vets who insisted on joining us. Cancer can do many things to the human spirit but it can't make boring people interesting. A pensioner in a baseball cap showed us pictures of his diseased organs, speaking of them with a curious twinkle like they were his grown-up children in Canada. He took out some pamphlets and spread them on the tabletop. 'There's something for every-one,' he said brightly, his perfect dentures gleaming incongruously from within his collapsed phizzog. 'I'll leave these with you, maybe you'll spot something that's up your street, cheery-bye the now.'

It struck me again how times had changed. Thirty years ago, he'd have been in a muffler, heading off to work with his greaseproof wrapper full of blubber sandwiches, humming welding shanties as he punched in for another day's clanging around the bulkheads. Now he was dressed like he played part-time in the Boyzone over-forty-five league.

I took a swatch at the leaflets. They were what you might expect. For burn-bellies like myself there was a weightwatchers' club where, presumably, everyone stood about hooting and applauding if you put on a pound that week. What tickled me was a theatre group for gay lung cancer sufferers called Fags Out. I showed that one to Donald and he tried to laugh but wasn't in the mood. His problem was that they were taking him in the next day. Not to operate, but to die. The chemo had failed to halt the spread and surgery was out of the question.

'Only about a quarter of lung cases are suitable for surgery and guess what, I'm not in the lucky quarter.'

I tried to cheer him up by showing him another leaflet, for the Cancer Fancy Dress Charity Ball. I suggested we take our wigs off, paint a couple of red dots on our heads and go as a pair of tits, but he still didn't crank to life. Ignoring the waitress to avoid a tip, I bought a fresh round of teas from the counter and a couple of Caramel Wafers. I didn't want a Caramel Wafer. I wanted Dairy Milk, or a Creme Egg, something that could be absorbed into the system without my digestion having to take an axe to it. Stupidly, I'd forgotten the middle classes are immune to the absurd potency of cheap confectionery anyway, so I ended up licking the chocolate off both biscuits, as demurely as I could, and rewrapping the offending stumps out of sight.

I doubted that Donald was a cancer bore, so I took a mental deep breath and asked him what was on his mind. I had him down as private and guarded and suspected, being middle class, he would only open up to his peers, not a lowlife like me.

'Regrets,' he said, almost before the question had left my mouth.

'About what?' I said.

He didn't reply and sat for a long time in deep, unruffled, selfish silence. This little unaccustomed chink in manners allowed in the glint of reality that told me his death was more or less imminent. He was on the deep sea bed, walking slowly and alone, while above him the lucky millions thrashed and laughed on the surface. That's how he saw it, anyway.

I tried again. 'Regrets about what?' I could make out his scrawny chest heaving up and down under his thick Burberry coat. I'd like to report he was on the point of unburdening himself when his mobile phone went off, but he wasn't. He took out the irritating little fucker and spoke into it.

'Hello, yes?' His tone softened and I could tell he was talking to a woman. He fixed me with a stare and I pulled a funny face till I realized he was just concentrating on his conversation. 'I can't, I'm not able to travel. I've a serious bronchial infection.' He gave a wink in my direction but I didn't react in case it wasn't meant for me. 'No, no, I can't,' he said, firmly. He was trying to close the call but the chat took a turn towards unit trusts and endowment schemes and he was drawn, enthusiastically, back in. I watched, feeling whatever closeness there was between us start to evaporate. I'd forgotten he must be worth a few quid. I looked at the half-sucked Caramel Wafers I'd bought to cheer us up and saw the class lines yawn open like the San Andreas Fault. I've never swallowed all this 'class is dead' pish. A society may have no class but that's not the same thing as being classless. He ended the conversation abruptly, put away his mobile and treated me to a thin smile. 'My accountant,' he said. 'It's important at times like these that we put our affairs in order.'

I nodded agreement, not knowing what else to do. What the fuck affairs did I have? 'Mary, look, there's my sock drawer. I've instructed my accountant to put it in order, so you'll have no worries there when I'm gone.' I decided to try one last plunge in to the moat before the drawbridge finally slammed shut. 'I appreciate you want to leave your family well fixed,' I said, 'very sensible.'

'Yes,' he said, 'now the worst is to happen I'd be foolish to die intestate, the matter would have to be dragged through the courts and in the delay the family would be sorely inconvenienced.'

I climbed back out of the moat. 'Fuck it,' I thought.

'Well, we can't have that, can we?' I said. 'Not the family inconvenienced. I mean you'll have enough on your plate lying six foot under a burst settee with an eye socket full of fish bait without worrying about whether the family can pay its club membership to Living Well on time.'

I could tell he didn't like the directness, not from me, and his little mouth puckered like an arsehole. 'What about these regrets, then?' I nagged. 'Come on.'

He thought for a moment then offered me another of his tedious little smiles. I saw it now, he was doing 'grace under pressure' acting, only it was coming out as smugness, which annoyed me because deep down he was better than that. He shook his skinny head on his skinny neck.

'I'm sorry,' he said, 'I shouldn't have spoken, I've already said too much.'

I felt my own spirits start to sag. I'd come to this meeting hoping to rediscover something, Donald being a living link with my past. We'd go way back, I thought, root out memories of books and relatives, exchange perspectives, however horrible, drink from that lost well. But this wasn't it, this wasn't it at all.

He shrugged and took a dutiful sip of cold tea. I could tell he was preparing to leave. 'Things change,' he said.

'In what way?'

Thin smile.

'Don't tell me,' I said, 'you've already said too much.'

He nodded. 'Correct.' He called for the bill, insisted on paying for the first round of teas. I pointed out there was no charge for conversation. 'Oh, yes, there is,' he said, buttoning up his Burberry, 'it's a high-cost commodity, is that.'

He stood up, catching me by surprise, leaving me fiddling with my teaspoon. It was one of those flattened ones, I noticed, probably trodden down by some shit-soled cook. I buttoned my jacket, for show, and he offered me his hand to shake. I took it.

'You know, Donald,' I said, 'there's something I've been meaning to divulge to you, a terrible family secret that's been concealed down the years.'

He looked startled. 'What's that?'

'It concerns your dear mother, my very own auntie and a certain incident.'

I had his attention. 'What incident?'

I was still clutching his hand. 'I'm sorry,' I said, 'I shouldn't have spoken, I've already said too much.' I stopped clutching and let it drop. He looked gratifyingly annoyed. 'You know what, Donald?' I said. 'I hope they put those words on your fucking tombstone.'

He picked up his change, leaving fifty pence for the waitress. 'You don't understand,' he said. 'You handle this your way and I'll handle it mine.' He shuffled off, looking glum.

I'd been a bit slap-happy with him, I knew that, but I didn't care. The way I saw it, he'd drawn a short straw and so had I. It was legitimate I should treat him to a kick in the nuts, we were level on points, I reasoned. I pocketed the fifty pence and shuffled out. Served her fucking right for the flat teaspoon.

*

The day after that, I did a foolish thing. Sometimes, though, it seems a foolishness is a sensible thing to do. I was creeping down Govan Road with two onions and a tin of chopped pork in my pocket, leaning on this aluminium walking stick they'd given me, and thinking, 'Fuck me, all I need are surgical stockings and a Rainmate and my humiliation is complete.' Across the street I saw Cotter and Andra Binnie heading for the Two Ways. The sight of them seized me with this great eruptive need for normality and I found myself swearing at the walking stick and sending it clattering into a close. Of course there were risks, I knew that. In my condition, a single drink might be enough to poison my system. On top of that, if I went on a binge, then coupled with the heavy painkillers I was on I could find myself in a permanent coma or having horrible convulsions on a chip-shop floor while drunks stepped over me calling for deep-fried pizzas. On the other hand, overwhelmingly, there was company and a good sixties juke box. As I stood, swithering, it occurred to me that Donald, at around the same time, would be climbing between his starchy hospital sheets, clutching his portfolio of investments under his arm, preparing to die. I went in.

I suppose, despite everything, I expected a big welcome. Nothing. Only a few smokers' coughs in bad suits and a weary-looking collie stretched out under a table in a Celtic jersey. I crept up behind them as they stood at the bar, which wasn't a good idea. I could hear the words 'cock-shaped wreath' and 'that skinny you could bury him in the holder for a snooker cue'. I nudged Cotter.

'All right, boys?' I tottered a bit but in the main was

making a fair fist of doing irrepressible ruddy-faced Micawber acting. Their faces fell.

'All right, Rab?' said Binnie.

'Great to see you, Rab,' lied Cotter, without missing a beat, 'what'll it be, the usual schooner of Fresh N' Lo?'

I shook my head. 'I'll have what you're having,' I said.

He looked at his pint, then back at me. 'Are you sure?'

I nodded. Six pints further on, we were standing on the pavement, swaying lightly in the breeze, eating chips.

'I must admit, I was pissed off when I first saw you, Rab,' said Binnie. 'I thought the big white look of you was going to take away the benefit of the drink.'

Cotter shook his head in vigorous disagreement, like a man who wouldn't hear a word of it. 'Fie and thrice fie,' he said. 'Rab's a Govan man, he was brung up decent. He knows you don't start flashing your terminal illness in the pub, it only spoils the night for others. Isn't that right, Rab?'

I accepted this tribute with becoming modesty. Binnie tossed his greasy paper aside and gave a short, cursory vomit, a gesture of culinary approval in our country.

'So how is the you-know-what doing, then, Rab?' he said, pointing to my belly.

I shrugged, fumbling for easy bland words that would not cloud the bright tropical sky of our minds. 'Well, they say if—' Explanation ceased, Cotter having clamped a cold, salty palm over my mouth.

'That's enough gory details, Rab,' he said, screwing up his mouth in distaste, 'you're making me sick.' I agreed, with a nod, to desist, and he removed the palm. 'Well, gentlemen,' he announced, 'it's been a delightful afternoon. Shall we conclude with a pish?'

This suggestion proved agreeable and we strolled to a nearby close where, in the custom of our culture, we relieved ourselves, en masse.

'Well, what do you think, Rab,' said Binnie, firing his arc with careless abandon, 'is it great being back on the swally or what?'

I laughed delighted agreement. 'I tell you, Andra, it's as if I've never been away. Do you know what, I think I could drink all bloody well night, ha ha!'

I did not, in fact, drink all bloody well night. Instead, I was conveyed, on a stretcher, from my home by two ambulancemen while Mary ran alongside berating me for a stupid bastard and the boys skulked and hid around the corner, in case there might be girls and they'd get red phizzers. Half-crazed by drunken pain, Mary's nagging and the thumping and jarring of the bovine paramedics in the china shop of our narrow closemouth, I tipped myself out and staggered, cursing, toward the waiting ambulance. I hammered on the rear doors shouting, 'Open up, you fuckers.' Within my fevered, random gaze, I saw thrilled pensioners feign shock and Kangoled youths kick their girls on the bum in delight. The telly was stinking and I was a godsend.

I awoke, in hospital, feeling chastened and hellish. Still too pished for treatment, I was allowed to mooch about the day room with the terminals, smoking and watching cricket, a one-day test, fortunately for some. I'd three fags left and no money, such was the hurried nature of my departure, and I decided to eke them out rather than mini-binge, though great was that temptation due to the consuming idleness.

At breakfast, a nurse had explained how fortunate I was to have been admitted. 'To be honest, we thought you were an emergency, really you shouldn't be here.'

I considered this information. 'I've an inoperable cancer,' I told her, 'I'm dying.'

'Yes,' she agreed, scraping some egg yolk from her tunic

with a fingernail, 'but you're dying slowly, that's not quite the same thing, is it?'

I asked her if I speeded up the process would I get a nicer bed away from the window, I wasn't big on air, I explained. She gave me a smile from the eyes that tickled the end of my tired old cock. 'We'll see,' she said.

It was a bigger hospital than the one I'd had the chemo in, and more lively, apart from the deaths. Every dressing gown seemed to have some human pipe cleaner in it, shuffling about, looking self-absorbed and pitiful. The quiet made me almost pine for the loony bin where at least some creamer might jump on the table and go 'Wooooooo!' once in a while, to help break the day up. Horrible hacking coughs abounded and people rasped and wheezed, making me feel uneasy. If you weren't ill before you went in, you sure as shite would be by the time you came back out. Except you didn't come out, which was rather the point of this particular ward.

For a couple of days I slumped in a Parker Knoll waiting for painful treatment that wouldn't work, to give me extra life to go on slumping in a Parker Knoll waiting for more painful treatment that wouldn't work. Some pastor fucker came round with some ugly bints and they got blasted into some hymns, totally uninvited, which peeved the tits off all us who'd more than half a pulse. I stuck it as long as I could, fuming and that, harrumping over my *Daily Mirror*, until I heard the tambourine come out and the sound of clapping and that's when I lost my rag. To pre-empt any fine theological hair splitting, I wheezed across the lino and, best I could, sunk my foot up the pastor's arse. 'Fuck off,' I shouted, 'there's people trying to die in here.' He went ashen in the face, then puce, and I swear his fist clenched and he made a little feint toward me. At the last nanosecond he remembered he was holy and that it wasn't

325

in the contract to swan about dishing out uppercuts to the infirm of body. I was still up for it. 'Come on, then,' I urged, 'you and me, for a square go.' He wasn't having any, which was just as well, as I'd spent my last shell hurtling across the floor to get at him. It would almost have been worth croaking to leave the next day's headlines: 'Minister Kicks Fuck Out of Cancer Victim' –'I was only trying to bring comfort,' sobs the Padre as he's led away with a blanket over his head. The ward sister gripped my elbow and whisked me, as a considerate pace, into a nearby administrative office. Here I was given a reprimand and warned about my disruptive conduct on the ward. It was also arranged, magically, that I'd have another endoscopy that afternoon.

'I've already had one,' I told them.

'Yes, I know,' she said, a bit fractiously. 'Well, now you're having another.' She shooed me out of the office and back into bed. I tried to work out what was going on. In the end, I concluded it was a procedural thing, this being a different hospital they were obliged to do their own tests. More likely they were trying to cover themselves in case I croaked on their manor, so they could say, 'Well, we gave him the best of micro-technology and he still pegged, selfish bastard.'

I steered a bit clear of Donald following our tête-à-tête in the cafe. He was in a corner bed, next to the radiator, way up the ward on the same side, so at least we didn't have to look at each other having our bedpans emptied and picking spilled mince out of our chest hair and that. Our ward was, unofficially, on open visit, which meant that, being croakees, close family could drop in at any reasonable hour. I'd already told Mary not to come. I'd done 'I don't want you seeing me like this' acting; but that wasn't the real reason, I just didn't fancy the strain of having to entertain anybody for an hour a shot. Scum aren't comfortable with speech, and after twenty minutes or so the chat tends to peter out and as host you feel obliged to carry the show. You sit there in silence, racking your sedated brains for something worth saying, while laughter seems to crackle out from every bed around the room. You know your lot are thinking, 'Fuck me, I wish I was visiting him over there, not this miserable cunt,' and out of panic you start juggling the oranges or something. So I told them all to stay back. When the end is nigh, I promised myself, that's when I'll give them the nod for a spot of sobbing. Let's face it, the boys would only start ogling the nurses or planning raids on the dispensary anyway, so it wasn't a grievous loss. One vow I did make to myself when the time came was to tell Mary how much I L'd her. I had a little speech prepared: 'Mary, you've been as decent a wife as an ugly bastard like me could probably get. In fact, all in all, you've been pretty good. PS. Cotter's got Aids but it's up to you.' It was a bit gushy, but it meant well.

Now and then I'd see Donald lying back, smiling beatifically while his no-nonsense wife and teachery kids sat around looking grim and respectful. The son was a bit pasty, like he'd been reared in captivity, but the girl was pretty and had a bit of spark, and kindly Uncle Rab would have humped her at a pinch. Except, of course, that introductions were never forthcoming. Having dutifully kept his appointment with me, Donald's horizons, under the relentless ticking of the clock, now extended no further than the tiny radius of his nearest and dearest. When a man knows he is to be downsized in a fortnight . . . Prove you could live a fortnight in this place and you'd qualify for a mortgage. Three of us would be dead within the week. Donald needed his family around him, I needed mine

327

out of sight, so I could prepare alone. As Donald had succinctly put it, 'You handle this your way, I'll handle it mine.'

It's not that hard to lay your hands on the drugs in hospital, if you know where to look. The average hospital is always having to turf out junkies who slink in off the street and are found roaming around corridors, trying to pick locked cupboards with dirty needles, so obviously, if you're already inside legitimately, you have a head start. The admin office where I'd been ticked off had a sort of mini-pharmaceutical shelf for soft-core drugs so that the night nurse, when occasion arose, could fetch some appropriate pill while still keeping an eye on the ward through a small square window. I won't pretend I had any criminal masterplan to gain access to the room by booting the Padre up the arse but since I was in there anyway, and since the bottle of Mogadon was sitting by itself, looking slightly neglected away from its mates, I'd taken the opportunity to furnish it with the company of my dressing-gown pocket. Sometimes in life, your instincts are way ahead of you, they know what you want long before you do and gradually, as I've said, I've come to accept that I've practically fuck all to do with being me. Basically, I'm just a set of thoughts in a scabby suit, the deeds are somebody else's department.

I didn't know how many tablets to take, never having committed suicide before, so I leaned on my elbow and under the mask of a mild coughing fit shook most of them out into a little tent I'd made under the blanket. I couldn't make out the time on the ward clock for the dark but I estimated, from the long intervals between passing cars outside, that we were around the smallest of the wee small hours. I had some water ready in a paper cup and I took a small sip, for show, in case the nurse was watching. She wasn't. She had her head down under the desk lamp and was picking her nose absently, with a pinkie. She was only a little buck-toothed slip of a thing in charge of all us wounded beasts and I remember hoping, albeit vaguely, that she wouldn't get a bollocking in the morning. If she did, well, tough titty, maybe the odd terminal stiffing out would help keep her conk out of *Marie Clare*. I started counting the pills into the water then stopped, realizing I was committing suicide and that the arithmetic was hardly my concern and could be left to some tetchy coroner they'd pull in off the golf course to root around my stomach contents with a set of tweezers. I swished my hand around the sheet, hoovering up every pill, including strays, and dropped them into the cup. Some water trickled out over the pillow and I took another sip to lower the level. 'Well, that's that, then,' I thought, profoundly. One or two people have asked me what it's like to be on the point of suicide, do you achieve any piercing insights and that? Maybe others do, all I know is that to me it felt like one more mechanical act, like eating a Polo mint or saying my prayers. Part of me wanted to be plucky, roguishly flippant, all of that, I mean me and Donald, the others too, we'd seen the movies, we knew what was expected of us, and some, like him, chose to oblige. For myself, in the end, I simply couldn't be arsed. The only thought in my head was that I hoped I'd wake up dead. My dread was that six months later I could be shuffling around the day room in a pair of Pampers, clutching a balloon and singing along to the Teletubbies. I had to do it properly. Duly resolved, I swished the dissolving mess around with a biro, took a last deep breath, and jumped off the edge of the world into oblivion.

After Donald croaked, I volunteered to gather up his belongings and take them down to the porter's office for his wife to collect. They knew I was, roughly speaking, family, and though they couldn't account for such a tragic evolutionary occurrence, didn't want to risk offence, so gave me the regulation bin bag bearing the stencilled words 'Patients' Clothes'. The spectacles, watch and wedding ring had been placed on top of his bedside cabinet and I put them, for safekeeping, into a little leather wallet he kept for loose change. Two pairs of socks, one tie (tartan), plain shirt, striped boxers, light grey flannels and wool blazer. I peeked at the label on the blazer. BHS. So he was human, after all. I sniffed the socks. A vague hint of talc. I realized Donald's socks smelt sweeter dirty than mine did clean. I didn't know what to do with his mobile phone and was about to put it in his jacket pocket when the fucker went off.

Not knowing what to do, I jabbed, in a cold sweat, at a bunch of buttons till eventually I heard a female voice say, 'Donnie? Hello, Donnie, it's Beverley, can you talk?'

I had just about worked out what end to speak into so, in a spirit of scientific enquiry, I said, 'Sure, go ahead.'

Beverley went ahead. 'Listen, I'm really sorry about last time,' she said, 'it was my fault, I was stressed out, Keith was quizzing me and—' She stopped. She sounded North Country, Yorkshire possibly, or more specifically, I surmised, Leeds. 'Don,' she said again, sounding suddenly alarmed, 'is that you?'

I floundered a bit. 'Yes, but I can't talk now,' I said, 'I'm dead.' I pressed a red button which I presumed meant 'off' and tossed the mobile into the bag. An uneasy thought struck me and I fished it out again and found the 'on' button. I tapped out one, four, seven, one, pressed 'send' and listened. Number withheld. I turned the phone off again, and slung it back in the bag. Don Juan could rest in peace, his legend still unsullied.

I was able to perform this dubious act of loyalty being myself less than dead. The trick with pills, I learned, is not to take them all at once; your system rejects them, as mine did. Ingesting the doses over a period of hours is the key to a happy conclusion. I'd lain there, deathly pale, except for a red face, while some poor cleaning bint was on her knees soaking two litres of semi-liquid pharmaceuticals off the lino with a J-Cloth. Needless to say, I received another stern talking to after I'd come round. Basically, this boiled down to: 'Don't think you can stroll around topping yourself just because you're terminal, you'll stay in line and die at the allotted tempo like everyone else.'

The little nurse with the snotty pinkie had saved me, it turned out. I was on my back and had let out a retch which alerted her. She'd rolled me onto my side and they'd had to wheel out the stomach pump which, at four in the morning, had boosted my popularity rating no end. Why did I do it? While all those other poor bastards were fighting to live, why did I suddenly point my hearse the wrong way down a one-way street? At the time, your Honour, it just seemed the sane and rational thing to do. Yes, sir, I know I'm a lifelong nutter, but this time I plead a mitigating circumstance: I acted while the balance of my mind was undisturbed.

The following afternoon I felt well enough to rise and shamble into the day room to savour my last fag. It was a bright, pleasant day and I'd expected it to be empty, thinking my colleagues would all be stuck at open windows, sniffing the roses, shedding bittersweet tears of regret and bequeathing small personal mementoes to couldn't give a fuck relatives who were probably all out jet-skiing in Corfu. To my irritation and surprise, the place was packed, with every chair taken. Even Donald had roused himself and was sitting in a wheelchair, looking poorly and smiling up at the telly.

At first I thought it must be some big European game on Sky, until pictures of a street procession came up. A tabloid headline on the coffee table reminded me that today was historic. It was the inauguration ceremony for the Scottish Parliament. 'Bravehearts Once More', it said. The wind of discontent that had blown through Scotland for a generation had at last found its expression in the lava-lamp form of Donald Dewar. He was sclaffing past Azad Video in his big specs and War on Want suit looking like he should be following the parade with a care worker rather than leading it. He didn't fill you with confidence. You wouldn't want him turning up at a world summit with a delegate badge marked *Hi, Donald Dewar, Caledonia PLC*. In life, geeks are always bullied. Gerhardt Schroeder would have him up on the table in no time, buzzing his ankles with a laser pen and making him do the Highland Fling. All the same, my fellow terminals cheered and stamped. Pictures of Tony Blair came up, making some arrogantly self-effacing remark from a podium then pausing for a round of applause. When it didn't come, Dewar started one off.

A terminal next to me in a tartan bunnet started weeping and sniffing. When I asked him what was up, he shook his head. 'I never thought I'd see this day,' he said.

Luckily, I'd nothing left in my stomach to vomit up. 'Well, you have,' I said, 'but I wouldn't go buying any weekend lottery tickets if I was you.' I lit my fag to quell my nausea. Someone shouted at me to put it out. 'We're allowed to smoke in the day room,' I said.

'No,' he said, 'not when others don't want you to, it's selfish.'

The logic of this baffled me. 'What the fuck are you quibbling about, half you fuckers in here have lung cancer anyway, what the hell difference will it make now?'

A grey-haired man pulled a dressing gown tight around his tracheotomy bandage. 'You make us cough,' he rasped.

'Yes, put it out or go outside,' said someone else.

I nipped the fag. Tony Blair said, 'Thank you, Donald Dewar.' Everybody applauded, on the telly and in the day room. I felt like an illegal immigrant who'd just climbed out of the laundry hamper. It was as if the whole country was engaged in a ceremonial mass wank or some vague tartan wet dream and if you didn't join in you were a prude.

'I don't know what you're all hooting about,' I said, 'that lot of second-rate fuckers won't matter a toss to us, we're all on our way out anyhow.' I was still fuming over the fag business.

Donald leaned forward in his wheelchair to make his wispy voice heard. 'The Parliament's for our children,' he said, 'and our children's children, for Heaven's sake think about someone other than yourself.'

I was shocked. I felt oddly hurt that he'd joined in, having a go, when all I'd done was introduce a tiny note of scepticism. To me blood is thicker than politics, even thin blood, like the stuff we shared. But that's the middle classes for you, no breeding. 'You should grow up,' I said, 'there's only one country now and that's the land of economics.' There was a bit of tut-tutting and shushing but I bombed on. 'Anyway, I'm from Govan,' I said, 'we do our bit. They'll only have to visit our Web site, Nesbitt dot cancer dot com, slash leaky trainer to know where to find the cheap labour.' I was shaking all over, it's hard enough swimming against the tide when you've your health and strength but if they came at me mob-handed I was fucked.

An old husk in a Black Watch tammy poked me with a walking stick but I picked up a Zimmer frame and wielded it. 'Do you want some of this?' I said. Someone tugged my elbow and I yanked clear, upsetting a vase of fabric flowers. The husk crapped out and took a convenient asthma attack, wheezing into his inhaler. What was I coming to, I wondered, threatening harmless padres and old men? I felt wretched and messed up inside and just wanted to get everything over with.

'For pity's sake, calm down, man,' wisped Donald. And I did. I lowered myself by instalments onto my hands and knees, trying to hide the gathering tears, and started to rummage about on the swirly Axminster, picking up the scattered flowers. A pair of female feet clinked into my eyeline. 'Oh, fuck,' I thought. I gave a precautionary sniff and looked up to find the ward sister wearing her Nurse Ratched face.

'Mr Nesbitt,' she said, evenly, 'Dr Baillie would like to see you, would you come with me please to his office?' I was pretty certain I knew what was coming. It was the three-strike rule, I was being expelled from the terminal ward. And yes, so too it proved, though not, for the life of me, under any circumstances I could have foreseen.

'We have the results of your endoscopy, Mr Nesbitt,' said Baillie.

'Oh yes, which one?'

Dr Baillie was younger than I'd imagined and though he didn't appear vexed, his manner did hint at some sort of awkwardness. 'The second.'

'I see,' I said, 'and should I give a fuck?' I excused myself the swear word, I'm old school, you don't diss the quack, but it just jumped out. Besides, any day now I was about to abandon ship, offshore, from the Land of the Given Fuck and slip noiselessly down to join Donald at the bottom of the Sea of Enforced Tranquillity.

His reply startled me. 'Well, yes,' he said, 'I rather think you should give a fuck.'

I half-raised the portcullis of one leaden eyelid.

'We think your first test resulted in something of a misdiagnosis.'

I cautioned the phrase on suspicion. 'Something of?'

He went on, 'As you know, Mr Crammond is a very experienced surgeon and highly—'

'Old?' I suggested. 'Are you saying he made a bollocks of it?'

They resisted the temptation to look at each other for support. Dr Baillie took the bollock by the horns. 'Absolutely not, not in the least. If anything he's been over-thorough in his treatment of your condition.'

I struggled to follow his stealthy progress through the corridors of deception. Over-thorough. What kind of a thing was that to say? What did that mean? 'What does that mean?' I asked.

He opened a thick medical tome marked at a picture page with a yellow sticky and hid behind his pointing finger. 'Illustration one,' he said, 'high-grade lymphoma, illustration two, low-grade lymphoma.'

I looked at two similar, squalid burps on belly innards. 'Fair enough,' I said, 'what's the difference?'

He shrugged. 'Well, life and death, basically,' he said.

The long and the short of it was that I'd been given extensive hard-core treatment to deal with a non-malignant lump. This was the nub of the 'over-thorough' conclusion. I had a low-grade not a high-grade lymphoma and as a result I was saveable. He explained about a bacterium called *Helibactor pyloris*. 'It's extremely common in Glasgow,' he said, 'it's often associated with overcrowding during childhood.'

I'm making sense of this now, of course, with hindsight, but I wasn't at the time. 'What about it?' I remember mumbling.

'Well, it's what caused your tumour. The tumour is a symptom, not the cause. If we treat the bacteria, as we can do, with antibiotics, then the tumour will gradually disappear.'

'Just like that?'

'Hopefully, yes, almost definitely.'

I didn't fancy the sound of this after the recent debacle. 'Get a grip,' I said, 'don't wheel out any almosts, is it yes or no?'

He made an expansive gesture with his hands. 'All right, then, yes,' he said, 'barring, of course, anything unforeseen.'

His qualifications were doing my nut in, after a shock like this I needed certainty, I couldn't be looping the loop every five minutes on the Big Bumper Corkscrew Ride of Death. I took several minutes, sitting dumbly, while I struggled to make internal adjustments. They told me to take my time. I was anyway. Then I said, 'About that daft old git—'

'He's retiring next month,' said Baillie.

'Oh yes?' I said. 'A bit late for early retirement isn't it, he's about ninety-three.'

Baillie perched on his desk. 'He's retiring next month,' he repeated, a bit quieter this time. It's all in the tone with these people. They knew what was on my mind, thoughts of the old legal redress. Their tone seemed to suggest sympathy as long as I made no mention of going down that road. If I so much as mumbled the word 'damages', they'd be fighting each other to do a Pontius at the hand basin behind them. It occurred to me that's why the ward sister was still hanging about, looking vigilant, as a witness to the conversation. I had no appetite for revenge, I was still too stunned at having my life mended and slung back at me like a patched-up pair of trousers. Besides which, if you sue these fuckers, your life's tied up in legal knots for years while they close ranks. Meanwhile, if you ever need to nip up the Out Patients for a quick running stitch, your heart's in your mouth in case you land for a convenient 'ten per cent extra free' offer with the anaesthetic. 'The court heard how a tragic error of judgement, blah,

blah . . .' 'Overworked staff, stringent new guidelines, blah fucking blah . . .' I wouldn't put myself through all that, not unless I had to. I mean, who's got the time? I looked up at him. 'Are you saying then . . . what are you saying, that I can go?'

He heard the bewilderment in my voice and nipped in quick with his let-me-guide-you-through-this-confusing-maze encouraging smile. 'Give us a little while longer,' he said, 'just to see how you respond.'

Unctuous fuckers. As a terminal, he wouldn't give me the time of day, I was a walking rebuke to the limits of his expertise. I might as well have been shuffling about wearing a big sign saying, *I win, the Doctor's a wanker*, but as soon as things change, and I'm revealed as an easy one, he's back on-side, feigning warm interest and clucking concern. I wasn't letting him away with it. 'Respond,' I said, 'I'll show you how I respond, I respond like this.' I stood up on my wobbly little legs, took off my dressing gown and pyjamas and threw them across his desk. Of course, the trouble with these big impulsive gestures is that you're left to live with the consequences. A naked man striding down a corridor in the full vigour of health can be a striking sight and a formidable symbol of protest against a hypocritical bureaucracy. A skinny fucker in a crap wig, on the other hand, sclaffing along in too-big leatherette slippers, just looks like an escaped saddo who's about to be gripped by the elbows at any second and escorted back to his soft toys.

I stood outside the swing doors of the ward and peeked through the glass, praying there wouldn't be any visitors. God answered my prayers and there were dozens of the fuckers. I had little alternative but to do what any man would in the circumstances. They say that if a woman is being mugged, strangled, or beaten to death, her instinct is always the same; to try and keep her skirt down. A man has his own equivalent. I'll bet those human skeletons that built the Burma railway did this, and Archimedes, who ran bollock-naked down the street shouting 'Eureka, eureka.' As soon as you know your cock's going to be under public scrutiny, you give it a brisk, enhancing, life-giving fluff. You've got to, it's the only memory people are going to take away about you. Imagine two old bints out shopping in Ancient Greece, in their togas and Rainmates. 'Here, Antigone, did you just see that Archimedes run past? He was shouting something about the rate of descent of a falling body.' 'Never mind that, Eurydice, did you clock his cock? Talk about all bloom and no stem, it was like a little walnut whirl in pink icing, tee hee, tee hee.'

I don't know what anything means any more. I don't even know what means means. I started off walking down the open road with friends, family and time by the sackful. Now the friends and family have all croaked or meandered off, I'm running out of time and I'm still shuffling along that same patch of dirty road, with that fucking Glasgow drizzle in my eyes. It took me a long time to realize I've been walking in circles, but what the hell, you've got to go somewhere and nowhere is as good a place as any.

Two days after the Archimedes incident I was standing by the porter's office, waiting for Mrs Donald to pick up her old man's kit. Having volunteered my services, it seemed appropriate to see the job through and gibber some sort of word of consolation or support before I left myself. I could see, through the serving hatch, two or three bags awaiting collection. People find hospitals bleak, depressing places and it's out of cowardice and panic that they bang on about nurses being 'angels' and doctors 'performing miracles' and that. It's an attempt to crowbar an element of spirituality into the routine mechanics of arrival, departure and all matters related. After all, you'd think if any set of people could find evidence for an afterlife, it'd be doctors, rummaging around, as they do, in brains and tripes all day. Yet I've never heard one complain about the occupational hazard of having to dodge flying souls, halfway through a failed bypass, speeding up through the polystyrene ceiling tiles to Heaven's gate, have you? Which leads me to assume that the preponderance of medical evidence for this everlasting life caper must incline toward the negative.

I could see straight out to the taxi rank and since nothing pulled up I took it she must have arrived by car round the side. She barged in the swing doors looking fraught and tired. Despite everything her clothes were still immaculate and her hair well groomed and tidy, but also curiously lank and lifeless looking, like it too was in mourning. I gave her a sort of half smile when I saw her, thinking that would be enough of an intro and that she, with her superior social skills, would switch smoothly onto auto to pick up the slack. Instead, she blanked me and brushed straight past on her way to the porter's window, She gave Donald's name and ward number and a moment later the window panel opened and this lazy bastard porter tried to stuff the bulky bag through to her. I stood, feeling a bit stupid, not quite knowing what to do. Thinking it was just possible she didn't, after all, know who I was, I sort of leaned in and decoratively helped negotiate the bag through the office door where it should have gone in the first place. I mumbled my name and flashed the family credentials and was relieved to see a little look of recognition come into her eye. I pressed on with my prepared words of succour and support, the usual useless twaddle that seems to be essential at hideous moments in life. She thanked me and headed for the door. Then she did a thing that threw me. She turned back from the door; stepped up and looked me full in the face. Being a mug, I was half preparing myself for maybe a tender touch of the hand, a heartfelt, 'You know, despite your different circumstances, Donald thought very highly of you, in fact he was always, blah, blah . . .' But she didn't do any of that. She just gave me this hard, even stare and a look of, how can I put it, contempt, as she finally got it off her chest.

'You know,' she said, 'I've been turning this back and forward in my mind, and for the life of me I still can't work it out. Just how is it that a decent, considerate, churchgoing man like Donald, who's paid taxes all his life and scarcely missed a day's work till his illness, could be taken from us, yet something like you can just get off scot-free? How is that? Can you explain that to me? Can you?' She stared at me with studied concentration, fierce tears gathering at the corners of her eyes. I didn't know how to react, other than to agree with her.

'I know, missus,' I said, 'I can hardly take it in myself, but let's face it, it's all a fucking lottery, isn't it?'

She let out a funny sort of startled wail at this answer, something that tottered on a high wire, with hysteria on one side and desolation on the other if she fell off. Unsure which way she would topple, I kept schtum. I watched her, not daring to help, as she forced the black bag, with an impatient scuffle, through the swing doors, onto the street and into the scarred deepening years of the rest of her life. When she was safely gone, I picked up my Safeway bag and walked. I stood outside the swing doors, feeling numb and dazed, not having quite cast off my role as Non-Malignant Bobby in the outstanding production of *Skinny Bastards* now playing in the hospital behind me.

Cars and buses roared and pulsed at traffic lights, a display of raw, mad appetite that clenched my delicate constitution. In the hospital forecourt a man in a white Mondeo was mouthing to me urgently from behind his windscreen. I stepped over and as he drew down the window, leaned my head in, timidly.

'Do you want a fucking taxi, or don't you,' he grimaced, his face a traditional, contorted mask of Glasgow welcome.

I declined. 'No thank you, coachman,' I said. 'I'll walk.' And so I did. With my bag in one hand and my wispy feather legs beneath me, down the drying grey pavement slabs toward Govan. It occurred to me that my dear wife, thinking me dead, would have nothing in for my tea. 'No matter,' I thought. 'I have a scabby suit, a shit attitude and a self that's worth expressing.' That would keep me going.